THE MAN WHO SHOT

SIEGFRIED SASSOON

A Novel

By

John Hollands

Quill Publications,
2, Orchards Farm,
Buckerell,
Nr. Honiton,
Devon, EX14 3GJ.

Email: john.hollands120@outlook.com
Website: www.johnhollandsbooks.co.uk

Cover design: Hara Davis
ISBN: 9780904596069

Printed and bound by:
Imprint Digital,
Upton Pyne,
Devon.

Also by John Hollands

The Dead, the Dying and the Damned
Able Company (US only)
The Gospel According to Uncle Jimmy
Never Marry a Cricketer
Never Marry a Rugby Player
Not Shame the Day
The Exposed
Poetry of the Korean War (contributions)
The War Poems of a Young Soldier
Blundellian Writers 1604-2004
The Court-Martial.

Memory and Imagination series:

Gran and Mr Muckey
What a Fag!
Heroes of the Hook

Acknowledgements.   My thanks are due to the following: Hara Davis, Lesley Pyne, Jonathan Hollands, Penni Cotton, June and Peter Holloway, Anthea Wynn, Christopher Price, Ken Fisher, and Mark Hollands.

Dedicated to Sir Christopher Ondaatje
One of life's great all-rounders

Banishment

I am banished from the patient men who fight.
They smote my heart to pity, built my pride
Shoulder to aching shoulder, side by side,
They trudged away from life's broad weald of light.
Their wrongs were mine; and ever in my sight
They went array in honour. But they died, -
Not one by one; and mutinous I cried
To those who sent them out into the night.

The darkness tells how vainly I have striven
To free them from the pit where they must dwell
In outcast gloom convulsed and jagged and riven
By grappling guns. Love drove me to rebel.
Love drives me back to grope with them through hell;
And in their tortured eyes I stand forgiven.

Siegfried Sassoon.

Wastage

Deaths continue in abundance
Leaving a silence hardly serene,
And generals with no conscience
Fuel the slaughter as routine.

Yet among men most gallant,
Who fall regularly in the cause,
Are poets of the rarest talent
Too precious to waste on wars.

D.J.H.

Contents

Author's Note

This is an historical novel, set during the Great War of 1914-1918. It is based on Siegfried Sassoon's Protest, a curious and unique occurrence in British military history.

My novel is based on actual events, augmented by my imagination. I aim to tell an entertaining story true to its times, rather than produce a so-called factual version based on personal recollections which are sometimes ambiguous and conflicting, with areas where there are no records at all. At times I have distorted historical accuracy in the interests of a coherent story. For example, Sassoon's commanding officers changed frequently, so to start with I have stuck with his main CO, Lt-Colonel Stockwell (Buffalo Bill), as though he was in command the whole time.

To this day, the Great War is riddled with unsolved mysteries. Siegfried Sassoon's Protest is probably the greatest of them.

Second-Lieutenant Siegfried Sassoon was a distinguished war poet and a dashing hero who served in the Royal Welch Fusiliers. In a bizarre attempt to stop the war he issued a public protest against the way in which it was being conducted. The general background to his Protest remains obscure, especially with regard to the influence of pacifists such as Bertrand Russell and Lady Ottoline Morrell. Likewise, many repercussions caused by Sassoon's Protest were never made public in the interest of national security.

Siegfried Sassoon's accounts of his service in the Great War (*Memories of a Fox Hunting Man, Sherston's Progress,* and *Siegfried's Journal* etc) were written years after the events took place and parts of his story were either omitted or were a mixture of fact and fiction. So wary was Sassoon of what he wrote that his first major work was anonymous, only for his cover to be blown by Charles Graves (the journalist brother of Sassoon's great friend Robert Graves).

By good fortune I have been able to draw on previously untapped sources of information, namely disabled veterans of the Great War who served in the ranks of the Royal Welch Fusiliers. Hitherto, these men (who I first met on a visit to the Rhondda Valley in 1960) have been ignored. It was as if their thoughts and knowledge were of no consequence, even though at least some of them were aware of what happened within their regiment

By writing this story as a novel, I am able to pry into the inner thoughts, ambitions, and machinations of those involved, even though this inevitably introduces a large degree of conjecture on my part. Likewise, a fictitious approach enables me to use dialogue to which I could not possibly have been privy.

I have modified a few military terms and tried to avoid details which would only confuse the non-military reader. The spelling of the Royal Welch (Welsh) Fusiliers has varied throughout their distinguished history, but I have stuck with the better known, and regimentally preferred, Royal 'Welch' Fusiliers.

British weapons in the Great War

The basic British platoon weapons in the Great War were Lea Enfield rifles and bayonets, Lewis light machine guns, and Mills hand grenades. These were usually referred to as bombs rather than grenades. They were larger than cricket balls and considerably heavier and the distance they could be thrown was approximately 40 yards. A bombing party was a group of men armed mainly with Mills bombs, used when raiding enemy trenches. They were often carried in satchels. Officers were armed with revolvers. Knives and knobkerries (African style coshes) were used by individual choice. Entrenching spades with short handles and sharpened edges were often used in hand-to-hand fighting. Periscopes were used in forward trenches in order to observe no-man's-land without risk of exposure.

Main Characters

Siegfried Sassoon	2nd Lt., Royal Welch Fusiliers
Lady Ottoline Morrell	Pacifist, intellectual and socialite
Robert Graves (von Ranker)	2nd Lt., Royal Welch Fusiliers
Davey Jones (618)	Young Welch Fusilier (autistic)
Rhys Jones (617)	Davey's twin, also a Welch Fusilier
Khyber Morgan	Fusilier, later promoted to RSM
Blodwyn Morgan	Wife of Khyber Morgan
Bertrand Russell	Pacifist, intellectual and socialite
Robbie Ross	Leading literary critic, agent
Megan Griffith	Cousin of the Jones twins
Lt. Col. Stockwell (Buffalo Bill)	Sassoon's commanding officer
Captain William Rivers	Army psychiatrist at Craiglockhart

Minor Characters

Captain Blakiston Houston	Cavalry Officer, 21st Lancers
Fusilier Butler	Sassoon's first batman
Captain Simpson	Defence Counsel, court-martial
Major Jordan	Prosecution Counsel, court-martial
Lytton Strachey	Member of Bloomsbury 'Lit. Set'
Phillip Morrell	Husband of Lady Ottoline
Sir Edward Marsh	Influential literary figure
Roderick Micklejohn	Secretary to the Prime Minister
Major Hunt	Company commander
Captain Vivian de Solta Pinto	Sassoon's second-in-command

SIEGFRIED SASSOON'S PROTEST

During July 1917 Second-Lieutenant Siegfried Sassoon, 1st Battalion, the Royal Welch Fusiliers, made the following protest against the continuation of the Great War. The war was heading towards a climax, with Germany enjoying a period of dominance on the western front. The protest was first made public in The Bradford Pioneer and was then publicised by national newspapers and raised in the House of Commons.

Sassoon's protest read:

"I am making this statement as an act of wilful defiance of military authority, because I believe the war is being deliberately prolonged by those who have the power to end it. I am a soldier, convinced that I am acting on behalf of soldiers. I believe that this war, upon which I entered as a war of defence and liberation, has now become a war of aggression and conquest. I believe the purpose for which I and my fellow soldiers entered upon this war should have been so clearly stated as to have made it impossible for them to change without our knowledge, and that, had this been done, the actions which actuated us would now have been attainable by negotiation.

I have seen and endured the sufferings of the troops, and I can no longer be a party to prolonging the sufferings of the troops for ends which I believe to be evil and unjust.

I am not protesting against the military conduct of the war, but against the political errors and insincerities for which the fighting men are being sacrificed.

On behalf of those who are suffering now, I make this protest against the deception which has been practised on them. Also I believe that it may help to destroy the callous complacence with which the majority of those at home regard the continuance of agonies which they do not share and which they have not sufficient imagination to realise."

PART ONE

KHYBER MORGAN

1

An Early Hero

Siegfried Sassoon was just my type of hero. From the moment I heard of him and his hair-raising exploits on the western front during the Great War, I was captivated. Our history teacher at Caterham Prep School devoted an entire lesson to him and even the excitement of the Battle of Britain, which was raging around us at the time, failed to divert my interest and admiration away from Sassoon.

It was mid-summer 1940 and due to our school's situation on the North Downs twenty or thirty aircraft were being shot out of the sky above us each day. Most of the other boys were engrossed in watching aerial dog-fights and collecting chunks of shrapnel, but although I did my fair share of both my main interest remained reading all I could about the trench warfare of the western front and the exploits of Siegfried Sassoon.

I never lost interest in him and he became something of an obsession with me. It was the start of years of research which lead to all kinds of revelations about Sassoon, in particular the consequences of his notorious and defiant protest. However, it wasn't until Christmas 1960 that my interest developed into something more tangible.

By then, I was in my mid-twenties, living at Elstead in Surrey, earning my living as a journalist and novelist. I was making enough money to enable me to propose marriage to a beautiful Welsh girl named Megan Griffith, a sales promotion lady with an expert knowledge of food-mixers, working at Bentalls Departmental Store in Kingston-upon-Thames. Her family home was at Ferndale in the Rhondda Valley, several miles north of Cardiff.

Over Christmas 1960 I drove down to Wales to stay with Megan in order to meet her parents, her two sisters, and her multitudinous relatives. Since I was the first Englishman to try to marry into the Griffith family I approached 55, Tip View Terrace, Ferndale with trepidation, knowing that I was in for a stringent appraisal.

In the early 1960s the area in and around the Rhondda Valley was the heartland of Wales: the coal mines were the base of the nation's wealth; it provided the power-house of their national rugby team; and the town of Treorchy boasted the best male voice choir in the world. Also, Megan had told me of what a proud and idiosyncratic race the Welsh were, so independent of mind that my future in-laws spoke Welsh more than they did English. Megan further warned me that although they would speak English in deference to me, they would soon revert to their native tongue if I failed to impress them. She advised me to concentrate on being a good listener: they were born raconteurs so I would impress them most if I laughed at their jokes and anecdotes and went along with their style of Christmas. This would include a monumental (male only) booze-up at the Old Comrades Club on Christmas Eve, a long Chapel service with a hell-fire-and-brimstone sermon from Mr Thomas on Christmas Day, and a trip to Cardiff Arms Park on Boxing Day to see Cardiff give the London Wasps their annual thrashing.

Having listened to Megan, and read Richard Llewelyn's famous novel *How Green is my Valley*, I thought I had a good idea of what I was letting myself in for, but what I encountered was quite beyond my expectations.

I must have impressed my future in-laws for not a word of Welsh was spoken during my visit. They could not have been more open and friendly; a delightfully happy lot who rarely stopped laughing and singing and who liked nothing better than to relate stories of bygone years, especially the days of the great depression when the miners were on strike and spent most of their time dodging and outwitting the Dorset Police who had been sent to the Rhondda to break up protest meetings and generally keep the natives in order - wonderful stories which were no doubt further exaggerated with each telling, but which were notable for never betraying any animosity towards the unfortunate English police who were only carrying out orders.

The afternoon of Christmas Eve was devoted to visiting Megan's relatives and drinking interminable cups of tea in front-parlours only ever used at Christmas and wakes. I was introduced to her relatives and I was aware of being eyed surreptitiously as they enquired into my interests, my background, and especially my future prospects.

The first indication I had that I was meeting with their approval came when an ancient great-aunt suddenly grasped her walking stick and thumped it on the floor. When she had everyone's attention, she said: "Never mind all this chit-chat. Can you hold your beer, bach?"

There was general laughter and later, as Megan and I walked back to her terraced home, she explained that what her great-aunt had in mind was the male-only booze-up at the Old Comrades Club. She emphasised that it was Ferndale's major social event of the year, so highly rated that everyone dressed up for it in their best suits. When I demurred, Megan made it quite plain that I had no option otherwise I would bring shame on the family. What's more, she told me that I would be expected to match them all pint for pint but on no account was I to get drunk; merry maybe, but not drunk. In Wales outward respectability was everything.

As Megan's father and I stepped out into Tip View Terrace, duly dressed in our Sunday suits, there was already a steady trickle of men making their way down the hill. By the time we reached the Porth Road there was a regular throng spilling out from terraced houses and sundry side streets like tributaries pouring into a major river. I began to wonder just how big the Old Comrades Club was and I dreaded to think of the chaos there would be at the bar.

I needn't have worried. The Club was enormous and the bar service was the swiftest I'd ever known. On entering everyone paid £2 into a 'kitty'. I was let in free. One of Megan's cousins explained to the doorman: "This is Megan's young man from London!" to which the doorman replied, "Oh, from London! That's all right then, look you."

In those days, anyone from the big smoke never failed to impress the Welsh. 'London' was a magic password that got you in free anywhere, apart from Cardiff Arms Park.

Once inside everyone made a bee-line for an enormously long bar on which pints of beer were already poured and awaiting collection. The club was soon crowded to capacity with well over three hundred crammed in. Everyone sat in family groups, leaving the bar free. So many were smoking (including me, a keen pipe-man) that the atmosphere was as dense as a London pea-soup fog.

To start with I felt very much an outsider as Megan's relatives exchanged family gossip. I feigned interest but my eyes wandered. The hall was festooned with Christmas decorations: paper chains, bags of tinsel, coloured balls, and glittering stars from Woolworth's. At the end of the hall was a stage and alongside it a huge Christmas tree, its branches sagging under the weight of boxed presents. It was all very different from what I was used to in England where my family spent every Christmas ensconced in front of a television set watching *The African Queen* and other repeat programmes whilst munching turkey sandwiches.

It was a relief when the conversation turned to rugby. Megan had obviously boasted about my prowess as a club-player with the Harlequins and how I was a friend of the slim young English sensation, Richard Sharp, who had run rings around the Welsh at Twickenham during his international debut. It gave my views credibility but in order not to appear partisan I referred frequently to past Welsh heroes such as Wilf Wooller, Vivian Jenkins, and Hayden Tanner.

As we pursued this common interest I became more relaxed. I was pretty sure that by now they had decided that Megan hadn't made such a disastrous choice after all.

Rugby talk went on until the singing started. The Old Comrades Club had its own choir and they formed up on the stage and led everyone in the usual repertoire of Welsh songs. I seized an early opportunity to visit the Gents. '*Sosfan Bach*' and other traditional airs were out of my musical range.

The crowd around the Gents was so solid that rather than get involved in the push and shove, I took a seat at an adjacent table to wait for the scrum to diminish. I found myself sitting next to a distinguished-looking man who I judged to be in his seventies. He exuded authority with an upright, square-shouldered physique; a hard man, a military man. "You must be Megan Griffiths's young man?" he said.

"That's right. How did you guess?"

"I can tell an Englishman a mile off." He smiled and revealed sparkling dentures. "And I know every one of the rogues who come in here every Christmas Eve."

"Yes, I suppose you would."

"I'm Khyber Morgan, ex-Welch Fusiliers. I've known Megan since she was a babe in arms. You're a lucky young fellow."

"I know."

He viewed me curiously, wondering why I'd chosen to sit there. "Not browned off with your new relatives already, are you?"

"No ... No ... I'm just waiting for a chance to have a pee."

"Oh, I see. Don't worry. The initial rush will soon thin out. They won't want to miss too much of the singing. You were in the Duke of Wellington's Regiment, I hear."

"Yes ... The 1st Battalion. Who told you?"

"Megan, of course. How come the Duke's? You're not a Tyke."

"A family tradition. My father and uncles were in the Dukes."

"Were they in the trenches?"

"Yes ... And Gallipoli."

"They survived?"

"Yes."

"Good for them!" He left it at that and drank deeply. I spotted an opening in the crowd around the Gents and I was just about to slip through it when he restrained me with a firm hand on my arm. "Hang on! I'll show you something that will interest you. You can get by without a leak for a bit yet. It will either make or break your Christmas, depending on your disposition. It's something you'll never forget, either way."

He waited until the choir broke off for liquid refreshments and then led me further down the room, towards the stage. As he stood up I was surprised by his height. He was at least 6 foot 3 inches tall with only a hint of late middle-age spread. As we walked down the room he paused at each table, making remarks of a personal nature that never failed to get a laugh or a friendly riposte. He was obviously a man of consequence in the Rhondda community.

When we drew level with the stage he went through a side door which had a temporary sign on it saying, 'Veterans'. It was another lounge bar with more Christmas decoration and a handsome buffet set out on a long trestle table. On the bar, pints of beer stood in readiness. Here however a male nurse in a white uniform stood by, ready to take the pints to the tables and regulate consumption. The reason for this was clear enough. The room was full of invalids, veterans of the Great War. Everywhere I looked there were empty jacket sleeves and trouser legs, all stitched back to shoulders or hips. Numerous crutches and walking sticks were scattered about the place, some just lying on the floor next to the owners. They all wore decorations, not just ribbons but the medals, often two rows of them. I immediately recognised a couple of Distinguished Conduct Medals and several Military Medals.

As soon as they saw Khyber Morgan a cheer went up. They were waiting for him and there were cries of "Here he is!" and "Good old Khyber!" He raised a hand in recognition. "Everything, all right, lads?" There were murmurs of assent and numerous ribald remarks. Nearly all of them raised their glasses to him and drank deeply.

We walked to the bar and helped ourselves to fresh pints, facing the veterans. They were a sad sight. Khyber told me about them, speaking softly and compassionately.

"These lads were all in the Fusiliers. From different battalions, mark you, but we all knew each other. There was a lot of interchanging among the battalions in those days. And these are the poor devils that never got over their experiences. They live in an Old Soldiers Home up near Mountain Ash. This is their annual Christmas treat. Those of us who were lucky to survive in one piece lay on a meal and a few drinks for them every Christmas. They're not allowed too much booze, of course, but this is their big night of the year. During the evening everyone drops in to have a word with them. There's nothing formal about it, just a gesture really. It's very difficult. With the shell-shocked it's impossible to know whether they want to reminisce over old times. Some do and some don't, and if you choose the wrong ones it does them more harm than good. I've known them for so long I reckon I know the form by now. We'll have a word with one or two of them in a moment."

I studied them unobtrusively. Many looked normal, but others appeared to have St Vitus Dance, their faces twitching or their bodies suddenly jerking, never still for more than a few seconds. Some were making heavy weather of raising their glasses and a fair amount of beer was being spilt. One man stood out in particular. He was sitting on his own and was obviously the odd man out, staring straight ahead, looking thoroughly bored, never blinking, just an empty gaze.

"Let's go round and see how morale is," said Khyber when we'd finished our pints. "Don't expect too much."

Khyber was an old hand at it. He was like touring Royalty: a word or two here and there and everyone was happy. He stopped at every table and made them laugh as he recalled past incidents. In reply they either referred to him as 'Sir,' or 'Khyber'.

As we passed down the room I asked him: "Were you an officer in the Fusiliers?"

He laughed. "Oh no, not me. I was a mere Fusilier when the war started, but I ended my service as the regimental sergeant major. Some of these lads served with me when I was a corporal, others when I was their sergeant, and just before the armistice, I was their company sergeant major. I didn't make RSM until we were on the north-west frontier. That's why I'm known as Khyber. Khyber isn't a Welsh name, in case you were wondering."

"I guessed that. I imagine it's something to do with the Khyber Pass?"

"Right! I've been up and down the Khyber Pass more often than any other serving soldier, so eventually it became my moniker. I've been Khyber Morgan to everyone in the valleys ever since."

We exchanged more banter with men at the tables, but when we reached the man who was on his own, Khyber walked straight past him. It was most unnatural. When we were out of ear-shot, I asked: "What's the matter with him?"

"Him? He's the saddest case of all. He never speaks. Not a word since 1918."

"A throat wound?"

"No, no. He was in France for four years and never got a scratch. It's a mental hang-up. They've never been able to find anything physically wrong with him. They even gave him electric shock treatment early on. A sort of torture. It was standard procedure then. They piled on the agony until men eventually spoke in order to avoid further pain. But they never got a word out of him, even though they damn nearly killed him. Now, he just sits around and never speaks. But in some respects he's quite normal. He reads quite a lot and plays chess up at Mountain Ash."

"Haven't you been able to help? You have the confidence of all the others."

"Me? Good God, no! He's Jones 617. Towards the end of the war we were serving together in the 25th battalion."

"What happened?"

"He's the Fusilier who shot Captain Siegfried Sassoon."

"The poet?"

"None other. He was my company commander."

"But Sassoon is still alive."

"I know. Jones shot him but he didn't kill him. He only grazed Sassoon's skull, hardly even a wound. If he'd shot him straight between the eyes, as he intended, he wouldn't be like he is now."

"You mean they would have strung him up."

"No, no. It would have been hushed up. Strictly speaking he was entitled to shoot him. The brass hats would have been glad to see the back of Sassoon at that stage. It would have been just another accident, a trigger-happy sentry shooting a man returning from no-man's-land."

"How can you be so sure it was intentional?"

"Because I saw everything that led up to it. Sassoon was a popular officer with his men but Jones 617 had a special reason for hating him."

As we walked on, Khyber tapped his nose with his right forefinger, a familiar gesture of confidentiality. "Say no more!"

Once we'd circled the room we retired to the bar for fresh pints. I was already feeling light-headed and I was very mindful of Megan's warning not to get drunk. As I pushed my glass aside, a group of men burst into the room, anxious to pay their respects to the veterans. Khyber nudged me and indicated that it was time for us to leave. He waved around as we made our way out, acknowledging more friendly remarks. "See you all next year, boys. Don't do anything I wouldn't."

There was general laughter and a chorus of replies: "That'll give us plenty of scope."

19

Khyber turned to me. "Sorry about the corny remark. I say it every year and they love it."

When I reached the door I stood aside to allow Khyber to go through first, but he stopped and looked towards the ceiling. He beckoned me to join him and pointed at framed photograph hanging above the doorway. It showed a young Welch Fusilier in uniform, smiling brightly, a chubby and happy-looking young fellow. The frame was expensive, surrounded by a strip of regimental ribbon. I looked at it in amazement. "Surely that's the fellow over there ... The starer."

"No, it's his twin brother, Jones 618. The 'starer', as you call him, is Jones 617. They were identical twins. No one could ever tell the difference, apart from the way they wore their caps. Their father was Jones-the-Bucket, a Ferndale family who lived just down the road from here." Khyber Morgan paused and then added: "In the Rhondda, Jones 618 is the greatest hero who ever lived. Even more than Jones 422 and Jones 491 who got Victoria Crosses at Rorke's Drift. "

I examined the photograph more closely. There was a simple caption beneath it: 'Fusilier Davey Jones, 618. Greater love hath no man than to lay down his life for a friend.'

"Was he a Victoria Cross as well?"

"Good God, no! They never gave 618 any medals, far from it." Then he added with bitterness: "The bastards!" His voice faded away, but the sight of the photograph had affected him. He pushed past me brusquely. There were tears in his eyes. One actually trickled down his weathered cheek. He brushed it away and walked on in embarrassment, the subject closed.

Once we were back in the main bar, he said: "Go and have that pee you were so desperate for. Then get back to Megan's menfolk before they think you're tired of their company."

We left the Old Comrades Club just before midnight. It was an unwritten rule that everyone returned home in time to wish the women (who were still up, waiting) a happy Christmas on the stroke of midnight. We were all pleasantly intoxicated, but none of us drunk. Megan and the other women were in the front parlour and as soon as we'd all piled in, more drinks were rolled in on a trolley and we toasted Christmas 1960 amid hugs and kisses.

Megan was anxious to know if I had enjoyed myself and who I had met and talked to. "He spent most of his time with Khyber Morgan," her father said. "He took him to meet the veterans from Mountain Ash."

"The singing was marvellous," I said, anxious to steer the conversation away from the unfortunate veterans. It seemed appropriate to keep things light and cheerful.

"Did you know any of the words?" asked Megan.

"A few, just here and there ... '*Bread of Heaven*' and things like that. But I didn't join in for fear of spoiling things."

In fact, whilst they were all singing I thought of little else besides Jones 617 and his twin brother's memorial photograph. It struck me as very strange that after so many years, and with the Second World War intervening, that the community in the Rhondda was still so obsessed by the Great War. Why not the veterans of WWII as well? I couldn't help feeling that something very odd had happened among the Welch Fusiliers in the trenches. A whole string of unanswered questions occurred to me.

Why should Jones 617 hate Khyber Morgan when the others so obviously admired him? Could it have something to do the shooting of Siegfried Sassoon? And why would Jones 617 have wanted to shoot him? And why did he fail to kill him? And how come he was entitled to shoot him? And why was his twin brother regarded as the Rhondda's greatest hero when he hadn't received any medals for gallantry? And who was the friend he laid his life down for: his twin brother? And what made Jones 617 lose his voice. And most puzzling of all was the vehemence with which Khyber Morgan had said: "The bastards!"

There was no midnight service in the local chapel, but no one showed any signs of going to bed. Just before two o'clock Megan's mother came in from the kitchen carrying a huge meat dish on which there was a turkey, dressed and ready for the oven, bulging with stuffing and with rashers of bacon draped across the breast. A cheer went up and Megan said to me: "Now you can go down with Dad and the others."

"Down where?"

"To Khyber Morgan's. He runs the local bakery."

She laughed at my quizzical look. "It's a point of honour in the Rhondda to have big turkeys. It's keeping up with the Joneses, literally. And the birds are always far too big for our ovens. So we take them down to Khyber and he puts them his bakery ovens. You'll see ..."

I joined what amounted to a guard of honour for the turkey and as we went out into the street I was again confronted by others trooping down the hill. The head of each household was holding their bird aloft, and there were lots of catcalls and friendly banter, each taking the mickey out of the other birds.

"So you're having pigeon pie this Christmas then, Dai?"

"I'll have you know this is a 20-pounder. Probably too big for even Khyber's ovens."

"Get away, man! We all know you've been soaking it in water for the last week."

When we reached the Porth Road we soon came across a double-fronted shop, lights ablaze. The shop's overhead sign proclaimed: "Morgan and Sons, High Class Bakers and Confectioners (Founded 1862)." Inside two young women and Khyber were tying labels on to the legs of turkeys to make sure everyone got their own bird back. We were at the rear of the queue and our turkey was one of the last to go into an oven. When Khyber slammed shut the final oven door, he called out, "Come back around one o'clock and they'll all be done to a turn."

"Don't forget to baste them well, Khyber."

"Don't tell me how to do my job, Boyo, or I'll have you on a charge."

"It wouldn't be for the first time."

"Nor the last, I can tell you."

We were about to leave when Khyber spotted me. He beckoned me over. "I've learnt something else about you, young man. From my missus this time ... You're a novelist ..."

"That's right."

"What are you writing now?"

"Nothing. I'm lost for a decent subject at the moment."

"Well when I told my missus I'd met you she gave me a right good telling-off. She said I should have told you everything that happened with Sassoon and the Jones twins. She says it's time the truth was aired. She's another

Jones, you see … A cousin. But writing about it won't be as easy as my missus thinks. Blodwyn has no idea how deep it all goes. I've never told her everything. But if you're interested in hearing the details, look me up next time you're down in the Rhondda."

"Right, I'll do that."

Megan and I were married that summer at Kingston-upon-Thames. Her parents could only afford to invite close relatives which meant that Khyber Morgan wasn't there. Consequently it was over three years before I met him again, and then only by accident.

Our first son had recently been born and Megan and I took him down to the Rhondda to show him off. By that time I'd forgotten all about Khyber and the veterans. However, during our visit I had occasion to call in at the local tobacconist to buy some Balkan Sobranie pipe tobacco, and who should be there but Khyber, also buying Balkan Sobranie. Our mutual love of this poisonous weed sparked off an animated conversation and we ended up smoking a couple of pipes together while enjoying a pint or two in the local pub. Inevitably, our conversation turned to the Fusiliers. He gave me a brief outline of the story about the twins and Sassoon but then added a word of warning.

"If you decide you want to write about it, you'll have to wait until everyone concerned is dead. And that includes me. The truth will only stir things up. And I don't want to be around when that happens. There will be too many denials, accusations, and counter claims. The Establishment of the Welch Fusiliers won't like the other ranks poking their noses in and telling what really happened. But don't worry, all those involved are dropping off like flies and you're young, so you can afford to wait."

As we finished our pints and prepared to leave, he added, "Next time you're down here I'll get out all my old maps, press cuttings, and even a photograph or two. I'll tell you the story in detail. Do it gradual, like. There's no hurry."

So every time Megan and I went down to Wales I made a point of visiting Khyber. We must have met dozens of times and we became firm friends as we delved into the past. He was a wonderful old soldier and a born raconteur. What made it even better was that as we sat in their tiny back parlour Blodwyn served up Welsh beef sandwiches with bread straight out of Khyber's ovens.

Khyber and I would round the evening off in the local pub; but whether in his back parlour or the pub we never left the western front. What he told me was so intriguing and so sad that I became determined to make it into a novel. I would aim to solve one of the many mysteries of the Great War and by so doing let future generations in the Rhondda know what really happened.

After each session with Khyber I went back home to Hayling Island and read up all I could about the Welch Fusiliers in the Great War. I not only wanted to check the accuracy of what he told me but also to get a more rounded picture of events. I read (and re-read) all the books by such writers as Robert Graves, Captain de Salvo Pinto, Colonel Stockwell, Robert Nichols, and the biographies of Lady Ottoline Morrell, Sir Philip Morrell, Bertrand Russell, and a host of literary figures on the fringes of the Bloomsbury Set, all of whom were involved. Eventually I was satisfied that I had the complete story.

One thing stood out above all else. Everything revolved around Siegfried Sassoon. He was a truly remarkable man. He had about him a mystique and an aura of distinction. He was a multi-faceted character: incredibly brave, absurdly reckless, impulsive to the degree of stupidity, and defiantly ill-disciplined. He had a talent for establishing friendships with his men at a time when familiarity between the ranks was very much frowned upon; but above all he was a poet, a man who never stopped composing fresh verses and who always had a novel or anthology of poetry at hand to read, never wanting to waste a single moment.

Yet he was also an odd-ball, a typical English eccentric, even though his roots were in the Middle East. The famous writer Richard Church claimed that he had a definite fissure in his personality, and Bertrand Russell declared him to be schizophrenic.

As Khyber Morgan insisted, I have waited until all the characters in the story are dead before publishing. Lady Ottoline Morrell, Bertrand Russell, Robbie Ross, and Edward Marsh had already departed. Sassoon went in

1967, aged 80, dying peacefully in bed just like the red-faced generals he so despised in his poetry. Robert Graves was one of the last to go. Only Khyber Morgan and Jones 617 were still alive when I finished writing the story to my satisfaction. Even when they died, in 1987 and 1989 respectively, I continued to wait, anxious to give plenty of time for the air to clear.

Megan and I attended Khyber's Memorial Service in June 1987. It was an unforgettable occasion; the biggest Memorial Service Wales had seen in years. He had, after all, been the regimental sergeant major of Wales's premier regiment and not many men could match his two Distinguished Conduct Medals, his Military Medal, and his three Mentions in Despatches. He also had six Welsh rugby caps and would have got many more had it not been for overseas service.

The singing at the funeral fairly raised the roof of Llandaff Cathedral. When the service was over and a lone bugler had sounded Last Post, we gathered in the Cathedral forecourt, reluctant to disperse, determined to swap stories about Khyber. I got into conversation with several Fusiliers who had known him during his days on India's North West Frontier. There were various theories as to how many times he had been up and down the Khyber Pass. Some said over fifty times, but others said that was a gross exaggeration.

"It doesn't matter how many times," said an ex-sergeant with all his medals up. "Khyber was the salt of the earth and he had more stories about the Fusiliers than anyone."

"And now the old bugger has taken them all with him," joked another.

I didn't say anything, but thought to myself, 'Oh no he hasn't.'

At home, on Hayling Island, I had every last detail of his most important story: the hitherto hushed-up account about the man who shot Siegfried Sassoon.

Here's what happened.

The Man Who Shot Siegfried Sassoon

PART TWO

SIEGFRIED SASSOON

2

Sassoon Joins the Colours

It was August 1914 and Siegfried Sassoon's life was in crisis. He was frustrated and disillusioned. His career as a poet had stalled and come to a juddering halt. One editor told him bluntly that he was a thoroughly spoilt, not-so-young man and that it was time he grew up. A close hunting friend advised him to get a job as a stoker in the merchant navy, convinced that he would never become a successful poet until he had experienced life in the raw.

He knew they were right. Since leaving Cambridge University he'd got nowhere. He'd written poetry of no literary merit; the ramblings of an immature pseudo-intellectual. Even his distinguished literary advisers, Edmund Gosse and Edward Marsh, were tired of trying to help him. His output had dwindled alarmingly and his early promise was not being fulfilled.

Sassoon moved to London, well away from Weirleigh, the family's country estate. He found living with his mother, surrounded by bowing and bobbing servants, suffocating. He hoped that London would liberate and inspire him, but it didn't. He produced even less poetry and the short book he brought out, *The Daffodil Murderer,* missed the mark as satire and degenerated into an empty pastiche of Masefield, with no originality.

All the time the years were slipping by. Rupert Brooke was younger than him and his career was roaring ahead. He was everyone's darling, the blue-eyed boy of English literature and the epitome of what Sassoon felt he should be. The final ignominy was that he was in financial difficulties with the prospect of having to ask his mother to bail him out.

Inevitably, he abandoned his London flat and slunk back to Weirleigh. Then, in a moment of frustration, he gathered together all his rejected and half-finished poems and burnt them, even pulling the chain on the ashes as an act of finality. Then he burst out of the house, jumped on his bicycle, and pedalled like hell, so mentally disturbed that he had no idea where he was going.

He ended up in Rye, having covered some thirty miles, but it was worth the effort. He revelled in the physical exertion of speeding along on his bike and he doggedly refused to dismount and push up any of the hills, and the harder he rode the more his mind cleared. It was always the same with him: hesitancy, doubts, and then a sudden burst of clarity, resulting in an irrevocable decision to take reckless action and to hell with the consequences.

By the time he found himself in a favourite tea shop in Rye his mind was made up. He would volunteer for the army. He would join the war against the Hun. He was convinced that with a short, sharp spell of combat, and a few daring exploits to gain him gallantry awards, his poetry would be transformed. He would make warfare his central theme and it would enable him to burst forth upon the literary scene.

Sassoon decided against joining the Brigade of Guards or a fashionable cavalry regiment. He wanted nothing to do with snobbishness, archaic military traditions, and high expenses. He would opt for a basic local unit, the Sussex Yeomanry. It was a relatively untried regiment formed during the Boer War, commanded by Lt-Colonel the Earl March.

Earl March regarded the Sussex Yeomanry as his personal regiment and insisted that all volunteers be interviewed by his adjutant, a bright, up-and-coming regular soldier seconded from the 9th Lancers named Captain Blakiston Houston. Earl March also stipulated that new recruits of high social standing, who might warrant a commission, should have a second interview at which he attended.

Earl March missed very little of what went on in Sussex and Kent and through the local social grapevine he heard that a Sassoon was about to volunteer at his Lewes depot. He knew all about the Sassoon family even though he had never met any of them. He was aware that one of the Thornycroft girls had married a Sassoon and had had three sons by him: Michael, Siegfried, and Hamo. He assumed that it was one of them who was about to volunteer, but he had no idea which one.

When Siegfried arrived at the Lewes Depot of the Yeomanry he, like the other recruits, signed on for the duration. They were then paraded before Captain Blakiston Houston and given a pep-talk about the merits of the regiment. Sassoon, to his surprise, was then taken to one side for a second interview. When he was ushered into the CO's office, Captain Blakiston Houston was at a desk in the centre of the room with Earl March sitting to the rear, intending to be a mere observer. Sassoon was invited to sit and he adopted a casual posture, leaning back with his legs crossed.

"Siegfried Sassoon?"

"That's right."

"I have a few questions," said Captain Blakiston Houston.

"Fire away!"

"Tell me something about yourself."

"Certainly. I was born in Matfield, near Tunbridge Wells. And I'm one of three brothers, our family residence being Weirleigh. My father died some years ago. I am aged twenty seven and I'm eager to do my duty towards King and country."

"And where were you educated?"

"Marlborough."

"And how did you fare at Marlborough?"

"Not very well. It was a ghastly place. I joined the Cadet Corps but didn't do too well in that either."

"And then?"

"Cambridge ... Clare College."

"What did you read?"

"Law."

"So you are now a qualified lawyer?"

"No. Law didn't suit me, so I read something else instead."

"What was that?"

"Medieval History."

"And did that suit you?"

"Even less."

"But you got a good degree, no doubt?"

"No. I came down early."

"Why was that?"

"I saw no point in it. Medieval History had nothing to do with my future career."

"And what career have you been following?"

"Poetry. I'm a poet."

"Really! Of any note?"

"I've had several things published."

"By whom?"

"I publish privately."

"How do you manage that?"

"I have private means."

"And since Cambridge what work have you done?"

"I've just said ... I am a poet."

"Nothing else?"

"No."

"And you make a good income from poetry?"

Sassoon laughed. "Five pounds so far. One publisher promised more, but he never paid up. But I get by."

"So you've never left home?"

"Yes, I left recently. I found living at Weirleigh somewhat claustrophobic. So lately I've been living in London. The capital is better for contacts and friends of influence in the literary world. It is where the decisions are made."

"And what other interests do you have ... Apart from poetry?"

"I hunt. We have our own stables at Weirleigh. I love hunting. I find it stimulating ... And I love a challenge."

"So you're a good horseman?"

"I like to think so."

"What else do you do?"

"I dabbled with polo ... I fish ... Play golf and cricket ... Cricket for either the village or the Blue Mantles."

Earl March interjected from the rear. "The Blue Mantles! I played against them years ago."

Having entered the conversation, Earl March felt obliged to continue. He was astounded by what he had heard so far. "If I understand you correctly, Sassoon, you had a singularly undistinguished career at Marlborough, you flunked out of Cambridge, and since then you haven't worked at all. You've spent your time hunting, fishing and playing golf and cricket?"

"I also write poetry."

"Don't you help to manage the estate?"

"We employ people to do that."

"So you've never done a real day's work in your life? And you're twenty-seven years old."

"As I've said, I have had numerous poems published, either in magazines or pamphlets. And recently a short book... *The Daffodil Murderer*..."

"Who published that?"

"John Richmond."

"Never heard of them ... Private means again?"

"Yes."

"And how many did it sell?"

"Not many. But it was critically acclaimed ... In some quarters."

"And in all this time you've only earned five pounds?"

Sassoon did not reply. The conversation had become repetitive. He also considered Earl March to be aggressive and unfair, indeed somewhat insulting. A silence ensued. Eventually Captain Blakiston Houston turned in his chair, wondering if Earl March wished him to continue with the interview. Earl March indicated that he didn't. He had heard enough.

"Sassoon, I mean no disrespect, but we are a very down-to-earth, working-class regiment, so with your lack of worldly experience, and your reluctance to knuckle down to anything worthwhile, I don't consider that you are a suitable candidate for a commission in the Sussex Yeomanry."

"A commission," said Sassoon. "I have no desire to be commissioned."

"You don't?"

"Certainly not. I want to serve my country as a trooper."

"I assumed that having been to Marlborough and Cambridge ..."

"The last thing I want are responsibilities. I just want to get to grips with the Hun, do my duty as best I can, and fight under the orders of those who are trained and competent in such things."

The Colonel's face flushed with annoyance. He felt belittled, as though he had lost an argument. "Very well, that's all."

Sassoon stood up and drew himself to attention, even though he was still wearing civilian clothes."

"Report back to the recruiting sergeant," said Captain Blakiston Houston. When Sassoon was out of the office the adjutant turned again to Earl March. "Well, sir?"

"Idle bounder! One of the landed Jewry. Still, he's probably a first-rate horseman with all that hunting. And that's the first requirement of any trooper. And he seems pretty keen to get stuck into the Hun."

"Yes, sir," agreed Blakiston Houston. "You're right." Then he smiled and added: "He'll go down a treat with the other troopers."

Sassoon's service with the Sussex Yeomanry was short-lived. It started with two pointless days in Lewes, marking time by doing domestic chores in the depot; sweeping, dusting and polishing as though he was one of the maids at Weirleigh. Their nights were spent with a single blanket on the bare floorboards of the local Corn Exchange, and when Sassoon found this intolerable and sought permission to stay at the local hotel instead, everyone laughed, apart from the sergeant. He said: "You'll do the same as everyone else, and if you don't like it you can lump it. Bloody hotel! You're in the army now, lad."

Another set-back occurred when Sassoon's groom at Weirleigh, Tom Richardson, travelled down to Lewes by train, together with Sassoon's beloved horse, Cockbird. As Richardson led the immaculately groomed animal into the depot stable yard asking for Mr Sassoon, his master's social status could not have been more emphasised. Those present stared in astonishment, wondering just what sort of a toff they had been landed with.

Due to the scarcity of mounts, Cockbird was allowed to stay and Sassoon took great delight in explaining to his new comrades how he and Cockbird had won numerous Point-to-Point races and how, at hunts throughout Sussex and Kent, they were renowned for tackling hedgerows and fences all others avoided.

On their third day at Lewes they set off on a journey to a temporary camp near Canterbury. There, they were under canvas and for several days they were put through basic training, learning how to march, salute, drill, and other elementary requirements. The weather was hot and sunny and to start with Sassoon enjoyed himself. His fellow troopers were a novelty, from a social strata he had never encountered - men with an earthy sense of humour who used language of which Sassoon was aware but chose to ignore other than in moments of stress.

Gradually, things began to pale, especially when the weather broke. Also, he realised that Cockbird was not cut out for a military life, being unable to cope with the weight of military equipment, and rather than see his beloved horse become a beast of burden, he sold Cockbird to one of the Yeomanry officers for his personal use.

For Sassoon there was no such escape. He found sharing a tent with twelve yokels increasingly irksome. Several of them snored loudly and one or two of the others had even more unpleasant personal habits. Sassoon longed for the privacy of his own room and his study at Weirleigh and the luxury of clean sheets, a soft mattress, and early morning tea in bed.

What surprised him, and greatly amused his comrades, was that they were far more able to cope with routine duties than he was. He was forever late on parades and he resented being punished for what he considered to be trivial infringements. Most of all, they laughed at his aversion to mucking-out, a task which at Weirleigh was undertaken by the junior stable lad.

His Squadron Commander was a thoroughly unpleasant disciplinarian who specialised in impromptu fire-drills. As he always put it: "I like to catch the men with their trousers down - their pyjama trousers in the middle of the night!" He also liked to spring emergency assemblies on them. These entailed saddling up and standing-to in full battle-order, ready to ride off at a moment's notice.

Sassoon accepted these things, knowing that they were inevitable in the army. What he found intolerable was the absence of proper conversations. He yearned for discussions about literature, music, and art, but all he ever got from his new comrades were lurid details of 'having it off' with tarts in Canterbury.

When their training progressed to the art of horsemanship, Sassoon came into his own. Then, he was able to out-perform his fellow rankers, forcing them to admit that his previous boasting about his hunting and Point-to-

Point successes was fully justified. NCOs came to rely on him to demonstrate how things should be done, especially how to treat their mounts, to nurse them along and get the best out of them.

Soon his Squadron Commander singled him out for training fresh horses, and at one point the adjutant took him aside to compliment him on his good work. This led to him being asked to ginger-up a new horse that was said to be lazy. With his love, understanding, and patience, Sassoon soon had the animal's confidence. It responded to him wholeheartedly and those who witnessed the transformation were filled with admiration. Sassoon was so exhilarated by his success that he exercised the horse every day, gradually extending it until it was as good as any horse in the regiment. Eventually, he became so proud of displaying what a good combination they were that on a routine squadron exercise he broke ranks and attempted a fence that was beyond the horse's capability. Sassoon was thrown and suffered a broken arm, an injury that proved slow to heal. It had to be re-set twice and eventually a silver plate was inserted to help the bone to knit together.

During his long convalescence, split between a Canterbury hospital and Weirleigh, he reassessed his situation. His greatest concern was that only a fifth of the troopers in the Sussex Yeomanry had volunteered to serve overseas. It meant that the regiment was unlikely to be sent abroad. They would sit at home, ready to repel a non-existent invasion, while others saw real action in Belgium and France.

That wasn't what Sassoon had signed on for. He wanted adventure and experiences that would give his poetry substance. The war was getting deadlier every day and he was desperate to be part of it. He longed to be in the trenches which now stretched from the North Sea to Switzerland.

He decided to quit the Sussex Yeomanry and join an infantry regiment. He made enquiries and was told that easiest way was to apply for a commission, which everyone told him he should have done in the first place; that the privileges of rank far outweighed any lack of responsibilities, and that, anyhow, his social standing deemed that he should be a leader. His main adviser was a family friend, Major Ruxton, a retired professional soldier still with influence in his old regiment, the Royal Welch Fusiliers. The major's advice was reinforced when Sassoon heard that a young man for whom he felt a physical attraction was also about to join the Welch Fusiliers.

Sassoon had got to know Bobby Hanmer through hunting with his sister Dorothy. She was a good-looking young woman and a fine and brave horsewoman, but Sassoon found her brother infinitely more appealing. He even feigned interest in Dorothy in order to ingratiate himself with Bobby, and eventually he became engaged to her, inspired by the same motive.

Such homosexual leanings were nothing new with Sassoon but his was a passive style of homosexuality. He was the type who stood back and admired, but he was so shy of making a first move that he never got into trouble with the law. He regarded his inclinations more as antipathy towards women than a desire for a physical relationship with another male. With Bobby Hanmer he fantasised about saving his life in heroic circumstances in France, not sodomizing him.

Consequently, Siegfried Sassoon utilized Major Ruxton's influence and applied for a commission in the Fusiliers. The Sussex Yeomanry raised no objections and the *London Gazette* duly recorded that he had been appointed a probationary second-lieutenant in The Royal Welch Fusiliers

3

A Farthing as a Tip

Rhys and Davey Jones were arguing as they walked down the hill towards the Army Recruiting Office in Porth. Usually they argued over trivial matters, one-sided arguments with Rhys holding forth and Davey hardly interested, silent apart from occasional cutting and uncalled for remarks such as "balls!" or "bollocks!" This time it was different. It was a serious argument. Davey was roused and when he was roused he was prone to give way to loud outbursts. Right now, he didn't like the sound of what Rhys was suggesting: it would all end in change and upheaval, two things he couldn't abide. For him everything had to be routine and predictable, or else he just couldn't cope and opted out with long periods of silence.

There was a pause in their argument. Rhys wasn't surprised. He knew all the signs. Davey was about to explode, maybe even become hysterical; so Rhys adopted a conciliatory tone. "Davey, unless we do something, and do something quickly, it'll mean a beating from Da. He'll knock the hell out of us. Our jobs of delivering meat for Cleaver Williams didn't come easy, look you. And persuading Cleaver to buy us a tandem was something really special."

They walked on in silence, but Rhys hadn't finished. "Davey, you should have taken the farthing and left it at that."

"A farthing as a tip!" exclaimed Davey. "Now there's generous for you!"

"All right, a farthing isn't much, but you should never have planted it in her front garden and said that with any luck it would take root and grow."

"Served her right."

"Maybe! But why make things worse with one of your silly limericks? It's sick to death with them, I am." Rhys's strong Welsh accent rang out loudly as he became increasingly exasperated. "Sick to death with them, I am!"

Davey chuckled, going from one extreme to another, as he often did. "It was a good one though, Rhys. But I only got half of it out before she boxed my ears. You should have heard the rest of it, then. It was a good one ... One of my best."

Davey was so proud of his riposte to the odious Mrs Wynford-Barclay that he recited it again, this time in full.

> *"There was an old bag from Mountain Ash*
> *Who looked just like a bloke with a tash,*
> *She'll go to her grave*
> *Still needing a shave*
> *But up to her fat arse in cash."*

It was a good one, but Rhys was never going to admit it. "That's enough, Davey! No more, now. No wonder she reported us to Cleaver."

Rhys and Davey Jones were identical twins. As the midwife who delivered them exclaimed: "There now, two peas from the same pod!" Their likeness was so uncanny that it made them minor celebrities in the Rhondda, especially since their Ma insisted that they dressed alike. Yet in character they were far from identical. Their personalities had nothing in common. Rhys was bright, aggressive and serious-minded, a scholar the local school in Ferndale was proud of. He played the piano beautifully and had a passion for singing, with a fine tenor voice, at sixteen the youngest person ever to pass an audition for the Treorchy Male Voice Choir.

On the other hand, Davey ... Well, Davey was an enigma. No one understood him, which made them either wary or downright suspicious of him. Small children, especially girls, were scared of him. They ran off when they saw him coming. Despite being identical to Rhys there was something very odd about him, something that made him stand apart. To some, it was the way his mouth always hung open, with others it was his penetrating stare. Both traits declared him to be a simpleton, an archetypal village idiot, someone who found it impossible to relate to others, a lad who spent most of his time in a world of his own.

No one was surprised. It ran in the family. His Uncle Desmond was still remembered. He had been institutionalized in early childhood and left to rot in an asylum for the rest of his life. During the fifty-five years he was incarcerated no one ever visited him. All his relatives were afraid that if they put in an appearance the authorities would minimise his difficulties and expect them to take him back home to care for him. When he eventually died, and the family saw the conditions in which he had lived, they were so ashamed that when Davey was born and found to be similarly handicapped they agreed that he should never suffer the same fate.

They were lucky: providence smiled upon them. His twin brother, Rhys, was perfectly normal and so bright and intelligent that his God-fearing parents concluded that he had been sent by the good Lord to look after his less fortunate brother. From early childhood it was deemed that he should be his brother's keeper: he had a contract for life as a minder.

Rhys assumed the role automatically. He knew nothing else and although he was never entirely successful in keeping his brother out of trouble, his love and devotion towards him enabled them to stagger from one minor crisis to another without anyone demanding that Davey should be locked away and forgotten, as his uncle Desmond had been.

Like most people in the Rhondda, Cleaver Williams was aware of the situation. Cleaver was well-off, the owner of several butcher-shops, and for years he had employed the twin's father as a part-time gardener at his home in Porth. Their father was such a good gardener that he won Cleaver Williams numerous prizes in local flower and produce shows, and this put him in such good favour with Cleaver that when the twins left school and were looking for work, he employed them as delivery boys. Really, he only had a vacancy for one, but Rhys and Davey refused to be parted. So Cleaver Williams splashed out on a brand new Rudge tandem and had it adapted with a large luggage rack on the front so that they could make deliveries up and down the valleys.

For a couple of years everything went smoothly but gradually the familiarity of the job, with the same old orders, the same old journeys, and the same old customers, made it boring and tedious. Davey became increasingly disgruntled and complaints against him multiplied. Customers found him sullen and abrupt, often downright rude, and the way he so often just sat on the rear saddle of the tandem, his feet barely reaching the ground, and left Rhys to do all the work, made customers contemptuous.

Cleaver Williams took a lenient view of the complaints and it wasn't until Davey was downright rude to the bank manager's wife, Mrs Wynford-

Barclay, that it became too much. Burying his tip in her garden was one thing, but when he dragged her handlebar moustache into the dispute, that left no alternative but the sack. Cleaver Williams gave them a week's notice and sent them packing, straight back home to face the wrath of their Da.

That was when Rhys had his flash of inspiration. Rather than go home in disgrace, sacked and unemployed, and due for the mother-of-all beltings, he decided they should enlist in the army. With the war only a few days old, the army was the perfect answer. Their Da would be furious at first, but he'd soon get over it, just so long as they had jobs to go to. Indeed, as far as Rhys could see, their Da would soon welcome them being in the army. It would get them out of his hair for good. The army would clothe them, feed them, and accommodate them. Their pay would be more than they got as delivery boys and even if Davey got them into further trouble the army would never sack them. They might confine them to barracks, or give them 28 days in the glass house, but never the sack. The army was a secure haven, a lot better than the only other option of going down the pits; and as far as the war was concerned, that wasn't anything to worry about. Everyone knew it would be all over by Christmas.

The Recruiting Sergeant for the Royal Welch Fusiliers at Porth spent most of his days standing formally at ease behind the plate glass window of his recently opened Recruiting Centre. He looked straight along the busy main street and to start with he had been full of confidence. He had expected a steady stream of jingoistic lads to come marching up the hill, all eager to join up; and with his fee of half a crown per enlistment he reckoned he would soon be rolling in dosh, able to booze away to his heart's content.

It just hadn't happened. The youth of the Rhondda had no idea why war had been declared and, as so many of them pointed out, they had no quarrel with the Germans. If it had been a war against the English pit owners, that would have been different, but since it was against the Germans only ten had volunteered in a fortnight.

Then the sergeant's eyes lit up and he was unable to conceal his amusement. He turned to his corporal who as was sitting behind him with his feet resting on their desk, twiddling his thumbs. "Well now, here's a tidy situation, Corporal. Look you at what we have here, then. The Jones twins."

The sergeant knew all about the Jones twins. He often saw them riding about the valley on their Rudge tandem, their huge luggage rack piled high with blood-stained paper packages containing everything from pig's trotters to fillet steaks. It made him wonder what the hell the world was coming to. The likes of the Jones twins would never sort out the Hun. He even doubted if they were old enough to enlist. They certainly didn't look eighteen.

Rhys led the way into the office, with Davey loitering well behind. As Rhys began to explain their presence, Davey wandered across the room and studied an enormous poster of Lord Kitchener on the far wall. He even offered the great man a sloppy salute. When Rhys saw that the sergeant was watching Davey, rather than listening to him, he went over to Davey and pulled him away. Then he explained to the sergeant that they'd come to sign on for seven years with the colours and five years in the reserves. The sergeant told him not to be so bloody soft; to go back to their Ma and Da and stick to riding Cleaver Williams's tandem. Then, as a joke, he added: "Don't you realise that delivering sausages is a reserve occupation? Anyhow, how old are you?"

"Eighteen last March," Rhys lied.

"And no birth certificate, I take it?"

"No, never had one. And my brother is the same age as me. We're twins."

"You don't say! Twins the same age ... Now there's a novelty for you."

Davey responded with a giggle. Much as he relied and doted on Rhys, he enjoyed seeing him belittled. The sergeant glanced at him, having heard various stories about him and he decided to have some fun at their expense. He turned again to his corporal and winked. "Well, what I suggest you do, lads, is take a trip down to Port Talbot. Rumour has it that down there they are forming a Welsh Bantams Battalion, a new unit designed for short-arses like you two who can't see over the top of the trenches. You're too short for the Fusiliers, even though the minimum height has just been lowered to five feet five inches."

"That's what we are," replied Rhys.

"In your socks?"

"Without socks."

"Boyos, you may not realise it, but you're volunteering for the Royal Welch Fusiliers. It's the finest regiment in the British Army. And apart from winning wars we are renowned for two things - winning the Army Rugby Cup and our singing. And with due respect, I don't fancy the chances of either of you under a Gary Owen. And our choirs need basses, baritones and tenors, not trebles."

"We're tenors," said Rhys indignantly. "And I've passed an audition for the Treorchy, look you."

The sergeant paused. That was difficult to argue with. No one was accepted by the Treorchy unless he really could sing. He racked his brain for another reason for sending them on their way. Then his corporal handed him a scribbled note. It said, 'Stop buggering about, Sarge! Just sign them on! We need the commission.'

The note jolted the sergeant back to the reality. Too right! He wasn't paid to pussy-foot about. The army needed recruits, and so did he. Two enlistments meant 5/- for him and his corporal, enough for a good night's piss-up. So he settled for a snide remark instead. He nodded at Davey. "Doesn't he speak at all?"

"Only when he wants to. I speak for us both. I'm the elder ... By twenty minutes."

"Oh, the son and heir ..."

"That makes no difference."

"And I suppose your Da is Jones-the-Bucket?"

"That he is, Sergeant."

"And does he know you are volunteering?"

"No, Sergeant. It's a surprise we're giving him."

"A surprise, indeed! Really? Well lads, he won't be half as surprised as you two are going to be. But since you're both eighteen and five foot five, sign here and you're in, subject to a medical."

"Medical?"

"Of course! But don't worry. It's only a quick once-over. And nothing mental about it. You're not paid to think in the army. Just so long as your balls jump when you cough, you're in."

"And what about the King's shilling?"
"Oh, and it's a barrack room lawyer you are already then, is it?"

4

A Taste of Action

By the time Siegfried Sassoon had been gazetted as a probationary officer in the Royal Welch Fusiliers and joined the 1st Battalion in France, Rhys and Davey Jones were already combat veterans. They had been in the trenches over six months and had taken part in the Battle of Loos, even though their contribution had been decidedly inglorious. As members of Seven Platoon, C Company, they had been the first to go over the top. They'd only gone a few yards when they came under fire from machine guns and within minutes half their comrades lay dead in the mud of no-man's-land. The twins and the other survivors dived into the nearest shell craters for cover.

B Company followed up swiftly as a second wave. Their officers and NCOs were desperate to rally the remains of C Company, ordering them to get back on their feet and re-join the sprint towards the German trenches. Major Baxter, the B Company Commander, actually paused on the lip of the crater in which the twins were sheltering. He pointed at them and yelled at them to get up and to follow him. Davey stumbled to his feet, obeying instinctively, but Rhys stayed perfectly still and defiant. Before Major Baxter could say anything else he was shot dead. He collapsed in a heap and his body rolled into the crater, coming to rest between the twins. They looked down at him in horror. There was no hope for him. He'd been shot straight between the eyes. There was a neat hole with blood trickling down his face to form a dark brown mask as it congealed.

"Get back down," Rhys shouted. "Get under cover … Lie flat …"

"But …"

"Get down, I tell you. We're not going anywhere."

There would be no heroics as far as Rhys was concerned. He'd got his brother into this horrific mess and now he was going to get him out of it. He'd promised his Ma and Da that he would look after Davey and take him home unharmed, so he wasn't going to let him walk into a hail of bullets.

He stretched his right arm up and grabbed Davey by the seat of his trousers, pulling him down into the mud. "Play possum," he yelled. "Pretend you're dead."

They stayed in the crater for the rest of the day, lying on their stomachs, faces in the mud. Major Baxter was between them face up, his sightless eyes searching the sky, arms and legs akimbo. Other companies pressed home the attack, a seemingly endless stream of men rushing past above them, heading for near-certain death. The bedlam of exploding shells and the rattle of machine guns continued, together with frequent exhortations by officers and NCOs to keep going and not to bunch. Then the impetus of the attacks evaporated. No-man's-land became so thick with bodies that survival became of the essence and more and more troops followed the example of the Jones brothers and sought shelter in the shell craters.

They stayed there for the rest of the day and well into the night. None of them were going to take any more chances. They remained tense and alert. Davey was the only one who slept. He snored as he always did, but amid all the battle noises no one noticed. Eventually, when things had calmed down, and it was obvious that the Battle of Loos was over, men sheltering in the craters began to stir. Rhys woke his brother and they joined others in crawling back to their own lines. The fresh Scottish unit manning the trenches watched the bedraggled figures emerging out of the darkness and they were so sickened by the sight of so many shattered men that they never queried what had happened. Their hearts bled for the decimated Fusiliers, so they helped to drag them in. They placed the wounded on stretchers and directed the others to the rear, telling them that the remains of the Fusiliers were in reserve, waiting to be reformed by an influx of reinforcements.

Siegfried Sassoon was among the reinforcements. He was the oldest of a dozen subalterns, the others being straight out of Sandhurst or their public schools. To the surviving senior officers in the battalion, they were simply a new in-take of 'warts', a term designed to keep subalterns in their place, so necessary for good discipline and a reminder that however willing they were to sacrifice their lives, they remained the LFL in the PBI, lowest form of life in the poor bloody infantry.

Sassoon didn't care what they called him. He was just happy to have at last joined the 1st Battalion with Bobby Hanmer and another subaltern, David Thomas, a remarkably handsome son of a Welsh vicar who he had first met at Cambridge.

Life in the war zone surprised them. They assumed they would go straight into the forward trenches and remain there for weeks on end, confronted by close combat, nightly patrols into no-man's-land, and under constant shell fire. In their innocence, it was what they were looking forward to: a chance to deal out death to the Hun. The old hands soon put them right. They told them that because conditions in the line were so bad, with freezing temperatures, torrential rain, thick mud, and rats and lice - never mind the Hun - units never did more than a few days in the forward trenches before being withdrawn for a rest; and that once out of the trenches they were able to get cleaned up, be de-loused, and billeted in local towns and villages which had been evacuated by the French civilians. The officers took the pick of the billets, and found ways of making themselves very comfortable. They established company and battalion messes and the availability of horses and limited motor transport meant they were able to visit local towns where they enjoyed meals and drinks in the hotels and bars that were still operating normally.

The other ranks made do with whatever billets were left over, usually in derelict farm buildings, but they also had liberal freedom and took advantage of it, visiting local bars where they drank until they were reeling or broke. In most towns there were even brothels: red light houses for the rankers and blue light houses for the officers.

Sassoon and David Thomas were in C Company under Major Hunt, billeted near Bethune. They soon got to know the men in their platoons. Sassoon found them very different from the men he'd served with in the Sussex Yeomanry. They were younger and more compliant and because most of them had been born and bred in the squalid conditions of the Welsh mining villages they had little difficulty in adapting to living rough, whether in the line or reserve. Shell-damaged billets and dugouts which were little more than holes in the ground, held no terrors for them. They were happy to endure anything just so long as they could sing. Singing to them was a

46

reflex action. Each company had a choir with an elected choir-master and so keen were men to give expression to their talents that when parties of them approached each other along a trench or a stretch of road, instead of passing the time of day with idle gossip they would launch into song, what they called question and answer duets. Their favourite was *On Ilkley Moor Bar 'Tat*, with one lot singing, 'Where hast thou been since I saw thee?' and the other answering 'On Ilkley Moor bar 'tat'. Once they'd sung a couple of verses they went their ways, laughing happily.

Sassoon, being English, and hardly able to sing a note, was a man apart, but that didn't stop his platoon respecting him. They looked up to him because of his social background, a natural leader of whom they expected great things, instinctively recognising the British class system as an ideal basis for running an efficient army.

Sassoon was amazed by the number of his men with the same surnames. Eleven of them were named Jones, five Davies, and three Williams. With the Joneses it was so confusing that they were all known by their last three army numbers. The only two Sassoon mastered were the Jones twins, Rhys and Davey - Jones 617 and Jones 618 respectively. It was such a formal arrangement that even the twins abided by it, referring to each other by their last three numbers. The first time Sassoon met them was on a foot-inspection. As he approached them Jones 617 said to his brother: "Here comes our officer, 618 ... Look up, boyo."

"I am looking up, 617."

"Well give him a salute when he reaches us."

"Of course I'll salute him, 617 ... Is it daft you think I am?"

"I know very well it's daft you are, 618. Just do it. "

After they'd saluted, 617 sighed in exasperation. "For God's sake, 618! There's no need to shake hands with him as well, man."

Sassoon's platoon consisted of three sections of twelve men each with Sergeant Matthews looking after routine activities and shouldering the main responsibility for discipline. He also appointed Sassoon's batman and runner, both of whom would share the platoon HQ dugout while in the line. Sassoon's batman was appropriately named Butler, a regular soldier with years of service; a God-fearing man married with two daughters. He was very quiet, industrious, and efficient, and Sassoon soon came to like and respect him.

Sergeant Matthews appointed Jones 618 as Sassoon's runner. This brought a protest from Jones 617 who pleaded that they should remain in the same section, but Sergeant Matthews would have none of it. He'd seen enough of Jones 618 to know that he couldn't be relied upon. Being platoon runner would be no push-over, but it was generally reserved for one of the less able men in the platoon. When 617 continued to protest, Sergeant Matthew snapped: "You're in the same platoon, for God's sake. What more do you want?"

"My Ma told me not to let him out of my sight, Sergeant. And it'll be the best for everyone if I keep an eye on him."

"Well your Ma doesn't run this bloody platoon, now does she? I do."

Despite the harshness of his rebuke, Sergeant Matthews had a word with Sassoon about the delicate relationship between the twins. "If Jones 618 isn't up to normal duties," said Sassoon, "he should be transferred to a rear echelon."

"It's not as easy as that, sir. As twins they refuse to be parted. And if 618 was transferred there is no way 617 would be allowed to accompany him. So we leave them as they are. With respect, sir, it would be best for him to be your runner and for you to keep an eye on him."

"Right, I'll do that," agreed Sassoon.

The 1st Battalion's commanding officer was Lt. Colonel C.I. Stockwell, an experienced and popular officer, even though notorious for strict discipline and occasional bullying. He was a dogmatic man, set in his ways, who expressed himself with a string of clichés which he repeated ad nauseam. He often threatened to shoot men who displeased him and at other times he would urge men 'to get stuck in' or accuse them of having 'cold feet!', or the 'vertical wind up'. It was never just 'the wind up' or the 'horizontal wind up' but for some reason always the 'vertical wind up'. He was adamant that no-man's-land belonged to the Fusiliers and that the Hun must be hounded mercilessly until they were too frightened to leave their trenches. He was known throughout the battalion as 'Buffalo Bill', the origins of which were unknown, although some said it was because of the way he cracked the whip, just as Buffalo Bill did in his capacity of ring-master at his circus.

Among the first officers Sassoon met from other companies was Robert Graves, one of the few subalterns to have survived the Battle of Loos. He had acquitted himself well during the battle but even that failed to improve his standing in the battalion. Everyone was suspicious of Graves. He had German blood, his full name being von Ranke Graves. He was further handicapped by his uncouth, scruffy appearance and his irritating habit of butting into other peoples' conversations with the air of a know-all, especially when the subject broached the arts. In the opinion of many of his fellow officers, Graves should never have been commissioned, despite being educated at Charterhouse, and he was often referred to as 'von Ranker Graves'.

Graves first met Sassoon after having a row with his company commander over the right of one of his Fusiliers to call his lance/corporal by his Christian name. Graves was so disgusted by such pettiness that he stomped off in a paddy and made for C Company officers' mess where things were more adult.

The mess was in a farmhouse and as Graves passed through the hall he saw tatty magazines, newspapers, and cheap novels with lurid covers scattered about on a table, most of them soggy because of the rain dripping through the shell-damaged roof. He eyed them casually and even thumbed his way through a copy of *John Bull*. Then he was amazed to see a copy of *'Essays'* by Lionel Johnson. It was a dry, well-preserved copy and Graves wondered who in the Fusiliers would be interested in such a book. He went into the mess still carrying it and glanced around. Several officers were sitting about, either talking shop or smoking, with an air of boredom hanging like a cloud. His eyes eventually rested on Sassoon. He was in the far corner, standing over a wart sprawled out in a battered armchair. Sassoon stood out, being several years older than the other warts. He was over six foot tall and well-built and had a plain face with a large nose and protruding ears; yet he had an inquisitive, intelligent look, not the usual bland expression of a youngster straight out of his public school. Graves's final clue to the ownership of *'Essays'* was that Sassoon was holding a

49

leather-bound copy of *Tess of the d'Urbervilles*, so Graves went straight up to him and butted into his conversation, ignoring Thomas. He held *Johnson's Essays* aloft. "Yours?"

Sassoon turned in surprise. "Yes. Why? You want to read it?"

"I already have. I just didn't expect to see a copy here."

"I didn't like to throw it away."

"No, you mustn't do that. It can stand being re-read - several times. I'm Robert Graves, A Company."

"Siegfried Sassoon ..."

"The poet?"

"Yes. How did you know?"

Sassoon was delighted. It was the first time a stranger had ever acknowledged him as poet. He smiled broadly, an infectious grin that often gained him speedy friendships.

"I'd heard that you were due to join the battalion," said Graves. "And it may surprise you to know that I've been following your progress: *The Daffodil Murderer* and all that. I write a bit myself as it happens, poetry mainly. But nothing published yet. Not like you. But I will be, you wait and see. When did you arrive?"

"Three days ago. And you?"

"Long time now. Or so it seems."

"Loos?"

"Yes."

"A bad affair, I hear?"

"Appalling! Utter chaos. No one had the slightest idea of what was happening. Everyone just milling about getting mown down."

"Things can only get better then?"

"Hopefully, but the carnage won't stop. It'll just become more organised and methodical." Graves laughed bitterly. "But don't take any notice of me. As anyone will tell you, I'm a cynic with the very suspect name of von Ranke. I've even been accused of being a spy, especially since I've got relatives fighting on the other side. I expect you'll get a similar reaction with the name of Siegfried. And being one of the Chosen Race won't help you."

Sassoon stared at Graves, taken aback by his directness.

"Never mind," continued Graves. "Why don't we walk into Bethune to let our hair down? Enjoy ourselves while we have the chance?"

"I'm afraid the brothels have no great appeal for me."

"I don't mean the brothels." Graves laughed mockingly. "Oh dear! You've formed a bad opinion of me already. I might look like a womaniser, but if anything I'm inclined the other way."

"But I'm told that's all there is in Bethune ..."

"Not at all. It's a nice little town. Or it was. And at the far end, beyond the brothels, there's a tea shop where they serve Earl Gray tea and cream buns at three times the proper price. Sometimes they even have Eccles Cakes. But never any Welsh Cakes, unfortunately. Anyhow, let's give it a try. Better than sitting around here. You can tell me what you think of *Johnson's Essays*. And you might be interested in what I've written."

Sassoon didn't reply. He'd never heard of Graves, let alone his poetry. Indeed he could imagine what his poetry was like: schoolboy doggerel, typical of a sixth-form classicist with no idea how difficult it was to get into print. Sassoon turned to David Thomas. "Shall we go?"

"No thanks," replied Thomas. "But don't mind me. You two go off and discuss Johnstone's *Short Stories*."

"*Essays*, actually," corrected Graves. "By Johnson."

"Whatever," laughed Thomas.

Sassoon and Graves walked into town. As they passed the red-light brothel numerous men were queueing patiently. As the two officers passed by most of them looked away, shame-faced, but others laughed and joked, full of bravado. One, near the front, already had his trousers off with them dangling over his arm.

On the far side of Bethune the tea shop was empty, just several tables scattered around covered with dirty tablecloths and surrounded by a hotchpotch of upright chairs. They sat at a table by the window and when a dishevelled French woman appeared they ordered tea and cakes.

"What kind of cakes she brings is in the lap of the Gods," said Graves. "They're invariably stale and she practically throws them at you. Hardly the service you get at the Waldorf. And the tea is ghastly on account of the suspect water supply. The Frogs have no idea. It always amazes me that they're our allies. We have much more in common with the Germans."

"You'd better not say that too often."

"I already have. And you're right. It didn't go down well."

As they waited to be served they were silent. It was not an auspicious start to what was destined to become one of the most significant literary associations of their time, a friendship that would greatly influence their lives and many others. The cakes turned out to be cream buns, as hard as Mills bombs and with some of the cream scraped away, as though the management thought the baker had been too generous.

"Looks as though the mice have been at them," said Sassoon.

Graves chuckled boyishly. It helped to thaw the strangeness between them. He asked what an Englishman was doing in a Welsh regiment. Sassoon told him about his brief experience in the Sussex Yeomanry and then explained his friendship with Bobby Hanmer and how they had applied for a commission together. Eventually they discussed *Johnson's Essays* and this broadened into a general literary review. Their opinions differed considerably but neither felt obliged to shift or compromise their views. Sassoon's interests were strictly traditional with a tendency towards satire, whereas Graves prided himself on a more avant-garde approach, being very critical and shocking Sassoon when he dismissed *Paradise Lost* out of hand.

Time passed swiftly and their conversation flowed smoothly, heralding a quick and easy friendship. Their dedication to writing created a bond and it was the first time either of them had enjoyed a stimulating, in depth discussion since joining-up.

They repeated their order for tea and cakes and they soon discovered that they had a mutual friend in Edward Marsh, the London critic and editor of *Georgian Poetry*. In literary circles he was a well-known homosexual but that didn't worry either of them. They were just thankful that he was eager to encourage young poets. They acknowledged the need for mentors if they were ever to make an impact on the literary world.

Eventually, Graves pulled a note book out of his breast pocket. It was full of samples of his work and he thumbed his way through them, reading out what he considered to be choice pieces. He was amazed when Sassoon matched him by producing several scraps of papers bearing experimental drafts.

"Do you jot things down all the time?" asked Graves.

"Yes … My billet is scattered with notes and ideas."

"Same here. Have you written about the war at all?"

"I haven't seen anything of it yet, but I intend to."

"Good! The war will be the making of us …"

"If we survive," smiled Sassoon.

"Oh, we'll survive all right. I have a feeling in my bones. We have a mission in life. We have to survive for the sake of literature."

"You certainly don't lack confidence."

"And neither must you. You have talent and there is nothing more tragic than unfulfilled talent."

"As with Rupert Brooke …"

"Indeed … One of our brightest stars, although I fancy his attitude would have changed with time. All this, 'A corner of a foreign field that is forever England', smacks of mawkish patriotism. We'll do a lot better than that."

"You're very hard on him."

"You have to be hard. Aim for perfection. And we must help each other. Be as critical as hell and never take offence. What we need is time to absorb everything, and then more time to express ourselves. The war won't last for ever. It's just a phase in our lives. But it will be the making of us. It will enable us to establish our names … Then we'll have years in which to write great poetry."

Graves spoke with such conviction that Sassoon couldn't think of a suitable response. It echoed his ambitions exactly, but he would never have dreamt of being so cocky. He stared out of the shop window, wondering what the future held. Bethune presented a cheerless scene. The shops opposite them were shuttered up and the cobbled road was wet and slimy, empty apart from several urchins playing football with a punctured ball.

Then Sassoon saw two men from his platoon splashing down the middle of the road. He pointed at them: "Two of my men. They're twins. The one on the left with his cap tipped back is the Company Choir Master and the other one is my platoon runner. "They're two of my eleven Joneses. Jones 617 and Jones 618."

Graves watched them draw nearer, noting their tubby physiques. They reminded him of garden gnomes and he marvelled at how two such unlikely-looking specimens had ever become soldiers in the first place. As the twins drew level with the tea shop they were singing, their arms about each other's shoulders, harmonising with the distinctive Welsh lilt.

"It's strange," observed Sassoon, "but when they sing I can understand every word. But when they speak I can hardly decipher what they're on about."

Graves smiled. "I know what you mean. Have you ever noticed how they say: 'It's a ridicalus siduation'?" He then gave a perfect rendering of Welshy-Welsh.

Sassoon laughed at Graves's mimicry. Then he called for their bill, to which Graves made no effort to contribute. Sassoon didn't mind. He was aware that everyone thought he was lousy rich. He wasn't, but he had no intention of shattering their illusions. It suited his image.

They walked back to C Company mess in high spirits, knowing that they were kindred spirits in the philistine world of the army.

5

618's Hidden Depths

When the Fusiliers were back to full strength they were deployed in the reserve trenches near Festubert, several hundred yards short of no-man's-land. There, they were comparatively safe but nevertheless had a hectic time. The Staff officers at Brigade decreed that the forward trenches needed more depth and that the barbed wire entanglements lacked density. The trenches also needed to be wider so that men could pass each other without difficulty, and the sides had to be reinforced with timber to prevent cave-ins. Duck boards were needed in the bottom of the trenches to combat the mud and fire-steps had to be far more robust. There were to be more saps (trenches extending into no-man's-land to enhance early detection of German patrols), and finally shelter bays at regular intervals between dugouts, into which men could dive for cover when German shells screamed in.

These tasks were to be carried out by the Fusiliers. As darkness closed in they went forward, usually in pouring rain and temperatures near freezing. Shelling and sniper fire posed a constant threat but they suffered very few casualties. In daylight hours, back in their reserve trenches, they were able to relax. Each man was expected to get six hours sleep, and for the rest of the time they were free to amuse themselves, once routine chores had been seen to.

During his spare time in his dugout Sassoon wrote poetry. After nights in the forward trenches his imagination was aflame, itching to burst forth; and thus inspired he sat at his desk for hours with words flowing freely. He had never experienced such urgency. He was only too aware of the importance of satisfying the demands of magazines and newspapers, ranging from *The Times* to the *Cambridge Magazine*. Getting into print and being noticed was what mattered. By-lines of *SS* or *Siegfried Sassoon* were a tremendous boost.

Before long, Sassoon had more support from influential mentors than any other poets and although he was determined to exploit this he was equally careful to maintain the aesthetic appeal of his work. It was only when he was convinced that he couldn't make a poem any better that he sent it off: then swiftly on to the next. He often wondered where his inspiration came from, amazed that he could write anything at all in such disgusting surroundings: a glorified hole in the ground, surrounded by leaking sandbags, the stink of overflowing latrines, and rafters housing a family of rats.

Apart from his poetry, it was a dismal and lonely existence with lots of petty duties and very few opportunities to talk to David Thomas or Robert Graves. The men in his platoon were of little help. They were good soldiers and happy lads, and he had no doubts that they respected him; but no matter how high their morale, and how often they burst into song, they were in such social contrast to Sassoon that it was difficult to empathize with them, especially since the army did its utmost to maintain the traditional barrier between officers and other ranks.

Butler went about his chores as batman in silence and apart from Sergeant Matthews calling in on duty matters Sassoon's most frequent visitor was Jones 617, keeping an eye on his brother. He came in so often it seemed he was in constant fear of a crisis overtaking his brother, and this aroused Sassoon's curiosity. Even if 618 lacked a few bullets in his magazine, why so much concern? It so intrigued Sassoon that he watched 618 more closely.

He was certainly very odd, no doubt about it. Indeed, his demeanour was often rather spooky. Sassoon had never known anyone like it. The lad had his own three-legged stool in a corner of the dugout and he sat on it for hours on end, never speaking. Most of the time he appeared to be asleep, his eyes closed, and in his livelier moments he did nothing but stare down at his boots. Yet every now and then he would smile and nod, as though he had come across some extraordinary inner-enlightenment; and he sometimes twitched and chuntered like a cat enjoying a dream.

After a few days of this curious existence together Sassoon felt it incumbent upon him as platoon commander to establish some kind of rapport with him. It struck him as ridiculous for two men to spend so much time together in a sort of self-imposed military purdah. For Sassoon it wasn't too bad. He was at least kept busy, but 618 was condemned to a life of solitude with everyone in the platoon treating him as one of life's unfortunate misfits. They didn't bully him or berate him: they simply ignored him. Sassoon felt so sorry for him that he made a deliberate attempt to change things. One afternoon, following a particular long spell of silence between them, Sassoon leaned over, touched 618's arm, and asked: "Are you asleep, 618?"

Without opening his eyes, 618 replied: "Asleep? Now why would I be asleep, then?"

"Boredom?"

"Boredom! I'm never bored, sir."

"Well what are you doing?"

"I'm hard at it, sir."

"Hard at what?"

"Organising my list of rhyming words, sir."

"You have a list of rhyming words?"

"Oh yes, sir ... Thousands and thousands of them. All logged in my memory."

"Memorised?"

"Oh, yes." 618 opened his eyes as though he had at last found a kindred spirit. "Do you know, sir, that among all the words I have stored away, not one of them rhymes with orange?"

"Really?"

"No, sir. Not one. But I'm still searching. The nearest so far seems to be lozenge, but that's not a proper rhyme, now is it? You try to think of one, sir ... Orange!"

Sassoon tried but failed.

It was the start of their short, strange and ultimately tragic relationship.

Rhyming words were 618's great passion in life. To him, there was nothing more fascinating and satisfying. They were far more important to him than they ever were to Sassoon, to whom rhymes were merely a facet of poetry, a framework on which he hung finer raiments. To 618 rhymes were the be-all and end-all, and his one great pleasure in life came from using them to create limericks. With limericks, a good, pertinent rhyme at the end of each line was vital and five lines was the perfect length for pithy wit, with no room for sloppiness. He was well aware that one wrong word was capable of ruining any limerick.

For a time 618 was reluctant to discuss his love of poetry with Sassoon. Having declared his interest he sank back into further periods of silence. He was still intimidated by his officer's presence, well aware that someone of his lowly rank was expected to keep in his correct place.

Sassoon wasn't so easily deterred. He was determined to draw out 618, but he was careful not to be too pushy. He played a waiting game, allowing the initiative to come from 618, letting him open up as and when it suited him, and then Sassoon would listen keenly.

"Do you keep records of what you write?" Sassoon asked when a suitable occasion arose.

"Oh no, sir. Nothing like that. But I mention them to the boyos sometimes when I think they might be amused."

"And are they?"

"Yes, but they never admit it. They never like to give me credit for anything. People are very strange, sir."

Sassoon understood perfectly.

By degrees an affectionate link was forged between them. When 618 got onto the subject of rhyming words and his mental store of them, his personality lit up; he became animated and erudite, and when they were alone in their dugout all barriers of rank and social standing melted away, poetry bridging their differences. Sassoon was so intrigued that he became determined to discover how 618's mind worked. Did he have a secret technique or was he blessed by a rare gift of recall - a photographic memory - that functioned instinctively and spontaneously?

Sassoon had to wait a week or so before he found out. He'd almost given up hope when 618 suddenly started to relate stories about the Rhondda and it wasn't long before he went off at a tangent and let it slip that he was devising a rhyming dictionary of his own, all in his mind, of course. Then he described how he first discovered his gift with words. As youngsters, 617 and he often scavenged local rubbish dumps and on one occasion 618 came across a battered copy of Chambers English Dictionary. As he flipped through the pages and saw the columns of words, he was fascinated. There were so many of them, reams and reams of them. Yet to his amazement he had no trouble in memorising them. He just read down a page and every word became firmly lodged in his mind. It called for no effort of his part. It just happened, so he took it for granted that it was normal; and thus encouraged, it wasn't long before his interest broadened out and he developed a passion for rhyming words, which in turn inspired him to write limericks.

His limericks always had a common theme. They were all crude, the product of a smutty, one-track mind; and the misogyny they betrayed was the direct result of the way girls in the Rhondda had always shunned him, even to the extent of running away from him in terror, screaming hysterically as though he was an ogre, the Ferndale bogeyman.

Unlike Sassoon, 618 had no literary ambitions. Ambitions were beyond him; his horizons were empty, with no desire to exploit his talent. The pleasure he derived from rhyming words was reward enough. Anyhow, he didn't see anything particularly extraordinary about it. It was just an integral part of his make-up, something to be taken for granted, rather like 617's gift for music.

As days passed, Sassoon's interest acted as a catalyst on 618 and the youngster became increasingly talkative. It was the first time anyone had shown an interest in him. Sassoon was the only person ever to accept that behind his vacuous and off-putting appearance, and his inability to socialise conventionally, there lurked a mind of hidden depths.

A feeling of mutual confidence and respect was established and before long 618 became positively garrulous. In staccato bursts he talked about anything that entered his mind. Very often he was so eager to launch into a new subject that he neglected to explain what he was talking about, taking it for granted that Sassoon would catch up as he went along, as he always did.

One of 618's favourite topics was life in the Rhondda: the ugly coal tips, horizontal rain sweeping down the valleys, the inhospitable mountains, and the black-faced miners trudging home at the end of their shifts, heading for galvanized tin baths in their back parlours where their wives scrubbed them from head to toes in an effort to rid them of ingrained coal dust.

Sassoon was fascinated: it opened up a whole new world to him, making him realise what a sheltered and privileged life he had led so far. There were many other things he hankered to ask 618 about Wales but he let him divulge things in his own time.

Soon, 618's schooldays featured prominently: how he was known as the school dunce and made to sit in a corner of the classroom with a tall, conical cardboard hat jammed on his head bearing the letter 'D'. He didn't seem at all resentful about it and he loved to relate pranks Rhys and he got up to. They made Marlborough seem very dull. His favourite story was about their piano lessons which their Da paid for out of the money he made from spare-time gardening. Rhys was dead keen, but Davey had no interest. So Rhys did the lessons for both of them. After each lesson he left the teacher, walked down the corridor, did a smart about turn, and walked straight back again with his face suitably contorted to fool the teacher into thinking he was Davey. The teacher never suspected a thing and at the end of the first term he wrote on Rhys's report: 'Rhys cannot match his brother Davey. He lags well behind in talent'.

618 often repeated his stories two or three times without realising it, like a senile old man, but Sassoon never corrected him. Most of them improved so much with each telling that they were well worth hearing again, as with the time the twins got locked up in the Guard Room of the local Military Police Barracks in Pontypridd. Every day they rode into the barracks on their tandem to make deliveries at the sergeants' mess and Davey was always upset by the way the RSM shouted at everyone. So one day, as the RSM drilled men on the square, he shouted back at him as they rode past, much to the delight of the squaddies.

"Shut your mouth, you horrible old man!"

The RSM couldn't afford to lose face, so he arrested the twins and locked them up in the Guard Room. Unfortunately he then forgot all about them and it wasn't until dozens of Cleaver Williams's customers demanded to know where their orders were that a police search was mounted. Eventually, well after dark, their tandem was spotted leaning against the guard room with a cloud of flies around the undelivered meat. Their disappearance and incarceration made headlines in the South Wales Echo and made them comic, one-day celebrities.

Sassoon also heard in great detail about the squalor of the miners' terraced houses and how most of them were nothing but hovels held together by layer upon layer of cheap wallpaper; and how 618 had been responsible for emptying the buckets in the outside lavatory. 618 even claimed that the greatest relief, relaxation and pleasure in the valleys was singing and inter-breeding, the latter resulting in an abundance of people named Jones, Davies, Williams, Thomas and Morgan, which in turn made amusing nick-names necessary, as with his Da, known throughout the valleys as 'Jones-the-bucket'.

"You see, sir," explained 618, "our Da is a compulsive worker ... Greedy, really. The old skin-flint is always after money. After a full shift down the Maerdy pit he does part-time gardening for toffs in the Porth area. He wins prizes for them, all by using top quality manure. And you know what that is, don't you, then?"

"No idea ..."

"Pit pony shit! None better, sir. It's because of all the Welsh cakes the men feed them. So Da always takes a shovel and a bucket down the shaft. Then he shovels up the pony shit and takes it with him on the bus to Porth. And that stinks everyone out. There's always a mad rush to get to the back, of the bus, away from Da. Anyhow, once when Da was about to catch the bus, someone called out: 'Watch it boyos. Here comes Jones-the-Bucket.' And that's how he's been known ever since."

Sometimes, as 618 talked, Sassoon continued to work on his poems. 618 didn't mind, indeed he hardly noticed. But one thing 618 spotted was that Sassoon often left half-finished or corrected copies of his poems lying around. He would wait until Sassoon was out and about in the platoon and then grasped the chance to read them, showing no concern for his officer's privacy. He even made fair copies of them in an old school exercise book he had. Butler disapproved and tried to stop him but 618 ignored him.

Sassoon realised what was happening but he didn't mind. He was flattered by 618's interest. One day he returned to their dugout and caught him at it red-handed. 618 was reading a poem out loud, as though that was the only way to savour it properly. Sassoon paused in the doorway and listened. The difference in his voice as he read was remarkable. It was rich and melodious and he interpreted the punctuation faultlessly. When 618 realised he was being watched he stopped and assumed a guilty look. Sassoon laughed and said: "Carry on. That's fine reading, 618."

From there on, Sassoon encouraged him as much as he could. He suggested that he should commit more of his limericks to paper instead of just mulling over them in his mind. At first, 618 would have none of it, but eventually he agreed and he would sit there, sucking his indelible pencil as he made copies. He even made corrections, not out of necessity but in imitation of Sassoon.

As this continued Sassoon fell to wondering what it was that 618 actually wrote. The fact that he could remember lists of words and read poetry beautifully was no guarantee that he could write well. Would it be trash, just childish doggerel, or something more worthwhile?

Sassoon didn't like to appear nosey and ask outright for a sight of his efforts, so he sent 618 on a bogus mission to battalion headquarters so that he, in turn, could read what his runner had left lying about. The first thing he discovered was that 618's limericks were pornographic, featuring women from various Welsh towns. The first one went:

'There was a young lady from Bridgend,
Who had a lusty and aberrant friend.
Having lifted her skirt
And warned it might hurt,
He took her straight up her rear end.'

Another one read:

'A young lady from Haverfordwest,
Was famed for a humongous chest.
It was known far and wide
And she flashed it with pride,
But where would it finally rest?'

Sassoon was stunned. They really were a bit much.

Then he had a change of heart. What the hell! They were certainly vulgar but that didn't stop them being damned good. He read them again and ended up laughing with delight. 618's vocabulary was dazzling and totally unexpected. 'Aberrant' was a brilliant word-choice which Sassoon would never have thought of and as for 'humongous', he had to look it up in his dictionary, discovering that it was a recent American word meaning vast and flabby.

Sassoon scribbled a note and put it beside the limericks, knowing that 618 would see it when he returned. It read: 'Now there's bootiful, look you!'

When 618 shuffled back down the steps of the dugout, Sassoon watched him out of the corner of his eye. As he settled on his stool and read the comment, a broad smile stretched across his chubby young face.

After that, they read each other's efforts all the time. 618's comments weren't as perceptive as Robert Graves's, of course, but Sassoon found them interesting all the same. Indeed, on one occasion he had reason to thank him. It concerned what eventually became one of Sassoon's most famous poems, *The General*. 618 suggested that instead of the line, '*He murdered them both*' he should modify it to, '*He did for them both*', which Marsh later hailed as a master stroke.

One day, 618 asked: "Do all your poems get published, sir?"

"Good Lord, no. Lots don't."

"What do you do with the ones that aren't, sir?"

"Just chuck them out. Or leave them lying around, like the ones you see. I suppose that in the end Butler chucks them out with the rubbish."

"Do you mind if I make copies of them, sir? I do sometimes, anyhow. But Butler says I have no right to."

Sassoon laughed. "Help yourself. But they're only rejects, not worth anything."

"They are to me, sir. I think they're all great."

Sassoon was genuinely touched. "Then copy them out by all means, just so long as you don't start claiming them as yours."

"No one would ever believe me if I did, sir."

From there on, instead of letting Butler get rid of all the scraps of paper left lying around, 618 went through everything carefully and when he found completed poems, or even two or three verses, he copied them into his school exercise book. Butler knew that Sassoon had given his permission so he let 618 get on with it.

Eventually, however, Butler became exasperated by sharing a dugout with two men obsessed by poetry. He didn't mind it with Sassoon because he was an officer, and his were proper poems which were published, but he despised 618's childish efforts. What made it worse was that 618 was gaining a reputation within the platoon. Men sometimes dropped into the dugout when they knew Sassoon was absent just to see what 618 was up to, and they had an absurd habit of calling out the name of a Welsh town or village, whereupon 618 would reel off another of his dirty rhymes. Butler got so sick of it that he tackled Sassoon about it.

"It's not a good thing, sir," he protested. "The others shouldn't encourage him. And when you encourage him as well it's even worse. It gives him ideas beyond his station. Just leave him alone, sir. Let 617 handle him."

"There's no harm in what he does," said Sassoon.

"Yes there is, sir, with due respect. And as his officer you shouldn't encourage him."

Sassoon listened politely to Butler's complaints but he took no action. Nor did he intend to. Indeed he was so intrigued by the way 618 made up instant limericks about girls from Welsh towns that he decided to try him out, to see if it really was true. After a quiet spell in the dugout, during which 618 had been sitting on his stool for twenty minutes or so, Sassoon suddenly called out: "Blueth Wells!"

618 opened his eyes and straight away recited:

> *There was a young lady from Blueth Wells*
> *Who had a weakness for bodily smells.*
> *When she mastered the art*
> *Of the malodorous fart,*
> *She went dizzy and cried: 'Hell's Bells!'*

Sassoon roared with laughter. Then he snapped: "Welshpool!"

618 responded even quicker this time.

> *"There was a young lady of Welshpool*
> *Who in most respects was no fool,*
> *But with men she adored*
> *Her judgement was flawed,*
> *Rating them all on the size of their tool."*

They continued in a similar vein for several minutes, their laughter becoming increasingly boisterous. Sassoon was astounded. He had always regarded limericks as trivial, but he was well aware that to reel them off without the slightest hesitation was quite remarkable, the stamp of exceptional talent. Furthermore, when 618 recited them his rich accent made them all the more melodious and amusing.

As 618 continued to meet all Sassoon's challenges, Butler could stand it no longer. He threw a fit of temper. He hurled a tumbler against one of the wooden supports, smashing it to smithereens.

"That's too much!" he yelled. "It's too much, Mr Sassoon. It's no way for an officer to behave."

Sassoon looked across in amazement. Such an outburst was completely out of character for Butler. What's more, he looked as though he was about to become violent. His chest was heaving up and down and his hands were out in front of him as though he was itching to throttle someone. Eventually, he managed to speak, but he was so breathless that he was barely coherent.

"Mr Sassoon! I have served you to the best of my ability. There's nothing I would not do to make you comfortable. But there's a limit. And I can't serve you any longer while that ..." Butler pointed at 618 with disgust ... "while that ..." He still couldn't bring himself to say what he thought of 618 so he changed tack. "I am a religious man, Mr Sassoon. I have attended chapel since I was a boy. My parents were among the most respected people in the Rhondda. And my lady wife is ... Well, she's a lady. And I have two young daughters ... Innocent young girls ... As a regular soldier I know what soldiers are like. And I understand their frustrations, but I cannot stand here and listen to this half-wit carrying on like that, especially with your encouragement. It's outrageous to talk about Welsh ladies like that, as though they're all sluts, just chunks of meat ... I'm sorry, Mr Sassoon, but I must ask for an immediate transfer to a rifle section."

With that, he stormed out of the dugout.

Sassoon waited for a time. When Butler didn't reappear he went looking for him. Shells were falling nearby but he ignored them. He found Butler squatting in one of the shelter bays. He looked totally spent, a man in despair, so lost and miserable that he was close to tears: a hardened, regular soldier about to crack up.

Sassoon saw no reason to apologise, but he did. He squatted down beside Butler and admitted that he was at fault, that he had been thoughtless; and then he tried to explain to Butler that 618's limericks didn't matter, that making up smutty rhymes was the only talent the poor fellow had. It was his sole way of expressing himself, of coming remotely near to a normal life. "Anyhow," he continued, "one can't stop crudity in the army. And his limericks aren't meant to be taken seriously, any more than jokes generally are taken seriously. And dirty jokes go back to times immemorial."

He failed to convince Butler. He again requested a transfer to a rifle section. Sassoon had no option but to agree.

Sassoon wandered off, feeling wretched. He went to see Major Hunt at company headquarters. He told him what had happened but Hunt shrugged it off as of no importance. Sassoon wasn't comforted so he went to see Robert Graves. He also advised him to forget it: he saw it as no more than a clash of personalities. Neither of them was wrong. It was just a matter of different points of view. No offences had been committed and there was, after all, such a thing as free speech. Then he added with his usual bluntness: "Is that all you've got to worry about, Siegfried?"

Then Jones 617 became involved. He appeared in the dugout and stood to attention in front of Sassoon and requested a formal interview. He apologised for his brother's behaviour. He agreed with Fusilier Butler that the limericks were completely out of order. He also emphasised that 618 needed to be guided and controlled in a responsible manner, not encouraged to follow the vagaries of his dirty mind. For 618's own sake it had to be stopped. 617 said his brother had no judgement as to proper behaviour and if he was encouraged to make up dirty rhymes there would be no end to it.

"With respect, I've been trying to stop him for years, and now you're encouraging him."

617 went on to explain that his brother deeply regretted what had happened with Butler. He liked Butler a lot and felt awful about upsetting him. He considered him a nice old bloke who had always been very kind to

him. "My brother certainly had no intention of offending him," explained 617.

"I know," said Sassoon.

"But he has no common sense."

"Really ..."

"It's the problem our family has always had with him."

"I understand."

"He means no harm."

"I know that."

"He just can't help getting into trouble. And it's always me that has to dig him out of it."

"I see."

"I need to be with him. Sergeant Matthews should never have split us up."

"Probably not."

"You must stop all this silly nonsense of his. Forbid him to make up any more limericks."

Sassoon's expression hardened. He wasn't going to let anyone push 618 around. He suddenly realised how fond he'd become of the lad. Their love of poetry had created a firm link between them. "It's not as easy as that. You may not realise it but your brother has a very rare gift. It needs to be encouraged, not throttled."

"But I know from experience ..."

"There's no harm in what he does," interrupted Sassoon. "No harm at all. And it brings him to life, out of his shell. It would be criminal to crush his spirit. And dirty rhymes don't matter. Good God, they go back as far as Chaucer ... And no doubt beyond that ... They're part of our culture. People like Butler just have to exercise greater tolerance."

"Then you don't intend to do anything about it?"

"No. But I'll arrange for Butler to have a transfer to a rifle section, of course. And if you want to keep a closer eye on your brother, I've no objection."

"Thank you."

"The best thing is for you to take over as my batman."

"Your batman!"

"Yes. I can't do without a batman."

"With respect, I have no desire to be your batman. I'm a soldier, not a servant."

"Well bad luck. If you want to watch over your brother, you've got no alternative. There's no way I'm going to have 618 serving in a rifle section. Is that clear?"

617 glared at Sassoon.

"Well is it?"

"If you say so ..."

"Well I do say so."

6

An Unwelcome Transfer

The Fusiliers were expected to move forward to confront the Germans within hours, but quite unexpectedly their orders were countermanded and the entire 7th Division was ear-marked for West Picardy for further training. It was a cause for celebration, but not without drawbacks. To reach their training area near Montagne they had several days of hard marching along boring, poplar-lined roads which tested the poor quality of their boots. Worst of all, every night brought the laborious task of finding somewhere to sleep, never knowing if they would have proper billets in French towns or villages or be left to improvise for themselves in derelict buildings or rat-ridden farm out-houses.

Their only consolation was that when they reached Montagne their billets had been pre-arranged. As soon as these had been allocated, the men slept for hours.

Montagne was a good posting, well away from the usual dangers. The battalion trained hard with Buffalo Bill sparing no-one. He was confident that the Germans were weakening and there would soon be a major breakthrough, so he geared their training to the mobile warfare he was convinced would follow. These exercises took place over the hills of Picardy and concentrated on platoon, company, and battalion attacks, with the emphasis on speed, timing, and team work. Buffalo Bill rode about the battalion on his favourite horse, a chestnut mare of sixteen hands. He loved to appear suddenly and unexpectedly out of woods and copses, always at the gallop, popping up here there and everywhere, full of his usual bluster, chastising men, threatening to shoot slackers, and accusing practically everyone, regardless of rank, of either cold feet or the vertical wind-up. Every third or fourth day their training switched to improving their marksmanship at an improvised rifle range or to perfecting their field craft, based on crawling about on their bellies, an art which most of them had already mastered out of sheer necessity.

Their billets around Montagne were good, as good as any in France. After training men were able to get dry and cleaned up, and then visit local bars in the area for riotous drinking sprees. Sassoon shared a billet with David Thomas. They were lucky to have a small, well-appointed cottage owned by a French officer serving at Verdun. It featured a large kitchen-come living-room with a recessed fire place, ideal for log fires over which they spent most of their free time reading. At other times they talked non-stop, recalling the past, Sassoon harping on about his hunting experiences and Thomas about his schooldays.

Their leisure hours were further enhanced when the Transport officer offered them the chance to ride a couple of horses that needed regular exercise. Sassoon took on a cantankerous beast with only one eye, known to the men as 'Old Dead-eye'. While everyone in Transport did their best to ignore the animal, or treated it harshly in an effort to make it shoulder its fair burden, Sassoon went out of his way to befriend it, just as he had with awkward horses in the Sussex Yeomanry. He soon gained its confidence and, together with Thomas on a friendlier mount, they enjoyed long rides in the surrounding countryside between the end of training and darkness.

Sassoon and Thomas normally dined in the C Company Officers Mess, but when Graves visited them they made an occasion of it and dined at a bistro on the road into Montagne, reached on horseback. The fare was good, the wine plentiful, and they invariably ended up in high spirits, pleasantly merry, staggering back to their horses with their arms twined about each other's necks, smoking cigars. With the war lurking in the background their aim was simple: to enjoy themselves, to laugh, smoke, eat and drink until their heads were spinning and nothing seemed to matter anymore.

When they returned they usually found that the company choir had set up a large brazier in the spacious, cobbled courtyard of their cottage and were in the throes of a rehearsal. Really, it was no more than a sing-song, but Jones 617, the company choir master, liked to give it an air of importance and dignity. After going through their repertoire of traditional Welsh songs, their favourite being *Men of Harlech,* they reverted to army songs, some going back to the Boer war, such as *Dolly Gray.*

Men from other companies often joined them, the choir under Jones 617 being the best in the battalion. Sometimes even Buffalo Bill and his field officers came round to enjoy the fun. The colonel always insisted that they sang *A Long Way to Tipperary* and then he and his officers roared with laughter as the choir went on to Jones 618's crude version of *The German Officers Cross the Rhine*. It always climaxed with everyone singing: *"Inky, pinky, parlez vous ..."*

That was the highlight of the evening, so successful that no one ever complained about 618's risqué words, least of all 617. He was too preoccupied with perfecting their harmonising. As conductor, he was in his element, his facial expressions changing all the time, with a full repertoire of bodily contortions; arms waving about wildly as he summoned-up various sections of the choir. The finale was always a solo. This was shared around and the best was Fusilier Morgan who specialised in Negro spirituals, his favourite being *Swing Low Sweet Chariot'*.

When the singing finished around midnight, the Jones twins shared the duty of extinguishing the brazier and tidying up generally. Then they would go into the cottage to ask Sassoon if there was anything further he needed, knowing that many of the officers would stay on for some late-night drinking, treating the cottage as an annexe to their mess. Once, when Robert Graves was there, he recognised the twins from the time in the Bethune tea house. He greeted them with his usual hint of sarcasm.

"Ah, the Jones twins. And which of you is the budding poet Mr Sassoon talks about?"

They stared back at him blankly, embarrassed to have been addressed directly in the presence of so many officers. Sassoon tried to put them at their ease, but he needn't have worried. Graves, who was in one of his loquacious moods, changed the subject abruptly and took it upon himself to read out one of Sassoon's recent poems, due to be published in London under the title *Redeemer*. 618 recognised it immediately. He could have recited it from memory with no trouble. Graves's voice boomed out dramatically, straining to do the poem justice.

> *"Darkness: the rain sluiced down; the mire was deep;*
> *It was past twelve on a mid-winter night,*
> *When peaceful folk in beds lay snug asleep.*
> *There, with much work to do before the light,*

We lugged our clay-sucked boots as best we might
Along the trench; sometimes bullets sang,
And droning shells burst with a hollow bang;
We were soaked, chilled and wretched, every one;
Darkness: the distant wink of a large gun."

A respectful silence followed. The other officers assumed that if von Ranker said it was good, then it must be.

Eventually, Graves held out his glass towards 618, expecting a refill, but 618 ignored him. He was reliving the night which the poem recaptured so perfectly. Graves shrugged and said, "Oh, well, never mind!" Then he topped up his beer from a bottle on the kitchen table. Having demolished most of it he made another effort to get a response from 618. "So what did you think of Mr Sassoon's poem, Fusilier?"

"Bootiful, sir. Absolutely bootiful."

"He's already familiar with it," said Sassoon. "He was there on the night."

"The real talent in the poem," declared Graves, not interested in whether 618 was familiar with it or not, "is the word-selection. I loved the use of 'clay-sucked boots' and at the end, the 'wink' of a large gun."

"That's thanks to Jones 618," said Sassoon. "I originally used 'flash' and then changed it to 'spark'. But 618 insisted on 'wink'. He also suggested, 'A coughing gun' instead of 'large' and I'm sorry now that I didn't take his advice on that as well."

Graves nodded sagely. "Well whoever thought of 'wink', got it right. It's perfect." He turned again to 618. "So you see a lot of Mr Sassoon's poems?"

"Yes, sir. He leaves them lying around all over the place. So I read them whenever I can. And I make copies of those he doesn't send to London. To keep and treasure, sir."

"So you're a real fan?"

"Indeed to goodness, yes. Mr Sassoon is going to be a very famous poet."

Graves was astounded. The gnome spoke with such authority. As the party broke up and Graves followed his fellow subalterns out of the cottage, he thought: 'Out of the mouths of babes ...'

Graves walked back to his billet deep in thought, obsessed by the gnome's verdict on Sassoon. However ignorant the young Fusilier might be, Graves considered his judgement on Sassoon to be fair comment. There was something about Sassoon's poetry that appealed at all levels, just as Kipling did; and Graves felt privileged to be a fellow officer and friend of a man so clearly destined for greatness. When Graves wrote poetry he had to fight for every word, but Sassoon was churning out poems at a prodigious rate, and he was getting them published. From what Graves had heard from his journalist brother, who was at the heart of London's literary grapevine, everyone was talking about Sassoon. "We are watching the growth of a Titan," had been Charles's opinion.

No one ever talked about Graves's poetry like that.

As Graves tossed and turned in his sleeping bag, another thought occurred to him. Once Sassoon's war experiences increased, a whole new vista would open up for him. If he could produce something like *Redeemer* after merely helping to stiffen the defences, what magical words would flow from his pen when he was really roused? To what heights would Sassoon then soar? For how many generations would he be the conscience of the world? Graves had wondered the same thing about Charles Sorley. He'd met Sorley when they were alongside the Suffolk Regiment at Loos, the day before Sorley died. They had compared poems just as he did with Sassoon and Sorley's genius struck him like a physical blow. He would never forget Sorley reading out what proved to be his final poem, *The Mouthless Dead*, which started:

> 'When you see millions of the mouthless dead
> Across your dreams in pale battalions go,
> Say not soft things as other men have said,
> That you'll remember. For you need not so."

Now, Sorley was dead, butchered like so many others. When Graves saw him buried, all that was left of him was a small brown-paper parcel. There, reduced to scrag ends, was a man who would have ranked alongside Tennyson, Blake, Keats and all the other immortals.

Graves's final thought before falling to sleep was that the same thing should never happen to Sassoon.

It didn't go unnoticed that Graves was continually hanging around the battalion officers' mess. All officers were entitled to visit the mess, but warts like Graves normally stuck to their company mess. What no one realised was that Graves was determined to have a confidential talk with Buffalo Bill. He wanted it to be on a casual basis, rather than a formal interview; but informal or otherwise he would have his say. He would not shirk his responsibility towards literature.

Graves soon got his opportunity. He was alone in the mess directly after breakfast when Buffalo Bill strode in. The colonel grabbed an old copy of *The Times* and settled in an arm chair. Then, from behind his paper, his face obscured, he demanded: "Why are you always hanging here, wart?"

"I was hoping to have an informal word with you, sir."

"What about? You haven't got cold feet, have you?"

"No, sir. It's got nothing to do with cold feet, or the vertical wind-up. I want a word about Mr Sassoon."

"Sassoon! Don't tell me he's got cold feet ..."

"Good Lord no. Far from it. He's desperately keen to get stuck into the Hun."

"Good ..."

"It so happens that he's a poet, sir."

"Oh God! Not another bloody poet ... And a poofter to boot, I'll wager. Anyhow, what about it?"

"Well it so happens that poets are a pretty rare breed, sir."

"Bollocks, wart. They are two-a-penny these days. We never used to have any at all. We left that crap to Kipling. Not that I've got anything against Kipling. In fact I quite like some of his stuff:

> 'Tommy this and Tommy that,
> And Tommy how's your father...'"

"Quite, sir. Stirring stuff. But Mr Sassoon is likely to become a poet every bit as good as Kipling ... In fact, better ..."

"Oh yes ..." Buffalo Bill turned the pages of *The Times*, his tone indifferent, a mere mumble. "Good for him. Just so long as he doesn't get cold feet."

"No danger of that, sir. He's as keen as mustard. That's the trouble. At times he's overzealous. It's partly because he lost a brother in the Dardanelles."

"That's natural enough then. Good luck to him."

"It's not as simple as that, sir. Sassoon is a man of such talent that the nation can't afford to lose him ..."

"Lose him? How do you mean?"

"He might get killed, sir."

"Of course he might. We all might. Most of us probably will the way things are going."

"Yes, but there comes a time when one must do everything possible to safeguard really exceptional men ... Men of genius ..."

Buffalo Bill lowered his paper, slowly and deliberately, his face assuming a purple glow. "What kind of bollocks are you talking, wart? We all take our chances, regardless."

"Not really, sir. You'd hardly have sent Shakespeare over the top if he'd been under your command, now would you?"

"Certainly I would. Why the devil not?"

"Well let me put it this way, sir. They won't let the Prince of Wales risk his life."

"Good God, wart! Are you comparing Sassoon to the Prince of Wales?"

"No, but to be quite honest I rate Sassoon's survival as more important."

"That's bloody treasonable. You'd better watch what you're saying."

"Sorry, sir. I have no desire to belittle the Prince of Wales. And I quite understand why he is special ... That's not what I'm trying to say."

"Then what the hell are you trying to say?"

"That if Sassoon is sent over the top and is killed, it will be rather like killing off Shakespeare, or Chaucer, or Bacon ..."

"Bacon? Who the hell is Bacon?"

"A seventeenth century philosopher, sir. Author of '*The Advancement of Learning*'... The father of British philosophy, the man who many critics think wrote Shakespeare's plays."

"Well if he wrote Shakespeare's plays it wouldn't have mattered a damn if Shakespeare had kicked the bucket before his time, would it? If one bloke doesn't do it, another one will. 'Cometh the hour, cometh the man', as someone once said."

"Shakespeare, sir."

"There you are then." Buffalo Bill raised his paper and disappeared. Then he muttered an afterthought. "We're all in the hands of fate, von

75

Ranker. If your time is up, your time is up. Your name on a bullet and all that ... And there's bugger all anyone can do about it. Tell the mess waiter to bring me a drink ... My usual."

Buffalo Bill, despite being a disciplinarian and bent on wiping out the Germans without mercy, was at heart a compassionate man and he was disturbed by what Graves had said. He was confronted by a decision and he didn't welcome it. After what he'd seen at Mons, the Marne and Loos, the death of so many fine young fellows appalled him. Naturally, he could never express his concerns, but he shuddered to think of where it would all end. If the war dragged on for years he visualised a whole generation being wiped out. They would win the war only to find out that they were left with no young leaders.

Yet a bloody wart like Graves had no right to tell his commanding officer who was expendable and who wasn't. Who the hell did he think he was? God would decide the fate of his men, no one else. Mere mortals simply had to do their duty and hope for the best.

Nevertheless, Buffalo Bill was still troubled by what Graves had said. Sassoon was certainly a queer fish, but could he really be so special, another Kipling? And if he was, did Graves have a legitimate point? What did one have to do? Equate poets with civilians on essential services? Surely to God poetry wasn't an essential service?

In the end, unable to reconcile the matter to his satisfaction, Buffalo Bill took the easy way out. He put the blame on Graves. He was the real trouble. The wart was a real 'alarm and despondency' man. Probably another bloody poofter, concluded Buffalo Bill. He decided to get rid of him, at least in the short term. Everyone would be glad to see the back of the blighter anyhow.

An ideal solution soon arose. An order came from divisional HQ that a junior officer from the Fusiliers with combat experience was to report to base to train reinforcements. Graves got the posting.

Buffalo Bill persisted with his training programme to enhance their skills at mobile warfare. With considerable difficulty he arranged for a combined exercise with a squadron of the 9th Lancers. They would be present when the Fusiliers did a battalion attack, and once the attack was successfully accomplished, the Lancers would do their bit, a cavalry charge to rout the fleeing enemy. It would be an object lesson to the men that the cavalry were far from superfluous, that they had a role to play just as they always had and just as they always would.

The exercise was a major success apart from the finale. When the Lancers appeared they were in superb condition. The mere sight of them made Buffalo Bill's blood tingle. They formed up, half hidden in a wood, horses groomed and glistening, champing at the bit, riders upright in their saddles, spurs gleaming, lances erect, ready to respond to the orders from their brilliant young Squadron Commander, Major Blakiston Houston. For Buffalo Bill it brought back memories of his first taste of battle: Omdurman in 1898 when the very same 9th Lancers won the day by decimating the Mad Mahdi's Dervishes with a charge of breath-taking audacity.

Now, the Lancers moment came when the Fusiliers completed their battalion attack. Major Blakiston Houston's orders rang out and his squadron emerged from the wood, first at the trot, then a canter, and finally, on the command 'Charge!', at the gallop. As the troopers levelled their lances, yelling and screaming as though part of a genuine attack, another horse appeared out of the wood. It was galloping faster than any of them, rapidly catching them up, the rider bent forward, flat against the horse's mane, urging his steed on, riding recklessly, his left hand pressing a hunting horn to his lips, notes shrieking out, and his right hand waving a revolver around above his head, firing live bullets into the air.

It was 'Old Dead-eye', the stubborn horse which had been on the verge of being sent to the knacker's yard. The rider was Sassoon.

When the Lancers completed their charge they wheeled around and reformed. They dropped down to a brisk trot and returned to their original forming-up spot in the wood.

Buffalo Bill and his adjutant had viewed the charge from a nearby hill. They had recognised Sassoon immediately. Neither of them said anything, just sat on their steeds in dumb amazement; but as soon as the Lancers reformed they simultaneously spurred their horses forward, heading for the wood. By the time they reached it, Sassoon and Old Dead-eye were also there, jostling around among the Troopers, Sassoon chattering away jubilantly, thrilled after such an exhilarating experience. Old Dead-eye wasn't in such good shape. She was foaming at the mouth and trembling with excitement.

Buffalo Bill was in a similar condition, but trembling with anger, not excitement. He rode straight up to Sassoon and accosted him. "What the devil do you think you're up to, wart? Why aren't you with your platoon?"

"I couldn't resist it, sir. A boyhood dream ... A cavalry charge!"

"You'll bloody soon be on a different type of charge unless you watch it, wart. Stick to your duties like everyone else. Return to your platoon at once. And get rid of that old nag. There's no place for anarchy in the army, Sassoon. Not in the army I run."

Sassoon rode off and Buffalo Bill sought out Major Blakiston Houston. "I'm sorry about that ... The bloody impertinence of it."

"Typical Sassoon, Colonel."

"You know him?"

"Know him well, Colonel. He was a trooper when I was attached to the Sussex Yeomanry. I never expected to see him here. But he's a damn fine horseman. He should never have left the cavalry."

"Shouldn't he by jingo? Well, you're welcome to have the blighter back."

Later, when the exercise was wrapped up, with the Lancers preparing to return to their camp, and the Fusiliers back in their billets, Buffalo Bill and Major Blakiston Houston shared a drink in the officers' mess. Their conversation soon turned to Sassoon. Buffalo Bill was full of more apologies, but Blakiston Houston would have none of it. He laughed it off and expressed admiration for Sassoon. "I thought it showed commendable initiative, sir. Unorthodox, I'll grant you. But that's Sassoon for you. There's no denying his keenness. And I'm glad he's got a commission. He was like a fish out of water in the ranks. He's a born leader."

"I'm amazed he managed to keep up with you on that old nag," said Buffalo Bill.

"It doesn't surprise me a bit, sir. He has a wonderful way with horses. He used to sort out all our problem-horses in the Yeomanry. He understands them ... Really loves them. He has a unique rapport with them. He talks to them and pets them. And to gain their affection he blows up their nostrils."

"Good Lord! I've never heard of that. I must get our men to give it a try."

"I wouldn't advise it, sir. One of our troopers did and he got the end of his nose bitten off. You have to know what you're doing."

"Is that so? Well, if Sassoon's so bloody marvellous there's only one thing for it."

7

Mad Jack

The following day Sassoon was relieved of the command of Seven Platoon and appointed Transport Officer. His only consolation was that he was allowed to take his batman and runner with him.

As Buffalo Bill issued the order he felt relief on various counts. Firstly, it would teach Sassoon a lesson, make him realise that couldn't just arse about, and that if he did he would be kept well away from any real action. Secondly it would ease his concerns after his conversation with Graves. He had no intentions of mollycoddling Sassoon, but if there was a genuine reason for redeploying him it was something he would not ignored; and if Sassoon had such a unique way with horses, then Transport was where his talents should be exploited. The Transport Company had long been one of the weak links in the battalion.

Sassoon protested strongly, but it did him no good. Buffalo Bill was not a man to argue with and he concluded a heated exchange in familiar style. "The only response I want out of you, wart, is 'Yes, sir! No, sir! Three bloody bags full, sir!' And if I ever get anything else from you I'll have you bloody shot ..."

Sassoon was bitterly disappointed to be deprived of what he considered 'his platoon' and he dreaded that he might never be reinstated. He hadn't volunteered for the army to end up as a Transport Officer in command of back-firing army trucks and farting horses. He'd volunteered to kill Germans and gain personal glory.

However, he had no option but to knuckle under and knock the Transport Company into good shape. A change of command was long overdue. Sassoon examined the horses individually. Many had been neglected and he lost no time in rectifying things. He instructed men in how to groom them properly and then made a list of other points which needed attending to, such as cracked heels, mud fever, and saddle galls.

His men responded well, glad of positive leadership, sensing that Sassoon knew more about horses than his predecessor ever did.

Sassoon had under his command a sergeant, numerous lorry drivers, a farrier, a shoe-smith, a saddler, a carpenter and a cook, all long-service men. In terms of equipment there were numerous motor vehicles, but the backbone of the unit were the horses. They were essential for drawing numerous large wagons, including a huge general service one, and others for carrying officers' kit, cooking equipment, water, and the quarter-master's equipment. Finally there were gun carriages and limbers for carrying machine guns, mortars, spare rifles, and vast quantities of ammunition.

Sassoon worked closely with the quarter-master. He gave Sassoon all the assistance he could, especially when it came to his first major test when the battalion was ordered to move from Montagne to Morlancourt, via Vaux and Point Noyells, a three-day journey which entailed all the carts and limbers clattering over cobbled roads. The battalion only stayed in Morlancourt five days. Then they were ordered into the trenches to relieve the Middlesex Regiment in the Bois Francais region, a stretch of the line where the Germans were no more than 75 yards away.

Once the battalion had completed the change-over, Sassoon's major task was to supply the companies with food, water, ammunition and other vital requirements. It entailed a nightly slog of over eight miles, always in pitch darkness and pouring rain. They were forever drenched to the skin and it was also a hazardous operation. Shells were a constant threat and snipers' bullets, although intended for those in the trenches, were still singing their way westward, picking off unsuspecting victims as they went.

Buffalo Bill watched Sassoon's progress carefully and was delighted by what he saw. He said nothing, just let him get on with it. Then he gave him ten days leave in England.

Sassoon's leave passed swiftly. He started with a few days at Weirleigh, trying unsuccessfully to comfort his mother over the death of his brother Hamo. Having done his best, he went to stay in London in order to enhance his contacts in the literary world. He dined and socialised with his mentors, Edmund Gosse, Sir Edward Marsh, and Roderick Micklejohn who was personal secretary to the Prime Minister. He also renewed a brief acquaintanceship with Robbie Ross who was destined to become his greatest help in getting his poems published.

Robbie Ross was an outright and predatory homosexual who had been involved in the Oscar Wilde case. Not that Sassoon was interested in the sexual peccadilloes of Ross, or any of the others. He was aware that their sexual activities made them criminals in the eyes of the law, but he found nothing repulsive or reprehensible in what they did. He just loved to be in their company, immersed in their world of culture and social eminence: to dine with them in their London Clubs where oak-panelled walls, portraits of famous statesmen, and wall-to-wall thick-pile carpets were the norm. They made such a wonderful contrast to leaking sandbags, floating duckboards, and scurrying rats. It was like a dream come true. He loved to lounge back in a leather arm-chair, his stomach over-full, a brandy to hand, puffing at a Havana cigar as they talked into the small hours. He was very much the junior among them but he never felt any inferiority. He was, after all, the creative spark among them. It was his poems that appeared in the newspapers and periodicals, and he was the one with red-hot news from the trenches; one of the heroic lads to whom they all felt so indebted. With a singular lack of modesty he told them of his war experiences, very often incorporating the deeds of his friends as well, claiming them for himself.

Repartee and witticism flowed and Sassoon contributed as much as anyone. They expected stories of adventure from him and they certainly got them. He also surprised them with details about the men in his original platoon, dare-devils like Corporal O'Brien and Fusilier Morgan. Some of his best stories were on the lighter side, about the number of men in the battalion named Jones or Davies, and how difficult it was for an Englishman to sort them out, especially his batman and runner who were identical twins, Jones 617 and Jones 618 respectively.

He told them about Jones 618's extraordinary gift for memorising lists of rhyming words. When he quoted examples of 618's limericks they chuckled with delight. Despite being men of eminence, their minds were just as one-track as 618's. Roderick Micklejohn was enthralled and Sassoon couldn't help wondering if 618's limericks would end up being repeated to Herbert Asquith as a warm-up before Cabinet Meetings.

When Sassoon mentioned how 618 could memorise page after page of Chambers English Dictionary without making a single mistake, and how he had organised a rhyming dictionary in his mind, Micklejohn led a sceptical chorus. It was only the intervention of Edward Marsh, who had personal knowledge of a similar case, that convinced them that the Welshman was in all probability an autistic savant, a person handicapped by a lack of socially acceptable behaviour but who was instead blessed by extraordinary mental gifts of a very rare nature. Edward Marsh explained that some autistic savants soared to the heights of genius on specialised subjects and it was a common mistake for people to assume that because of their strange, withdrawn, social ways they lacked intelligence and were mere simpletons.

"The best way to view them," he said, "is as people whose brains have been wired up differently."

Marsh's insight into autistic savants helped Sassoon to understand the strange happenings in his dugout but it came as no surprised when Marsh added that the boy should never have been drafted into the army in the first place. He concluded: "It's bound to cause complications."

Micklejohn was still unconvinced and threw out a challenge to Sassoon. "All right then, Siegfried. When you get back, ask your young Welsh friend to make up an instant limerick about a girl from Rhosllanerchrugog."

Evenings like that left Sassoon glowing with contentment. He was a big hit with these men and their interest in him grew all the time. Following the deaths of Charles Sorely and Rupert Brooke, he was now their blue-eyed boy. He was the one to sponsor in a market crying out for poetic war experiences. Robbie Ross was particularly keen to get his hands on anything he wrote.

The extent of Sassoon's growing success became evident when he received a very strange letter. It was post-marked 'Oxford' and as he went to open it his head was jerked back by an overpowering waft of perfume. The letter was on very expensive notepaper and in a hand full of extravagant flourishes. At first he couldn't believe it was genuine. He thought it was someone playing a practical joke. In the most bizarre syntax he had ever read, it referred to a poem of his which Ross had placed with *The Times*

Sassoon skipped to the end of the letter. It was from Lady Ottoline Morrell. He read it two or three times, sunned by its contents. By any interpretation it could only be seen as a first, audacious love letter. She expressed her admiration for his poem but soon forsook highfaluting comments about imagery and symbolism and became far more personal, more concerned with his magnificent and youthful physique, and his bravery in the front line. She had obviously unearthed a photograph of him and was conversant with his background, such as the wealth of his family, his home at Weirleigh, and his mother being a Thornycroft.

When he mentioned the letter to Ross, his new mentor smiled knowingly. He explained that that was the type of letter Lady Ottoline usually wrote, being a very flamboyant character with a passion for poetry, music, art, gardening, and all things beautiful, especially young men, even though she had a long track record of affairs with men well into middle-age.

"She lives at Garsington Manor, near Oxford," Ross explained, "and her ambition is to turn her splendid country estate into a commune, a haven for the arts and the finer things in life, including women's suffrage, pacifism, and universal promiscuity. Next time you're on leave I'll take you to meet her. You'll find her charming and a great help with your writing. She's bizarre, but show her respect and treat her seriously. Never regard her as a joke, or try to take advantage of her, like so many of her so-called friends do. Send her a polite reply and enclose copies of other things you've had published."

"I don't want any complications," said Sassoon. "I'm already engaged to Dorothy Hanmer. Not that it means much. Her younger brother is a great friend of mine and to be honest I'd much rather be engaged to him."

Ross chuckled with delight, his suspicions confirmed, his hopes boosted.

"Being engaged stops a lot of questions," explained Sassoon. "It makes me appear normal, like all the other subalterns. They're forever talking about their girl-friends."

"I understand perfectly. But don't worry. There will be no complications with Lady Ottoline. At the moment she is fully occupied. She's known in her circle as Lady Utterly Immoral. She's not only married to Sir Philip Morrell, the pacifist Liberal MP, but she's also carrying on with the artist

Henry Lamb while at the same time being the full-time mistress of Bertrand Russell."

"Russell, the pacifist? Surely he's well past it?"

"Far from it. He's a randy old goat." This time Ross laughed out loud. "Don't worry, Siegfried. Everyone in Ottoline's circle is up to something or other. They've got the morals of alley cats."

"They're not alone in that."

"Touché," laughed Ross.

Sassoon returned to France in early March and resumed his duties as Transport Officer. He was delighted that during his absence the winter had lifted. Spring was in the air. What delighted him even more was to be back with David Thomas and to find that Robert Graves had returned to A Company after his spell as training officer at divisional headquarters.

Then tragedy struck. David Thomas was killed. A sniper's bullet hit him in the throat and he died a few hours later. Statistically, it was just another death; the sort of thing which was happening to hundreds every day, but to Sassoon and Graves the loss of their dear friend had a devastating impact. For Sassoon it was the first time the horror of war had struck home personally; far more than with his brother's death, which had been cushioned by its remoteness. He swore revenge and straight away arranged an interview with Buffalo Bill at which he pleaded to be put back in command of Seven Platoon. Buffalo Bill was so impressed by his persistence that he agreed. As battalion commander he was reluctant to hold back anyone so desperate to see action and the truth was that Sassoon's replacement had been a disaster. He had such cold feet that he was in danger of frost-bite.

When Sassoon resumed command of Seven Platoon it was like being back among old friends. The first thing he did was go around the platoon to speak with each man. He found them in good spirits, eager to have a go at Fritz. So keen, in fact, that he realised the time had come for him to stop day-dreaming. Now was the time for action. He had to prove himself. He had to act, and act swiftly, not only to cement the men's faith in him, but also to justify all the boasting he had done back in the London Clubs with his mentors. It was a matter of self-respect.

The German unit facing them was the 31st Bavarian Regiment. They were a timid lot, bent on a quiet life. They made no attempts to dominate no-man's-land and they relied on their gunners to keep the Fusiliers on their toes. It was Sassoon's final incentive to get stuck in. He called an orders group and told Sergeant Matthews and his section commanders that he would be going out on a reconnaissance patrol that night. He would go over the top at 2300 hours and would be in no-man's-land for at least four hours making a detailed survey of their frontage, during which time they were to fire Verey light flares every quarter of an hour to give him reasonable visibility.

Next, he told Sergeant Matthews to have the two best men in the platoon standing by for further patrols on subsequent nights. Matthews had no hesitation in recommending Corporal O'Brien and Fusilier Morgan. O'Brien was Irish, but born in Cardiff's Tiger Bay, reputed to have been a contract man in civilian life. He had been with the battalion since landing in France and he had already survived four major battles, Mons, the Marne, Festubert and Loos. His nick-name was 'The Bear' on account of his hairiness, with some claiming that he even sprouted small feathers on his shoulders. He had such a thick head of hair that he had no forehead, a mat of tight curls stretching to within a whisker of his eyebrows. He looked so primeval that Sassoon reckoned he would scare the Hun to death.

Fusilier Morgan was in stark contrast: tall, powerfully built and in such perfect proportions that he looked smart even when covered in mud. He had about him an air of dependability, a man who should have been given stripes long ago, and would have been but for a drunken spree while in reserve. Before volunteering to join the Fusiliers on the first day of hostilities, he was tipped to get a Welsh rugby cap, having already played for Cardiff before his nineteenth birthday.

Jones 617 stamped down the steps into the dugout. He stared hard at Sassoon who was sitting at his desk. "So now you're going to start looking for trouble, are you?"

News certainly travels fast, thought Sassoon. His orders group had only finished ten minutes before. He didn't like 617's tone, or his aggressive expression. "We're going to seize the initiative, if that's what you mean."

"That's exactly what I mean ... Looking for trouble.

Sassoon found 617 increasingly tiresome. From the moment he'd become his batman he'd gone out of his way to be obdurate. He carried out his duties but with a total lack of enthusiasm, and above all he made it quite clear that he did not approve of Sassoon's increasing influence over 618. He resented the way Sassoon assumed he was the only one who understood him; that he was 618's saviour, leading him out of his reclusiveness into something approaching normality, just because he could write limericks and recite Sassoon's highfalutin poems.

Sassoon understood 617's attitude. After so many years of being 618's guardian, he felt his authority was being usurped and he resented it. When Sassoon heard 617 tell his brother that he was not to compose anymore limericks, he remained silent, pretending he hadn't heard. He knew he should have contradicted 617 then and there, but he took the easy way out. He waited until he was alone with 618 and then told him: "Don't worry about what your brother said. He'll soon calm down."

"You want a bet, sir?"

As Sassoon prepared for his reconnaissance patrol he found he lacked one thing, a torch. He turned to 617.

"Do you by any chance have a torch?"

"Yes ... A good one... My Ma gave it to me before I left home... "

"Can I borrow it?"

"My torch ... You can't go out in no-man's-land flashing a torch about. It's not a walk in the park, now is it?"

"I need it for making notes about the lie of the land."

"It's dead flat. Just a few dead trees, otherwise nothing but mud and shell craters."

"It's the craters that I'm interested in. They provide cover."

"You don't have to tell me that. At Loos I spent nearly twenty-four hours in one. Why don't you just leave the Hun alone, like they do us?"

"So you're happy just to sit here and be shelled?"

"We have no option about that, now do we?"

"Of course we do. Instead of sitting here dodging whizz-bangs we could be out there harassing them ... Bombing raids and that kind of thing."

"Their wire is as thick as a jungle ..."

"Maybe, but I don't intend to go through their wire. That's when the trouble starts. Anyhow, we might just as well get killed out there as here, doing nothing. Don't you want to kill a few Huns?"

"Certainly not! Mind you, I will if I have to. But I've no desire to kill Fritz for the fun of it. And I don't fancy crawling around in all that mud. I really hate that mud."

"Getting muddy is a small price for cracking a few German skulls."

"There's blood-thirsty for you, now ..."

"We owe it to Mr. Thomas."

"You getting killed won't help Mr Thomas, now will it?"

Sassoon let the matter drop. 617's intransigence was made obvious by the way he never called Sassoon "sir". There was something about him that Sassoon didn't like. He was too dogmatic, and too engrained in bossing 618 about; too obsessed with being the man in charge.

Later that night, when Sassoon went over the top, a small knot of men gathered to see him on his way. Among them were the Jones twins. There were murmurs of "Good luck!" but to a man they all wondered what the hell he was up to. Was he bloody crackers? All he was taking was a revolver, a torch, a sketch pad, and 618's indelible pencil. He took no grenades, no knobkerrie, and no knife, the most essential weapon of all if he encountered a wounded German in a crater.

Once Sassoon disappeared through the narrow gap in their barbed wire, Jones 617 turned to the others and said: "That's the last we'll ever see of him. Mad as a bloody hatter."

618 contradicted his brother. "He'll be back. He's got great potential."

"Great potential, my foot!" snapped 617. "All he'll do is stir-up trouble. It's the likes of him that gets others killed and wounded."

"Now you mustn't look at it like that, 617."

"Yes, I bloody must, 618 ... He hasn't the faintest idea what he's letting himself in for. Or others for that matter."

An argument continued between the twins as the group of men headed back to their dugouts. It always amused the others when they argued, especially when their voices became raised. It made their Welsh accents all the more pronounced, with cries of 'look-you' and 'Boyo' cropping up all the time; and the truth was that ever since 617 had become Sassoon's batman, they were arguing more frequently. Everyone was waiting for the day when they fell out in a big way. Then what would happen?

Sassoon wasn't as foolhardy as they thought. He wasn't looking for trouble, not yet! His priority was to get things properly organised. It was inevitable that the trench system would be like a maze but he saw no reason why no-man's-land should be as well. It was crying out for a plan naming landmarks, plotting all the craters, and grading them according to the cover they provided, the hazards they presented, and the field of fire they afforded. This lack of basic information made him wonder if anyone ever used their intelligence. New ideas seem to be regarded as a sin against the Holy Ghost. To Sassoon it was little wonder that the war was a stalemate.

Once Sassoon got clear of their barbed wire he paused. What confronted him was surreal. It was as though he had slithered into hell. He felt like an ant, a tiny, insignificant creature lost in a vast, hostile and alien world. The darkness was relieved every few seconds by exploding shells and their momentary flashes created a kaleidoscopic affect. All the trees were dead, tall and naked, rearing up like ugly spikes, splintered branches dangling as though in sorrow.

Although nothing much had happened on this stretch of no-man's-land since the Bavarian regiment arrived on the scene, Sassoon soon discovered that it hadn't been like that in the past. Everything indicated a recent battle ground where the devil had enjoyed a merry dance, leaving a nightmare scenario of dead and rotting bodies synonymous with the western front.

As he slid into each new crater he tried to ignore the contents. What little he saw made him want to vomit. At the bottom of each was a miniature lake - liquid filth in which bodies and fragments of human remains floated or protruded through the slime. The dross of modern war was everywhere: discarded weapons, boots, and bits of equipment and clothing. In one there was an upturned British steel helmet floating and rocking gently.

The steep sides of the craters were slippery and treacherous and on numerous occasions he had to struggle to stop himself slipping down into the flotsam. Often he was startled by sudden noises as gases escaped from corpses, or as they slid down the slopes into the morass to be hidden for ever. At other times, when he directed his torch beam in the direction of movement, he picked out dozens of scavenging rats.

Visibility continued to be variable. Heavy clouds scudded across the near-full moon causing flickering shadows to come and go. The first of the Verey light flares soared into the sky. Sassoon froze, perfectly still apart from his eyes. They darted from side to side, searching for movement and noting landmarks. When the flare died he crawled into the nearest crater and took out his sketch pad. By the light of the shaded torch he started the laborious task of plotting everything that surrounded him. Once he had completed this, he crawled forward to the craters nearer the German trenches. He leapfrogged stealthily from crater to crater until he was within twenty yards of the German barbed wire.

After Sassoon had been in no-man's-land for four hours no more flares went up. It started to rain, sheets of it slashing across from the west. Total darkness engulfed Sassoon, giving him no option but to return. He answered the challenge of the sentry and dropped down into the trench. 618 was waiting for him. He was drenched and bedraggled, not even using a ground sheet to keep the rain off. Yet he sparkled with delight on seeing Sassoon back safely. He forsook his usual reclusive and withdrawn attitude and leapt forward to give his officer a congratulatory slap on the back, a gesture no other Fusilier would have dared to make.

Sassoon led the way back to their dugout. 617 was sitting there, as dry as a bone. "Your brother is wet through," said Sassoon.

"I'm not surprised," replied 617. "I told him to stay where he was. But he wouldn't …. Said he was anxious about you … It's the first time he's ever defied me."

618 was already back on his stool. Sassoon waited for a few minutes, until 617 wasn't looking, and then smiled across at him and gave him the thumbs-up.

In the morning, Sassoon summoned Corporal O'Brien and Fusilier Morgan to his dugout. He suggested that the three of them should embark on nightly patrols to harass the Germans and they agreed readily. They spent the morning cloistered together. Sassoon gave them copies of his map of no-man's-land, complete with arrows that marked the best routes to the German lines, with each crater designated a number for easy identification. They were greatly impressed. They had never seen such attention to detail.

"Drawing and sketching is a hobby of mine," said Sassoon, obviously proud of his handiwork. "And sketches like this should be standard issue. But it's not meant to provide short cuts. There is to be no dashing from one crater to another. We crawl all the way ... And we never adopt the easy crouching run, hoping for the best. And none of these new steel helmets with their distinctive shape and harsh outline."

He told them that their patrols would have two objectives. On the first two nights they would aim to knock out German machine gun posts and then, on their third night out, they would spring an ambush on the Hun. He reasoned that having been bombed two nights in succession, the Hun would send out a patrol to try to intercept a third sortie.

"On the first two nights we will crawl to within bomb-throwing distance of the Hun lines. But before we get there we will separate. Two of us will be in one crater to do the bombing and the other will go to another crater some distance away. He will then act as bait, rather like staking out a goat when tiger hunting. But instead of our goat betraying itself to the tiger by smell, our goat will attract the attention of the Germans by yelling insults and abuse at them. There are few more unnerving things than yells coming at you out of the darkness. It will make them wonder what the hell is going on. And their immediate reaction will be to open fire in the general direction of the voice. Whichever of you acts as our goat can insult them as much as you like, but you remain under the cover of the lip of the shell crater.

"As soon as the Hun opens fire," continued Sassoon, "the two of us in the other crater will see the barrel flashes. We'll then stand up and hurl grenades at them. We'll have to stand up to get the necessary distance. You can't throw a grenade properly if you are lying down. And remember, the Germans will be looking in the other direction, at the man still shouting abuse at them. Once we've bombed them, we pull back smartly, all three of us taking different routes, as shown on the plans I've given you. But still crawling, no dashing back. On the third night I'm banking on the Hun sending out a patrol to intercept us. So we'll take out a bigger patrol early on and wait for them to appear."

That night they went out just after midnight. Sassoon briefed Sergeant Matthews carefully so that the sentries would be alert for their return. Corporal O'Brien volunteered to act as the goat. Shouting abuse at Fritz appealed to him. Sassoon agreed readily enough, confident that Morgan and he could hurl the grenades hard enough to reach the German trenches.

"Even if we don't knock out any," said Sassoon, "we'll certainly make them nervy, knowing that we're after them. We'll travel light, revolvers and grenades only. No cumbersome rifles. Lightness will be essential."

Sassoon led the way over the top. O'Brien and Morgan followed, slightly to his rear, one on each flank. They stopped every twenty yards or so, slid into a crater, and listened. When convinced the way was clear they moved on, leaving snake-like trails in the mud.

They halted just short of the German barbed wire, in the last of the craters Sassoon had marked on his plot. They waited again. No sounds came from the German trenches. Sassoon tapped O'Brien on the shoulder and the Irishman slipped out of their crater and headed for another, some forty yards away. It took him ten minutes to crawl over to it. While he edged along Sassoon and Morgan organised their grenades. They lined them up in front of them on the lip of their crater. Then they waited. They were beginning to think that something had gone wrong when the silence was shattered by O'Brien yelling out at the top of his voice.

"Hey! Fritz! Where are you, you yellow bastards? Show yourself. We've got a present for you, you murderous swine-hounds ..."

O'Brien became increasingly blasphemous and personal, knowing that at least a few Germans would understand English. Voices were heard coming from the German trenches. Orders were shouted and they sent a flare soaring into the air, illuminating everything. O'Brien should have 'frozen', but he chose to move about, deliberately attracting their attention. He heard cries of: "Achtung! Achtung!"

When the flare faded away, O'Brien resumed his shouting and immediately came under machine gun fire. He ducked down and watched spouts of mud leap up in front of him. Sassoon and Morgan had no difficulty spotting the barrel flashes; small yellow and red sparks coming from the German trench some forty yards away, mounted on the top of their trench wall.

It was a long throw with heavy Mills bombs but they were confident they could make it. They stood up, risking exposure, and then threw their grenades with all their might. Sassoon's fell short. He saw them exploding several yards in front of the German trench. Morgan was more successful: his grenades landed in the trench. The explosions of his grenades were muffled, with no extravagant fireworks. They heard yells of panic and warning, indicating that at least some men had been wounded, if not killed. The machine guns stopped firing.

O'Brien slithered across to the rear of his crater and started the long crawl back to their lines, ignoring the spasmodic and inaccurate rifle fire from the German trench. Sassoon and Morgan gathered up their unused bombs and did likewise. They took different routes back and when they reached their lines Sergeant Matthews and others were waiting for them. O'Brien was already there, grinning broadly. Jones 618 was among those waiting.

"618!" barked Sassoon.

"Sir?"

"My hunting horn."

"Sir!"

618 ran off, laughing gleefully as he guessed what Sassoon was going to do. When he returned, Sassoon climbed on to the firing step of the trench, his head and shoulders exposed. He took a deep breath and sounded several hunting calls. With the notes still reverberating across no man's land he jumped back into the trench. He turned to his men who had watched in amazement.

"Just blowing them a raspberry! The Hun won't appreciate that."

Nor did they. Machine gun bullets soon raked the Fusilier's front. Sassoon and 618 squatted in the bottom of the trench, knowing that they were safe. 618 took hold of the hunting horn and tried to blow more raspberries. Sassoon laughed when all he succeeded in doing was to spray gob far and wide.

Everyone in the platoon thought it would be madness to repeat the patrol the following night, but Sassoon was adamant. They went to a different part of the German line. This time, since Morgan had proved better at throwing grenades, Sassoon concentrated on pulling out the pins and then handing them to Morgan, who then threw them as quickly as he could. It proved a more efficient system and while O'Brien went through his shouting routine they were able to get three or four grenades in the air at the same time. Consequently, the two machine guns that opened up on O'Brien were both silenced.

Jones 618 was waiting for their return, holding Sassoon's hunting horn.

The scene was then set for the final phase. Sassoon took out a dozen men. They went over the top as soon as it was dark and took up prearranged positions on the lips of two craters some distance from each other. Between them was a wide gap, an obvious route for the Hun to take as they came looking for them.

They didn't have to wait long. The Hun came out early, intending to set up an ambush in the very craters in which Sassoon's men were waiting. In the flashes of intermittent shells they watched the Hun approach, dark and shadowy, huddled together, crouching low, their leader constantly turning, beckoning his men on. When they were some twenty yards away Sassoon gave the order to fire. It was a minor massacre. As the leading Germans were shot, so others were revealed like targets popping up at a shooting gallery. There was no cover for them. The nearest craters were fifteen or twenty yards away.

In the short, sharp, small-arms battle that followed, the outcome was never in doubt. Six Germans were shot dead or wounded and the others fled as fast as they could, disappearing into the darkness.

Sassoon ordered men forward to retrieve the bodies, hoping to get a wounded man as a prisoner. There was one, but he died when they lowered him into their trench.

Half an hour later, after retaliatory whizz-bangs had died away, Sassoon had visitors. As Major Hunt and Buffalo Bill came down the steps of the dugout, the Jones twins were told to make themselves scarce. The two senior officers sat at the table, relegating Sassoon to 618's stool. He carried on pulling off his muddy clothes, his exertions making the candles flicker and threaten to go out. Buffalo Bill and Major Hunt watched impatiently.

"You're a bit high, Sassoon," said Buffalo Bill.

"An occupational hazard, sir."

"So what have you been up to?"

"We ambushed a German patrol. Seven of them dead."

"Who ordered you out?"

"No one, sir."

"Then what the devil do you think you're playing at?"

"Using my initiative, sir. It was no more than a routine patrol."

"Routine?"

"Yes, sir. Surely we don't need special orders to kill a few of the Hun? I thought the whole idea was to get stuck in?"

Buffalo Bill glowered. He was incensed that one of his favourite clichés was being quoted at him. "According to Major Hunt, that's the third night running you've swanned off into no man's land on your own initiative ..."

"That's right, sir."

"Well for God's sake, Sassoon, don't you believe in letting people know what you're up to?"

"Not really, sir ... It's my front ... My responsibility."

"What would happen if you lost your way coming back in?"

"Hardly likely, sir." Sassoon leaned across the dugout, took hold of a copy of his plan of no-man's-land off the table, and handed it to the colonel. "We go by this, sir ... A great help to know the exact layout of things. We all memorise it, of course."

Buffalo Bill studied the plan, the like of which he had never seen. Then he turned to Major Hunt. "Have you got a copy of this?"

"No, sir ... News to me."

There was silence as Buffalo Bill tried to think of an appropriate comment. Eventually, he said: "A good idea, Sassoon, but for God's sake let people know what you're up to."

"There was no secret about it, sir. Everyone who mattered knew. I had an orders group in the normal way. And we had a section of men standing by to help if we got into trouble."

"Well in future keep your company commander informed. Understand? And you only do things like that with his approval. Is that clear?"

"Yes, sir."

"Good! Anyhow ... Well done. The Hun must be kept in his trenches."

"Quite right, sir ... No-man's-land belongs to us."

Buffalo Bill stared at Sassoon incredulously. The bloody wart was taking the piss! That was another of his clichés: no one else's. He didn't know whether to explode furiously or laugh at the wart's damned cheek. He took the easy way out and left the bunker in silence, his facial expression inscrutable. Major Hunt followed after him, unable to restrain a smile.

As they went down the trench Buffalo Bill chuntered away grouchily, but the only words Sassoon picked up for sure were: "Pure bloody anarchy! Get a grip of him, Hunt. We must have discipline. God knows what the army is coming to. Anymore of that behaviour and I'll shoot the blighter - and I mean it this time. Mad young bastard!"

The matter didn't end there. Several men scattered along the trench as sentries heard Buffalo Bill's verdict on Sassoon and they grinned in the darkness. They saw the remark as complimentary, not derogatory. In the trenches madness was laudable.

Jones 618 was one of those who overheard the remark and it inspired him to write another limerick. This time he committed it to paper. For once it had nothing to do with misbehaving Welsh young ladies and 618 was so pleased with it that he left it lying around for Sassoon to see. He didn't have to wait long for a reaction. When they were alone in the dugout, Sassoon held it out in front of him and read it aloud:

> 'Sassoon won't take any old flack.
> He'd sooner sally forth on attack.
> So he goes out each night,
> Enjoys a damn good fight,
> And now we call him 'Mad Jack!''

618 remained on his stool, eyes tightly closed, dreading what further comment Sassoon might make.

"Very good, 618."

618 opened his eyes, his face beaming.

"And I'll tell you what I'll do," added Sassoon. "I'll send it to the *Wipers Times*. They'll love it ... Right up their street."

"You really not minding then, sir?"

"Not a bit. And if the *Wipers Times* use it you'll become a published poet."

"The same as you, sir."

"Yes ... Well, sort of ... Similar, anyhow."

8

A Lone Rescue

The nick-name of 'Mad Jack' stuck. It was a natural.

The limerick appeared in *The Wipers Times* and attracted widespread attention. The field officers in the Fusiliers were furious. They saw it as a Fusilier openly ridiculing an officer, but to their dismay their protests only served to give the limerick greater prominence.

Jones 618 pinned copies of it on the platoon notice board and on prominent timbers throughout the platoon. Then he went back to his dugout and spent most of his time re-reading his first excursion into print, tormented by the thought that instead of the last line being, 'And now we call him Mad Jack', it would have been better as, 'And now his nick-name is Mad Jack.'

As for Sassoon, he loved it. It meant everyone was talking about him and the limerick did, after all, sparkle with respect. Indeed, he was so proud of the sobriquet that he wrote to Ross and March, enclosing cuttings and a highly fictitious account of his antics, knowing they would pass it on.

A week or so later Sassoon had an opportunity to justify his boasting. A rumour spread that they were about to mount a major raid on the Germans. Buffalo Bill talked about it openly and the only thing that caused surprise was that he was highly critical of the idea. Indeed, he was so opposed to it that men joked that he had cold feet. Not that anyone really believed that. They knew him well enough to realise that if he had reservations about a raid there must be sound reasons for it.

C Company was made responsible for the raid and Major Hunt all but promised Sassoon that he would command it. They often discussed it and both expressed the hope that if it was successful they would get gallantry awards. The other officers in the company were only too willing to let them get on with it, valuing their lives far more than medals.

Buffalo Bill explained the aims of the raid at an orders group. Even though he tried to dress it up as a new, spectacular initiative it was clearly no more than a routine operation, an effort by brigade staff officers to boost the men's morale by capturing a prisoner to reaffirm that the unit confronting them was the Bavarian 31st Regiment, the so-called soft touch.

Buffalo Bill surprised everyone by appointing Birdie Stansfield to command the raid. Stansfield was the senior subaltern in C Company but not the most charismatic of officers. Sassoon was given the minor role of counting the raiders back into the trenches. The entire force was to number twenty-seven men, consisting of four parties of five men each and an evacuation party of seven to deal with casualties and any unforeseen complications. The plan was for two snatch parties to go through separate gaps blown in the German wire by trench mortars. Once in the German trenches, the snatch parties were to make their way towards each other, mopping up the Germans sandwiched between them, making sure that at least one of them was kept alive as a prisoner. Those waiting outside the German wire were to give them covering fire as they withdrew.

The raid was due to take place at dusk the following day, the trench mortars having blown gaps in the German barbed wire during the afternoon. At last light, just as the raiding party was preparing to go over the top, the Gunners would lay down a smoke screen in front of the German wire, giving the snatch parties as much protection as possible as they sprinted through the gaps and dropped down into the Hun trenches.

Sassoon felt betrayed at not having been put in command of the raid. He knew he was far more suited for it than Birdie Stansfield and although he realised that the decision had been Buffalo Bill's, he resented that Major Hunt had not spoken out more forcefully in his favour.

Another thing that annoyed Sassoon was the lack of originality in the plan. It was a straight replica of training exercises: crawl across no-man's-land, dash through gaps in the wire under cover of smoke, go mad, bomb everything in sight, grab a German, dash out again and return to their trench to see how many had survived. Surely to God, thought Sassoon, they could dream up something more original than that.

When Buffalo Bill concluded his orders group he piled his papers together and looked around at his officers. Finally, he made the usual obligatory remark: "Any questions?"

He didn't wait for a response. He moved away from the table and started to speak to his second-in-command, Major Compton-Smith. Everyone was startled when Sassoon called out: "Just one if you don't mind, sir."

"Not at all ... What did you have in mind, wart?"

"Why don't we try doing something original, sir?"

There was silence among the officers. They didn't consider that a question: they saw it as insubordination.

"Such as?" asked Buffalo Bill.

"Something that has never been done before, sir."

"Such as?"

"Attacking them from a quarter least expected, sir."

"Such as?"

"The rear, sir. No one has ever attacked the Hun from the rear."

The second-in-command laughed scornfully. "It may have escaped your notice, Sassoon, but before you can get to the Hun's rear you have to go through their front line trenches to reach it."

"On the contrary," countered Sassoon. "We get to their rear by taking advantage of the modern means at our disposal."

"Such as?"

"Parachutes, sir."

There was general laughter. "What about submarines?" called out the second-in-command.

Sassoon ignored him. He continued to stare at Buffalo Bill, waiting for him to respond. When he didn't, Sassoon added: "Colonel, all we need are two good men who are prepared to drop by parachute behind enemy lines."

"The Flying Corps aren't even issued with parachutes," said Buffalo Bill.

"That's only to stop them from bailing out prematurely, sir. Dropping men by parachute is perfectly feasible. When the Observation Balloons are threatened by German planes, the observers always jump to safety by parachute. So all we need to do is get the Flying Corps to drop two men by parachute behind the Hun lines. Then, in darkness, those two men slip through the German lines, locate a suitable man for snatching in their front trench, and then whisk him back to our lines."

"And how will they get through the Hun wire?" asked Buffalo Bill.

"We will already have cut their wire in the usual way, with trench mortars. The only difference is that our two parachutists will go through the Hun wire from their side to our side. And once our men are on their way back with their prisoner, we lay down a smoke screen to help them safely back. "

As the officers digested this, the only sound was of the barn doors creaking as they swung to and fro. "Have you ever jumped by parachute, wart?" asked Buffalo Bill.

"No, sir."

"Then what makes you think you can?"

"Any fit person can, sir. There's no secret about it. And everyone has to have a first time." Sassoon looked around defiantly. Graves was sitting next to him but he offered no support. Indeed his cynical grin seemed to say, 'Now you really are stirring things up!'

 Like a salesman clinching a deal, Sassoon added: "If you like, sir, forget the parachutes. The Flying Corps could land two men behind the enemy lines. As you can see from our aerial photographs, there are plenty of secluded spots behind Hun lines. And having landed the men they could then take-off again."

Buffalo Bill stood up, having heard enough.

"I'm not saying it would be easy, sir," continued Sassoon. "It might not even work, but at least it would be worth a try ... Something different ... Not the same old doomed routine."

Sassoon sat down, knowing it was pointless to say anymore.

"Thank you for your idea, Mr Sassoon," said Buffalo Bill stiffly. "But that's all it is, an idea. It would take months to organise something like that, even if the Flying Corps proved willing to co-operate. Tomorrow's raid goes in at last light. Everything is all set. The brigadier has to have a full report of the outcome before he goes to see the divisional commander for dinner tomorrow night. Any more questions?"

There were none.

The following afternoon the trench mortars bombarded two twenty-yard stretches along the Hun lines until the barbed wire was broken down, leaving a clear run into the German trenches.

In C Company Major Hunt and Birdie Stansfield selected the men to go on the raid. Final details were then settled. Corporal O'Brien was to lead one snatch party and Fusilier Morgan the other. Birdie Stansfield was to control the two sections giving covering fire. The third, reserve party was under the command of an experienced sergeant.

After a lunch of bully beef and hard biscuits, the raiding party assembled for a weapons inspection. Two Lewis guns were to be taken and each man was expected to carry a minimum of four Mills bombs. The men helped each other to blacken their faces with burnt corks. Everyone wore cap-comforters, not helmets, and pockets were emptied to prevent security leaks. The more blood-thirsty among them sharpened their bayonets and checked that their knobkerries were in sound condition.

By 1600 hours every detail had been seen to; everything had been checked and re-checked. There was nothing to do but wait.

The waiting was the worst part. They just sat around in the reserve trenches. None of them spoke. The raid hung over them like a guillotine. It dominated their minds, but to discuss their chances of success and survival was taboo, something that would only tempt fate. So they smoked one Woodbine or Wills Whiff after another, secretly ruminating on the prospect of death and eternal darkness.

Sassoon was among the most restless. He smoked so many pipes that his tongue became raw and burnt. He tried to improve a half-finished poem, but nothing came right. Even basic rhymes evaded him. All he produced was a jumble of meaningless words. He was smouldering with resentment at having no part in the raid. What had he done to deserve such treatment? And why had Buffalo Bill been so hostile to his idea of attacking from the rear? How could he be so blind and stubborn to ignore the use of parachutes? Didn't they want original ideas?

Eventually Sassoon became so frustrated that he walked round to the forward trench where men would be going over the top at last light. He was keen to see what kind of a job the mortars had made of flattening the German barbed wire; just how wide the gaps were and whether the wire had been properly flattened or merely rearranged. When he reached the departure spot he saw men clustered around the main periscope used to view no-man's-land. They were some of the men going on the raid and Sassoon was horrified to see that Butler was among them. Sassoon hoped to have a word with him but, like the others, Butler turned away abruptly and hurried off when they saw him approaching. It was an uncharacteristic reaction, as though they were up to no good. As Sassoon stepped forward to look into the periscope he heard someone move behind him. It was Fusilier Morgan.

"They were looking to see if the ribbons are up yet, sir."

"The ribbons?"

"Yes, sir. When we blow holes in the Hun wire they know exactly what we're up to. That we're going to raid them by going through the gaps. So they crawl out and tie red ribbons on the wire at each end of the gaps, as markers. Not that they needed markers. They know where the gaps are without markers. It's their way of telling us that they know what we're up to. That their machine guns will be ready for us ... That we'll get that far, but no further."

"You make it sound like a death trap," said Sassoon.

"It is, sir. We all know that. Have a look for yourself."

Sassoon looked into the periscope. It was just as Morgan said: red markers were fluttering in the breeze. "Does the colonel know about this?"

"Of course. He knows better than anyone."

"Then in God's name ..."

Morgan laughed, just a sad chuckle. "It's the system, sir. That's the way things work. And despite everything we have been known to get the odd prisoner."

Sassoon didn't know what to say. This was something new to him, something entirely different; not war at all. It was mass suicide: sending men out to die, to be shot to pieces.

"Just one other thing, Morgan," said Sassoon. "Is Butler going on this raid?"

"Yes, he volunteered. He's keen to see action after all that time as a batman."

Sassoon walked off, leaving Morgan to examine the ribbons. As he strode through the trenches a sensation akin to prickly heat overcame him, more an attack of panic, anger and frustration due to things having slipped beyond his control. He was appalled that an old soldier like Butler, a family man, was going on the raid. If it hadn't been for the ridiculous nonsense over 618's limericks, Butler would be safely in the dugout, going about his rightful duties.

As Sassoon strode along the trench he could still visualize the ribbons blowing in the wind. Quite apart from Butler, none of the others would stand a chance either. He shuddered as he thought of men like Morgan being sacrificed for the sake of a prisoner, some poor, wretched young German who would contribute nothing new or worthwhile.

Sassoon quickened his pace, heading for battalion headquarters, to the barn where he knew he would find Buffalo Bill, the adjutant, and the usual sprinkling of field officers. He pushed his way through the double doors and saluted. They were standing around a large map spread across the table. They looked up, curiously. They had never seen a man so pale and drawn. Buffalo Bill guessed what was on his mind.

"Are the ribbons up already?"

"Yes, sir."

"You've never seen them before, I suppose?"

"No, sir."

"Come outside ... A word in private."

A couple of shells landed nearby but they ignored them. They stood directly opposite each other, the same height, eye-ball to eye-ball, like a confrontation between a drill-sergeant and a recruit.

"Those markers make the raid bloody senseless," said Sassoon.

Buffalo Bill was in no mood for protests or appeals. "Sassoon, when you've seen more action out here you'll realise that markers on the wire are quite normal. You'll also learn that the general staff likes to go by the book. No matter what you or I may say. So don't think things are going to change just because you happen to come up with a bright idea."

"One can but try ..."

"Good God, do you think I haven't tried? Do you think I haven't told them that they're just wasting good men? Do you think my heart doesn't bleed for the lads? But I have to obey orders the same as you do."

Sassoon suddenly felt sorry for the colonel, realising that despite his outward belligerence he valued his men just as much as anyone else.

"I'd like to volunteer, sir. I must take the same risks as the men."

"The answer is 'no'. You'll do as you're bloody well told. Now get back to your dugout and stay there until it's time for the raiding party to go over the top. Then count them as they come back in. Under no circumstances are you to go out into no-man's-land."

The evening light was fading fast.

Nervousness among the raiding party became increasingly tangible. Company cooks took mugs of tea around, but there were no takers. They were waiting for Major Hunt to appear with the carboy of rum. That's what they needed and plenty of it; and right away so that it had time to take effect.

The sun slipped towards the horizon. The huge, red orb was surrounded by livid storm clouds. Those with watches kept looking at them. Everyone was itching to get started. Major Hunt appeared with the rum and handed out double rations. Then Buffalo Bill and the adjutant came round to wish them all good luck, a gesture known to the men as 'the final farewell'. The Colonel singled out Corporal O'Brien for encouragement. He was the men's champion, the man who could be trusted to sort the Hun out no matter what was thrown at them. He was always so lucky that others followed him instinctively. He was the man to be with when the shit began to fly.

The sun disappeared and thunder rumbled. It was murky, just right for a snatch operation. Buffalo Bill uttered some final words of encouragement. "Any second now, lads. I know you'll all do your best. Act on Mr. Stansfield's whistle. Then move as fast as you can, and keep going straight ahead. Don't miss the gaps."

"No danger of that ... They're marked clearly enough."

There was nervous laughter.

Buffalo Bill pretended not to hear.

Smoke shells landed accurately just in front of the German trenches. Stansfield watched it spread. It was perfect, blowing it the right direction, drifting at the right speed. When the German trenches disappeared, Stansfield looked down at the twenty-seven men in the trench. The white of their eyes and teeth stood out against their blackened faces. He raised his whistle to his lips and blew with all his might. The men leapt on to the

105

firing step and then scrambled over the top. In a trice they were through their own wire, heading for the gaps, doing their best to sprint across 75 yards of mud; but the harder they tried the deeper their boots sank into it amid loud squelching noises.

Sassoon and his men were lying on the parapet, knowing that bullets would soon be flying in all directions. It started to rain. Sheets of it sluiced down. The smoke drifting along no-man's-land fused in with it to form a uniform and impenetrable greyness. The raiding party disappeared into it and for a few moments there was a spooky stillness.

Then pandemonium: the noise of infantry weapons rent the air. There were also human cries and yells, voices of mixed emotions: anger, hatred, desperation, jubilation, fear and pain. The orders of Stansfield and Corporal O'Brien rose above all else. German voices followed until they were all drowned out by a cacophony of assorted battle-field noises: Mills bombs exploding, Lewis guns chattering; the sharp report of Lee Enfield rifles; and above all the dreaded rat-a-tat-tat of the German machine guns.

A collective shudder went through Sassoon and the men watching. There was nothing they could do apart from hope and pray for their mates.

Sergeant Matthews slid in beside Sassoon and nudged him. "Someone is coming back in, sir. He's wounded. He's limping like mad."

Sassoon spotted him. He leapt out of the trench and dashed forward to help the man. He grabbed him and carried him back to the safety. He was one of Corporal O'Brien's snatch-party. He had two bullet wounds in his right leg. He was jabbering hysterically, well-nigh unintelligible. While a medic slapped dressings on his wounds, Sassoon tried to decipher what he was saying. He related how they had sprinted after O'Brien only to find that the gaps in the barbed wire were no longer gaps. Under cover of the smoke the Hun had placed pre-fabricated barbed wire barriers along the length of the gaps. They were like portable road blocks, wooden structures, each one about fifteen feet long and a mass of wire.

"They were feeble," the man said. "But it was the surprise that did us. And we had no wire cutters. We got in a hell of a tangle. It was pathetic. And when Fritz opened fire men went down like ninepins. Just about everyone was hit, even Corporal O'Brien. Then Fritz turned on Mr. Stansfield's lot ... It was murder ... All we could do was run for it ..."

His words were soon borne out. More men appeared out of the darkness, stumbling and staggering all over the place as they ploughed through the mud and fought against the wind and rain. Many were wounded, dragging themselves along or being helped by others. Small arms-fire was still coming from the Germans. Bullets hissed and cracked above them, sweeping across no-man's-land, taking an inevitable toll on the retreating Fusiliers. Every now and then a man would go down face-first into the mud: smack, splosh, never to rise again.

Sassoon again leapt out of the trench. A few others followed him. As they helped the wounded back in there were desperate cries for stretchers. The survivors told how the bulk of the raiding party were still stranded in no-man's-land. They were wounded and taking cover in shell craters, waiting for the small-arms fire to tail off before attempting to make their way back. Sassoon realised that unless he acted swiftly they were doomed. They would either bleed to death or slide down into the bottom of the craters to drown in the liquid mud. He pulled out one of his plans of no-man's-land and the survivors showed him the craters in which their comrades were sheltering. Fusilier Morgan provided the most reliable information. He was one of the few not wounded. He helped Sassoon to organise a small rescue party and they lost no time in going over the top again, back towards the German lines.

In all, Sassoon led out four sorties, bringing back wounded men each time. They crawled about in the mud under continuous fire but miraculously they suffered no more casualties. In three of the craters into which Sassoon slid, he found only dead men. He left them there and concentrated on saving the living. Among them was Corporal O'Brien. He had arm and leg wounds and a bullet through his stomach. He proved the hardest of all to help. He was so weak through loss of blood that he had slithered down the slope of a crater until he was half-submerged in the slimy bog, gradually disappearing, being sucked under. He was such a dead weight that they couldn't budge him and those tugging at him found that they too were in danger of slipping into the mud. Sassoon had no alternative but to return to their trenches for a length of rope. When he got back they looped it under O'Brien's arms, climbed back on to level ground and then hauled him up the side of the crater. Finally, Morgan hoisted him on to his shoulders and carried him back in a fireman's lift.

When they lowered O'Brien on to a stretcher he opened his eyes. He smiled at them, coughed up blood, and died.

With the death of O'Brien, Sassoon and his men thought their task was over, but when they checked on the known dead and the wounded they found there was still a man unaccounted for. It was Fusilier Butler. No one had any idea of what had happened to him.

They discovered an hour later.

Everything had gone quiet, a hiatus after the uproar. Sassoon was in his dugout, his nerves still on edge, amazed that he had survived, unable to do anything but swig tots of rum. Then Sergeant Matthews hurried down the steps. "You'd better come, sir. Something odd is going on out in no-man's-land ... Over by the Hun wire."

They hurried along the trench until opposite the site of the raid. Several men were there, peering over the top of the trench. One of them 'shushed' Sassoon and Matthews as they approached. They all stood stock still and listened. Across the muddy strip a voice called out, a weak, plaintive cry. It was Butler. "Shoot me. For God's sake shoot me."

Gunnery flares soared into the sky. They burst into life just below the clouds and their brilliance was reflected downwards. Night was turned into day. Butler's cry continued: "Shoot me! Shoot me!"

Through his binoculars Sassoon could see Butler plainly. He was flat on his back amid the German wire, wounded and unable to move. Sassoon was surprised the Germans hadn't already finished him off. He wondered if they were waiting for his comrades to come out to rescue him, deliberately holding off on humanitarian grounds. Or perhaps they were lusting after more victims if a rescue party was sent out. Sassoon guessed the former: such things had happened in the past. At times there was a weird, ill-defined sense of chivalry between the two armies. Those who were victors often became magnanimous towards enemy wounded, especially if none of their own men had been hurt.

Sassoon glanced around the men surrounding him. They were silent, implacable, watching him. It was his decision. He was the platoon commander. He stared at Sergeant Matthews, willing him to tell him what to do, but Matthews didn't respond. Then Sassoon caught a glimpse of 618. He was at the back of the group. When they made eye-contact 618 said nothing. He didn't need to. His eyes said it all. They were pleading: 'Save him, sir. Please, please save poor old Butler.'

Sassoon recalled his dispute with Butler and how his batman's morality and decency had driven him to volunteer for the raid, and Sassoon felt an overwhelming responsibility towards not only Butler but his wife and daughters. As he studied Butler again through his binoculars he felt something pulling at his sleeve. He looked down. It was 618, tugging away like a dog pawing his master for attention. He was carrying a pair of wire cutters. He held them out towards Sassoon.

Sassoon didn't hesitate. He took the cutters and climbed out of the trench. He was unarmed apart from the revolver in his holster.

"Keep the flares going," he ordered.

He set off, walking as briskly as he could through the mud, standing upright, making no attempt at concealment, knowing that he would soon find out the intentions of the Germans. If they were going to shoot him they would wait until he was at least halfway across, an easy target. Then a sniper would take pride in shooting him with Teutonic precision, a single shot straight between the eyes: instant death.

He got halfway. Fresh flares burst into life. He could see Butler plainly. He was still calling out, now little more than mumbles and grunts. He was oblivious as to what was happening. Sassoon thrust the wire cutters out in front of him in order to make his intentions clear to the Germans.

A rifle shot rang out. The bullet sent up a spout of mud to Sassoon's right. He kept walking, the cutters now above his head. Then came another shot: another spout of earth, only an inch or two away this time.

A German voice called out in broken English. "Vatch your step, Tommy! No tricks!"

Laughter came from their trenches.

"Keep going in a straight line, Tommy."

Sassoon realised that to them it was a macabre joke. It was a good sign. Fritz had a weird sense of humour. In a 'them or us' situation they were vicious and ruthless, without mercy, but in rare situations like this, they often surprised everyone, just as they had done on Christmas Day in 1915. They were soldiers, not murderers, especially the Bavarian lot.

Sassoon reached the barbed wire. He called out to Butler. "It's Mr Sassoon, Butler. I've come to get you. Hang on!"

There was no response. Butler either didn't hear or he was past understanding. He was embedded deep in the wire, hopelessly tangled up, clothing ripped and blood everywhere. Sassoon got to work with the wire cutters. They worked beautifully. Taut strands of wire fairly sprang away and he soon had Butler free. He threw the cutters aside and pulled Butler upright. Then he hoisted him on to his shoulders in a fireman's lift. As they started back, Butler started to jabber, but Sassoon had no idea what he was saying. He wasn't even listening. He was waiting for another shot, even though he realised that if they shot him now, he would never hear a thing.

Then there was another shot, another near miss, another spout of mud.

A chorus of broken English comments came from the German trenches.

"Vatch your step, Tommy."

"You're not home yet, Tommy."

"It's a long way to Tipperary."

"Keep right on to zer end of zer road ..."

"Do zer same for us one day, Tommy ..."

There was laughter and cheers, but their jests soon became fainter. They were more than halfway back. Sassoon knew they were safe.

The raid had been an abysmal failure. Ten men were dead and eight wounded. Nor was there any reason to believe they had inflicted any casualties on the Germans.

Buffalo Bill was distraught. He held a de-briefing shortly after daybreak. All the fit survivors attended and the consensus of opinion was that they had been outwitted by the Hun. No one argued with Sassoon when he said it was high time they abandoned stereo-type tactics which seldom, if ever, worked. When Buffalo Bill questioned men individually about the rescue operation it was estimated that at least six men had been saved by the rescue parties from certain death, Butler included.

When the debriefing ended, the adjutant told Sassoon to stay put. He stood to attention before Buffalo Bill.

"So you went out into no-man's-land anyhow, wart?"

"Yes, sir."

"Against my specific and repeated orders ..."

"Yes, sir."

"Why?"

"Because men's lives were at risk. I wasn't going to leave them to die. They deserved better than to be abandoned."

"It could have cost us more casualties."

"Of course it could. But it didn't."

"They tell me you saved Butler off their wire. That you went out openly and alone?"

"Yes, sir."

"For Butler? Your batman."

"He's not my batman any longer. He requested a transfer to a rifle section and then volunteered for the raid."

"You were damned lucky the Hun didn't shoot you."

"I know that. It was a gamble. But they could see what I was up to ..."

"And I suppose you would have done the same for them?"

"Of course ..."

"I bet you would, too. One of these days your luck is going to run out, Sassoon."

"Quite likely, sir ... We all take our chances."

It was another of Buffalo Bill's favourite clichés. He recognised it immediately. The young bugger was at it again. Buffalo Bill was of a mind to give him a right-royal rocket, but in view of what he was about to say he had no option but to ignore Sassoon's impertinence.

"It seems that Fusilier Morgan was something of a hero?"

"Yes, very much so ..."

"I'm going to recommend him for a Military Medal."

"With respect, sir, a Distinguished Conduct Medal would be more appropriate."

"I'll decide on that."

"Of course, sir."

"As for you, wart ... You disobeyed my orders, repeated orders. You deserve a bloody good kick up the arse. But I have to admit that you were incredibly brave. So against my better judgement I'm going to recommend you for a Military Cross ... Or perhaps you think it should be a DSO?"

"That's up to you, sir."

"It certainly is! And another thing that's up to me. If you ever disobey my orders again you'll get something a damn sight more memorable than a MC or a DSO ... You'll get a fucking FGCM ..."

"What's a 'fucking FGCM', sir?"

"A Field General Court-Martial. And when they find you guilty of disobeying direct orders it won't be me who will shoot you, like I'm always threatening. It'll be the real thing, a firing squad."

9

Lady Ottoline's Letters

Sassoon was amazed by the difference a Military Cross made. From there on, everyone viewed him in a new light. Never again was he called 'wart'. One glance at his distinctive purple and white ribbon (which he had sewn on at the first available moment) and even senior officers took notice of him. They actually listened to what he said.

It took a week or two for the award to be confirmed but there was such little doubt about it that news of it was bandied about freely. It was, after all, a new medal, designed especially for junior officers and regarded as their next best thing to a Victoria Cross.

When Sassoon wrote to his mentors in London he slipped the news in surreptitiously, playing it down, pretending to be modest and asking them to be discreet and not mention it to anyone, knowing perfectly well that with men like Ross and Micklejohn, the more secretive he made it sound the quicker they would bandy it about; and sure enough it was only a matter of days before every editor and publisher in town knew about it. Nor was news of the award confined to the literary pundits. Ten days later Sassoon had another letter from Lady Ottoline Morrell.

He smiled as he opened it, recognising the perfume and the elaborate handwriting. He recalled everything Robbie Ross said about her, especially her nick-name, Lady Utterly Immoral. He wondered if her letter would live up to such a derogatory insinuation. The first few lines confirmed that it certainly did. Even as he skimmed through it he marvelled at her boldness. She started off by addressing him as 'My darling Siggy!'

'Siggy!' he thought. Good God, what a damned cheek. They hadn't even set eyes on each other and she'd already settled on a soppy name for him. As for 'darling ...' that was pretty muted compared to what followed.

"Siggy, you are such a brave, brave boy, and when you get more leave, you must visit me at Garsington as soon as possible. Urgent! Pronto! I'm simply longing to welcome you with open arms. To embrace and hug you!

And you'll find Garsington absolutely divine. You must stay with me as long as you can. With my husband forever in London, doing his duty in the House, the master bedroom, overlooking our delightful lawns and my Italian gardens, will be available. Oh, how truly delightful it will be, Siggy! So in the meantime you must take care of yourself and not get up to so many of your daring escapades about which the whole of London society is talking. Robbie was told by Robert Graves that you deserved something even greater than a Military Cross. A Victoria Cross ... What a brave boy you are!"

And so it went on. A real humdinger of a letter which amused, shocked, scandalized, and flattered, all at the same time.

Sassoon was delighted that Robbie Ross and Graves were doing their best to promote his activities but what amazed him was that his first invitation to share a lady's bed should come from one he'd never met and who, from all accounts, was very nearly old enough to be his mother. As he folded the letter and put it in his map pocket, he concluded that behind all Lady Ottoline's brazen 'hoo-ha' there just had to be an ulterior motive.

Towards the end of June Sassoon and others were given a brief spell of leave. It was only for five days and known as 'Farewell Leave', it being common knowledge that there was a 'Big Push' in the offing to get rid of the Hun once and for all. Five days gave him small chance to do anything much and in the end he contented himself with visiting the Thornycrofts in order to please his mother and cement family relationships.

When he returned to France, his duty done, it was like a tonic. He had never known the battalion in such a happy and carefree mood. The Jones twins got back from their leave on the same day and they too were in an ebullient mood, especially Rhys. The praise and thanks lavished on him in Ferndale for having brought his brother back home safely made him a hero. No one seemed to realise that it was merely a short leave and that when they went back they would have to face even greater dangers. The way people in the Rhondda saw it, if Rhys could do it once, he could do it again.

The reunion between Sassoon and Jones 618 was quite extraordinary. Sassoon was already in his dugout when the twins came down the steps, arguing as ever. 618 entered first and as soon as he saw Sassoon he stopped dead. They looked at each other for a moment and then 618 burst into a smile, rushed at Sassoon and gave him a bear-hug, burying his head on Sassoon's shoulder. It was all so sudden that Sassoon could do nothing to restrain him.

617 was so shocked that for a moment he just stood and watched. Never before had he seen his brother do such a thing. Not even with his Ma or Da, and certainly never with him. And hugging an officer ... He would be damned lucky if he got away with that. 617 darted forward and yanked his brother away, expecting to get an earful of abuse from Sassoon; but Sassoon merely laughed. Then, recalling the challenge Micklejohn had suggested in London months before, he called out: "Rhosllanerchrugog!"

Jones responded:

> "There was a girl from Rhosllanerchrugog
> Who liked nothing better than a good snog.
> She found all men charming
> But what was so alarming
> Was how soon they turned back to a frog."

They laughed, delighted to have fallen straight back into their old ways.

Jones 617 was mortified. At the earliest possible moment he took his brother aside and rebuked him in no uncertain manner. He was as harsh on him than he had ever been, not only berating him verbally in foul language but physically shaking him to drive home his anger. He had to understand that any type of close relationship with Sassoon was thoroughly unhealthy. It went against all military and social conventions and if he ever did it again it was bound to cause trouble, maybe even worse than the Butler tragedy. He had to realise that Sassoon was a slippery, two-faced, stuck-up, mongrel Englishman whose obsequiousness was nothing but a pathetic attempt to gain popularity and become one of the boyos.

10
The Somme

The battalion was in reserve and the late June weather had turned hot. The men spent most of their off-duty hours swimming in a pool they had created in the nearby river. Sun-tanned and naked, they arsed about until the heat went out of the sun. Then they turned to playing touch-rugby or punting balls about. Those who took the game seriously and harboured ambitions of playing 1st class club rugby took lessons from Corporal Morgan on Welsh side-steps and how to bamboozle the opposition with dummy passes, the secret being all in the eyes.

Jones 617 soon had the C Company choir back in action. Every night he organised an al fresco concert around a huge bonfire well away from the river so that they didn't get eaten alive by mosquitoes and midges. For 617 it was a way of forgetting his troubles with his brother, and with the rest of the company it helped to banish from their minds the likelihood of perishing during the rumoured Big Push.

By now everyone knew the coming offensive was a certainty. There was plenty of hard evidence: mountains of ammunition being hoarded by the Gunners; fresh units flooding across the Channel from Dover and Folkestone; and the narrow French roads choked with marching troops, the rhythmic beat of their hob-nailed boots ringing out on the cobblestones. Senior officers didn't even try to disguise what was in store. They explained that a major offensive was essential, not only to drive the Hun back, but to relieve the pressure on the French who were suffering agonies at Verdun. Everyone was assured, and accepted the assurance, that this would be the Big Push to end all Big Pushes. The planning was so detailed, and the use of massed artillery so advanced, that it was confidently predicted that objectives ten miles into Hun territory would be captured on the first day.

Buffalo Bill was in his element, restless and excited, hardly able to sleep at nights in his eagerness for the big day. He had been so humiliated by the failure of the raid on the Bavarian Regiment that he was now determined that when the Big Push came they would erase all memories of that debacle.

To ensure this he embarked upon a reorganisation of the battalion. He was more convinced than ever that mobile warfare would take over and when that happened it would be the experienced and well-trained officers who would win the day, not a bunch of wet-behind-the-ears subalterns, which was a pretty fair description of the replacement officers coming across from England.

He planned accordingly. When the initial attack came, the replacement officers would be right there in the front, leading the cannon-fodder into the inevitable early slaughter. In reserve would be his proven veterans, ready to deal out death and destruction when the Hun fled in full retreat, ripe for annihilation. That was when real skill would be needed, and Buffalo Bill was determined that the Fusiliers would still have a full complement of good young officers to provide it.

Sassoon was among the subalterns kept in reserve. Without any explanation he was put in command of the battalion's sniper section, leaving Seven Platoon and Sergeant Matthews in the hands of a pathetic youngster who had been a bank clerk in Newport. Once again Sassoon was allowed to take the Jones twins with him, which he found a great comfort. He knew that if 618 stayed in Seven Platoon, no new officer would understand his shortcomings; no one would dream of shielding him as Sassoon had done over the past months.

Sassoon found the Sniper Section in excellent shape. It ran itself under Sergeant Burgess. His men were so skilled that they didn't need an officer. They were masters of concealment and camouflage and all of them were accredited marksmen with experience at Bisley. Sassoon's only task was to adjudicate on genuine 'kills' to ensure that daily reports sent back to battalion were reliable. Not that he ever had reason to doubt any of the claims. The snipers knew instinctively when they'd made a kill, and they had made so many that they had no reason to exaggerate.

Sassoon grasped the opportunity to become a sniper himself, anxious to see if he could match them. He was a good shot, though not an accredited marksman, and - as always - he couldn't resist a new challenge. He selected a spare Lee-Enfield rifle with a new telescopic sight, which had been ranged-in by Sergeant Burgess. All he then had to do was select a hideout, camouflage himself and be patient.

He was amazed by how much more he saw through the telescopic sight. He could even pick out rats scurrying about on the top of the German trenches. He felt like shooting a few of them, but he resisted the temptation and waited for something more worthwhile. He didn't have to wait long. The Hun were remarkably careless in exposing their heads when they threw slops and rubbish out of their trenches, and others among them never bothered to duck down when they passed along a low stretch of trench where their heads and shoulders were momentarily exposed. They just dashed across, as though it was a game and they were issuing a challenge.

It wasn't long before Sassoon had several victims to his credit and as his successes mounted he became more selective about the men he shot. He would pause, trying to decide if the man deserved death. If he was a gnarled, hardened veteran or an NCO, or a square-headed Prussian, he shot him quite happily; but if he was a young, fair-haired lad who had obviously been pressed into service, like so many of the Fusiliers, then Sassoon spared him and bided his time.

His most memorable kill was a rabbit. That amused him greatly. He visualised himself relating the incident to Ross and Marsh and the others either over dinner at one of their clubs or the Savoy Grill, or the Café Royal. Through his telescopic sight he saw a young bunny hopping along merrily near the top of the Hun trenches. How it got there was a mystery and it showed no signs of nervousness, with its white tail making it an easy target. Then another player entered the scene. A German head popped up over the top of their trench and eyed the rabbit greedily, carried away by the prospect of rabbit pie for supper. Suddenly the Hun jumped out of the trench and tried to grab the rabbit. It evaded him easily enough and Sassoon could have shot the German without any difficulty; but he didn't. He was one of the young, blond-haired brigade so Sassoon shot the rabbit instead. His bullet took the poor creature's head clean off. The German froze, horrified by his stupidity. Then, realising that by rights he should already have been dead, he smiled and waved in Sassoon's direction. He then grabbed the remains of the rabbit and jumped back into his trench.

Finally his hand and arm appeared above the trench wall as he waved his thanks. Sassoon hadn't felt so pleased in a long time.

The Big Push was scheduled for July 1st. At an orders group, Buffalo Bill made it clear that Sassoon was to stay with the snipers, with no role in the attack. Sassoon was so infuriated that he applied for an interview and lodged another of his vehement protests, but it brought him no satisfaction, just another kick up his backside and the terse comment: "Sassoon, I'm sick to death with you and your friend Graves pestering me as though you have a divine right to advise me on how to utilize your limited skills. I'll be the judge of where you are best employed. And I dare say that when I decide your time has come and send you on a suicidal mission, you'll be damned sorry you didn't keep your trap shut."

In the very early hours of July 1st Sassoon and the Jones twins made their way forward to the front line. Sassoon couldn't stand being in the rear, not knowing what was happening. So he sought out Major Hunt and he confirmed that the Fusiliers were to stay in reserve. The Manchester Regiment, made up of 'Pals' battalions, had the task of making the initial breakthrough. They were already lined up at the start line, hordes of them crouching in the front trenches, supping their final tots of rum, supposedly to boost their confidence before their first taste of action, but just as much to numb the pain when they were wounded. They were told that after the pounding the Germans had taken from the artillery, there would be very little resistance. The Germans who survived would be nervous wrecks and only too pleased to surrender.

When daylight broke the front line was covered by mist. It was ideal for the attack and seen by the men as a good omen. It was even better than a smokescreen which the planners at base had deemed to be superfluous. God was helping them even if the brass hats weren't. Major Hunt, Sassoon and the Jones twins took up a position on a high ridge behind the front trenches where they would have a good view of the launch of the offensive. They lay down on the bare earth, Hunt and Sassoon armed with binoculars. The mist was still swirling about. Nothing else stirred. Three great armies, the crème-de-la-crème of European civilisation, were about to tear each other to pieces.

At zero hour whistles all along the line shrieked out in perfect synchronisation. Shouted orders followed, the NCOs cursing men to get on with it and junior officers encouraging their men with cries of: "Follow me, chaps!" and "Keep spread out!"

Kitchener's New Army was on the move. The Battle of the Somme, the Big Push designed to change everything, was underway.

The wind changed direction. The mist swirled and curled upwards. Then, within seconds, it disappeared, vanished as though by magic. It left the troops feeling naked and exposed. Doubts flooded their minds, but officers and NCOs kept urging them on. They responded, keeping up a steady pace, shoulder to shoulder, moving forward methodically, thousands of them, battalion upon battalion, a solid mass for as far as the eye could see, their rifles thrust out in front of them, their long bayonets glinting in the sun.

"What a spectacle," muttered Sassoon, staring through his binoculars.

Then the British shelling stopped with the advancing troops still well short of the German lines. It gave the Hun plenty of time to emerge from their deep entrenchments. Loud, guttural cries rang out; orders urging haste to mount their machine guns. At first, when their machine guns opened up, Sassoon didn't hear them. He was too busy watching the relentless advance of the Pals battalions. It wasn't until large numbers of them began to fall over for no apparent reason that he lowered his binoculars, wondering what the hell was going on. Then he became aware of the familiar 'RAT-A-TAT-TAT' of machine guns and he cursed the Pals for the way they were diving for cover at the first hint of danger. Yet when he studied them more carefully he realised they weren't diving for cover: they were being annihilated, scythed down as the machine guns traversed from side to side. When the truth dawned on him he went numb. He couldn't believe it: hundreds of them were falling, never to rise again. Some shuddered and squirmed about for a moment or two, but most of them just collapsed and remained perfectly still. The middle of no-man's-land was suddenly a carpet of khaki.

Beside Sassoon, Major Hunt gasped: "Christ, mass murder!"

Sassoon watched in silence. He could only pray that those who survived would dive into the craters, but very few of them did. They had tunnel vision, their eyes concentrating on the trench directly ahead of them. It wasn't until men right beside them fell that they understood what was happening, and then it was already too late: they were doomed. They went down in a vast ripple, human dominoes.

Eventually, too late, those who survived broke into a desperate sprint. Scattered pockets of them burst through the flattened barbed wire and dropped down into the German trenches. They disappeared from sight but small-arms fire, exploding Mills bombs, and the screams and cries of men engaged in desperate, life-or-death, hand-to-hand fighting, told exactly what was happening.

When news was rushed back to those in command that the Germans were still in possession of their trenches and that the Pals battalions had been all-but wiped out, reinforcements were ordered forward. Experienced units, which had been scheduled to go over the top in the late-afternoon to exploit the initial breakthrough, found themselves going over the top in the early morning. They were hardly aware of what was going on, only that they were churning through piles of their dead comrades. Many of them joined the dead as the German machine guns continued with their deadly fire, but one regiment, the West Yorks, made it in sufficient numbers to clear a stretch of a German trench. Jubilant shouts were heard and men climbed out of the trench and waved back, as though announcing that the way ahead was now clear.

Then a new factor came into play. A recently constructed German pillbox on a hillock known as Wing Corner sprang into action. The pill box was a large, concrete structure, dug into the hill, invisible apart from two apertures or weapon slits, overlooking the German position, giving the machine gun crews a perfect enfilade shoot along the length of the trench.

The West Yorks were trapped, packed into the trench like sardines in a tin. Before they could respond they joined the multitude of dead and ended up lying higgledy-piggledy, one on top of the other in the bottom of the trench.

The slaughter Sassoon witnessed never left him: it became more than a memory, it was a macabre apparition indelibly printed in his mind which remained with him for the rest of his life.

He spent the afternoon in a dugout with the Jones twins. They were in full battle kit, ready for anything, even though the Fusiliers were still being held in reserve.

For hours, the familiar battle-noises continued. The trench outside their dugout reflected what was happening. First, it would be choc-a-bloc with men: silent and pensive, waiting to go forward as the next wave of cannon-fodder. Then there would be sudden bursts of shouting with NCOs ordering men to look lively and get moving. Boots and tightly bound putties shuffled past the doorway of the dugout, and no sooner had all the men disappeared than another lot replaced them. Just as regularly they heard the shrill note of whistles signalling men over the top, into the hail of bullets that still swept across no-man's-land. In the dugout not a word was spoken, apart from 618 who kept up a repetitive moan of: "Why? Why? Why?"

Major Hunt stepped down into Sassoon's dugout. "The Fusiliers are next," he said, "but not us, just Able and Baker Companies. They've got to knock out that pill box at Wing Corner."

The men of Able and Baker soon packed the trench. A few of them were singing in their traditional way, but the words of '*Men of Harlech*' were subdued and lacked spirit. A couple of subalterns (friends of Sassoon's) came halfway down the steps of the dugout and had a few words with him. Neither of them said farewell, even though that was the point of their mission.

Major Hunt suggested to Sassoon that they should watch the attack, as they had done with the main assault in the morning, but Sassoon declined. There was no way he could watch men he knew so well being killed. He could go with them, and die with them, but he couldn't watch them being shot down knowing that he was safe.

He refilled his pipe, drawing on it aggressively. 617 made tea again, about their fifth cup. 618 continued to mumble to himself. Sassoon's pipe went out and he knocked it against the heel of his boot, clearing it for a refill. It took him three matches to get it going again but then he lost interest in it as they heard more whistles being blown. He visualised men going over the top. He couldn't stand the thought of what would happen to them. He searched desperately for some way to relieve the tension. He turned to 618 and challenged: "Port Talbot!"

618 didn't even look up. Instead, he repeated: "Why?"

An hour later the battle noises ceased. Major Hunt re-entered the dugout, two steps at a time. He sat at the table opposite Sassoon. "They were magnificent!" he exclaimed. "I have never seen men so well drilled and so disciplined. It was like a training exercise, a perfect outflanking movement. It ended with young Edwards from Able Company crawling up beneath the firing aperture and tossing bombs in. He killed them all. The lads went in and dragged them out. There'll be no more trouble from those bastards at Wing Corner."

"What about elsewhere?" asked Sassoon.

Major Hunt shrugged his shoulders. They both knew things had only just started, that the battle would go on for weeks, possibly months; indeed that it would eventually graduate from a battle into a campaign.

For the next three days the Fusiliers played a major role in clearing the Germans from a series of woods. Robert Graves later described it as, "Just like another Loos, utter chaos." Most of the time it poured with rain which made things even worse. Units were shuffled about as though they were a pack of cards. First one lot was supposed to take a wood, then another. Then all units were drawn back due to the severity of the German shelling. Men lost count of the number of times they were stood-to and then stood-down: military confusion at its worst.

Sassoon was ordered to report to battalion headquarters. Buffalo Bill, the adjutant, and one or two others were huddled around a map. "Your time has come, Sassoon!" called out Buffalo Bill without looking up. "You've been volunteering for God knows how long and now's your chance."

Buffalo Bill's orders were crisp and precise. Sassoon was to lead a party of bombers against a machine gun post which had been holding everything up and causing heavy casualties. It had to be cleared before there was any hope of advancing further in order to consolidate their hold on Fricourt. Once the machine gun post had been cleared Sassoon was to report back to battalion headquarters before re-joining C Company.

Sassoon gathered together a squad of bombers and they advanced towards the machine gun near Wood Trench, adjacent to the termination of another trench known as 'Quadrangle Trench'. When they drew near they came under fire and sustained casualties. Among them was Corporal Gibson who Sassoon had always held in high regard. His death so sickened Sassoon that he made one of his typically foolhardy decisions. He told Corporal Morgan to take command of the men whilst he did a lone assault on the machine gun. If he silenced it, he told Morgan to report back to Major Hunt.

Despite Morgan's protests, Sassoon jumped to his feet, sprinted across a shallow valley, his men giving him covering fire with their rifles. He scrambled up a steep incline and then struck lucky. A gully in the hillside meant he could move unobserved in dead ground. It took him to within thirty yards of the machine gun. Then he went flat on his stomach, hugging the ground, and crawled forward. The Germans could see him but they were unable to depress their machine gun sufficiently to shoot him. It gave him the chance he needed and after throwing two grenades which were near misses, his third went straight through their aperture. There was a resounding explosion and the machine gun was silenced.

Below him and to his rear, Sassoon could still see his team of bombers so he waved to them in excitement. Then he glanced to his left, looking down the hillside into Quadrangle Trench. He saw a party of thirty or forty Germans turn a corner in the trench and start trudging towards him, unaware of his presence. The temptation was too much for Sassoon. He drew two more Mills bombs from his satchel and threw them with all his might. Again, he was on target. Some Germans at the front fell, and those behind them hesitated and took cover. Sensing their indecision, Sassoon reached to his trouser pocket and pulled out his hunting horn. He sounded it as loudly as he could and without further ado he charged down the slope towards the end of Quadrangle Trench, still blowing his horn. He paused to throw two more grenades and then charged forward again. As he jumped down into Quadrangle Trench the Germans were in full flight, certain that they were confronted by a large party of Tommies.

Sassoon found himself alone in the trench with no sign of the enemy, apart from a few dead bodies. He laughed aloud in his excitement, amazed that he had yet again been lucky and was still in one piece. He climbed on to the firing step and looked for signs of his bombing party, but they were nowhere to be seen, having gone back to C Company as ordered. He then remained on the firing step to regain his breath. He was in the most advanced position the brigade had yet managed but he was all alone. He debated what to do next. He thought it inevitable that the Germans would try to recapture the trench so he took up a position by a 'dog's leg' where he would see them coming and be able to toss bombs at them before making his escape.

No Germans appeared. He stayed there for two hours and nothing happened. After half an hour or so he got bored and pulled out his anthology of British poems from his map pocket and dipped into it at random. Eventually, having decided that none of the poems were as good as his, it occurred to him that Major Hunt and the others might be wondering what was happening. He pocketed his poems and his hunting horn, picked up his satchel of Mills bombs, and made his way back to C Company at the double.

Major Hunt told Sassoon to report to battalion headquarters, knowing that he was about to get a hostile reception. It was so hostile that Sassoon was staggered. Having wiped out a machine gun post single-handed, then captured the Quadrangle Trench and put at least forty Germans to flight, he felt justified in expecting praise, even the promise of another decoration.

When he entered battalion HQ, Buffalo Bill looked up sharply. Sassoon saluted and stood to attention.

"So! Explain yourself ..."

Sassoon hesitated. "Hasn't Major Hunt told you what happened, sir?"

"Not satisfactorily."

"Well, sir ... Things went pretty well, even if a bit unexpected. My bombing party proceeded against the machine gun nest, but when we had some casualties I thought it best to try a solitary assault ... A greater chance of surprise, sir ... And that's how it turned out. There were several holed up there, but I was lucky enough to get a bomb through their aperture and that soon sorted them out."

"I'm aware of all that," said the colonel impatiently. "That's what Major Hunt told me. What I want to know is why, having accomplished your mission, you didn't obey your orders by reporting back here before re-joining your company?"

"Because I could see that the Quadrangle Trench was empty, apart from a party of Germans approaching from the far end. So I charged them. Bombed them for all I was worth ... I really let them have it ... It just seemed the right thing to do."

"Blowing your hunting horn, no doubt."

"Of course! It made them think there was a large party of us. And they just high-tailed and ran." Sassoon managed a nervous laugh. "Cold feet, sir."

"And then?"

"I waited."

"Waited!"

"Well, I lined up several bombs, all set to get them when they reappeared. But they didn't."

"And?"

"And nothing."

"Nothing! For two solid hours you did damn all? Just sat there, leaving everyone to wonder what the hell was going on? Whether you were dead, alive, captured, or whatever. If you'd obeyed your orders we could have consolidated the gain you'd made. As it is, the Hun is back in Quadrangle. And to make matters worse the Corps artillery was waiting to lay on another concentration. And I had to tell them to wait because I didn't know where the hell you were or what you were up to."

"Sorry about that, sir."

"Sorry! For God's sake man, don't you have any idea of discipline and following orders? What you did was enough to get a Victoria Cross twice over, but you go and cock-up it up because you think you know best. You must be mad! Bloody bone from the neck up, Sassoon ... Anarchy ... that's what it is, pure anarchy. And I'll tell you this, Sassoon. I'm not going to recommend you for a damned thing. As far as I'm concerned all you deserve, and all you're going to get, is a damned good kick up the arse. You're lucky I don't throw you out of battalion ... So just clear off."

Sassoon returned to C Company in deep depression.

When he had a chance to think about things, he decided the colonel was right. He had cocked it up. He had a chance to win a VC and he'd tossed it away. His thoughts alternated between hatred for himself and resentment towards Buffalo Bill for his 'by the book' attitude. Right or wrong, and anarchy or not, he'd still managed to silence a deadly machine gun and rout out forty-odd Hun ... All single-handed. How many VCs had ever done that?

Over the next few days the Battle of the Somme roared on, but remained a stalemate. The Fusiliers went back into reserve, to an unpleasant, flooded area by the River Ancre. Sassoon was billeted in a dilapidated cowshed with the Jones twins.

617 was proving more intransigent every day. He took one look at the inside of the cowshed and gave up on it without even trying to make them comfortable. This displeased 618 as much as it did Sassoon and he went into one of his prolonged sullen moods, and to make matters worse he kept dashing out of the cowshed and reappearing several minutes later looking pale and ill. Eventually, Sassoon asked him if he was all right.

"Got the shits, sir."

"Oh dear. Go sick."

"That's no use, sir. 617 says everyone gets the shits. And all the MO does it tell you to put a cork in it."

11
Mametz Wood

The failure of the Somme attack sent men's morale plummeting. Many regiments had taken over 60 per cent casualties every time they'd gone into action and the high command clearly had no idea of how to deal with the situation. Their sole response to each new disaster was to launch another fruitless attack, regardless of casualties. While grumbling had always been a tradition in the British Army, things were getting out of hand. The men's grumbling was bitter, really bitter.

The Fusiliers were constantly on the move, marching from area to area without ever being told the reason why. It was nothing for them to march anything up to twenty five miles a day. 618 was particularly hard hit, still suffering from the shits. Sassoon kept telling him to go sick but 617 always intervened and persuaded him otherwise, dreading that once he was sent back to a hospital he would never reappear and they would be parted for ever, with 618 ending up in another regiment as an ordinary rifleman.

It meant that as they marched along, 618 was taken short every couple of miles or so and forced to break ranks to dash to the nearest bushes or squat in the roadside ditch in order to relieve himself. He got precious little sympathy. As he caught up with the rest of the platoon again he was greeted by cheers and ribald remarks.

Eventually, the Fusiliers stopped marching and were given the task of clearing the last of the woods, the notorious Mametz Wood. Together with other units they captured it after days of ferocious hand-to-hand fighting in which over half of the 2nd battalion was wiped out. It was during these struggles that Robert Graves was first of all wounded and then reported killed after a shell landed right beside him.

Graves's death was a devastating blow for Sassoon: it destroyed him spiritually. He felt alone and empty, his morale gutted. Graves was the closest friend he had ever had, a man with whom he had gelled instantly and the one man he could laugh and argue with and tear each other's work to ribbons without any animosity. And now he was gone for good, just like

Charles Sorely, Rupert Brooke, Graham West, and Julian Grenfell; all slaughtered as they approached their prime. As Sassoon wrote to Eddie Marsh shortly afterwards, "So I go my way alone again."

To lose a close friend or relative was the cruellest blow of all. Some got over it, but most didn't. Often, as if by choice, such men soon joined the dead they so deeply mourned. Sassoon wondered how long it would be before it was his turn. At times, he didn't care. He would be happy to embrace death so long it was quick and painless.

The battalion MO, Captain Dunne, was quick to see a difference in Sassoon. He took him aside and asked him what was wrong.

What a bloody silly question, thought Sassoon, but he didn't betray his annoyance. He was determined to show no weakness. He believed in stiff upper lips, especially among officers. He mentioned Graves's death but claimed it meant no more to him than the death of others. He pretended to shrug it off like a true veteran. When Dunne persisted about his run-down condition, Sassoon made a feeble excuse. He blamed it on the first thing that occurred to him. Subconsciously he thought of 618. "I've got the shits," he told Dunne.

"I'd say you are also anaemic," said Dunn. "You look totally washed out. You'd better go to the New Zealand Hospital for a check-up. And that's an order."

The New Zealand hospital turned out to be a mere 'staging' hospital and Sassoon eventually found himself in the much larger and better equipped hospital in Rouen. He was then seen by a Welsh doctor who was sufficiently nationalistic to follow the fortunes of the Fusiliers. There was hardly a thing he didn't know about them. "And you must be 'Mad Jack' of Wipers Times fame?"

"I'm afraid so ..."

"So what's the trouble?

"The shits."

"Dysentery?"

"I'm never quite sure of the dividing line."

"I know what you mean? But bad?"

"Bad enough."

"I saw in The Times that you were awarded the MC."

"Yes."

"And according to your doctor you should have got more. Why don't you wear the ribbon?"

"I did originally, but it seemed inappropriate ... Others were doing exactly the same and getting nothing."

"That's hardly fair on yourself. Still, never mind. Let's run the usual tests."

He gave Sassoon a check-over: pulse, temperature, blood pressure, and finally his stethoscope came into play as he listened to Sassoon's heart and lungs. It was all done in a kindly manner, with sympathy rather than the customary cynicism of army doctors. Sassoon's reputation had preceded him and the doctor was of the opinion that he had done more than his fair share and was due for a rest. Eventually he stood back, put a comforting hand on Sassoon's shoulder, and said. "It's Blighty for you, young man!"

"Because of the shits?"

"There's more to it than that. There could be spots on your lungs."

It wasn't until Sassoon was on a train heading for a hospital ship that it dawned on him that he had effectively worked his ticket. He knew there was nothing wrong with him; he certainly didn't have the shits and the talk of spots on his lungs was nonsense. Knowing this, his escape from the front was tantamount to desertion, the most despicable crime of all. How the hell could he leave his men to their fate? What would become of Sergeant Matthews, Corporal Morgan, and - most of all - Jones 618?

Yet Sassoon's regrets remained secondary. He convinced himself that fate had dictated events. His evacuation wasn't premeditated. He was just another washed-out soldier whose circumstances had unfolded to his advantage: very similar to being given a cushy posting. Anyhow, perhaps the Doc was right ... Perhaps he did need a rest. As he sat in the train, watching the countryside roll by, his thoughts continued in a self-justification mode. What he had seen on the Somme had changed his attitude towards the war. After his early enthusiasm and blind jingoism, he now saw things in a truer perspective. It was as though he had entered

Limbo, a void in which he had no judgement or power of decision; everything pending, in the hands of providence.

There were also personal factors he could not ignore. He couldn't forget his row with Buffalo Bill and the more he dwelt on it, and the more he recalled the colonel's insults, so his feeling of personal responsibility towards the war evaporated. God knows, he'd done his best, but instead of his efforts being recognised, all he got was a severe reprimand.

His thoughts went on and on, round and round in circles, so inconclusive that their repetitive nature finally exhausted him and he fell into a deep sleep. Within hours he was back in England and the pros and cons of the situation became irrelevant.

Ironically, the Rouen hospital had been so unhygienic, with such poor food and contaminated water that the first thing Sassoon did on setting foot on dear old England was dash for the Gents.

The Man Who Shot Siegfried Sassoon

Part Three

The Protest

12

An Auspicious Meeting

Lady Ottoline Morrell woke first, just as she always did, no matter who she was sleeping with. She was a light sleeper, but there was more to it than that. She invariably woke in a state of frustration, far from happy with the outcome of her nocturnal activities.

The night she'd just spent with Bertrand Russell was typical: hours of lust and passionate endeavour, but with only Bertie achieving fulfilment. Whilst he snorted and quivered joyously, she lay beneath him unmoved, amazed that a man of his enormous intelligence could act in such a selfish and animalistic manner.

It had been like that for as long as she could remember and it left her full of resentment. Why couldn't she react like that? It sickened her that while she was able to satisfy her lovers, and always did, none of them ever satisfied her. Most of them just didn't try. They took their pleasure and then called it a night without a thought as to how she might feel: they seemed to think that as a woman, her satisfaction was of no importance.

Her first experience of it was when she lost her virginity in her early twenties. Since then it had become such a regular pattern that she had even begun to fear that it was her fault. Not that she was prepared to accept that. She knew she was responsive and this self-knowledge convinced her that she had every right to share her lovers' satisfaction; and of late, as she became older and more conscious of her declining allure, she had been looking further afield in order to find her sexual grail. She was convinced that men of maturity and experience (reputed Lotharios) were grossly overrated; so now she was of a mind to try men with youth and virility, wellendowed athletes with firm bodies and erectile stamina.

She eased the bedclothes upwards, releasing a waft of warm air, the odour of which rekindled memories of the night. She looked down at their middle-aged torsos. It was a nauseating sight. They were naked and in stark contrast, as unlikely a pair physically as most people thought they were mentally. She was heavy and ponderous, her bosom and stomach lying flat in wodges, spreading outwards like lava that had flowed and cooled; whereas he was all skin and bone, small, sinewy and knobbly-kneed, and so miniscule and shrivelled that his short-comings as a lover were hardly surprising.

Early rays of sunshine burst through the gaps in the French brocade curtains, flooding the master-bedroom in light. It was going to be another glorious summer's day. The prospect helped to lift Ottoline's gloom. She decided to spend the day in the garden, planting annuals in her herbaceous borders. Bertrand would no doubt get on with his writing, or prepare another of his lectures on pacifism that were going down so well in London's Wigmore Hall, every one of them packed to capacity.

Breakfast at Garsington Manor was correct and formal, an extravagant start to the day, never a matter of appearing when convenient and helping oneself off a sideboard. Servants were there to serve. They were also expected to know what the guests required and then attend to them with discretion, showing no interest or surprise in who they had slept with.

On this occasion, Lady Ottoline and Bertrand Russell were alone at breakfast, something the staff were accustomed to. Her husband, Phillip Morrell, stayed in his London flat during the week, handy for the House of Commons, where he was an increasingly influential back-bencher championing the cause of pacifism.

They sat at opposite ends of the long dining table in the manner of husband and wife. Their indifference to any form of morality or discretion surprised no one. From the scullery maids upwards they all knew what the form was: that Ottoline's marriage was 'open' and she slept with whoever she fancied; and that for several years now Bertrand Russell had been her unfaithful lover, a man who spread his seed far and wide and had no hesitation in taking his pleasures whenever available with no concern for the pain he caused others.

The morning post arrived as they consumed their cereals. They heard the crunch of the postman's bicycle tyres on the gravel drive and then they saw him go past the dining-room side window, cocking his leg over his saddle as he dismounted. At Garsington there was an abundance of mail delivered three times every day, bar Sundays.

The butler brought the early delivery into the dining room on a silver tray, spread out fan-like for easy identification. Lady Ottoline was offered the tray first so that she could appraise what was going on in her household, and after she had claimed her letters and gleaned as much information as possible from the other envelopes, the butler distributed letters to other addressees who were present in what he judged to be order of seniority.

On this particular morning Bertrand Russell's eyes lit up in anticipation as he saw a small, brown-paper parcel on the salver. He knew immediately what it was: an early copy of his new book, *The Justice of War*, the book that would have a major impact on everyone; perhaps become even more sensational than his previous book, *The Principia of Mathematica*. He was so keen to get his hands on it, to open it up, to feel it, and even to smell it, that he took no notice of the bundle of envelopes Ottoline received, especially one from France bearing a HM Forces stamp. Nor did she remark on it, preferring to wait until she was in the privacy of her study before gloating over its contents.

Russell flourished his book above his head. "This is where we become serious," he declared. "Once this has been read and digested, we must move on from the theoretical to the practical. This book proves our argument with pure logic, so it's time to stop all this endless talking. We must make them realise that we can no longer tolerate the barbarous slaughter that is being inflicting upon us by our politicians."

"Yes, Bertrand."

Ottoline had heard it all before. For all his reputation, Bertrand did tend to bang on a bit. For months she had been listening to him reading out sections of the book whilst it was still in manuscript. She found no faults in his arguments but it riled her that he would never acknowledge that she had been way ahead of him in the pacifist cause. She and Phillip were the founders of the Union of Democratic Control which now boasted over 300,000 members, on top of which Phillip headed the parliamentary opposition to the new Conscription Bill.

Furthermore, for all Bertrand's talk about rousing people into action, she had already taken the first steps towards achieving that end. Whilst he talked, she acted. Whether it succeeded or fizzled out remained to be seen.

The letter she'd just received from France could be the key to the whole thing.

Ottoline rose from the breakfast table and made for her study. As she hurried along the corridors her heavy skirt and petticoat rustled loudly. Once seated at her mahogany-veneered bureau she slit the envelope open with her ivory-handled paper knife. She prayed that it would fulfil her hopes and that Siggy - having written to her twice - would now have the confidence to open up and tell her what he really thought; that he would follow her example and write intimately, and that in particular he would agree to visit Garsington during his next leave. After the glowing reports she'd had about him from Ross and others, she couldn't wait to meet him: to see him in the flesh, to feel his flesh.

The letter both delighted and disappointed her.

Her delight came from the poems he enclosed. He called them his unpublishable avant garde poems and they clearly demonstrated that his attitude to the war was on the turn. Disillusionment was setting in. Probably, she concluded, influenced by the death of his great friend, Robert Graves, obnoxious young upstart though he was reported to have been.

In his covering letter Siggy said: "These are rough, random efforts, just dashed off for you, Ottoline. They're what I would love to publish but would never dare to. Also, you may be amused by more illustrations."

She read the poems thoroughly and then read them again, even more thoroughly. They were brilliant, flashes of inspiration devoid of the convolutions so common among lesser poets. They were more striking than anything she had ever read on the virtues of pacifism. They summarised everything a true pacifist believed in.

She was overwhelmed by pride in him, loving him all the more because of his talent. Inwardly, she wept, wishing that she had met him years ago, when she was in her prime and he was in his early twenties, embarrassed by repeated erections and ripe for moulding into the perfect lover. Then, in a world at peace, devoid of dangers and agonising partings, it would have been perfect.

She singled out three of his poems as her favourites. She started with the longest, headed:

The Sniper.

Now sits a man within my sights.
He's smiling and relaxed, at leisure;
Sublimely unaware that his frail life
Lies entirely within my pleasure.

He basks in the sun and waffles on,
No doubt regaling his friends and cronies
With the rights and wrongs of army life,
And denouncing all officers as phonies.

What crazy duty demands that I should kill
This man who cannot remotely matter?
If I shoot the poor sod, what comfort in that?
To see his skull implode, then shatter?

So I'll have done with this evil slaughter:
And seek an end to mass insanity.
With the Lord granting me peace of mind
As I strike a blow for humanity.

The second was:

Wake up to Reality.

Don't you ever rue that your countrymen are dying?
Aren't you sickened as they perish in a senseless war?
Don't you ever wake up at night to hear men crying?
Can't you grasp that our efforts are rotten to the core?'
Isn't it time to cast your smoking gun aside?
And by so doing end this pointless genocide?

The third one went:

The Warning

We Tommies at the front suffer, sir.
We Tommies in our trenches die,
And all in the name of freedom, sir,
Though we all know that's a lie.

Your fight for the flag is bogus, sir
In the end war always wins.
Notice the cross-bones of death, sir,
And the skull above it that grins.

She marvelled at their controlled bitterness and they inspired her with optimism. Here was a man of intellect with sufficient courage to speak out loudly and clearly, to rebel against the views of the Establishment. She was convinced that once she'd had a chance to talk to him he would join them in their fight against the endless slaughter, and especially to oppose the Conscription Bill going through the Commons.

What disappointed her about Siggy's letter was that it was so impersonal. He made no attempt to return her affection. It lacked playful flirting and flattering innuendo. There was no reciprocal pet name for her, and no indication that he harboured thoughts of embarking on a great adventure of unsurpassed physical delights: no excitement, no romance, no impetuosity, no longing to indulge in rampant wantonness.

There wasn't even any reaction to her repeated invitations to stay with her at Garsington Manor. He wrote stiffly, like a distant relative angling for a favour, so unlike the dashing and gallant young man she so desired. He addressed her as 'Dear Ottoline' and signed off, 'Yours sincerely', one of the most formal letters she had ever received. She wondered if this was out of loyalty to Dorothy Hanmer, but she rejected that and instead put it down to shyness. The poor boy was self-conscious, inexperienced with women due to having two brothers and no sister, exacerbated by his education at Marlborough.

He obviously had no idea of her depth of feeling towards him. She tried to persuade herself that it was rather sweet, so typical of a highly-educated, well-bred young Englishmen. She decided she was expecting too much, too soon, letting her exuberance and lust get the better of her. After all, he had at least sent her a bundle of wonderful poems with some beautiful and amusing illustrations. To a virginal young sportsman that probably seemed endearment enough.

She concluded that for the moment, anyhow, her yearnings for a relationship would have to take second place to promoting their cause. Her first duty was to foster his pacifist inclinations, knowing that once that link was firmly established love would blossom and lead to a rollicking affair, back to the glorious days of humping at the least excuse: night-time, day-time, indoors, outdoors and whenever it took their fancy.

She couldn't wait to tell Bertrand the good news. She headed out into the garden, knowing that he would be over by the tennis court, swinging gently on the garden hammock in the shade of the copper beech, admiring his new book and checking it for the inevitable misprints which so infuriated him.

He heard her approaching, running towards him with her arms and legs flapping. "Do calm down, Ottoline," he admonished her as she reached him, hopelessly out of breath. "A female over forty at the gallop is not an edifying sight."

She took no notice of him. He was such an old prude. As she had suspected, he was already halfway through Chapter Two of his beloved book. "Bertie, I have some really wonderful news ..."

"Can't it wait until lunch?"

"Certainly not. It's very important. You know what you said over breakfast ..."

"Of course I know. It was only a few minutes ago."

"Well I've stumbled across the very person to help promote our ideas, to take matters from the personal to the professional."

"Do you mean from the theoretical to the practical?"

"Yes, of course ... And do stop trying to pick holes, Bertie. I'm well aware of how clever you are."

He smiled indulgently, knowing how he could at times be a trifle pompous. "Go on, then. Tell me all about him ... From your blushes it's perfectly obvious it's a 'him' ..."

"As a matter of fact, yes ..."

"Well before you get carried away by some frisky young Romeo, you must understand that what we need is a sacrificial lamb. Someone to put the good of the cause before his self-interest ... Someone who has been involved in the fighting ... Not a brass hat ... A young officer who has been in the trenches ... A hero ... A well-known and respected personality."

"That's him exactly."

"Who?"

"Siegfried Sassoon."

"The young poet?"

"Yes, and a close friend of Robbie Ross."

"Oh God! Not another poofter ..."

"Nonsense! Not all Robbie's protégés are homosexuals. Siggy is perfectly normal. He's even engaged to Dorothy Hanmer ..."

"And who might she be?"

"Oh, she doesn't matter ... She's just a flirty young wench. They hunt together. He'll soon get over her. He has a brilliant future as a poet and I think you should meet him as soon as possible."

"You meet him by all means, my dear. But not me. He mustn't get the impression that we are recruiting him. He must come to us of his own accord. He must see himself as an innovator, a man of conscience. Not a pawn of those who have already been heard."

"Well I intend to meet him as soon as possible."

"And I am sure you will, my dear. There's no harm in that. By the sound of it, he will never suspect your motive to be anything other than amorous."

"Bertrand, you really are impossible."

"I might be difficult ... But never impossible. And I'll tell you what. You must send this young man a copy."

"A copy? A copy of what?"

"My new book, of course. He'll need to read it in order to form a coherent and convincing argument, based on pure logic."

A week later Ottoline was overwhelmed with joy when she heard that Sassoon was back in the UK suffering from enteritis. What made it even better was that he was convalescing very handily at Somerville College, Oxford. She lost no time getting in touch with Robbie Ross, insisting that as soon as Siegfried was fit enough he should bring him to Garsington Manor. She also posted off a second volume of Bertrand's book to Somerville College, realising he would never get the one she had already sent to France.

Ross and Sassoon travelled down to Garsington Manor by horse-and-buggy, delighting in being old-fashioned. The weather was ideal and as they jogged along they discussed how best to exploit the new poems Sassoon intended to produce now he was away from the trenches. They also gossiped, mostly about Ottoline. Ross spoke of her with great respect, explaining that she was a member of the aristocracy, her forbearers being Bentincks and Montmorencys, the former owning Welbeck Abbey, a monstrous pile in the best British traditions. He then added that she married beneath her, choosing a solicitor named Phillip Morrell who was a Liberal Member of Parliament.

"Hence, in one way or another," said Ross, "she has an entrée into the most notable families in the realm."

"And you make full use of those contacts?"

"Of course I do. And I intend to go on doing so. And you must as well. We all use each other, Siegfried. There's nothing wrong with that. And Lady Ottoline is no exception. She'll help you but she'll expect something in return. Knowing her, I expect it will be something physical, despite your flapping ears and ugly mug."

Sassoon laughed. "Maybe .... She's already calling me 'Darling Siggy'."

"Splendid! Then you must play along with her. And whatever you do, don't let her know that you are of an unconventional moral outlook ..."

"Oh God ... You sound like poor old Graves. He always referred to it as 'our different disposition'. I prefer to call a spade a spade ... A homo is a homo ..."

"I take your point. I'm merely suggesting that you be discreet about it. And as a matter of interest, how is your engagement to the Hanmer girl going?"

"Farcical, but it's still on."

"Good! Then work it into the conversation with Ottoline. Her enthusiasm for you won't be damped a bit by knowing that you have a fiancé. She never has any concern over aggrieved wives or fiancés ... And according to the Garsington grapevine there is friction with Russell. She's looking around for someone younger, more virile."

"What am I supposed to be, a gigolo?"

"Not at all. All I am suggesting that you play along with her. To what extent is up to you. And don't get hoity-toity with me, young man. The Sassoon dynasty wasn't created by shrinking violets."

As they drew into the forecourt of Garsington Manor a groom hurried out to greet them. He grasped the bridle and steadied the horse as Ross and Sassoon alighted. As he prepared to lead the buggy away, Ross said: "I wonder what kind of dramatic appearance her ladyship has in mind today? She loves the spectacular."

The groom overheard the remark and laughed. "Lady Ottoline is in the studio, gentlemen. A footman will take you round there. Her ladyship is sitting for her portrait."

"That will be her third or fourth," Ross muttered. "But none of them have ever satisfied her. Augustus John did the first one. They became lovers while he made his first sketch of her. There's even a rumour that he's done a self-portrait of them in the act."

The footman soon appeared and led them through the gardens to a large outbuilding which had once been a cow shed with a hay loft. It had been renovated with the ground floor now guest-accommodation and the loft a studio still accessed by a stout, wooden ladder.

Lady Ottoline heard them approaching. She rose from the chaise longue on which she was reclining in an insouciant pose. She crossed the studio to the easel, behind which her friend Dorothy Brett (the deaf daughter of Lord Esher) was standing on a step-ladder, working on a mammoth, nine-foot high portrait of Ottoline in one of her most extravagant ensembles.

It had been Ottoline's intention to invite Ross and Siggy to climb the ladder into the studio to admire her portrait; but when she saw it she was so appalled that she changed her mind. It made her look like the 'Madam' of a Tangier brothel. She hurried over to the doorway and prepared to climb down the ladder to welcome her guests.

Sassoon's first glimpse of her was her size nine shoes with worn-down heels. She was feeling her way cautiously down the ladder, rung by rung. Next to appear was a pair of well-turned ankles in thick, purple stockings. Then her ample back-side emerged. She was so tall there seemed to be no end to her coming down the ladder. Everything about her was baggy and flowing, especially the three-quarter length, pale pink, Turkish-style trousers which did nothing to conceal the width of her posterior. When she reached the bottom of the ladder and turned to greet them, she spoke in a deep and melodious voice whilst patting her lustrous auburn hair into place.

"Welcome! Welcome!" she cried. Then, totally ignoring Ross, she flung her arms open wide, skipped up to Sassoon and embraced him, giving him wet kisses on both cheeks.

"Siggy, at last ... It's wonderful to meet you. Is your diarrhoea better?"

It was not the greeting Sassoon had anticipated, but Ottoline's straight-forwardness made them laugh.

The day was a great success.

Robbie Ross, having formally introduced them, made himself scarce. He wandered over to the Garsington Farm to further his friendships with Aldous Huxley and the other pacifists who were avoiding military service by working as farm labourers for the Morrells.

Lady Ottoline took Sassoon on a tour of the house and gardens and he was entranced by everything. He saw it as the perfect country residence. It was spacious, without being monstrously large and unmanageable, and it was beautifully furnished with an abundance of imported items reflecting Ottoline's character. Brilliant and unexpected flashes of colour were everywhere yet there was never a sense of money having been spent recklessly. As they passed from room to room Sassoon was increasingly dazzled.

The gardens were just as striking. The influence of Ottoline's early days in Italy had given rise to one of the finest Italianate gardens in Britain. They settled on the hammock beneath Bertrand Russell's favourite copper beech tree and later on strolled about the lawns surrounding the swimming pool. Both lunch and tea were served beneath the copper beech and there was never a strained or awkward moment between them. As they explored each other's minds, Sassoon realised he was in the presence of an extraordinary person and he soon forgot about her zany appearance. He also grew accustomed to the casual way she rested her hand upon his knee or thigh. He put that down to her demonstrative nature, never imagining that it was for the thrill of feeling the muscular flanks of a horseman and athlete.

As they spoke, they both harboured an agenda. Sassoon harped on about his poetry and his need for a permanent top-class publisher; and although she responded with plenty of praise and flattery she was more interested in discovering to what extend he was willing to back up the dissent he felt towards the war, as came across so clearly in the poems he had sent her. He smiled evasively, assuring her that they were experimental and certainly not intended for publication. He steered the conversation back to all the famous names she kept dropping and she explained how most of them were in the habit of popping into Garsington without formality, often staying for several days at a time, and she urged him to do likewise so that she could make appropriate introductions.

He also spoke of his experiences in the trenches and he was surprised that she had a good understanding of what it was like, how one had to equate the horrors, the human waste, and the sadness with the camaraderie of the men and their devotion to duty. He told her of Morgan, O'Brien and the Jones twins, especially 618. He explained how he was an autistic savant with a rare gift of memorising words and rhymes and how, every now and then, he came up with brilliant suggestions. She showed little interest in a budding Fusilier-poet, being more anxious to hear about his Military Cross. He smiled and glossed over the details, merely telling her that he was lucky to have been awarded one at all, with his colonel castigating him for his lack of discipline and a tendency towards anarchy.

"And are you an anarchist?" she asked.

"I suppose I am. I find it very hard to accept the sluggish mentality of professional soldiers. Especially their refusal to adapt to new situations ... And I hate the way they accept total disasters and huge casualties as an acceptable price ... How they just shrug their shoulders and then call up more reserves and make the same mistakes all over again."

"More cannon-fodder ..."

"Precisely! Like in the Big Push on the Somme."

He went on to tell her what he had witnessed on the first morning: the mass slaughter of the Pals Battalions and the fate of the West Yorks, and the way it had been best summed up by Jones 618 who was reduced to cries of: "Why? Why? Why?"

As Ottoline listened she shed tears. "You must never go back, Siggy."

"I don't have any choice," he laughed. "My ailment can't last very much longer, and then it'll be back to join my men ... Not that I'm in a hurry to return, I must admit."

145

13

A Long Recuperation

Sassoon's diarrhoea lasted several months. He managed it very well. It came and went at his convenience. Every time he went before his monthly medical board he explained how he was prone to sudden stomach cramps which led to the original trouble starting all over again. Consequently, since the doctors seldom doubted the word of officers, especially those decorated for gallantry, he was repeatedly signed off for a further month. He wasn't even confined to a hospital and was able to spend time at Weirleigh with his mother, or take advantage of the hospitality of friends in London, or visit (and occasionally stay overnight) at Garsington Manor.

It was a good life, made all the better when the near-miraculous happened. News came via Eddie Marsh that Robert Graves was still alive after all. Sassoon's joy was unbounded. There couldn't have been better news as far as he was concerned. Graves had been wounded by artillery fire and everyone who saw his crumpled, blood-stained body wrote him off as a 'goner'; but after a day of lying unattended on a stretcher it was discovered that he was still breathing and the doctors at the New Zealand Hospital were able to save him. Indeed, he returned to England on the same day as Sassoon and they were quite unknowingly hospitalized within a few miles of each other.

Once Graves had recovered sufficiently from his wounds, and was allowed out of hospital, it made a tremendous difference to Sassoon. Carousing about as a pair was so much better fun than when alone, and during his early visits to Lady Ottoline at Garsington the presence of Graves made it much easier to forestall Ottoline's increasingly bold overtures. Graves found it hilarious. "I never thought I'd end up as a chaperone. As the men in my old platoon would say, 'It's a ridiculous siduation'.

On Sassoon's initial visit to Garsington he had promised Lady Ottoline he would visit her regularly just as soon as he had the chance, and now he was a free agent, able to come and go as he pleased, he kept his word. He dropped in perhaps once or twice a week and as their friendship developed so they became more adventurous and met either at the Ashmolean Museum or at a quaint pub in Burford frequented by his Uncle Hamo. Sometimes they even met at her London flat in order to visit various art galleries and theatres. On these occasions he found it expedient to turn up late and then depart early in order to stay at Weirleigh where he tried unsuccessfully to comfort his mother who was still suffering nightmares on account of his brother's death at Gallipoli.

As time passed, he found Ottoline's company increasingly stimulating and amusing. She was full of original ideas and he was delighted by the way she kept to her word and introduced him to numerous famous and influential men and women. Thanks to her, a new world opened up for him, an entrée into the heart of British culture; a circle of friends far broader and more creative than his mentors, a coterie of talent he treasured for the rest of his life. There seemed to be nobody of note she didn't know and although they all had their favourite stories about her eccentricities, there was no doubt of their admiration and respect for her as the hub of their social and cultural whirl.

He looked forward eagerly to their meetings and they found themselves in agreement on everything they discussed which made them more relaxed and open with each other. He accepted her coquettish ways: how she held his hand or clung to his arm and was forever making bodily contact, like a cat pleading to be fed; and his natural conceit meant that he enjoyed the way she paraded him from one group of friends to another, all the time singing his praises, talking endlessly about his poetry.

Of course, in the risqué environment of Garsington Manor their closeness gave rise to gossip and this worried Sassoon. Whilst he regarded her as a dear and valued friend, there was no physical attraction as far as he was concerned. He had no urge to grab her and hug her, or to encourage her advances. He simply accepted anything physical in a spirit of neutrality. He entered into the normal male/female ritual of kissing cheeks on meeting and departing but his contact with her warm and soft skin failed to stir his red corpuscles.

When snide remarks about them persisted at Garsington he decided to visit her less often. He also postponed his promised long stay and when he did make it he took Graves with him. Lady Ottoline was far too polite to object, but she wasn't at all pleased. She regarded Graves as an intruder, knowing that his presence would hinder the prospect of a relationship with Siggy. Furthermore she resented the smug way in which he imposed himself upon them. He was far too opinionated; a brutish, uncouth young man who she wasn't at all surprised to learn was a keen pugilist.

The dislike was mutual. When alone with Siegfried, Graves mocked her strange appearance and pacifist sentiments, and when Siegfried sprang to her defence Graves suspected that Sassoon was falling for her so-called feminine charms. He was aware of the hazards presented by a besotted female and he was equally alert of Sassoon's naivety and vulnerability. He feared that if Lady Ottoline succeeded in seducing him it would drive a wedge between them and end their friendship. The very thought of Sassoon sullying himself with a mature woman of infinite experience made Graves irritable and resentful.

Lady Ottoline's lack of progress with Siggy, and the strained atmosphere caused by Graves, wounded her deeply. She felt isolated, as though she was being ostracised in her own home. She imagined conspiracies springing up against her and she saw the utopian world she hankered for slipping away from her. In her determination to fight against this feeling of doom, she arranged a dinner in Siggy's honour to which she invited her closest friends, including Virginia Woolf, Carrington, Dorothy Brett, D.H. Lawrence, Katherine Mansfield, Middleton Murry, Aldous Huxley and several notable pacifists working on the farm, all of whom she knew would be delighted to meet Siggy.

What she didn't reckon on was her husband suddenly appearing. A division in the House of Commons had been postponed and when he returned to his nearby flat he found that he had neglected to pay his electricity bill and it had been cut off, so he headed for Garsington Manor. If he had been aware of Ottoline's plans, and the possible birth of a new affair, he would have done the decent thing and stayed at a hotel; but Garsington Manor was, after all, his home and Lady Ottoline his wife.

Sassoon met Phillip Morrell for the first time over pre-dinner drinks. He was unimpressed. He concluded that the MP was a weak, insignificant character who should have stayed loyal to his vocation in life, that of a small-town solicitor.

With Phillip's arrival, Ottoline hastily rearranged her seating plan, placing Phillip in his rightful place at the head of the table and moving Siggy to her immediate left where she would be able to devote herself to him; to chat to him in confidence and to lay her hand on his thigh beneath the table without anyone seeing. However she made the mistake of placing Robert Graves only a few places away on her right, within shouting distance of Siggy. This meant the two of them kept swapping military stories which left everyone else less than enthralled.

By the time the ladies withdrew from the dining room for coffee, allowing the gentlemen to pass the port around and smoke cigars, Ottoline realised that all her scheming had failed. Led by the example of Graves, the gentlemen became drunk and boisterous and started playing childish army mess games, and the ladies, hearing their raucous behaviour, soon despaired of the gentlemen ever joining them and drifted off to bed in high dudgeon, Ottoline being the last to retire.

The following morning Ottoline did her best to pretend that nothing untoward had happened and after presiding over a large gathering at breakfast she invited Siggy into her study to resume her efforts to win him over. She showed him all her personal treasures, including signed poems that Thomas Hardy had given her. She kept offering him small presents and although he protested and tried to restrain her, he saw such hurt in her eyes that he succumbed to her generosity. He understood how she felt. Unrequited love was no stranger to Sassoon. He had had similar experiences with David Thomas and Bobbie Hanmer: a longing to revel in the softness and warmth of their flesh and to love them heart and soul, only to realise that there was no hope of fruition.

When Ottoline forced a first edition (Volume I) of Gibbon's *Decline and Fall* on him, he showed his appreciation by spending over an hour illustrating copies of the poems he had sent her, signing them 'with deep affection, Siggy'.

For the time, that pleased her well enough.

After their visit to Garsington, Sassoon and Graves went to stay in London with Robbie Ross at 40, Moon Street, Piccadilly. There, an extraordinary character named Nellie Burton kept a lodging house that specialised in looking after and protecting single gentlemen of a 'different disposition'. The house was full of charm and guests came and went and indulged their predilections in the knowledge that no questions would ever be asked.

Having had their fill of Moon Street, they went to stay at the Graves' family home in Harlech and there they lived close to nature. They roamed the rugged coast line, paddled along golden sands, and splashed about in rocky pools like children. They plunged naked into the raging Atlantic surf, roamed the hills in the hinterland, and finally retired to Graves's basic, tumbled-down cottage in which they talked, read and wrote poetry deep into the witching hours.

From Wales they went to Weirleigh but here they struck trouble due to the way Sassoon's mother kept them awake every night, wandering the house and crying out in despair as she tried to contact Hambo, her dead son, a racket which Graves claimed made it worse than being back in France. It was the closest they ever got to falling out until Graves decided to get married.

Later on, during Sassoon's convalescence, there were two major developments concerning his writing. In September he published a collection entitled *Morning Glory*, and then, through the joint efforts of Robbie Ross and Ottoline, his future literary career was assured when they persuaded the publisher, William Heinemann, to bring out a commercial edition of his work.

The significant role Lady Ottoline played in this meant Sassoon replied to her letters regularly and assumed a more tender and appreciative tone. He even included the occasional endearment and signed off 'with love' in the same way as she did; a sentiment he found impossible to express when confronted by her face to face.

Sassoon still had to attend a monthly medical board. By this time, his claims that his diarrhoea attacks kept reoccurring had grown a trifle thin and he found it expedient to concentrate on the possibility of lung trouble, claiming to have a persistent cough. It gained him another month on the sick list but he knew in his heart that his prolonged 'holiday' was about to end. It had, after all, lasted the best part of nine months and anyone seeing him regularly, or hearing of his outings with hunts scattered about Sussex and Kent, knew perfectly well that he was as fit as the proverbial fiddle.

He was eventually passed fit at much the same time as Graves and they once again found themselves at Litherhead, waiting for a new posting abroad. They shared a room for nearly two months on light duties, which gave them plenty of time to enjoy themselves.

14

More Troubles for Ottoline

While Sassoon and Graves idled away their days at Litherland, Lady Ottoline had a difficult time. Her chief concern was Siggy, of course. She realised that now he was fit again he would soon face another spell on the western front, and that meant a high risk of him being killed. The mere thought of his beautiful body being torn to shreds reduced her to tears and every time she gazed at his photograph she rued the way her designs on him had been thwarted. It left her bereft of all confidence. She grew certain that she had lost her appeal to younger men.

Every morning she examined herself in the nude in the long mirror in her bedroom and she was horrified by what confronted her. Then she would dress in all her finery, complete with one of her outlandish hats, seeking reassurance; but all she ever saw was a middle-aged crone.

She still slept with Bertie, but she wondered why she demeaned herself. His gall was sometimes beyond belief. He boasted openly about his other love interests, namely an American woman, Colette Malleson. Even as he lay side by side with Ottoline, ready for another laborious fornication, he confessed to having slept with this awful woman and then, as though that wasn't enough, he had the audacity to assure Ottoline that he still loved her, and that he always would, but that a man of his sensibilities was quite capable of loving several women at the same time.

Bertie's pitiful boasting convinced Ottoline that she was alone in the world, simply an appendage being used by so-called friends; that no one loved her, that selfish men took advantage of her and her female friends secretly despised her. Love and loyalty seemed to be a thing of the past.

Her nights with Bertie became increasingly perfunctory. He took his pleasure and then, if he didn't just turn over on his side and fall asleep, he subjected her to a brief interrogation about Sassoon. Had the young man read his book yet? If not, why not? And if so, had he been impressed? Had he shown any signs of becoming a genuine pacifist? And if so, why had he returned to his regimental depot to await another posting to France? As a final insult he demanded to know if she had slept with him yet, and if not, why not?

"Surely that's the best way to secure his support?" he suggested.

"Oh God, Bertram, you're so uncouth."

"Not at all. What you must realise is that I will never succeed all on my own. No matter how good my lectures are, and how well attended they are, and how many standing ovations I get, we need a military sacrificial lamb, someone who is prepared to put the success of our cause before all else. We need headlines ... Protests ... Mass demonstrations ... Endless publicity ... And this man Sassoon sounds just the fellow. So there's no point in wasting time. Use your feminine charms on him. You've done more than enough for him. That contract with Heinemann will be the making of him."

Ottoline had heard it all before and she was tired of it. She would never desert the cause of pacifism but there were other considerations, first and foremost her personal happiness, and she knew that if she was ever to secure that through an affair with Siggy it would have to be based on genuine love, never on duplicity and entrapment as Bertrand suggested.

She saw Bertrand studying her in a thoughtful way, clearly on the verge of adding something else. He took her hand and said: "You don't have to worry about being unfaithful towards me, you know."

She looked at him with contempt and didn't grace him with a reply.

She wrote to Siggy every day. She poured her heart out to him; love letters oozing with sincerity and pleading for a similar response, all couched in her flamboyant style, sealed in pink envelopes, and humming with perfume.

The post corporal at Litherland always handed them to Sassoon at arm's length, and Graves laughed at Siegfried's inability to control facial contortions and bodily shudders as he ploughed from one risqué paragraph to another, wondering what on earth would come next.

At first Sassoon refused to divulge their contents, but when beautifully wrapped parcels arrived as well as letters he had no alternative but to open them in Graves's presence, and this led to his secretiveness gradually dissolving. He took to reading out choice snippets and before long he was holding nothing back. In a way, it helped to convince Graves that Sassoon was not interested in Ottoline's protestations of love and found her advances highly embarrassing.

Among the presents Ottoline sent were copies of poems by famous writers. There was also an exquisite sandalwood trinket box, to say nothing of various books, and several petit-point tapestries which she had created with loving care and which she suggested would go splendidly on the walls of his hut, but which ended up as bedside mats.

Ottoline's letters were a daily highlight for them. Graves insisted on having a hand in formulating Sassoon's replies, so her letters became a regular sport, something which they discussed at length as they strode the golf links at nearby Crosby, Sassoon playing whilst Graves went simply for the exercise. Sassoon insisted that his replies should not be unkind and Graves suggested that the best way to cool her Ladyship's ardour was for Sassoon to pretend that he thought the gifts were intended for both of them. So they devised short, polite notes of joint appreciation, knowing full well that they were a far cry from what the poor woman was so obviously hoping to receive.

One of Sassoon's early replies went:

> *"Dear Ottoline,*
> *Robert and I were delighted to receive your latest letter and presents. It is so kind of you to think about us both. Your generosity towards us is far more than we deserve. We will treasure your gifts and will derive great pleasure from the books and poems you have sent us. When we have time to write more poems, we will certainly send you copies, even though we have no hope of competing with the ones you enclosed ..."*
> *With fondest regards, Siggy and Robert.*

These replies were final proof to Ottoline that everyone was conspiring against her. Troubles just went on piling up. The only person to take any interest in her was Middleton Murry. He wrote to say that he thought he was in love with her. That only infuriated her. She liked Murry but felt no physical attraction towards him; and how could he only 'think' he loved her? Either he did or he didn't. With love there were no half-measures, as she knew only too well, and the very thought that the wrong man might be in love with her left her more desolate than ever.

Then, at last, she had a personal letter from Siggy. It was devoid of any mention of Graves. He wrote to her out of a sense of duty and fair play. He had just received a new posting to rejoin the Fusiliers in France and he felt obliged to tell her, face to face, knowing that on the law of averages alone he could well be killed. He was prepared for his fate but he knew it would cause unacceptable hurt if he died without one last visit to the two women to whom he was inextricably bound, his mother and Ottoline.

In his letter he explained that he would shortly be in London for the day so perhaps they could meet for lunch. She was overjoyed. She replied immediately and made arrangements to stay at her flat at 38 Bloomsbury Street, certain that his heart had softened and that he was anticipating spending the night with her.

They lunched at the Café Royal and then visited the National Gallery. Sassoon made an effort to be talkative and cheerful and he welcomed the way she either held his hand or took his arm as they wandered around. Initially he had cringed at her outlandish attire, especially her ridiculous hat with a long ostrich feather that kept brushing people's faces; but in the end, as she weaved about trying not to spike people, he could only laugh and admire her courage at being so eccentric.

They had tea at the Waldorf Hotel. She knew it well, of course. She had been there many times to show off a host of different men, be it Walter Sickert, Herbert Asquith, Roger Fry, Henry Lamb, Augustus John, Phillip Morrell, Bertrand Russell and numerous others long forgotten. She always remembered the stir she had made when she went there with burly Augustus John, still in his smock with daubs of paint all over it.

The Waldorf tea lounge hadn't changed a bit. Despite the war it still boasted a small string orchestra, suitably muted in the background, and it remained the rendezvous of London's leading society hostesses, all of them anxious to keep up with the latest intrigues. Lady Ottoline was a hostess equal to any of them, but she only graced the tea lounge in order to show off her latest conquest. When she entered on Siggy's arm she had never felt so proud. It proved to her wide circle of friends and enemies that she wasn't past it; that she was still capable of attracting young men and embarking on affairs with them.

She was delighted by the expectant hush that greeted their entrance and she revelled at the way the maître d' kept them waiting before showing them to a table on the corner dais where they would be seen to the best advantage. She basked in the limelight, knowing that Siggy, in his close-fitting uniform, with his burnished Sam Browne, and the purple and white ribbon of his Military Cross, would cause a major stir. She was declaring to London society that she didn't have to scrape the bottom of the barrel with an old has-been like Bertrand Russell. She was there to make her bitchy friends squirm with envy; to make them marvel that she was able to mesmerize a famous young poet who had been featured in The Times as a future poet laureate, and rumoured to be line for a Victoria Cross.

She had no idea that many of those present knew more about Sassoon than she did. They too had well-informed contacts. While Robby Ross had gone to great lengths to hide from Ottoline the truth about Sassoon's 'different disposition', others among the Garsington crowd (notably Clive Bell) had been happy to whisper the word to rival hostesses that Sassoon was a homosexual who was known to have stayed at Half Moon Street; and that his much-trumpeted engagement to Dorothy Hanmer was a mere blind aimed at enhancing his chances with her younger brother, Robert.

It made Ottoline's appearance with Sassoon all the more intriguing. Smirks flashed between the tables as those present became more convinced than ever that the recent ridicule heaped upon Ottoline was fully justified. Her appearance on the arm of a poofter was a delicious piece of gossip, destined to do the rounds in Belgravia and the country-houses.

Afternoon tea at the Waldorf was very much a 'little fingers up' occasion and Sassoon, in common with most other men present, maintained a bashful, embarrassed profile, daunted by so many doyennes of social distinctions. Lady Ottoline on the other hand smiled around patronizingly, and whenever she spotted anyone she particularly wanted to impress she waved gracefully, no matter how distant they were, usually getting at least a dozen waves in return from tables between them where others thought they were being singled out.

By the time Sassoon settled their bill and they prepared to leave, Ottoline was happy that she had done herself justice. As they meandered between the tables towards the foyer, they paused every now and to exchange words with those of real note. One of them asked: "And are you now off back to Garsington, Ottoline?"

"My dear, we can't possibly wait that long. We're heading for my flat and then perhaps the theatre afterwards ... If we still have enough energy ..."

She had no idea of what a fool she was making of herself.

Sassoon had been uncomfortable at the Waldorf but back at Ottoline's flat he was even more on edge. Her remarks over tea forewarned him that they were heading towards a crisis in their relationship. Ottoline had had enough of his stalling and was no longer prepared to be fobbed-off: as far as she was concerned the time had come for him to commit. There was a steely determination in her demeanour. The way she bustled about, rearranging the bedding and asking him what he would like for breakfast made her intentions perfectly obvious.

In alarm, his mind worked feverishly, seeking a way to extricate himself. He knew that this time there would be no easy way out. As a first step he told her about his new posting to France, making it sound as alarming as possible, the most likely outcome being death. His intention was to make her realise that a relationship would be unwise and only invite the prospect of inconsolable misery. When he continued in this alarmist vein, describing how he could easily be horribly maimed, or blinded, or shell-shocked and reduced to a cabbage-like existence, she flung her arms around his neck and hung on to him with all her strength. Far from being put off, she led him over to her Chesterfield. As they settled down on it, she entwined her arms about him and encouraged him to talk about being reunited with his old platoon and meeting his fellow officers again. They talked on and on and when it grew dark they didn't bother to switch on the lights or draw the curtains, and in the dim intimacy of the room she became convinced that, despite his initial hesitancy, he would stay the night and enjoy the type of farewell all soldiers longed for.

She felt her body responding in anticipation and as her sexual desires surged she became more voracious and demonstrative, forcing him to edge back along the Chesterfield until he could go no further. She kissed him tenderly on his cheeks, and then, for the first time, she succeeded in kissing him on the lips, which encouraged her to press home her advances even more boldly. He was so embarrassed that he had no option but to bring things to a halt. He shot his left hand forward and looked at his watch.

"Good God, look at the time!"

He stood up so abruptly that he tore himself from her arms. "I must be off, old girl. Otherwise I'll miss my train."

"Train? What train?"

"I'm going back to Weirleigh."

"What on earth for?"

"To tell my mother about my posting."

His words were like a dagger to her heart. His mother! Dear God! Did he equate her with his mother? He could tell his mother any time: telephone her, write to her, or send her a blasted postcard! As his heartless disregard for her feelings sank in, and she realised that he intended to abandon her, she tried to be playful and skittish, pulling him back onto the Chesterfield as though it was all a big tease. When he didn't respond and remained poker-faced she said: "You must stay, darling Siggy! Don't be such an old fuddy-duddy."

When that failed to galvanize him, she begged him to stay. She became desperate, her words wild and disjointed. It was inconceivable to her that after such a joyous day and hours of cuddling, he could be so cruel, using his neurotic mother as an excuse. She kept declaring her love, promising that if he stayed it would be an experience he would never forget; but he just smiled back, a strained and artificial grimace that made it clear to Ottoline that his mind was made up.

After all the favours she had done him he realised how ungrateful his behaviour must seem to her and in his embarrassment he tried to convince her that he had an inescapable duty to tell his mother personally of his posting, and when she laughed this off as juvenile, he fell back on a wild and improbable theory that men's experiences on the western front did nothing to enhance their enthusiasm or capacity for love-making. She didn't understand what he was driving at and it left him with no alternative but to be more explicit. Stuttering awkwardly, he explained that he could never be more than a friend to her, that he would always be a good and loyal friend, and he would remain eternally grateful for all her kindnesses, but now, with his future so uncertain, any intimacy between them would be most unwise.

He was damned if he was going to be more explicit than that, and for her part she realised that her worst fears were being fulfilled: he was rejecting her because of her age; that he saw her as a wrinkled old prune. She knew it was bound to happen eventually, but surely not this soon? Rejection was something she had never experienced. She was aware that numerous men had slept with her simply for the kudos of another conquest, but even the more recent ones had never hesitated or failed to perform. She was so fazed by the thought of being physically repulsive to Siggy that she felt paralysed, not knowing what to do or say.

She watched in silence as he clambered into his mackintosh. Then, frantic to do something - anything to make him change his mind - she acted unthinkingly. She dashed into her bedroom and rummaged around in her jewellery box until she came across one of her most treasured pieces, a large, polished opal pulsing with shifting colours. She hurried back to him and pressed it into his hands.

"Oh no, Ottoline! Not more presents ..."

His disdainful expression told her that she had made an error of judgement; that he didn't see the opal as an act of love but as a tawdry bribe to overcome his rejection.

"It's just a good-luck charm, Siggy," she said by way of justification. "Take it with you to remind you that I'll always be with you in spirit. But stay tonight, Siggy ... That will be your greatest treasure and memory ... Please!"

When she realised that he wasn't going to change his mind, she dashed forward and pressed her back against the door, barring his way. "Don't go, Siggy. Don't go!"

He tried to return the opal but she refused it. She pushed it back into his mackintosh pocket, begging him to keep it as a symbol of her love. As she continued to plead, with tears now rolling down her cheeks, he gave her such a pitying look that she suddenly realised the futility of her efforts; that she was simply humiliating herself. Reluctantly she gave in and opened the door for him, her head bowed in misery.

He held her by the shoulders, at arms' length, and then leaned forward and bestowed light kisses on her wet cheeks. He was of a mind to hug her but he couldn't bring himself to do it. He remained stiff and mannerly, as though she was a distant aunt. He was so lost for appropriate words that he simply turned and left, closing the door behind him. She hurried upstairs and from her bedroom window she watched him stride down the street. She gave him a final wave, but he didn't respond. He didn't even look back and she could tell by his hurried gait, and how he was looking around for a taxi, that he couldn't get away quick enough.

She collapsed on to her bed, convulsed by sobs, convinced that she would never see him again.

15

A Sudden Reappearance

Within a couple of days Ottoline became very ill. Her doctor declared her to be so run down, so depressed and so weak and anaemic that he insisted that she should stay at a famous 'hydro' in Harrogate. While there, recovering very slowly, she was totally isolated. She had no visitors and not one of her so-called friends kept in touch with her. Her only letter came from her personal maid, recounting the chaos at Garsington Manor with the usual misfits chasing around the place playing 'musical beds'.

She heard nothing from either Phillip or Siggy. With Siggy it was understandable. He was no doubt back in the front line, but with Phillip there were no excuses. He was her husband and even allowing for his duties as an MP there was no reason why he could not have written. Eventually, he sent her a post card of Big Ben, on the back of which he related that their cowman had committed suicide, drowning himself in the village pond by tying a brick to each foot.

It wasn't until Christmas that her doctor allowed her to return to Garsington Manor. Had he known that Phillip had invited a crowd of guests, he would never have sanctioned it. As it was, Ottoline had a wretched time. Amid the guests' high jinks by night, and their hypocritical displays of religious respect in the village church by day, gossip was once again rampant. Ottoline was told by three reliable sources that Bertie was now having an affair with Katherine Mansfield, as well as still sleeping with the Malleson woman. This disloyalty, coupled with the demands placed on her as hostess, meant that she became ill again, so ill that she had to go into a nursing home for what her friends referred to as, 'Yet another of her cures'.

While there, she heard that two novels were about to be published with characters based on her. The first was by Gilbert Cannan, which didn't worry her, but the second was by D.H.Lawrence, a close friend, and that distressed her no end. She saw it as an outright betrayal, no doubt done under the influence of Lawrence's odious wife, Frieda.

Then, to cap all her woes, she was visited by Aldous Huxley and Carrington. With unconcealed delight they told her that they had been to the Palladium the previous night and seen Phillip in the audience with an unknown young woman who was very pretty and full of giggles. When Ottoline confronted her husband he admitted that it was true, and as his confession unwound it revealed horror after horror. He had two mistresses and they were both pregnant. One of them insisted that unless she and her child were acknowledged and provided for she would make everything public and cause such a scandal that it would ruin his political career, even force him to resign from the House.

Sparked off by all this, Phillip started to behave in a very peculiar manner. This came as no surprise since there was a long record of mental breakdowns in his family, but the most unsettling thing for Ottoline was that he repeated to anyone who cared to listen that he was the intelligent one in their marriage and that Ottoline was completely dependent on him. Things became so bad, and his behaviour in the Commons so erratic, that Ottoline and her brother Henry made arrangements for him to be certified, a move that proved unnecessary due to a swift and unexpected recovery.

Amid all this, Ottoline turned to Bertie for help, only to be met by indifference. He claimed he had his own life to lead and was far too occupied with furthering the pacifist cause, stopping the war, and sorting out his love affairs, to become involved in her personal complications.

Ottoline sank to her lowest ebb. She had been betrayed by her husband, deserted by her lover, and had so far heard nothing from Siggy, the man with whom she was crazily in love and who she longed for most of all. She lost interest in herself. She didn't care who came and went at Garsington Manor and she got up in the morning not caring what the day held in store. Far from inspecting her naked figure in in her full-length mirror each morning, trying to convince herself that she was still desirable, she just rolled out of bed, flung on any old clothes, and didn't even bother to use make-up or attend to her hair, which had always been her greatest pride. In the course of a few months she went from a proud, distinguished and aristocratic lady, always highly conscious of her appearance, to being scruffy and unkempt.

It was into this situation, only a few weeks later, that Siegfried Sassoon suddenly reappeared.

Once again he was a hero, but this time a wounded hero. He had lived up to his reputation as Mad Jack. There was even renewed talk among the Fusiliers that he was due for another gallantry award. Graves instigated most of this talk, insisting that if Sassoon had been killed he would have been awarded a posthumous VC; but because he was only wounded and the attack he led had fizzled out, he had so far been ignored.

Ottoline first heard of Siggy's return from Robbie Ross. He drew up unannounced at Garsington in a taxi and told her the latest news he had gleaned from Robert Graves, who was also back from France. She was ecstatic. All her past humiliations were forgotten. She could only thank God that he had been spared, that he was still alive and his wound was not a ghastly mutilation. He had been hit by a sniper's bullet which had entered at his neck and gone into the top of his right shoulder, missing his jugular vein by a fraction. Ross said he was now recovering in a hospital at Denmark Hill, London.

Lady Ottoline dropped everything, smartened herself up, and joined Ross in the taxi waiting to take him back to Oxford. There, she caught an afternoon train and by early evening she arrived at the Denmark Hill Hospital. It wasn't visiting hours and the matron was reluctant to let her see Siggy; but Ottoline was so insistent that the Matron eventually relented. She then had the shock of her life. She walked through a ward full of badly wounded and heavily bandaged men, and when she reached Siggy in a private side-ward she at first didn't recognise him. He was propped up by a bank of pillows. His head had sunk back into them, making him a mere shadow of his real self. He was deathly pale and his hollow cheeks made him appear half-starved. He was fast asleep - the sleep of a man drained of all energy and vitality. She drew a chair up beside his bed and took his right hand, which was on top of the bedclothes.

"You mustn't wake him."

She looked up and saw a nurse standing over her.

"I'm Robert Graves's sister," she said. "This is the first time I've met Siegfried. But I've heard so much about him. Robert is devoted to him, his best friend. Mr Sassoon has lost a lot of blood. After he was shot, they made him walk a mile to the nearest aid post and that nearly finished him off."

"Can I stay for a time?"

"Fifteen minutes, but don't wake him."

Ottoline stayed for fifteen minutes exactly, all the time holding his hand, sometimes dabbing her cheeks with her handkerchief to stem her tears, all their past differences forgotten, her love for him deeper than ever.

Sassoon made slow progress, much slower than his doctors anticipated. It was psychological trouble more than anything else. Whilst the flesh healed normally, the trauma of his experiences persisted and the doctors lacked any effective treatment. They could only watch as his recovery came about naturally, with time.

Ottoline visited him regularly and found him very disturbed. He was either in the depths of despair and reluctant to enter into a normal conversation or bumptious and boastful, harping on about his reputation as 'Mad Jack'. She made due allowances and put a brave face on things, playing along with him as much as she could. With the help of Nurse Graves, and a doctor who had known Sassoon at Cambridge, she arranged that once he was fit enough he should spend his convalescence at Garsington Manor. There, she assured them, he would enjoy peace and quiet, with comforts lavished upon him.

When he arrived at Garsington Manor his frailty shocked everyone and they all noticed how he kept glancing around as though expecting something violent to happen; how he kept flinching unaccountably. He never got up until lunch time and in the afternoons he wandered around the gardens on his own. If it was fine he would rest on the hammock beneath the copper beech tree, reading the Thomas Hardy novel that never left his grasp.

He dined with Ottoline and her other guests but he had a very small appetite and spent most of his time looking around the table, staring at each diner in turn with an air of accusation. He went to bed as soon as the ladies retired for coffee and the gentlemen set about demolishing another decanter of port.

It wasn't until his fourth night at Garsington that he told Ottoline what had happened in France. Late each night she peeped into his bedroom, a perfunctory and motherly check to make sure he was sleeping soundly. To her surprise he was still awake. He was sitting up, as though waiting for her. He beckoned her across and motioned her to sit on his bedside. She hurried over and took his hand. He was shivering but his hand wasn't cold.

"I keep seeing dead bodies," he said.

"Here? Now?"

"Yes. Not this very moment, but when in the garden. I see them in all kinds of places, especially when I was in London. And the smell of death never goes away. It's often so strong that when I turn a corner or go round a bend I expect to be confronted by more bodies. And at dinner, when I look around at the others, they're always injured in some way or other, covered in shell dressings, all blood and dirt and muck ..."

"Oh, you poor boy ..."

"But that's not the worst thing ..."

"What else?"

"They've crapped all over me."

"Who have?"

"My senior officers, the colonel, the brigadier and his staff generally. God knows, I did my best but I got no thanks from them. I won't be getting any decorations for that last show, any more than I have done for most of the other things I've done ... They brushed it aside by saying that it was not a decisive action ..."

"Tell me what happened."

He told her, but his account was so disjointed that she found it hard to follow. He started by describing how being shot was like being kicked by a carthorse; and how the sight of so much of his blood flowing out of his neck and shoulder convinced him he was about to die.

"It was as though I was watching myself melting away, being poured down the drain."

Then he went back to the start of the action: how the colonel had called him forward and ordered him to organise a bombing party of 30 men. It was to be a special mission, as though he'd kept it in reserve especially for him. They were to reinforce a battalion of the Cameronians whose attack had just been repulsed with heavy casualties. As he set off with his party of men for the Cameronians the colonel's parting words had been: "Now's your chance, Mad Jack. Let's see how good you really are."

When they found the Cameronians, their officers were sitting in their headquarters dugout doing nothing. They then gave him a lot of confusing orders; tasks they should have done themselves, their dirty work, not his. "And I'll never forget their colonel," said Sassoon. "He had the gall to say: 'Well old chap, it looks as though you're really for it this time.' It was as though they were all trying to get rid of me."

Then, hardly pausing to take breath, he described the attack and how he had got wounded just as they achieved their objective.

"And what have I got to show for it?" he concluded. "Bugger all! And I'll tell you something ... I'll never go back to France. I've done all I'm ever going to do."

He spoke on, well into the small hours. To Ottoline he seemed semi-delirious. He was obsessed by gallantry awards and as she sat there, squeezing his hand, she saw him in a new light. She already knew that he was disillusioned with the war, that he was a man on the turn; but now she was convinced that his conversion was complete. A previously gung-ho warrior had had enough. He had seen the light.

Ottoline heard her guests going to bed. The Garsington floorboards were notorious for their loud creaking. Siggy was still talking, his voice quiet, little more than a mumble. She had little idea of what he was talking about but she sensed the importance of letting him ramble on, even if he went on all night. He needed to talk it all out of his system.

It was four o'clock in the morning when his eyelids began to droop and his voice to slur. When he fell into a deep sleep she rearranged his pillows, made sure he was tucked in securely, and prepared to tip-toe out of the room, hoping that she would not be heard by any of her guests. She took a final look at him and kissed him lightly on his forehead and stroked his cheek tenderly with the back of her fingers. Then she paused. It occurred to her that she could spend the night with him. She could undress and snuggle up against him in bed, give him the comfort and reassurance he so richly deserved: let him wake up already in her arms, flesh to flesh, ready for the most natural thing in the world, to have an experience he would never forget.

She was shocked by her own lasciviousness. Now was not the time for sexual gratification. It would be indecent to take advantage of him. He was physically exhausted and mentally sick, a man who had been through something she would never comprehend; a man who had seen so many foul deaths that the human body was no longer a thing of beauty to him, merely butchered blood and guts. It was little wonder he suffered hallucinations, and even less surprising that he had so often shied away from her. She understood now how a man could fail to become engorged and rampant with desire when he never escaped the vision of torn limbs and maggot-filled corpses.

Everything became very clear to her. Patience was needed above all else.

She went to her room as silently as possible. Then she lay perfectly still in her bed. She didn't sleep. She was deep in thought. She would wait. She would wait for as long as she had to. She would no longer harass him or try to entice him. She cursed herself for having been so thoughtless and pushy. She would devote herself to helping him recover, and when his mind had cleared and his hallucinations ceased, she would steer him in a new direction, lead him to such delights of physical intimacy that memories of past horrors would be obliterated.

Meanwhile, one comment he had made stuck in her mind.

'I mean it. I'll never go back to France.'

Bertie would be delighted to hear that.

16

A Fateful Dinner

In the morning Sassoon and Ottoline went into the gardens. They strolled about the manicured lawns and watched her daughter, Julian, playing at the side of the swimming pool. Their discussion during the night wasn't mentioned. She doubted that he even remembered it. Anyhow, she was more concerned with persuading him to extend his stay at Garsington until he was fully recovered, and she was delighted when he grasped the opportunity.

He stayed for over a month and in that time his health and general attitude improved day by day and he entered fully into Ottoline's way of life, getting to know her friends and accepting their strange mixture of love and bitchiness, the way they gushed over each other one minute and then criticised each other outrageously behind their backs the next. He had frequent visits from Robbie Ross and Robert Graves which helped to balance his existence and he also loved to wander over to Garsington's farm to discuss the war with the conscientious objectors who worked there, many of whom had interesting tales to tell. At other times he would take the pony and trap to Oxford to visit coffee houses, have lunch at various taverns, and admire the wonderful architecture of the colleges, so reminiscent of his days at Cambridge.

He had no more hallucinations, yet the battlefields remained in his mind. He maintained a regular correspondence with Cotterell, Dunn, and others, and he kept abreast of the exploits of the Fusiliers, noting with sadness the steady erosion of old friends. He often wondered how long it would be before they were all gone.

Ottoline watched over him carefully. Since her all-night vigil she was motivated by two desires: to advance their relationship so that when the time was ripe he would welcome its consummation, and to make sure his disenchantment with the war did not decline. She never forgot her assurance to Bertrand that he was just the man they were looking for and she was determined that her judgement should be proved correct. She knew that to bring both things to fruition it would require all the delicacy and understanding that she could muster.

Sassoon made the most of the opportunity to write more poetry, all of which was published, yet he was increasingly frustrated by the lack of impact his poems achieved. He loved to see them in print, and to read and re-read the praise lavished upon them by the critics, but he hated the way they then just disappeared overnight and were seemingly forgotten, one day wonders which lacked any real influence on the way the war was being so appallingly conducted. The fighting just went on and on. Like Ottoline he was convinced that something sensational needed to happen, something to shatter the country's complacency.

He discussed this with Ottoline and she suggested that he should meet Bertrand Russell. She assured him that Russell, for all his faults, was the country's greatest hope, that only he had the capability to lead a mass and successful movement against the war. He operated on a national scale through his lectures. She also suggested to Siggy that he should become more journalistic and instead of writing poems he should produce articles on the need for peace talks. He tried it but Robbie Ross was unenthusiastic and none of the articles ever appeared in print.

Matters came to a head by accident, completely unplanned. Sassoon gave it no careful thought, nor did he consult with anyone else. It was just an instantaneous, reflex reaction which surprised him as much as it did others. He acted on impulse, as he invariably did; a knee-jerk reaction which he was unable to control.

There was a sizable gathering for dinner with twenty-four people around the table. Bertrand Russell was among them. It was the first time Sassoon had met him and his reputation as a philosopher, mathematician, and lecturer, to say nothing of his book, *Justice in War,* put Sassoon in awe of him.

He also met the conscientious objector Lytton Strachey for the first time. His reaction towards him was quite different: total abhorrence. He was weedy and bearded and always playing a part, assuming feminine traits as though he was the Queen of Queens, and forever dragging his piles into the conversation as though they were a prize possession and an affliction which only he ever had to endure. Sassoon saw through him straight away. He was no more than a pseudo-intellectual whose acid wit was always cruel and biting; a poseur who made Sassoon feel contrite about his homosexual tendencies.

At dinner, Sassoon sat opposite him and straight away there was a clash of personalities. Strachey was jealous of Sassoon's literary successes and was determined to belittle him, to drag him back to his true station in life as a struggling amateur who was merely milking his war experiences.

"Ah yes," he greeted Sassoon, "Mad Jack, the saviour of the Somme." His sarcasm made Sassoon sound like a warmonger bent exclusively on personal glory.

Robert Graves was also present and he didn't help. He was in one of his provocative moods and when he sensed friction between the two men he did his best to goad them, laughing uproariously as they became increasingly rude to each other, ensuring that everyone's attention was soon focused on them.

What irked Sassoon more than anything was how Strachey persistently referred to him as 'Mad Jack' and dismissed his poetry as doggerel. Sassoon retaliated by asking Strachey what his claim to fame was, knowing that his only achievement was a very second rate book entitled *Landmarks in French Literature*. Eventually, when the maids cleared the table of the main course dishes and distributed the sweets, Lytton Strachey turned once more to Sassoon and asked: "So, Mad Jack, now you are fit and well, can we rely on you to unleash your madness by going back to France to win the war for us?"

"No, I'm afraid not."

"What are your plans then?"

"Certainly never to go back to France ..."

"But it's not up to you, surely, Mad Jack? A soldier goes where he's posted, rather like letters in the hands of the Royal Mail."

There were guffaws around the table. All evening they'd been laughing at Strachey's witticisms. They always did. It came automatically with virtually everything he said. Sassoon's face flushed in anger and it was in that instant that his subconscious mind took over and words spilled out spontaneously without regard for the consequences.

"Normally, of course," Sassoon admitted once the laughter died away, "that would be the case, but not this time. I intend to defy the military authorities. They can post me where they like, but I'm afraid their orders will get lost in the post. I'm not going to France or anywhere else."

"Oh, come now, Mad Jack ... How can you be so sure?"

"Because I intend to make a public declaration condemning the war and urging all British troops to lay down their arms and refuse to fight any longer. I will appeal to the government to open up peace negotiations. And I will do that from my home at Weirleigh. Then tell them to go to hell."

"High treason!" cried Lytton Strachey, his voice soaring several octaves as he strove for more laughter.

"Possibly."

"Then they'll court-martial you, Mad Jack."

"I hope so."

"And they'll find you guilty."

"No doubt."

"Then they'll shoot you, Mad Jack."

"Could well be."

"Won't you mind?"

"Well, I won't be overly pleased. But one has to be true to oneself, doesn't one? Not that I can expect you to understand that."

All eyes were on Sassoon. No one was laughing any more. The jokes were over. A spiteful little tussle between two writers had escalated to a point of no return. Sassoon had made a commitment virtually impossible to revoke.

"Mr Strachey," said Sassoon, "since you are a conscientious objector who is well-known for having to take your air cushion with you wherever you go, and a man who has never been anywhere near the front, or got your hands dirty farming, or driven an ambulance, or indeed done anything in the least unselfish, and a person who lives off dividends from arms manufacturers, you may be surprised to hear that on the first morning of the Somme, in a matter of half an hour, I saw four to five thousand men walk straight into the path of machine guns and drop down dead. They sacrificed themselves in good faith, acting on the orders of high-ranking morons who told them to walk, not run, an order they obeyed thinking their superiors knew what they were talking about. As you can imagine, that sight made a lasting impression on me. So now, I have to stand up for what I believe in. You believe in a comfortable life scrounging off others, and treating everyone as your servant. Well, so be it. That's your choice. I can't do that. After my experiences in France I believe in something totally different. I believe that the death of those men on the Somme, and elsewhere, was futile and unnecessary, that things like that must never be allowed to happen again. Unlike you, I intend to do something positive about it, regardless of the fury it might bring down on my head, and I will willingly face the consequences, in just the same way as those men on the Somme did. They knew they would probably die by machine guns or bayonets or high explosives, and I know that I will probably die in front of a firing squad. I will face it willingly, not caring a jot if the likes of you call it treason, high treason, mutiny or anything else. I call it dying in an effort to stop human madness. So when they blindfold me, tie me to a stake, and shoot me, I will depart this life quite happily, hoping it will convince others that I am right and they are wrong. When I think of all those who have died so needlessly, and all those who might still be saved, I will act without fear or hesitation."

Sassoon's tirade hung in the air, his true mettle revealed.

Bertrand Russell broke the trance that engulfed them. He leapt from his chair, rushed around the table to Sassoon, slapped him on the back, and congratulated him. Then he assured him that all pacifists would give him their utmost support. Others hurried around the table to add their congratulations. Only two men were left sitting, Strachey and Graves, the former routed and shamed, and the latter wondering what the hell Sassoon had let himself in for now.

Ottoline rose like the others, only to collapse in a faint as she visualised Siggy being shot at the stake. Everyone crowded around to help her and it was only when smelling salts were waved beneath her nose that she recovered. Bertrand Russell then took her into the privacy of her study in order to reassure her.

It had been the most remarkable dinner he had ever attended, but he pointed out to Ottoline that whilst they had all been mesmerized by Sassoon's inspirational outburst, and his resolve to face any consequences, what they had to remember was that Sassoon was a poet, and the essence of being a poet was to let oneself be carried away, to cast off restrictions and inhibitions, let the mind run riot, and to leave others breathless with admiration. Rants from the heart such as Sassoon staged were bound to have a startling effect, but in the aftermath they needed to be evaluated coolly and dispassionately.

The first thing Russell did was to promise Ottoline that there was absolutely no possibility whatsoever of Sassoon being shot by a firing squad. He scoffed at the very idea. He laughed at it. He explained that even if Sassoon went ahead with a protest and was court-martialled and found guilty, there was an abundance of sentences available to the court, all far removed from execution. For a start, not one person, officer or other rank, had yet been executed in Britain, no matter how heinous their crime. Furthermore, Sassoon's record of heroism would be taken into account; and he had dozens of influential supporters, to say nothing of famous relatives, who would rally around and pull appropriate strings. Even the press would be sympathetic and because Sassoon was such a popular poet the army would never countenance anything as drastic as an execution.

"Can you imagine the reaction of the British people if we execute our most promising poet and a hero to boot? Can you honestly visualise the headline, 'Mad Jack Shot at Dawn'?"

Furthermore, he explained, if the British authorities were stupid enough to execute a decorated officer and a member of the upper classes, it would be the biggest publicity coup the Germans could hope for. It would be a sure sign that Britain was cracking up.

"Just think of the number of influential men we can call upon," Bertie continued. "Your friend Siggy even has a relative in government, and another on Haig's staff. And the Thornycrofts control industries that are vital to our war effort. We can even go as high as Churchill and the Cabinet, for support - to the Prime Minister himself. I'm not saying that he won't be court-martialled, but even if he is, and even if he's found guilty, they'll only conclude that he is suffering from this new-fangled shell-shock. They will probably end up giving him more sick leave. Another nine months of hunting, as with his diarrhoea. And it will only do our cause a power of good. Whatever happens to Sassoon, his protest will register not only with the public, but the troops as well. The seed will have been sown. So we must welcome it and exploit it as much as we can."

Once Ottoline was convinced, Russell paused and smiled to himself. Sassoon's eloquence had been superb. It had certainly put that squirt Lytton Strachey in his place, and not before time. Russell reckoned that in all probability that had been Sassoon's intention in the first place.

Russell and Ottoline were jubilant. Everything had turned out perfectly. They now had the figure-head they so desperately needed: an infantry officer who was young, brave, decorated, badly wounded, and a national figure on account of his poetry.

Russell didn't waste any time. He suggested to Ottoline that they should invite Sassoon to a meeting with a few 'select' people to finalise their strategy. He nominated Middleton Murry and the left-wing journalist HW Massingham, making five of them in all. They met at Murry's London flat and they were delighted to find that Sassoon had already made a draft of his protest. They were not greatly impressed by it. It was weak, almost apologetic, and blamed all the wrong people, obsessed with condemning the crusty, intractable, old-foggy generals like Haig, Plumber, Rawlinson and Gough. It was as though he'd been reading too many of his own poems.

Bertrand Russel knew exactly what was needed. To blame the military would only alienate the public and reduce Sassoon to a whinger. It was essential to blame the politicians and business profiteers, the people everyone distrusted and hated. Middleton Murry and Massingham had their say as well, of course, and their discussion went on for nearly three hours as they quibbled over words and phrases; but eventually they produced a clarion call to end the war without specifying a mutiny or any hint of treason; they merely dressed it up with phrases people could hardly argue with, such as 'I can no longer be party to prolonging the suffering of the troops'.

"That's a splendid sentiment," declared Russell. "No one wants to prolong the suffering of our troops."

The final statement was clear and convincing. It was bound to appeal to a large proportion of the population who were sick to death with the war. There always remained the possibility of the protest landing Sassoon in an actionable position, but it also showed him as a man of reason and compassion. It was cunning, as only Bertrand Russell could be cunning.

Sassoon welcomed the final draft as a great improvement on his original effort and it was agreed that he should take it back to Weirleigh, leave it to 'mature' for a day or two, and then produce a final copy, written in his style, not that of a committee. He would then send copies to the others for their endorsement before Russell sent it to the Labour MP Lees-Smith so that he could raise the matter in the House of Commons at an appropriate time. Meanwhile Sassoon would refuse to re-join his regiment at Litherland and write to his colonel explaining his actions, then await further developments.

Ottoline was present when they devised the protest but she hardly said a word. She felt too emotionally involved. She was prouder than ever of Siggy, but she still dreaded him getting into serious trouble. What a hero he was! Not just a heroic soldier, but a man far braver and more principled than the rest of them put together, including Bertie.

Her love for him was so profound that later on, as she went about her daily routine at Garsington, she often misquoted Dickens to herself, crying out: "It is a far, far better thing he does than anyone has ever done before."

Then she would giggle and feel happy, really happy. She saw Siggy as a man of great fortitude, perhaps an historic figure who would change the course of world events; and if that came about their relationship would go down as one of the most celebrated love affairs of the century.

To Bertrand Russell fell the task of maximising the publicity and then exploiting the national debate that would follow. He intended to make capital out of Sassoon's protests at his lectures where his audiences would regard the protest as a major scoop. He would also circulate everyone on his 'Pacifists' and 'Conscientious Objectors' files, putting it all under the flagship of the *Non-Conscription Fellowship* which was, by now, well-known nationally and gaining members daily. Above all, he would rely on his good contacts in the newspapers and persuade Lees-Smith to spread the word in Westminster by means of a dramatic statement when he judged the moment to be right.

He lost no time in visiting the offices of the *Fellowship* where all his printing was done. He spent several hours with them, discussing the design and content of the pamphlets. They settled on some of his best-known and most successful slogans, all of which would be supported by some of Sassoon's anti-war poems, the ones Ottoline had so triumphantly passed on to him. He gave them a central position on the pamphlets, knowing that their message would have far more impact than anything else he had ever had published. He left them anonymous, just as Ottoline had insisted, but he wasn't worried about that. Sassoon's style would be obvious enough to those who mattered, and if the authorship leaked out ... Well, that would be just too bad.

Russell placed an order for several thousand pamphlets and then turned his attention to the best means of distribution. A lot would be seized upon at his lectures and he had a gang of supporters who would be only too pleased to distribute them by hand on street corners. As far as he could see the only ones that would have to be sent through the post would be to Sassoon's personal contacts and army units serving in France and Belgium.

Sassoon was keen to contribute in whatever way he could and he spent two days at Weirleigh making out a list of people he thought would be interested and sympathetic. He wrote a personal letter to each of them, explaining his protest and appealing for their support.

The only snag he encountered was the non-arrival of the Fellowship pamphlets. A copy of each pamphlet was supposed to be included in each of his letters. After waiting four days he contacted Russell over the telephone. Russell was full of feeble excuses and in the end Sassoon told him he would send all his letters to the Fellowship so that they could insert their pamphlets with each of his letters and then post them, thus saving valuable time. It never occurred to Sassoon to insist on seeing the pamphlets first to check what he was putting his name to. He took it for granted that they would be suitable.

Sassoon's list of contacts was predictable: all his writing acquaintances, his mentors, his relatives, his old hunting and cricket friends, one or two old school chums, and selected fellow officers in the Fusiliers, men like Cotterill, Dunn, Graves, Hanmer, Major Hunt and even Buffalo Bill (now a brigadier), the last just for the hell of it, to let him know that anarchy was still alive and kicking.

Then an additional thought struck him. He laughed out loud, as though suddenly inspired.

Why not put Jones 618 on his list?

He often thought about 618. He had no difficulty in conjuring up the image of his chubby face and he recalled with absolute clarity 618's return from leave when the youngster had been so pleased to see him that he'd flung his arms around his neck. It made Sassoon wonder how he was getting on; whether he was still writing limericks or if he had succumbed to his brother's discipline and was just sitting on his three-legged stool, waiting for his next running assignment. Sassoon knew that the arrival of a letter would do his morale a power of good. It would be something for him to flaunt in his brother's face, proving that there was at least one person who recognised his talents.

So he added 618 to his mailing list, and whilst he was about it he threw out a new challenge to him, another Welsh town to test his rhyming skills. He decided on Ebbw Vale. He knew 618 would love that.

Replies to Sassoon's letters posted by the *Fellowship* came several days later. Without exception they deplored what he intended to do and pleaded with him to have second thoughts, even though several grudgingly conceded the essential truth of his protest. Sassoon was bitterly disappointed by this lack of support but it was too late to do anything about it. He had already written to Colonel Jones-Williams at Litherland telling him that he refused to carry out any more military duties. His letter stated: 'I am doing this as a protest against the policy of the government in prolonging the war by failing to state their conditions for peace. This protest has already been made public and has been widely distributed.'

As Sassoon opened his mail over breakfast every morning, he quailed at the scorn heaped upon him. One of the first replies to arrive was from Bobby Hanmer, who wrote: "What is this bloody nonsense? For God's sake, Siegfried, don't be such a damned fool."

An even more critical reply came from another fellow-officer who wrote: "I note your invitation to stick your protest in a prominent place, but the only place I'm liable to stick it is up your arse."

Eddie Marsh wrote to deplore what he intended to do, pointing out that now the Americans had entered the war, his reasoning was misguided. Joe Cotterell, speaking for many of the Royal Fusilier officers in France, sympathised but was adamant that the war had to go on and warned Sassoon against falling under the evil influence of pacifists.

Sassoon had hoped for unqualified support from Robbie Ross, but he was disappointed. Instead, Ross wrote, "I am quite appalled by what you have done." Likewise, Roderick Micklejohn said he thought the protest was utterly irresponsible. Robert Graves, who was aware of the development, told Sassoon that he was completely mad to have taken the matter that far. Giving Lytton Strachey a piece of his mind was one thing, highly commendable and long overdue, but making a public protest was neither good form nor the action of an officer and gentleman. He had a contract with the army which he should honour.

So it went on, letter after letter, all of them condemning him. Sassoon did not hear back from Jones 618, but then he hadn't expected to.

Bertrand Russell only half-believed his assurances to Ottoline that Sassoon was in no danger of execution. He knew perfectly well that they were in virgin territory and nothing was certain. It would only take the president of a court-martial to be a stickler for discipline and things could turn very nasty. Sassoon could end up being condemned to death no matter what others in high places thought or said, and that would leave an appeal as his only hope. Small risk though it was, it was nevertheless a real one. So he was delighted and relieved when all the predictions he made to Ottoline turned out to be accurate.

As the news of the protest spread the military Establishment made it clear they intended to minimise the whole affair, to treat it as a mere aberration on the part of a badly wounded young officer. Likewise, all Sassoon's friends and relatives rallied to his support no matter what they thought of his protest. The first off the mark was Robert Graves. Having told Sassoon exactly what he thought of him - that he was a bloody fool - he obtained leave of absence from Osborne on the Isle of Wight where he was convalescing and sped up to London. His first call was to Edward Marsh who had a wider sphere of influence than anyone. Then Graves wrote to the commanding officer at Litherland and pleaded with him to be lenient with Sassoon. Another letter he wrote was to Evan Morgan, a family friend who was private secretary to the Minister of Labour, suggesting that when the case was raised in the Commons by Lees-Smith the War Office should adopt a conciliatory attitude; that they should summon a medical board rather than a court-martial.

Ross was also very active. He went straight to the top and pleaded Sassoon's case with Prime Minister Lloyd George, having got access to him through Roderick Micklejohn who owed him more than a few favours. Eddie Marsh meanwhile was seen going in and out of the War Office several days in succession and he ended up by involving the influential Winston Churchill.

The Establishment, having been fully mobilised, was unstoppable. The message went out to the military authorities that the case was to be treated with kid gloves, despite resistance in certain quarters of the Legal Department of the War Office. Everything was to be hushed up. It was to be a white-wash job.

Sassoon was already over a week late in reporting for duty at Litherland and it was no surprise when he received a stern letter from the adjutant telling him to report without further delay. He went north by train and was greatly relieved to find that Colonel Jones-Williams was on leave, with Major Macartney-Filgate standing in for him. The major was a charming old buffer and extremely friendly. He still saw Sassoon as a hero rather than a miscreant.

They sat opposite each other for a time without saying anything. Eventually Sassoon asked: "Are you going to arrest me?"

"Arrest you? Why should I do that?"

"Because of my protest."

"Oh, that! Yes, I've heard talk about that, but I've never arrested anyone yet so I'm not going to start now. Mind you, if you want to make a retraction you're always welcome."

179

"No thanks, sir. It must stand I'm afraid."

"So be it. Have a fag, young fellow."

Sassoon declined the offer. In the circumstances it didn't seem right to accept, but when the major thrust a box of choice Havana cigars towards him - his idea of fags! - Sassoon weakened, not wanting to cause offence or to miss out on one of his favourite luxuries. The major cut it and lit it for him and then did the same for himself. For a time they smoked contentedly. Such fine cigars deserved complete attention.

"So what happens now?" asked Sassoon eventually.

"You had better book in at the Exchange Hotel. That's where everyone goes these days."

"And then what?"

"Just wait and see what happens. Something will crop up, as Mr Pickwick always said."

"Mr Micawber, surely?"

"Really? Oh well ... Whoever ... It makes no difference. Something will crop up."

Sassoon booked into the Exchange Hotel and that evening several subalterns came in and had drinks with him at the bar. None of them knew about his protest. Later on they were joined by Litherland's adjutant. When he left he handed Sassoon a sealed envelope. Inside was a railway warrant and an order to attend a medical board at Chester the following day; but Sassoon had no intention of attending a medical board and he tore up both the order and warrant. He was determined to be court-martialled; to get his protest maximum publicised.

For three days nothing happened. Sassoon sat about the hotel writing poems. Then Colonel Jones-Williams appeared. They sat together in the lounge of the hotel and the colonel demanded to know why Sassoon had cut the medical board. When Sassoon explained that he would settle for nothing short of a court-martial, he was taken by surprise. Unlike Major Macartney-Filgate and others, who excuse his protest as a mere aberration, the colonel was all in favour of him being court-martialled, hoping that he would have to face the full consequences of his treachery.

"You may not realise it, Sassoon, but opinion in the regiment is very much against you. Your civilian conchie friends might support you, and all your friends in high places, but the rank and file in the army most certainly don't. If it was up to me, I'd throw the book at you. But unfortunately your case has been taken out of my hands. But I assure you that I will do my utmost to make sure you get your comeuppance in the end. Just you mark my words."

There was more waiting. Sassoon became so bored that he went to Formby and paced about the sand dunes, ending up at the mouth of the Mersey where he ripped the Military Cross ribbon off his tunic and threw it into the water. When the little bit of ribbon floated and drifted out to sea, he realised what a pathetically futile gesture it was.

When he got back to the Exchange Hotel Graves was waiting for him. They spent the evening discussing developments. Sassoon was astounded by how involved his friend had become and how he was determined to thwart his protest and safeguard him, claiming that he had got everything under control.

When Sassoon reiterated that he would strive for the right to be court-martialled, Graves became increasingly concerned. He knew that a trial had to be avoided at all costs; that an unbiased court-martial would very likely give him a long jail sentence or even death by a firing squad.

Despite his fears, Graves maintained an air of calm. "It's got nothing to do with what you want, Siegfried. The army has already decided not to take your protest seriously. Why the hell should they? You are nothing but a wart! You can demand what you like but they won't take any notice. And if you go on being awkward they'll simply have you declared insane."

"You mean shell-shocked ..."

"No! Bugger shell-shock. If you don't agree to a medical board they'll get two doctors to sign on the dotted line. Two signatures and that's the end of you, mate."

"How can you be so sure?"

"Because of all the contacts we've made. Siegfried, the Establishment has made its decision about you. The word has been passed round. There's not a hope in hell of you being allowed to spout your conchie views at a court-martial with the national press in attendance. No matter what the colonel has been feeding you, your future has been decided and you've got no alternative but to agree to a medical board."

"Are you prepared to swear to that?

"Certainly I am."

"On the Bible?"

"I haven't got a Bible."

"If you had one, would you swear on it?"

"Certainly I would."

Graves had no religious beliefs so swearing on a Bible wouldn't have made any difference to him. He was quite prepared to lie through his teeth; anything to persuade Sassoon to accept the verdict of a medical board which would arrange for him to lie fallow in some medical establishment or other until everything had calmed down and been forgotten.

"You've done as much as you can, Siegfried. Now leave things to Russell and his fellow pacifist."

As an experienced campaigned, Bertrand Russell forestalled the war office at every turn. He made sure Sassoon's protest was broadcast far and wide. He alerted the national and provincial press to what was about to happen and when the Bradford Pioneer won in the wild scramble to spread the news the floodgates opened. Practically everyone in the country knew about Sassoon's protest.

Russell's faith in the Labour MP Lees-Smith was also justified. To a packed House of Commons he read out Sassoon's declaration. The shock and concern was palpable, most of the members yelling comments and waving papers to demonstrate their disapproval. When the uproar subsided, the Secretary of State for War, instead of denouncing the protest, adopted a softly-softly approach and referred to Sassoon's splendid war record before appealing to the House to sympathise with a gallant young officer so cruelly affected by severe wounds.

The following morning most of the national papers ran editorials speculating on whether this was the start of mutinies such as the French had suffered. This speculation caused such alarm that Scotland Yard was put on alert. Due to their experience in dealing with disturbances caused by Bertrand Russell and his cohorts they lost no time in sending Chief Inspector Stoddart and forty-two constables on a dawn raid to the printing press and offices of the *Non-Conscription Fellowship* in Limehouse. When the caretaker was slow to open up they beat the front door down and flooded in. Then they rampaged through the building deliberately causing as much havoc as possible. The only incriminating evidence they found was 100 leaflets of Sassoon's protest. These were immediately impounded and Chief Inspector Stoddart was well-pleased with their raid, assuming they had prevented the distribution of any pamphlets. It was only later, when they examined other papers they had removed, that they discovered the *Non-Conscription Fellowship* had already fulfilled an order for 5,000 copies and all but a hundred had been posted off, among them a batch to selected units on the western front.

The police were too late. Widespread distribution of the pamphlets was assured.

Sassoon's medical board sat again the following afternoon. It couldn't have been more contrived. Graves gave evidence on Sassoon's behalf and made a fool of himself. He broke down into tears three times, making one of the members remark that perhaps he needed a medical board as well. Only one of the members cast any doubts on the outcome. He was suspicious of Sassoon's Germanic Christian name and thought that several of Sassoon's poems he had seen in the Cambridge Magazine were distinctly pro-German. A psychiatrist on the board was the only one to grasp the situation and he mentioned the excellent work of an establishment in Scotland known as Craiglockhart. The other members took their lead from him. Their final report concluded that Sassoon was of a nervous disposition, that he stuttered and talked incoherently in staccato bursts, and that he had a family history of neuropathy. As such they recommended that, in the short-term at least, he should be sent to Craiglockhart War Hospital near Edinburgh.

As soon as Sassoon was admitted to the Craiglockhart he felt impotent and outwitted. It was as though he had walked into a trap set by the army. They now had him exactly where they wanted him, isolated and well and truly muzzled. There was no way he could ram home his protest whilst incarcerated in a hospital for extreme cases of shell-shock. As far as he could see, his protest was all over: a dead duck.

His room at Craiglockhart was comfortable and the food adequate, even though eating amongst the shell-shocked was often unpleasant, with food slopped around and men often being sick. He was assigned as a patient to Dr William Rivers. He had his first interview with him on his second day.

Rivers, who held the rank of captain, was friendly and they talked freely for a while before going through a few necessary formalities about his medical history and army service. Eventually, Sassoon became impatient. "What's the point of keeping me in this place - *Dottyville*?"

"That's a good name for us," smiled Rivers. "I think I will enjoy having you here. You are obviously a man of originality. And I've heard about your poetry. Now that you're with us, I will make a point of reading it."

"You haven't answered my question ..."

"I'm sorry. That's probably because it's normally my job to ask the questions, not answer them."

"How long will my treatment take?"

"You aren't going to get any treatment. There's nothing wrong with you so there is nothing to treat. You're sound of mind and in fine physical shape. The nearest you have to any form of ailment is survivor's guilt. You saw so many men die that in your subconscious you are feeling guilty because you are no longer sharing the hardships and dangers of those still out there. My job is to persuade you to retract your statement. As soon as you've done that you will be discharged from here."

"But I'll never do that..."

"Never say 'never', Mr Sassoon. None of us know what the future might hold."

Part Four

The Court-Martial

17
Mutiny!

The summer of 1917 didn't improve things for the men in the trenches. It was at least warm but rain poured down as hard as ever so that when the sun shone everything went mouldy. Flies hung about in clouds and mosquitoes competed with lice in making men scratch until they were covered in raw patches.

The war became worse, not better. As the unburied dead multiplied the stink became insufferable. The fortifications on both sides deteriorated under continuous bombardments and a new form of terror came about when the art of tunnelling beneath each other's positions was perfected, resulting in huge explosions that literally blew everything sky high.

For months, Fusilier Davey Jones (618) had been so depressed by the conditions that he looked back on their early days in France with nostalgia. Three years ago, being abroad had novelty value. It was part of an adventure, even if a dangerous one. Now, he felt as though he couldn't stand another day of it. He would willingly have traded his life just for a few months back in the Rhondda. The disappearance of Mad Jack was one of his chief regrets. That had changed everything. There were no laughs, no limericks, no chipping in with odd rhyming words, and no fantastic and daring exploits; just the war becoming more desperate, nothing but endless slaughter.

There were more raids and more 'Big Pushes', none of which achieved a damn thing. All the time it was move here, move there, and then move somewhere else: march here, march there, and then march back again. Each new location was worse than the previous one, and all the time lives were dripping away even when things were 'quiet'. All but three of the old platoon had been killed or so badly wounded that they'd never been seen or heard of again, just like Butler who had died of his wounds; and with the disappearance of the old crowd team spirit and pride in the regiment had vanished. The new lads were nothing but untrained cannon-fodder. No one sang any more.

They had had six different platoon commanders since Mad Jack disappeared. Three had been killed outright by shells, one whilst going over the top, one knifed in a shell crater, and the sixth finished off by the Germans as he lay wounded on their wire. There was no Mad Jack to mount a rescue mission, as with Butler.

618 knew it was only a matter of time before he died as well. It was a toss-up whether he was blown up by a shell or picked off by a sniper. When it happened he reckoned it would be just his luck to lie there and watch himself bleed to death; even lie there and see one of his legs ten yards further down the trench; or perhaps his balls hanging on a snag on the trench wall as had happened with Fusilier Allsop.

618's depression was so obvious that others tried to cheer him up. They assured him that he and his brother were indestructible, just like Sergeant Morgan. Some felt so protective towards him that when they saw him trudging off on one of his running missions they'd take his message pad and complete the task for him. He never refused their help. To him, wandering about the trenches was pure hell. In most places the walls were broken down, as often as not with decaying body parts sticking out which couldn't be removed for fear of the trench collapsing. Then there was the foul smell of the latrines and rats running along the bottom of the trench as though they owned the place.

The only thing that stopped 618 from deserting was the presence of his twin brother and the beady eye he kept on him. Otherwise he would have headed to the coast to look for a ship going back to Blighty.

Their latest platoon commander was Mr Latimer. He was a full lieutenant transferred from the 2nd battalion. He was a professional soldier who went by the book and had firm ideas as to how things should be run. One thing he changed was the collection and distribution of mail. Previously, mail had always been brought to the platoon by the company clerk once or twice a week depending on a decent amount having accumulated. This wasn't good enough for Mr Latimer. His young wife wrote to him every day, so rather than be kept waiting and receiving her letters in batches, Latimer detailed 618 to go to battalion HQ every afternoon to collect the platoon's mail.

This went smoothly and to everyone's satisfaction. 618 enjoyed seeing who had received mail and he liked to smell each envelope in the hope of detecting perfume, his theory being that the stronger the perfume the sexier the sender would be. He soon concluded that Sergeant Morgan must have the time of his life when he went on leave.

618 never got any mail. It was hardly surprising. He'd never had a letter in his whole life. His Ma and Da's letters were always addressed to Rhys, which meant 618 had to sit and wait whilst his brother read them. Then he suffered the indignity of 617 reading them out to him as though he was a halfwit, unable to read them for himself.

He had been collecting the mail for a couple of weeks when he had a major surprise. There was one there for him. A letter actually addressed to 'Fusilier D. Jones (618), 1st Battalion the Royal Welch Fusiliers, France'. It was in a large brown envelope. He could hardly believe it. He was so surprised it unnerved him. He couldn't bring himself to open it. He hurried back to Seven Platoon and even as he distributed the letters to the others he kept his hidden in his map pocket. The one thing he wasn't going to do was show it to 617. It was his letter, nothing to do with 617.

It wasn't until later that night, when 617 was on a recce patrol with Mr Latimer, and 618 was alone in the dugout, unlikely to be disturbed, that he took the letter out. He smoothed it down on the table then steeled himself to open it. He pulled out several sheets of printed paper. He glanced through them swiftly without absorbing any details. His attention was riveted on the top sheet which had been torn off one of the old company message pads. It was headed: 'To:' and 'From:' and at the bottom, where it said, 'Signed' and 'Rank' was Mad Jack's signature.

A letter from Mad Jack! He laughed aloud in sheer delight. It was the finest surprises of his life. The message on the pad read:

> *"Just to keep in touch. Hope you are well and still writing.*
> *Enclosed are some papers that need to be displayed. Put*
> *them on the company notice board."*

Then, beneath this message were two words in capital letters: "EBBW VALE!"

618 went into fresh peals of laughter. He was suddenly gloriously happy. His woes vanished magically. Oh, what it was to have a friend, a *real* friend

who thought about him enough to write to him. He admired Sassoon more than ever. He'd always seen him as a great man, but this really put him in a class of his own. He wasn't just a hero and a poet, but a fantastic human being: a man of loyalty, with no side or snobbishness.

Straight away 618 started to compose a new limerick based on Ebbw Vale.

> 'There was a young lady of Ebbw Vale,
> Who was forever flaunting her tail,
> Men formed a queue
> 'Cause everyone knew ...

Then, to his amazement, he dried up. For the first time ever he was stuck for a good final line. He was so excited he couldn't think straight. He tried several lines, but none of them gelled. Beaten by Mad Jack after all, he thought. He was almost glad. Mad Jack would be delighted at having stumped him.

As 618 continued to struggle for a final line, he glanced casually at the other sheets of paper enclosed in the envelope. He couldn't make head or tail of them. Not that he tried very hard. They were something to do with the *Non-Conscription Fellowship* and signed by someone called Russell. He couldn't understand why Mad Jack would want to send him pamphlets about conscription. He wasn't a conscript. He was a volunteer.

618 looked again at the message pad and confirmed that it was an order to stick the papers on the company notice board. He done that often enough in the past, usually for Major Hunt, so there was no difficulty there. He always put things alongside Part II Orders which everyone was expected to read. There were plenty of drawing pins on the notice board and if the bumph didn't interest anyone, the company clerk could always throw it all away. He would have done his bit so he'd be in the clear: 'keeping his nose clean', as 617 always put it.

He decided to act right away, before 617 and Mr Latimer returned from their recce patrol. He knew they'd be wet through and covered by mud, expecting him to supply refreshments; cups of sweet tea and Welsh Cakes sent by Mr Latimer's wife.

He grabbed the papers and went out into the trench. As he slithered along the duckboards his mind was still working overtime on his Ebbw Vale limerick. He tried several more last lines, but still without success. He decided that the only thing was to go through his entire repertoire of rhymes, everything that rhymed with 'vale' and 'tail'. There would be hundreds of them. He started to mutter them out loud: hale, jail, nail, male, mail, pale, wail, fail, shale, female, high-tail, entail ...

He was still going through them as he pinned the pamphlets on the notice board. He arranged the sheet tidily alongside Part II Orders. Then he made his way back down the trench, still puzzling over his limerick. He was just short of his dugout when the last line came to him.

"Bloody hell", he cried aloud. "I must be going scatty - sale. That's it!"

He recited the whole limerick out loud, testing it for rhyme and rhythm.

> There was a young lady of Ebbw Vale,
> Who was forever flaunting her tail.
> Men formed a queue,
> 'Cause everyone knew,
> Her prize asset was always for sale.

Beat you again, Mad Jack!

When Mr Latimer and 617 returned everything was quiet. Their patrol had been uneventful. 618 made tea and laid out the Welsh Cakes. Then he helped them out of their sopping clothes and he watched them as they did their best to clean themselves up before settling down to sleep.

They were still asleep when the platoon commanders from Eight and Nine Platoons clattered down the steps of the dugout to see Latimer. He was none too pleased to be woken, but there was no avoiding them. They were highly excited and talkative, itching to explain what had happened.

They told him about the pamphlets and Sassoon's protest on the company notice board, and how Major Hunt had immediately associated them with Seven Platoon, if only because it was Sassoon's old platoon. They were full of theories about what had happened. They kept on about the bloody cheek of someone to put such mutinous drivel on their notice board. They warned Latimer that he was bound to be questioned about it.

"It's damn all to do with me," exclaimed Latimer. "Just because Sassoon was in Seven Platoon it doesn't implicate any of us."

"It's a question of who pinned it all on the notice board ..."

"Search me," said Latimer.

"Whoever did is automatically an accessory."

"An accessory to what?" asked Latimer.

"Treason, for heaven's sake! Or mutiny at the very least ..."

"Oh, don't talk balls ..."

"Wait until you read it all. It appeals to everyone to lay down their arms and surrender. According to Major Hunt, it's a court-martial as sure as eggs for whoever is spreading it around."

618 was at the back of the dugout, unnoticed by the others. At the mention of a court-martial his scalp began to itch and a feeling of panic overwhelmed him. He scratched his scalp vigorously. Until that moment it had never occurred to him that he had done anything wrong. He'd been far too busy thinking about his limerick to bother about anything else. And anyhow, he'd only done what Mad Jack had ordered. What was wrong with that?

The three subalterns continued to discuss Sassoon's protest and the supporting literature. As they speculated on the consequences, 618 slipped out of the dugout and strode about the trenches. His mind was in a whirl, wondering what he should do, trying to invent ways of proving that he'd had nothing to do with it. He wasn't even going to admit it to 617. It was none of his business.

Around noon a proper enquiry got underway. Major Hunt and his second-in-command toured the company questioning men, starting in Seven Platoon. They all denied any knowledge of it, including 618. Regimental policemen were called in. Two of them were posted to each platoon to question men further and to make sure no one suddenly disappeared. Then the brigade-major appeared and there were more questions. Latimer suggested to him that everything should be torn up and forgotten. The possibility of anyone in Seven Platoon laying down their arms was just too preposterous for words.

"Too late for that," replied the brigade-major. "The matter has already gone to division and the message has come back to stamp it out - Pronto! Whoever did it has to be caught. Then hung drawn and quartered I wouldn't wonder ..."

One of the regimental police, who had been a detective sergeant in the Glamorgan Constabulary in civilian life, sought out the brigade-major and explained that the subversive material must have arrived in the post. The introductory letter had a date on it, the 27th of July, and since the battalion went back into the line before that date, and no men had been on leave, there was no other way it could have got to C Company.

Accepting the logic of this, the brigade-major questioned the battalion post corporal. He explained that he no longer delivered mail to Mr Latimer's platoon. For the past few weeks it had been collected by Fusilier Jones 618. The corporal said he still saw and handled all the battalion mail as it came in and he remembered seeing a large brown envelope because of its type-written address; but he had no knowledge of who it was addressed to or who it was from. He said he had handed everything over to Jones 618 whose duty it was to take the mail back and then distribute it.

Jones 618 was ordered to report to battalion headquarters for questioning by the colonel and the brigade-major. By now he was terrified. He still didn't understand what he had done wrong, yet from all the remarks flying around it seemed that he was in deep trouble. At first he just stood in front of the two officers and said nothing, his head jerking from side to side as they fired questions at him. Eventually, he stammered out a reply: he denied that he had done anything, but neither of them believed him. They dismissed him and ordered two regimental policemen to escort him back to C Company. They took him to Sergeant Morgan's dugout and told Morgan not to let him out of his sight. He was to keep him there until further orders. For a long time Morgan and 618 sat in silence. Morgan could see that 618 was in one of his non-communicative moods, head nodding, worried sick and out of his depth.

Then, totally unexpectedly, 618 spoke. "What am I supposed to have done wrong, Sarge?"

Morgan ignored the question. He put one instead. "Did you do it?"

618 shook his head.

"Don't lie to me, boyo. I know you did. Mr Sassoon would never have sent a letter to anyone except you or me."

Morgan knew that 618's only hope of extricating himself from the mess he'd got into was to confess his offence and hope the colonel would have sufficient sense to realise that whatever he had done, he was innocent of any evil intent.

"Davey," said Morgan, deliberately using his Christian name to let him know he was talking as a friend, not his platoon sergeant, "if you've done nothing wrong, just say so. Were you trying to help Mad Jack?"

"I just did as I was told, Sarge."

"Look, I'll tell you what I'll do. I'll turn away ... A blind eye as they say... And you slip out quietly, go back to your dugout, and get rid of anything that looks bad for you. If you did anything wrong, get rid of the evidence. Then the whole thing will just blow over."

At first, Morgan wondered if 618 understood what he was suggesting, but when he turned away he heard 618 slip out. He reached his dugout without anyone seeing him, but it did him no good. He was too late. The dugout was full of regimental policemen. They had collected together all his belongings, including his limericks and the copies he'd made of Sassoon's poems: every scrap of paper they could find. They even had the envelope in which Sassoon's message and protest had arrived. The return address was hand-written on the back: 'If undelivered, return to *The Non-Conscription Fellowship,* Limehouse, London.'

The sharp-eyed ex-detective sergeant from Cardiff spent more time studying the papers than anyone. Eventually he approached the brigade-major. "Excuse me, sir. But I've come across a curious thing. Some of these poems we've found among Jones's papers are definitely seditious."

"So I've noticed."

"But have you also noticed that some of them are identical to the verses that appear on the *Non-Conscription Fellowship* pamphlets?

"No, I hadn't."

"Well they are."

"Really. And are they attributed to anyone? Sassoon by any chance?"

"No, sir. No by-lines. But the poems we found in Jones's kit are obviously originals, all in his handwriting."

"Indeed! Interesting, very interesting."

Within minutes Fusilier Jones 618 was escorted back to brigade headquarters by two regimental policemen. There, he was held under close arrest. Senior officers then studied and evaluated the evidence they had unearthed before deciding on appropriate action.

18

A Capital Charge

A few days later the Fusiliers were withdrawn from the front line for a period of rest. Talk in the battalion centred on Jones 618 and what lay in store for him. Initially, details of what had happened were obscure, but everyone assumed that whatever he had been up to would be dealt with as a minor offence. No one saw Jones 618 as a criminal.

The attitude adopted by the legal department of the War Office in London was in stark contrast. They bitterly resented the way in which Siegfried Sassoon's protest had been taken out of their control and placed in the hands of influential politicians, Establishment figures, and Sassoon's rich relatives and friends. If the professional soldiers in the War Office had had their way they would have thrown the book at Sassoon right from the start. Recent mutinies in the French Army were still fresh in their minds and they were so fearful of the same thing happening in the British Army that all units were ordered to be on the lookout for the first signs of trouble and then to crush any threats ruthlessly. An example had to be made of any potential mutineers.

Due to Bertrand Russell's efficiency as a rabble-rouser, copies of the *Non-Conscription Fellowship* pamphlets soon appeared throughout Britain and the western front. They cropped up in all kinds of places: on public transport, in pubs, in the foyer of the Drury Lane Theatre, in public conveniences, and retrieved from countless dustbins. Also, numerous army units in France and Belgium received copies. These were intercepted by eagle-eyed adjutants and consigned to the nearest wastepaper baskets. The only case of an individual member of the forces being targeted by the *Non-Conscription Fellowship* was Fusilier Jones 618.

The first indication to the men of the Royal Fusiliers that their regiment was about to be involved in a major scandal came when 618 was placed under armed guard in a large barn near battalion headquarters. It was surrounded by barbed wire and patrolled day and night by regimental policemen, a clear indication that no chances were being taken. Then it became known that the adjutant was preparing a summary of evidence. He was interviewing everyone who had been involved in the incident. On completion of the summary, 618 was hauled before the colonel and told that he was to face a Field General Court-Martial. He was to be charged with, 'Conspiring to incite a mutiny,' a capital offence.

When the news leaked out a collective shiver went through the battalion. It just didn't seem possible. It was the sort of thing that happened in other regiments, not the Royal Welch Fusiliers.

The legal department of the War Office in London did not consider the trial of Fusilier Jones warranted the appointment of a judge advocate, but in an effort to establish their fairness and impartiality they appointed a legally qualified officer to act as his defence counsel, rather than leave it to the more usual junior regimental officer. In the meantime Jones remained under close arrest and he was told that military law stipulated that he had no choice but to plead not guilty due to it being a capital charge. He was allowed two visitors a day and these never varied, his brother and Sergeant Morgan. The former spent the whole of each day with him and the latter called in whenever his other duties allowed. Two regimental policemen were present the whole time.

Captain George Simpson of the East Surrey Regiment was the defence counsel. He was a middle-aged solicitor, commissioned at the outbreak of the war. He was posted to the army's legal department in the War Office on the strength of his previous employment with the successful London Law Partnership of Swanson, Collins and Cuthbert. Legally, Simpson was a man of limited experience. Due to an early and unfortunate error of judgement he had never been trusted with anything other than domestic conveyancing, a task confined to the laborious checking of details. At the War Office his duties had been equally as mundane, arranging the compulsory purchase of land for training purposes.

Due to his lack of military experience he had no idea of how essential it was for the army to maintain ruthless discipline with no room for leniency. Before leaving for France he was briefed about the Jones case and handed a copy of the summary of evidence, which gave him the opportunity to devise what he hoped was a sound defence. When he arrived at the Fusiliers the first thing he did was seek further information from the adjutant.

"It's a sad case," was all that the adjutant was prepared to venture.

"Yes, of course," said Simpson, "but any theories on the likely outcome?"

"Never mind theories," replied the adjutant. "The army never convenes courts-martial unless they are confident of success. But it would be best if you judged for yourself when you meet the accused."

The regimental police guarding the accused were more forthcoming. When Simpson put much the same enquiry to them, one policeman said: "The bloke is bonkers, sir. As daft as a brush! And wait until you meet his twin brother. They spend their whole time arguing. His brother is the aggressive and dictatorial type. It's only when Sergeant Morgan is present that they calm down."

When Captain Simpson set eyes on 618 he was staggered. He concluded right away that he should never have been in the army let alone facing a capital charge.

Jones 617 and Sergeant Morgan were also present. As Captain Simpson took a seat at their table, opposite the two brothers, he couldn't help thinking of Tweedledum and Tweedledee. They looked so anxious that he decided the first thing to do was instil some confidence into them. He told them that having read the summary of evidence he had every hope that he would be able to secure a 'Not Guilty' verdict, although nothing could be guaranteed.

Morgan and 617 exchanged glances. They were not impressed by such optimism. Being guilty or innocent was only part of it. They knew the army loved to make examples of men, and there was no better way of deterring men from crimes such as cowardice, desertion or inciting a mutiny than by shooting someone.

As a first step, Captain Simpson started to go through the summary of evidence. It was essential that Jones 618 should know what he was up against. They'd only got through the first few pages when Captain Simpson stopped and turned to Sergeant Morgan. He suggested that they should step outside for a brief word. Once outside, he said: "Sergeant, is the accused all right?"

"Why do you ask, sir?"

"That's pretty obvious, surely? He's in a world of his own. He's not listening to a word."

"I know, sir. According to Mr Sassoon, who was his original platoon commander ..."

"Never mind Sassoon. I'm asking you."

"Well, Jones 618 is what they call autistic. He has been since birth. Don't ask me what that means exactly, but he often doesn't speak for hours. At other times he has bouts of anger, or frustration, especially if his routine is upset. Yet in some ways he's talented. He and Jones 617 are twins, of course. You must have noticed. They've never been parted. They joined up together and now they share a dugout with Mr Latimer, their platoon commander. 617 is his batman and 618 is his runner. It was arranged that way ages ago so that 617 can keep an eye on his brother."

"Not close enough an eye by the sound of it."

"No, sir. Seems not."

"Is he fit enough to plea?"

"He's not insane, if that's what you mean, sir. Like I said, he's what they call ..."

"Yes, yes, you said ... Autistic ... But if he's autistic he should never have been accepted for service."

Morgan shrugged. "You know how it is, sir. They sign-on anyone. Halfwits are two a penny in the infantry."

"Any question of shell-shock?"

"No, sir. No trouble there."

"And how old is he?"

"Eighteen, sir. They lied about their ages when they joined. Like so many others."

"How do you think the accused will react if I suggest he's unfit to plea? Frankly, one only has to look at him to realise that he isn't."

Morgan nodded glumly. "Put it to his brother first, sir, and see what he says. You'll have to convince him."

Captain Simpson knew it wouldn't be easy. No man liked to be told he was insane. Once back in the barn, he hedged around the question slowly and gently. Jones 618 just sat there as though unaware that he was under discussion. On the other hand his brother followed every word keenly, a deep frown across his brow.

When Captain Simpson finished, 617 asked: "If my brother was found unfit to plead, what would happen to him?"

"He'd be sent back to the UK ..."

"To a home for the insane?"

"Yes ..."

"A bloody loony bin!"

"Well ...Yes."

"Among a whole lot of nut cases?"

"He'd be well cared for."

"Don't talk daft, sir. What you're suggesting is that in order to get him off you'll be happy to send a perfectly sane man to live among murderers, psychopaths, schizophrenics and God knows what else."

Captain Simpson was taken aback but at the same time impressed by 617's outburst. What he said was perfectly true, but something Simpson was not prepared to admit.

"Well let me tell you this," continued 617, his tone sharper, a forefinger wagging. "Davey and I had an uncle. Like Davey, he was retarded. But no more than that. And our family, rather than be responsible for him, had him committed. They condemned him to spend his life in an asylum. And when he died and our parents went to the asylum and saw what he'd had to endure, they were so ashamed that they swore they would never let it happen to Davey. That's why I've spent my life so far looking after him - my life, my whole life. Maybe I've made a mess of it, but he's not going into an asylum. There has to be another way to get him off. He's not guilty and you've got to prove it."

There was a long silence. Then 617 put another question: "If Davey is put in an asylum how long would he be kept there?"

"He'd be detained at His Majesty's Pleasure."

"That means for ever. You know that as well as I do. And after a few months of living with a bunch of loonies he'll become as mad as them, just as his uncle did."

198

"Fusilier Jones, please don't think that I am unsympathetic," replied Simpson. "My heart aches for you both. But I have to be realistic. You know what the alternative is ..."

"They'll shoot me!"

Their heads swivelled sharply as they faced 618. It was the first time he'd spoken. Suddenly, without warning, he jumped up and pushed his chair back so hard that it toppled over and crashed to the floor. "They'll shoot me!" he shouted again. "That's what they'll do. I'll be tied to a post and shot." He spat out the words. "I'll be slaughtered just like all those men were on the Somme."

Sergeant Morgan retrieved the chair from the floor and made 618 sit down again. He put a hand on his shoulder to comfort him, but it was brushed away. Captain Simpson buried his head in his hands, realising he'd been landed with a horrendous mess.

Jones 617 was accustomed to such spates by his brother and was able to calm him down. "No one is going to shoot you, Davey," he said. "Don't be so bloody daft, boyo. Captain Simpson is going to get you off, and at the same time we're going to put the blame where it really belongs, with Sassoon." 617 turned to Simpson and asked: "So where is Sassoon now?"

"He's in the Craiglockhart War Hospital near Edinburgh."

"An asylum?"

"No. It specialises in helping the shell-shocked."

"Then can't Davey become shell-shocked? Can't he go to this War Hospital as well? Or to a similar one for other ranks?"

"I'm afraid not."

"Why not?"

"Because he is not shell-shocked."

"And Sassoon is?"

"Apparently."

"What balls! He was perfectly all right when he left us. He was wounded, but not shell-shocked. Mad Jack shell-shocked? Don't make me laugh! He's been in England for months without being kept in hospital. Then, as soon as he makes his protest, he becomes shell-shocked."

"Sassoon's case is entirely different."

"In what way?

"He's being treated by psychiatrists."

"So they'll never shoot him then?"

"I shouldn't think so."

"Why not? They bloody well should. He's the one who started all this business. He made the protest. All Davey did was pin some pamphlet on the notice board, unknowingly. That bastard Sassoon deserves to be strung up ..."

"Look here, Fusilier," interrupted Simpson. "It's no good ranting on at me about Mr Sassoon. I don't sympathise with him one bit. I thought his protest was amazingly stupid and misguided. And I'm just as appalled as you are at his soft treatment. But it's not for us to judge."

"Oh yes it is! We're the ones he is betraying. He's nothing but a bastard and just because he's a Jewish millionaire, and a published poet, and an officer, and his Mummy's family make weapons, he thinks he can do what the hell he likes. And he's damn right, the bastard."

Jones 618 again jumped to his feet. His chair crashed backwards, louder and more forcefully this time.

"Rubbish!" he yelled. "That's rubbish! Mr Sassoon is the bravest man I've ever known. He's done things no one else would ever have dared to try. He saved Butler. Went out all on his own and saved him. There's never been anyone as brave as Mr Sassoon. And he listens to me. Really listens."

"Oh shut up, Davey. You don't what you're talking about ..."

"Yes I do. He's a great poet. And a great man ..."

"Great man my arse! And he only saved Butler because it was his job as platoon commander."

"He did it for me ..."

"Bollocks! All he ever does is cause trouble and then bugger off and leave others to face the music. He's invented a whole lot of rot about a protest and a pound to a penny he's now wallowing around in the safety of some hospital writing poetry and playing golf."

"He's a great poet! You ask Mr Graves. I won't have a word said against him."

"He's a scrimshanking bastard," 617 said bitterly. "He's the one who should be here, facing the music, not you."

They were soon embroiled in another fierce argument. It became personal and abusive. Their voices soared as they stood toe-to-toe, on the verge of exchanging blows.

Sergeant Morgan intervened. He shouted them into silence. He pushed his way between them and held them apart, forbidding them to speak as they stood to attention. Then he strode to and fro in front of them until they calmed down. Simpson just sat there, as though frozen, appalled by such behaviour, longing to be able to escape it all.

"Dragging Mr Sassoon into all this won't help a bit," Morgan said. "Now sit down, both of you, and try to face up to things sensibly."

They obeyed meekly. Captain Simpson picked up the conversation again. "All I can tell you with regard to Mr Sassoon is that the War Office, in their wisdom, decided that he should face a medical board."

"And the medical board let him off scot-free," interrupted 617. "Just said he needed treatment, is that it?"

"That's right."

"Then give Davey a medical board."

"Things don't work that way. Sassoon's medical board was the War Minister's personal decision. The decision to court-martial your brother is conventional, taken at brigade level."

"So it's one rule for officers and another for other ranks. Is that it?"

"Yes, that's about the size of it," admitted Simpson. "It always has been, and I expect it always will be. But it's nothing to do with me. It's not my job."

"We all know it's not your job," declared 617, his voice full of rancour. "Your job is to find a way of proving my brother innocent."

"I'm well aware of that. And I'll certainly do my best."

"And your best had better be good enough, Captain Simpson. Otherwise blood will flow, I promise you."

Simpson gathered his papers together and walked out. He wasn't prepared to take any more. He knew a direct threat when he heard one. The whole thing was beyond belief. He was getting out, and getting out quick! No one could be expected to act for a man with a threat of bloodshed hanging over him if he failed. He had every right to refuse to handle the case. Jones 618 would have to defend himself, or get a regimental officer to defend him. Captain Simpson was just about to pass through the gap in the barbed wire where a regimental policeman was stationed when Sergeant Morgan came running out of the barn. Simpson paused to hear what he had to say.

"Don't take any notice of him, sir. He's a hot-head and always has been. And he's under tremendous strain."

"That was a direct threat."

"Yes, sir, but not a threat directed at you. It was against Sassoon. And anyhow, it was an empty threat. No more than his temper coming out."

"Well I'm sorry, but I can't help Fusilier Jones."

"Sir! You can't just abandon a lad like 618."

Morgan's appeal was heart-felt that Simpson's conscience stirred.

"At the very worst you could go for clemency," pleaded Morgan. "There are grounds. Please give it a try. Without you the trial will be a fiasco."

Morgan's desperation struck home. Simpson hesitated and then, against his better judgement, said: "I'll call back tomorrow. So long as you're here. Can you make it?"

"In the morning, sir."

"Right, I'll see you then. But get those two under control."

"I'll read them the riot act, sir."

"Good. And I'll do all I can to get him off, but don't expect miracles."

When they met the following morning nothing was said about the row. Sergeant Morgan's riot act had done the trick. The Jones twins were meek and mild.

Simpson hadn't slept at all. He'd been up all night working on the case and had come up with an approach which he considered to be both original and convincing. He felt much more confident and it showed. The first thing he did was complete their examination of the summary of evidence.

"This will give you the basis of the accusations we're facing," he said. "But don't worry about it. As a legal document it's worthless. It was drawn up by an officer with no legal experience. He failed to caution Fusilier Jones and, incredibly enough, he didn't get any worthwhile evidence from him. The whole thing is totally biased. He even ends up by warning Fusilier Jones, 'Anything you say can be taken down and used in evidence against you.' And that's tantamount to a threat. The most useful thing about it is that it reveals the attitude we're up against. All they want is a guilty verdict."

Simpson didn't go into any details of the tactics he would use. He switched to his greatest worry about the case: the poems and limericks found among 618's belongings.

"The poems they found among your kit might prove very tricky," he told 618. "Most of them are harmless, but one or two poems are highly subversive and seditious. Just the type of thing you would expect from someone planning to persuade others to mutiny. And they're all in the same handwriting, so first we have to establish whose handwriting it is."

Captain Simpson looked enquiringly at Jones 618. "Am I right in assuming that the handwriting is yours?"

618 didn't reply. Simpson turned to his brother. "Ask him if that is the case?"

"Davey, you've got to answer Captain Simpson," said 617. "He's trying to help you. Is the handwriting on the poems and the limericks yours?"

"You know it is. You know my writing."

"But *you* have to tell Captain Simpson. You must tell him everything, whether it's obvious or not."

The logic of this registered with 618. "Yes, sir, all those things are in my writing. But Mr Sassoon wrote the poetry. I just wrote the limericks. All I did with the poems was make copies of them. They were rejected poems and ones he intended to throw away. But I thought them great, so I copied them. Mr Sassoon never minded. He knew I did it."

"So to get this quite clear," resumed Captain Simpson, "which of Mr Sassoon's poems did you copy?"

"All those that the regimental police found. All the proper poems were his."

"Including the ones that were also featured on the printed pamphlets?"

"Yes. All of them."

"That's good. Excellent. That'll be all right then. You just wrote the limericks ..."

"Yes."

"Limericks are all he's capable of," laughed Jones 617. "He can't write proper poetry any more than I can. All the proper poems are bound to be by Sassoon no matter whose writing they are in. It's bloody obvious."

"Fine," said Simpson. "I only want to be quite clear about this because one or two of the poems are so incriminating. If we can prove that Sassoon wrote them it's quite possible that the powers that be will change their attitude towards him and court-martial him after all."

"Could they do that at this stage?" asked 617.

"Oh yes. It's certainly possible. There were plenty of people who were furious that Sassoon got off so lightly. And there is nothing binding about the decision of a medical board. It's not like the verdict of a court-martial which can only be changed on appeal. They can scrap a medical board decision at a whim and start again from scratch. And some of Sassoon's poems found among your brother's papers are far more incriminating than his protest ever was. All added together they're really explosive."

"Then we should shop the bastard," exclaimed 617 gleefully.

"Don't worry," said Captain Simpson. "A full transcript of your brother's court-martial will automatically go to Haig's Headquarters and also to my superiors in the legal department at the War Office. So who can tell, Sassoon might still get the court-martial he always said he wanted."

"Bloody Sassoon on the receiving end," chortled 617.

"Possibly," agreed Captain Simpson. "But we still have to prove that the poems were originally Sassoon's. And the best way to do that is to call him as a witness. But we mustn't be too confident. He'll be within his rights to refuse to answer some questions on the grounds that he might incriminate himself."

"He wouldn't have the bloody cheek ..."

"You never know," hedged Simpson. "Men can behave very selfishly when they're in a tight corner."

"Not even a bastard like Sassoon could do that to Davey."

"Well let's not speculate too much. It's also quite possible some of the poems have already been printed in England, probably in the Cambridge Magazine. If so, that will put the matter beyond doubt and it won't matter even if Sassoon does refuse to incriminate himself. I know someone on Fleet Street who can help me out on that. Anyhow, we'll see. One way or another I'm sure we'll be able to convince the court that Sassoon wrote the poems, not your brother."

"Just so long as we nail that bastard Sassoon," muttered 617.

"Quite," agreed Simpson. "Put the responsibility where it belongs - on Sassoon."

"Bloody right."

Throughout the exchange Jones 618 said nothing. As usual, he didn't appear to be listening, but he was. His mouth may have been open, indicating boredom, but he was listening to every word, absorbing and understanding everything. And he was sickened, utterly sickened, by their attitude towards Mad Jack. They had no idea of what a truly great man he was.

618 came to a decision, a decision that no one, not even 617, would ever shake.

19

Not Guilty

On the morning of the court-martial it was raining hard with a westerly wind blowing at near-gale force. The old school building in which the court was to be held was a sombre sight with two bedraggled regimental policemen in water-proof capes standing on guard by the rusty wrought iron gates.

The president of the court was the first to arrive. His name was Burrows, a Lt. Colonel serving in the Ox and Bucks who had been deprived of his command of the 3rd battalion by a nasty leg wound which made him limp heavily and use a walking stick. He had a walrus moustache, a ruddy complexion, greying hair, and sparkling blue eyes, making him look exactly what he was, a traditional regular officer with a fine military record. It was the first time he had ever presided over a General Field Court-Martial and he was not looking forward to it. He knew his limitations.

He returned the salute of the senior regimental policeman and passed inside. He'd only just removed his riding mackintosh when four other officers joined him, the other board members, three captains and a major.

Colonel Burrows welcomed them and they took their seats at the long table at the end of the school's assembly hall. In front of them, tables and chairs were arranged for the prosecution and defence teams, and the sergeant who was to act as recorder. To one side was a very make-shift witness box. At the far end of the hall were two rows of wooden, collapsible chairs for the use of any interested parties, which amounted to the officers of the Royal Welch Fusiliers.

Colonel Burrows delved into his briefcase that contained the summary of evidence, the charge sheet, King's Regulations, and a copy of the Manual of Military Law. He then lost no time in going through a ritual of legal requirements: that all members of the court were qualified to serve and that the charge sheet was in order and had been signed and verified by the convening officer, the colonel of the Royal Welch Fusiliers.

Then they waited for 0900 hours, by which time all other participants had arrived and were assembled in adjacent rooms: the prosecution, the defence, and the witnesses, all kept separate to prevent collusion. Colonel Burrows then ordered that the court should be opened. A regimental policeman took delight in relaying this information to everyone by shouting loudly in the best Old Bailey tradition and everyone took up their respective positions. The accused was the last to appear. He was marched in, flanked by escorts. Once the witnesses had been sworn in and all other formalities satisfied, Captain Simpson nudged Fusilier Jones 618, indicating that he should stand to attention at the side of the defence table.

Colonel Burrows then read out the accused's full name, rank, and number. "Are you that person?" he asked.

Simpson had to nudge 618 twice more before he replied: "Yes, sir."

Simpson sighed with exasperation. He had rehearsed 618 as best he could but he was under no illusions about the hard time he was going to have with him, especially when he was in the witness box. Simpson decided that the best thing was to enrol 617 as an official part of the defence team so that he could be present in court the whole time. That would comfort 618 and boost his confidence, and 617 would be helpful in devising suitable questions and coaching his brother on how to handle his cross-examination.

It wasn't an easy decision for Simpson to make. First he would have to get the court's permission and then he would have to accept that he would no longer be able to call 617 as a witness; but with Sassoon all set to arrive from England, supported by his Fleet Street friend, Haughton, and with Major Hunt held in reserve, he considered it a risk well worth taking.

While Colonel Burrows was shuffling papers about, preparing to read out the charge, Simpson rose from his chair and coughed artificially. Then he addressed the president in a very respectful tone. "On a point of order, sir, before we get underway, I would ask permission for the accused's brother Fusilier Jones 617 to be present in court throughout the case as a part of the defence team. As the court may have noticed, the accused does occasionally have minor difficulties, diagnosed these days as autism, which means that his brother's presence and support could prove beneficial to all concerned, especially the court itself."

Colonel Burrows had no idea what autism was, but he could see readily enough that Fusilier Jones wasn't quite all there. "Does the accused have a diagnosed medical condition?"

"No, sir. He is classified as A1. His difficulties are bound up with social behaviour and human relationships, not a medical condition in the normal military sense. He is not under any form of treatment. His brother's presence in court would be more a matter of expediency than anything else."

Burrows looked across to the prosecuting counsel, Major Jordan. "Do you have any objections?"

Attention focused on Major Jordan. He was a one-armed major in the Coldstream Guards. Since recovering from the loss of his arm the army had employed him as a prosecutor at Field General Courts-Martial. He was a hard man, a disciplinarian who was shrewd as well as ruthless; a man who showed no sympathy and demanded maximum penalties allowed by military law.

"No objections, sir," he replied. "I think my colleague, the defence counsel, has a valid point. It is, of course more usual for an additional member of the defence team to be a junior officer, but there are precedents of other ranks assuming this type of role. My only proviso is that it must be clearly understood that Fusiliers Jones 617 will forfeit any right of audience. He cannot be a witness if he is present in court the whole time as part of the defence team."

"Very well … Permission granted. I'll now read out the charge. Fusilier Davey Jones you are charged with endeavouring to incite a mutiny relating to the enemy contrary to section 31(1) of the Army Act in that in C Company of the 1st Battalion the Royal Welch Fusiliers you urged men to lay down their arms and refuse to fight by means of posting seditious literature on the company notice board and also that you are the author of other subversive material. How do you plea, guilty or not guilty?"

"Not guilty, sir."

618 remained standing until he felt Major Simpson tugging on his sleeve. He sat down and the prosecuting counsel rose instead.

Major Jordan had a thunderous voice which defied anyone to oppose him. "Sir, I will outline the case confronting us. In many ways it is simple and straightforward. The case starts with the accused's previous platoon commander, Second-Lieutenant Sassoon MC. Mr Sassoon recently took it upon himself to make a protest against the conduct of the war. This was duly dealt with by the appropriate authorities in the UK and Mr Sassoon is now a patient at Craighlockhart War Hospital near Edinburgh. However, before being confined there, he sent letters and other written matter supporting his views to various individuals, seeking their support. One such letter was sent to the accused, Fusilier D Jones, 618. He in turn attached the material to the C Company notice board without reference to anyone, a clear indication that he agreed with the contents and hoped to gain the support of other men in his company. The literature was spotted and, because of its seditious nature, was ordered to be removed. At the same time Fusilier Jones's dugout was searched. More subversive material was found, establishing further links with the *Non-Conscription Fellowship,* namely various poems and limericks. The poems were explicit in their opposition to the war, calling for men to lay down their arms and surrender. Significantly these poems were identical to those quoted on the *Non-Conscription Fellowship* pamphlets.

"A summary of evidence was then held and the accused was later placed under arrest. In presenting the case for the prosecution I will call five witnesses. The accused is represented by Captain Simpson, a qualified solicitor serving with the War Office in London. With your permission, sir, I will now call the first witness.

There was more shouting, a consequence of which a regimental policeman stepped into the witness box. Having been identified and sworn in, he related how he had removed the seditious material from the company notice board. "When I arrived on the scene there was a gathering of men around the board. They appeared to have read the papers and were discussing them. They were laughing and joking and passing such remarks as, "Mad Jack strikes again!"

Major Jordan had no further questions for the witness and Simpson declined to cross-examine him.

The second witness was the regimental police sergeant who had alerted his superiors to the fact that the literature must have been delivered by post. Again, Captain Simpson declined to cross examine the witness. The third witness was the battalion post corporal who verified that a type-addressed envelope had arrived for the accused whose job it was to collect mail and then distribute it within his company.

"And am I right in saying," asked Jordan, "that this was a strictly personal letter, addressed to Fusilier Jones, not to anyone in authority in the battalion?"

"That's right, sir. A purely personal letter."

"Thank you, that's all."

Captain Simpson again asked no questions.

The next witness called was Brigadier-General CF King. His identity as the second-in-command of the British Army legal department in France was established.

"Brigadier, were you consulted by the commanding officer of the Royal Welch Fusiliers about this case?" asked Major Jordan.

"I was. I was asked to confirm, or otherwise, that the written material displayed on the C Company notice board and the poems found in the accused dugout constituted an incitement to mutiny."

"And what did you conclude?"

"That they most certainly did. The views of the *Non-Conscription Fellowship* are well known to us. But the poems found in the accused's effects throw a new light with regard to the support the *Fellowship* has within the armed forces."

"And what advice did you give the Royal Welch Fusiliers?"

"I advised that a summary of evidence be set up. Then, subject to its findings, immediate action should be taken to scotch the matter."

"Thank you, Brigadier. No more questions. I now present the findings for the examination of the Board."

While the evidence was passed forward, Captain Simpson once again confirmed that he did not wish to cross-examine the witness.

The fourth witness was the Brigade-Major who had been in charge of the search of Jones 618's dugout. He explained how he had come across copies of various poems and limericks. "There was a fundamental difference between the two," he said. "The poems were serious, very anti-war, and plainly mutinous. On the other hand, the limericks had no military significance, simply crude doggerel."

An orderly stepped forward again and placed exhibits before the president. As they were examined by the members of the board, Major Jordan continued with his examination. "Major, please tell the court about the hand-writing of these exhibits."

"They were all written by the same person, sir."

"And can you identify whose hand-writing it was."

"No, I have no way of knowing, but I assumed - and still do - that they were written by the accused, but I have never seen other examples of his hand-writing."

"I have other examples here, Major. Would you care to look at these and tell the court if you can be certain it is that same hand-writing?"

The orderly handed several pieces of paper to the brigade-major. "Oh, yes. That's the same writing all right. No doubt about it."

"There's one more example for you to look at, Major. Please look at the writing on the letter written to the accused by Second-Lieutenant Sassoon. It's the letter that was recovered from the post. In your judgement, are the two sets of writing different?"

The brigade major examined the samples handed to him. "They're definitely different. No doubt about it. No resemblance at all."

"So in your opinion, were the poems and limericks written by the same person? By the accused?"

"No doubt about it."

"No more questions," said Jordan

Captain Simpson got to his feet to cross-examine for the first time. "Major, let's forget about the hand-writing just for the moment. The Defence does not deny that *all* the material recovered from the accused's belongings was in his hand-writing. But having read the poems and limericks are you of the opinion that ..."

"Objection!" Major Jordan sprang to his feet. Objections were his speciality. He loved to yell out as loudly as conditions permitted, shattering the calm of the court, aimed at unnerving his opponent. "The witness's opinion is not admissible."

"Sir," retorted Simpson, turning to the board members, "since the witness has so far done nothing but give his opinions I see no reason why he shouldn't continue to do so, especially if it helps us arrive at the truth."

"Point taken," muttered a smiling Colonel Burrows. "We will continue to consider, but not necessarily accept, the major's opinions."

Captain Simpson went on with his cross-examination. "Having read all the material, would you agree with me that although the poems and limericks are all in the same handwriting they were not necessarily composed by the same person? I suggest the poems and limericks were the work of two different people."

"That never occurred to me. I assumed then, and still do, that they were written by the same person. I reckoned that one lot was written when he was in a serious frame of mind and the limericks as a bit of fun, working-off his frustrations."

"But surely it is perfectly possible that some of the copies could have been actually composed by a different person?"

"Well, yes ... I suppose it is possible, but hardly ..."

"Thank you, Major. No more questions of this witness, sir."

The president called an adjournment for lunch. Sandwiches and cups of tea were served in one of the old classrooms. The board members, the prosecution and the defence team remained in separate groups. Jones 617 was present and stood beside Simpson while 618 loitered at the table on which the sandwiches were laid out. 617 was not at all happy. "Why didn't you query a few more things early on?"

"There was no need."

"Everything seems to be going against us."

"It's early days yet. When things get going they won't have it all their way."

"I bloody well hope not," said 617. "We'll have to prove that Davey ..."

"I know what we have to prove ... Just trust me. I know what I'm doing."

"I bloody well hope so," repeated 617.

"Go over and make sure he remembers what he's got to say."

"He knows. He's not all that stupid."

"Fine ..."

"And what about Sassoon? Are you going to call him as a witness?"

"Yes. I've told the prosecution and I've applied to the president for him to be called."

"What happens if they don't call him?"

"They have to. They have no option. He'll be here tomorrow. I'm also expecting a telephone call from my friend on Fleet Street as to whether or not any of the Sassoon poems copied by your brother have already been published in London. If they have, then end of argument."

617 accepted this without comment.

"I've done everything I can. And we've got a solid defence. So stop worrying."

When the court reassembled, Major Jordan made sure the board members all had copies of the incriminating poems which had been referred to earlier and then informed the president that he had completed the case for the prosecution.

Captain Simpson then rose to present the case for the defence.

"The defence case is in two parts, sir. We will first of all demonstrate that the accused committed no offence in displaying the material of the *Non-Conscription Fellowship* on the company notice board. We will then prove that the accused was not the author of the poems which were found in his belongings. That he was only the author of the innocuous limericks. Also, at no time did he promote these poems and he only kept them because of their literary merit. In order to support this I will call three witnesses. First the accused, Fusilier Jones, and then, as you and the prosecution have already been informed, Mr Sassoon. He will be available to give evidence tomorrow afternoon, for which delay I apologise. However, I ask for your indulgence since his evidence will form a vital part of the defence's case. My third witness will be Mr Haughton, an editorial member of the Morning Post. With your permission I will now call the accused as a witness."

Jones 618 looked worse than usual. The high-sided witness box meant that only his head and shoulders were visible. His hair was closely cropped and he had several red blotches where he had scratched mosquito bites. As always his mouth hung open. As he was sworn in, he looked terrified. Captain Simpson smiled at him, trying to reassure him.

The previous evening he and Jones 617 had rehearsed him and organised his questions so that in most cases he could just answer 'yes' or 'no'. They also impressed upon him that when it came to being cross-examined by

Major Jordan he was to answer as briefly as possible and never be drawn into lengthy discussions or explanations. Above all he was never to become over-excited or aggressive. If he got into difficulties he was to plead confusion and keep saying: "I don't understand" or "Could you rephrase that question, please". In short, at the first sign of trouble he was to slow everything down and play for time. That way he would far less likely to be forced into mistakes.

Captain Simpson put his first question. "Am I right in saying that for three years you were Mr Sassoon's platoon runner?"

"Yes, sir."

"As such, were you accustomed to placing messages, instructions and orders on the C Company notice board, alongside Part II orders?"

"Yes, sir."

"After three years of being Mr Sassoon's runner, what happened?"

"All sorts ..."

"Of course, but as far as you know, is he still a serving officer in the Fusiliers?"

"Oh yes, sir."

"Were you surprised when you received a letter from him?"

"Yes, sir."

"Why was that?"

"Because it was the first letter I've ever had in my life, from anyone. So I was amazed then, wasn't I?"

"Was it actually a letter - a personal letter that is - or instructions from an officer to a subordinate? In other words, an official communication? "

"Official, sir. On one of our pads."

Simpson broke off to address the president again. "Sir, as you'll see from the exhibits placed before you, the order pad was indeed made out in the usual way. The only irregular thing is that at the bottom of it there is a reference to Ebbw Vale." Simpson turned back to 618. "Please explain to the court the significance of Ebbw Vale."

"It was a bit of fun we used to have, sir. Mr Sassoon would call out the name of a Welsh town and I would make up an instant limerick about it."

"Do you often write limericks?"

"Yes, sir. I'm good with rhyming words."

"Hence all the limericks found in your kit by the regimental police?"

"Yes, sir."

"So when you received this order, what did you do?"

"I opened it."

"Yes, of course. Did you read everything in the envelope?"

"No, sir."

"Isn't it strange that you didn't read the pamphlets as well?"

"No, sir."

"Why not?"

"Because Mr Sassoon's orders were quite clear. Just stick them up, he said. And an order is an order. Always obey the last order."

"Quite," agreed Simpson. "Didn't you think it a bit odd that you had received a letter from England from your ex-platoon commander?"

"No, sir. It was an order, telling me to stick everything up."

"And you say you didn't read the printed matter?"

"Well, I glanced at it. But it was none of my business."

"What made you think that?"

"Because it was from some lot called the *Non-Conscription Society or Fellowship*, or something. So I thought it was something for the boyos who are conscripts to read."

"Did you see who signed all these papers?"

"Yes, someone named Russell, but I'd never heard of him."

"So you're not aware that Bertrand Russell is a well-known pacifist, a man dead set against fighting the war?"

"No, sir. I wouldn't know if I've never heard of him, now would I? Like I said, I thought it was meant for the boyos who are conscripts. And I'm not a conscript, sir. I was a volunteer."

"How soon after the declaration of war did you volunteer?"

"A few days, sir."

"Because you felt it your duty to support the war?"

"Yes, sir."

"Have you ever been in any trouble whilst in the army?"

"No, sir."

"Did you go over the top at Loos?"

"Yes, sir."

"And were you stranded in no man's land for nearly twenty four hours?"

"Yes, sir."

"And were you involved in the raid on German lines when Sergeant Morgan won his Military Medal?"

"Yes, sir. Sort of."

"And were you among the reserves during the battle of the Somme, ready and keen to go into action, had you been so ordered?"

"I wasn't very keen, sir ... But I was there and ready."

"So for three years you have been in the thick of the fighting?"

"Yes, sir."

"And once you had obeyed Mr Sassoon's order, and placed the material on the company notice board, did you hang around to speak to any of the men who were bound to pass by and read it?"

"No, sir."

"Have you, at any time, ever spoken to anyone about disobeying orders and laying down their arms?"

"No, sir."

"Have you ever been reprimanded by any officer or NCO for not doing your duties properly?"

"No, sir."

Captain Simpson was silent for a time, referring to his notes. Eventually, with all eyes on him, he asked if he might approach the board. Colonel Burrows beckoned him forward, together with Major Jordan.

"Sir, if I might have your indulgence," started Simpson, "the defence is content to let the combat record of the accused speak for itself. But I now intend to turn to the matter of the poems found in Fusilier Jones's kit. We submit that these poems were not composed by the accused. And as you and the prosecuting counsel are aware, sir, I have applied for Second-Lieutenant Sassoon to appear as a witness to clear up this matter and establish the true authorship. And unfortunately there might be a delay in Mr Sassoon arriving ..."

Colonel Burrows interrupted by clearing his throat unnecessarily. He also looked highly embarrassed. "Sad to relate, Captain Simpson, but we have received a message to say that your request for Mr Sassoon as a witness has fallen on stony ground. I am afraid Mr Sassoon will not be able to take the stand."

Simpson looked astounded and highly indignant. "May I ask why not, sir? It is a perfectly reasonable and legitimate request."

"I grant you that, Captain. And his non-appearance is certainly no reflection on you, I can assure you. You are perfectly within your rights to seek his presence. And we were prepared to await his arrival. But unfortunately when the court applied for Mr Sassoon to be made available, we were informed by the legal department at general headquarters that Mr Sassoon is an inmate of Craiglockhart War Hospital. This hospital is devoted to the treatment of mental disorders. And anyone who is currently under psychiatric treatment is automatically classified in Military Law as an 'idiot' witness. And an 'idiot' witness is barred from giving evidence. Even if Mr Sassoon appeared, we would have no alternative but to declare his evidence inadmissible."

Colonel Burrows reached for his copy of the Manual of Military Law. He had already ear-marked the relevant pages about idiot witnesses. "It comes under 'Competence of Witnesses, Paragraph 100'. Perhaps you would like to read the full text for yourself?"

"That won't be necessary, sir." Captain Simpson stood there, stock still, so taken aback that he didn't know what to do or say.

"I'm afraid there is nothing I can do to help you," said Colonel Burrows, realising Simpson's difficulties. "Perhaps you would like an adjournment while you reconsider your position? And then you can conclude your examination of the accused in the morning?"

"Thank you, sir."

The two counsels returned to their desks and Colonel Burrows declared: "The court is adjourned until 0900 hours tomorrow."

20

618's Decision

"**A**n idiot witness!" exclaimed Jones 617. "What crap."

The Jones twins and Captain Simpson were back in the barn, sitting around the table.

"I've never known such bloody rubbish!" continued 617. "If there is one thing Sassoon certainly isn't, it's an idiot."

They were discussing the day's events and thrashing out their next move when the court reassembled in the morning. They were well aware that without Sassoon's evidence their case looked thin to say the least. As usual 618 was unconcerned. He might just as well not have been there. For their part, Simpson and 617 ignored him and frequently referred to him openly without regard to his feelings.

"How reliable is this newspaper friend of yours?" asked 617.

"He'll be okay," replied Simpson without conviction.

"He'd better be."

Simpson changed the subject. Because of the time factor involved he knew that Haughton's contribution could well come too late. "The shame of it," said Simpson, "is that so far your brother has given evidence very well."

"And he will again," said 617, "just so long as he knows what to expect."

"Well I've told him what questions he'll most likely get when the prosecution cross-examines him. The most important thing is that he makes a firm denial that he was author of the poems. He's got to be quite definite that he just copied them. And he mustn't allow himself to be intimidated by Major Jordan. The major will undoubtedly pour scorn on your brother's claim not to have read the pamphlets properly and say that he knew perfectly well what he was pinning up."

Simpson was terrified by what might happen during 618's cross-examination. It would be the crux of the trial. It would open up unknown territory, and however much they rehearsed 618, Jordan would never be satisfied by 'yes' and 'no' answers. One slip by 618, and Jordan would tear him to shreds. A careless admission or an unwary contradiction and it would open the floodgates.

"Bloody idiot witness!" 617 cursed again. "Surely to God they're never going to believe that Davey wrote those poems. It's bloody obvious that he didn't."

"It might be obvious to you, but not necessarily to them. And it's the prosecutor's job to show that he did write them."

"But it's well known that Sassoon is a poet. The bugger never stops bragging about it."

"I know ... I know ..."

"Then call me as a witness. I'll bloody soon tell them. I shared a dugout with them and I saw Davey copying them out, didn't I?"

"You've no right of audience. You know that."

617 stood up and strode about the room for two or three minutes. "So what happens if they don't believe us and they find him guilty?"

"We've been through all that before, Jones. There's no reason why they shouldn't believe him, especially if Haughton comes up trumps. Your brother is a good, honest witness. And however pessimistic you want to be they are never going to shoot him. We've given them enough evidence of your brother's good combat record to scotch anything like that."

"They've shot plenty of other men out here, no matter what you say."

"Only men that deserved it like deserters and cowards. Davey is in a different category. And don't forget that there never was a mutiny. And whilst the intent to cause a mutiny remains a capital offence, the fact that it never happened could exonerate him ... Moderate his guilt, what we call mitigation."

"So what's the most likely to happen?"

"Imprisonment. Probably around five years. And that won't be the end of the world. Not with good behaviour. In fact he could well be better off in the glass house. At least he'll be safe."

"And in the meantime Sassoon gets off free. And we could have stitched him up good and proper. But I'll get him one way or another."

Jones 617 broke off and paced about again. He just couldn't keep still. He kept punching the open palm of his left hand with his clenched right fist, seeking relief from his frustration and anger, muttering all the time: "Idiot witness my arse ..."

"Jones, give it a rest, for heaven's sake."

The court-martial reconvened at 0900 hours. The Fusilier field officers occupied the chairs at the back of the assembly hall. The case was heading for an intriguing climax and although they couldn't see how it would be achieved they were longing for a not guilty verdict for the sake of the regiment.

Captain Simpson was keyed up to resume his examination of Jones 618. His questions were laid out in numbers in his notes, all so simple and straightforward that he didn't see how he could fail, despite the setback with Sassoon. He intended to emphasise 618's limited mental ability and get him to stress that he had never before written any poems, let alone ones which could be mistaken for those of Sassoon.

What Simpson lacked, however, was any idea of the state of 618's addled mind. He had no inkling that 618's first loyalty was now with Sassoon: that his obedience to his brother and respect for the truth had become minor considerations. Nor did Simpson appreciate 618's determination to escape the front line. He had no idea that since the Somme the youngster had often been tempted to desert; that to him life in the trenches was worse than death itself; that the noise, the blood, the agony of the wounded, and all the putrid bodies lying around the place, were more than he could stand.

So now, with the prospect of only a few years in jail if found guilty, and the certainty of saving Mad Jack from the severe punishment of a hostile court-martial, 618's decision was easy. The safety and reputation of a great man was paramount; it dwarfed everything else. As for jail, it held no terrors for 618. He had already endured far worse.

Even so, as his examination by Simpson re-started, 618 felt his heart pounding. As he stood in the witness box and the inevitable questions about the poems approached, he steeled himself to tell his lies. His chest felt about to burst as he fought for breath.

"Please confirm to the court," said Captain Simpson, "that you are not the author of the poems which were found in your kit."

618 was still gasping for breath, unable to answer.

"Do you understand me?"

"Yes."

"Then are you, or are you not, the author of the poems found in your kit?"

"Yes, I am."

"You are what? You mean you only wrote the limericks, not the serious poems?"

"No, I wrote them all."

"Not the poems ..."

"Yes I did ... I wrote all of them."

"You wrote all of them?"

"Yes ... All of them ..."

"I don't think you understand the question ..."

"Yes I do."

"I'm talking about ..."

"I know what you're talking about. I wrote them all."

"But you've previously made statements that you didn't."

"I was all mixed up, wasn't I? But I did. I wrote them all."

"That's just not true."

"Yes it is."

Simpson realised he faced disaster. He had no idea how to respond. He was totally bewildered by what the young fool was playing at. Simpson just stood there, his notes shaking in his hand. In desperation he turned to Jones 617, sitting at his side. "You tell him ..."

"Objection," cried Jordan. "Fusilier Jones has no right of audience."

Before Burrows could respond, Simpson shouted back: "In this case surely it is perfectly reasonable ..."

"Objection, sir. This is most irregular. Jones 617 is not permitted as a witness. He has no right of audience."

"Sustained."

Jones 617 jumped to his feet, inflamed by anger. "Sustained?" he yelled at Colonel Burrows. "What the hell are you talking about? You want the truth, don't you?"

"Be quiet, Fusilier."

"Why, for God's sake?"

Colonel Burrows had no gavel so he rapped the table with his knuckles to restore order. "Fusilier, you are not allowed to speak. You cannot address the court."

"That's daft, sir. I know exactly what happened. I know he didn't write those poems. Sassoon did, and I often saw my brother making copies of them."

"Objection, sir," roared Major Jordan.

"Sustained."

"But I tell you. ..."

"Be silent, Fusilier," shouted Colonel Burrows. "Just sit down and keep quiet."

"Damned if I will ... I know ..."

Colonel Burrows reached for his walking stick and crashed it down so hard on the table that everyone reacted as though a shell had landed. Then, almost as loudly, Burrows shouted: "Contempt! Contempt! Contempt of court! You're in contempt of court, Fusilier."

"I don't give a damn what I am ... I know..."

Colonel Burrows whacked his walking stick down again. "Orderlies, get that man out of here. Detain him outside for the rest of the trial. And everything he has said is to be struck from the records."

Two regimental policemen rushed forward and grabbed 617 by the arms. Despite his resistance and repeated cries of, "I know ..." they dragged him out of the court. Even then, 617 could be heard protesting: "Do you call this justice? It's a ridiculous farce."

He was still shouting as he was locked away in what had once been the headmaster's study.

In the courtroom everyone was agog, frozen in silence. No one had anticipated 618's startling rebuttal or the rough house which followed. Now, they just couldn't imagine what would happen next.

Major Jordan was the first to recover. He rose and addressed the president. "Sir, may I point out that the accused has been put forward by the defence as a reliable and truthful witness and under military law that means counsel is duty-bound to accept his answers, as indeed is the court. And the witness has now said six or seven times that he wrote all the poems found in his kit."

The president looked enquiringly at Simpson.

Simpson was out of his depth, devoid of any answers. He could only curse himself for having sacrificed 617 as a witness. Without Sassoon and 617 as witnesses he was reduced to the unpredictable Haughton, with Major Hunt only any good for a character reference.

All eyes remained on Simpson, waiting for him to respond.

"Well, Captain Simpson?"

"This new evidence comes as a total surprise to me, sir. It contradicts entirely what the accused has previously sworn to. And what I know to be the truth. I would ask for your indulgence by granting another adjournment."

"Objection," shouted Jordan.

"On what grounds?" responded Burrows.

"On the grounds that the evidence has already been given and therefore has to be accepted," said Jordan indignantly. "The defence can't expect to have an adjournment to reconsider things, simply because they didn't like the answers they got."

Colonel Burrows hesitated, betraying his legal inexperience. For the first time he felt the need to withdraw with his members in order to discuss things at length, and in total privacy. He consulted with his members and they all agreed. Burrows order the court to remain in session whilst they retired to a disused classroom.

Once settled in the classroom, Burrows said: "Gentlemen, legally I think things are becoming rather complicated. It's a great pity a judge advocate wasn't appointed to advise us on a point like this. As far as I'm aware, neither King's Regulation or the Manual of Military Law gives us any guidance on the matter. Do any of you have any comments?"

The junior captain spoke first. "What worries me, sir, is why they insist on a compulsory plea of not guilty"

"It's to ensure a full, fair and thorough trial," replied Burrows.

"But I don't see any sense in Jones pleading not guilty when he knows perfectly well that he is guilty. Surely, it's just an open invitation for the defence counsel to concoct a false story. Only to find in this case that when it comes down to it, the accused in not prepared to lie under oath."

"You're surely not suggesting that Jones is capable of having written those poems?" queried another member.

"Why not?"

"Because he's not all there, that's why not."

"What about Chatterton? He wasn't all there, either. But he wrote better poetry than Jones ever could. And Chatterton was only seventeen when he committed suicide ... He was probably an autistic like Jones."

"Who is Chatterton?" asked the major.

Burrows had no idea and chose not to show his ignorance. Nor was he willing to allow a pointless discussion to develop. Instead he wound things up swiftly by saying: "Legally, I think we are very much in the dark over all this. So I suggest we simply try to ensure that justice is given every chance to operate. If we are wrong in granting another adjournment at least our intentions can only been seen to be honourable, concerned with fairness and unearthing the truth."

Everyone stood as the members filed back into court. Once seated again, Burrows announced: "The court will be adjourned for an hour."

As everyone started to leave the courtroom Major Jordan was heard to sigh deeply, convinced he had been thwarted by ignorance. Captain Simpson grabbed 618 by the sleeve and went in search of Jones 617. When he discovered that he was in the headmaster's old study, he bluffed their way past the guard standing at the door, telling him that their contact with Jones 617 was quite in order. Once inside, Simpson dumped 618 in a chair and then explained to 617 what had happened. Finally he told him in no uncertain terms that he had an hour to bring his influence to bear on his brother; to straighten him out once and for all, to make him promise to tell the truth and stop playing silly buggers.

Simpson then stormed out, slamming the door behind him.

For a time he remained in the passage, listening at the door. He couldn't make out what was being said but 617 was doing all the talking. That was a good sign. Simpson had half expected them to start arguing, but 618's voice never came.

Inside the room Jones 617 strode about in front of his brother, telling him in blunt language that every man was responsible for his own actions and must be prepared to accept responsibility for the consequences of all he did or said or wrote; and since Sassoon wrote the poems - as they both knew perfectly well - so he and he alone had to answer for them.

"Those poems are none of your business, Davey," he yelled. "Do you understand? They're not your concern."

He felt like giving his brother a violent shaking, as he had so often done during childhood, but he knew that wouldn't do any good, that it would only send Davey into one of his tantrums or revert to silence. So he forced himself to calm down, to become reasonable, even up-beat. He did his best to make his brother smile and laugh; to give him something to look forward to. He told him that once he'd told the truth and been acquitted, and the war was over and won, he would go back to the Rhondda as a hero, and it would be a different world to the one he had known before as a butcher's boy. It would be a new world fit for heroes. All the old prejudices and inequalities would be swept aside by a new social order, with guaranteed jobs for all veterans.

"By the time you get back home you will probably have been promoted to lance corporal!" he said brightly. "A lance-jack, look you, Davey! Your prestige will soar. You'll be someone special, a man of account. Even the girls will welcome you back. No more being shunned, Davey. No more watching them run away screaming. You'll be such a hero that they'll drop their knickers for you whenever you want, won't they, then?"

618 laughed and chortled.

"So you go back into that court, Davey, and answer Captain Simpson honestly. No more silly nonsense, pretending you're a proper poet to protect that bastard Sassoon. Right, 618?"

"Right 617!"

Jones 618 was led back to the defence classroom by the orderly. As he and Simpson waited for the court to be recalled, the defence counsel said: "So your brother has put you right then? You know what you've got to say?"

"Yes, sir. I know."

After that nothing was said until another orderly entered the room and told Simpson that someone had been trying to contact him over the telephone from London. "Why didn't you come and tell me?" demanded Simpson, knowing it could only be his journalist friend, Haughton.

"It was a very bad line, sir. It always is, and a staff officer kept interrupting from Division, demanding to know if it was a priority call. So in the end the caller said he'd phone back in about half an hour and dictate a message for you, giving full details."

"Okay, that's fine. If I'm in court when it comes through make sure someone delivers it right away. It's very important. In fact, vital."

"Right, sir. I'll do it myself."

Simpson turned to 618. "You heard that?"

"Yes, sir."

"Well that will be my journalist friend from Fleet Street, giving the dates when Sassoon's poems were published ... Full details ... Do you know what perjury is?"

"Yes, sir. Telling lies under oath."

"Then just remember that. Or you'll only get into even more trouble."

Simpson's threat didn't worry 618 a bit. He knew that none of the poems in question had ever been published. Anyhow, he didn't give a damn even if he got a year or two more in jail for perjury.

When the court re-convened the back of the court-room was even more packed with officers, with orderlies bringing in extra chairs. The Fusilier officers were anticipating high drama. None of them believed that Fusilier Jones was a traitor but as things stood they knew Simpson would have to pull off a master stroke if he was to win the day; and they just didn't see how that was possible.

As Fusilier Jones was escorted to the witness box he was trembling. Fear shone from his eyes. The trappings and formality of the court bore down on him and he had to fight hard to keep his nerve, to maintain his resolve to defy military law and to lie and lie and stick to his lies. He kept telling himself that they were not evil lies. His lies were worthy lies, inspired by his determination to protect a really great man, and he was convinced that in years to come everyone would thank him.

Captain Simpson put his first question. "Fusilier Jones, please tell the court which of the poems and limericks found in your kit you were responsible for writing?"

Everyone saw 618's Adam's apple bob up and down as he swallowed. Eventually he managed to gulp: "All of them."

A perceptible murmur swept through the courtroom. Everyone was amazed that the adjournment had made no difference. At the prosecution desk, Major Jordan was unable to suppress a smile. He didn't understand what was going on any more than anyone else did, but he could not have been more delighted. The defence was winning the case for him.

Captain Simpson kept looking towards the doorway of the courtroom and very soon, to his enormous relief, he saw the orderly. He was waving a piece of paper above his head to attract attention. A broad grin spread across Simpson's face as he anticipated being saved at the very last second.

"If it pleases the court," he blurted out, "a message has just arrived for me from London that could have a vital bearing on the case. With the court's permission, might I have a moment or two to read it?"

"Very well," agreed Burrows. "But keep it brief."

The orderly hurried forward and handed the slip of paper to Simpson. He read it just as hurriedly. The message was plain and simple. It said: *"The poems you queried are all unknown. Extensive enquiries show that none of them have ever been published."*

Simpson was devastated. He was left high and dry, metaphorically as naked as the day he was born. He had no idea what to say. There was no way he could put the same old questions to Jones yet again.

In defeat, he crumpled the message up and thrust it into his trouser pocket. The roof of his mouth was dry and cracked. He was so devoid of ideas that when Colonel Burrows looked at him and enquired: "So, captain?" all he could do was resort to a guileless appeal, the sort of amateur touch a junior officer acting as counsel for the first time would have reverted to.

"Sir, we all know perfectly well that Jones didn't write those poems. He simply isn't capable of writing them. ..."

"Objection, sir." Major Jordan's voice was louder than ever, a note of triumph bursting through.

"Sustained."

"But, sir ... We all know in our hearts that Jones couldn't possibly have written them."

"Objection ..."

"Sustained. Captain Simpson, courts do not function on what we feel in our hearts. We are guided by evidence and evidence alone. Do you understand?"

"Of course, sir."

"Very well, then. Proceed with you examination."

"I have no further questions, sir."

"Are you sure?"

"Perfectly."

"Will you be calling any other witnesses?"

"My only possibility is Jones 617, sir."

"He's in contempt and has no right audience. That can't be changed."

For Simpson it was the end. "I understand, sir."

"Then we must proceed. Major Jordan, do you wish to cross-examine?"

"I do indeed, sir."

Jordan rose slowly. He needed time to reorganise his approach. This was a chance he had never dared to anticipate. He knew perfectly well that 618 hadn't written the poems, but that was no concern of his. His duty was to win the case and demonstrate to everyone that any attempt to mutiny would be stamped out ruthlessly. He intended to seize his chance with alacrity. He showed no mercy. He made no allowances for 618's distressed condition. He ignored the way he was drooping in the witness box, dribble edging down his chin.

Jordan tore into him and cut him to shreds. It was exactly what Simpson had originally feared. He took 618 back to the beginning when he had received his letter from the *Non-Conscription Fellowship,* and due to his relentless questioning and Jones's pathetic replies, he was able to twist everything grotesquely; he threw a whole new light on the situation, making it appear that 618 was well aware of the contents of the pamphlets and had deliberately selected the company notice board as the best way of gaining everyone's attention.

He made Jones contradict himself. He fed him leading questions to which the Fusilier readily succumbed, and he slipped in trick questions which brought admissions which damned Jones out of hand. And never a single 'Objection' came from the crushed and hapless Simpson. On frequent occasions, when 618 just stared back at Jordan, his jaw sagging, not knowing how to answer, the major passed on quickly to other questions, attacking him even more aggressively from another angle.

"Now about these poems you wrote," stormed Jordan. "Let us be perfectly clear about the messages behind them. There must be no room for any doubts. Do you confirm that you wrote the following words:

Now sits a man within my sights,
He's smiling and relaxed, at leisure,
Sublimely unaware ...."

Major Jordan bellowed the words out. It was his idea of how all poetry should be read: the louder the better, sheer volume underlining meaning and substance. 618 was so contemptuous of such a crass rendering that he interrupted, determined at least to give Sassoon's verses dignity. For a few moments the voices of 618 and Jordan rang out simultaneously. Then, quite unexpectedly, Jordan gave way to the accused. He didn't do it in anger or in protest. He went silent because he sensed that 618, in his sudden determination to be heard, was about to condemn himself out of his own mouth.

Jordan's hunch proved correct. As 618 recited the poems alone a feeling of amazement swept over the court. A dramatic change had overcome Jones; he was standing erect, his bearing suddenly full of pride; and the lyrical quality of his Welsh accent enhanced Sassoon's words, making them flow and echo around the courtroom. His voice rang out with such clarity that not a single word was missed and the humanitarian message of the poems was unmistakable. His previous dithering in the witness box was forgotten. Now, everyone was fascinated, reflecting on the implications of each poem.

"Now sits a man within my sights
He's smiling and relaxed, at leisure,
Sublimely unaware that his frail life
Lies entirely within my pleasure.

229

He basks in the sun and waffles on,
No doubt regaling his friends and cronies
With the rights and wrongs of army life
And denouncing all officers as phonies.

What crazy duty demands that I should kill
This man who cannot remotely matter?
If I shoot the poor sod, what comfort in that?
To see his skull implode, then shatter?

So I'll have done with all this evil slaughter:
And seek an end to mass insanity.
With the Lord granting me peace of mind
As I strike a blow for humanity."

618 went straight on to another poem. He didn't refer to any notes, nor did he seek permission from the court. His voice flowed on, challenging every man-jack of them to defy the truth and wisdom of Sassoon's masterpieces.

"Don't you ever rue that your countrymen are dying?
Aren't you sickened as they perish in a senseless war?
Don't you ever wake up to hear men crying?
Can't you grasp that our efforts are rotten to the core?
Isn't it time you cast your smoking gun aside?
And by so doing end this pointless genocide?"

Still Jones hadn't finished. He recited a third poem. All eyes were fixed on him. There were no objections from Jordan or the president.

"We Tommies at the front suffer, sir.
We Tommies in our trenches die,
And all the name of freedom, sir,
Though we all know that's a lie.

Your fight for the flag is bogus, sir
In the end war always wins,
Notice the cross-bones of death, sir,
And the skull above it that grins."

Silence settled once more over the courtroom, but it didn't stop 618's words echoing in the minds of those present. None of them had ever witnessed such a transformation in a man's personality, and lingering doubts about his claim of authorship vanished. His word-perfect fluency was tantamount to proof of authorship.

Major Jordan waited, exploiting the dramatic pause. He glanced across at Colonel Burrows and his members, making eye contact with each of them in turn, implying that Jones had just proved his point for him: that a mutineer had been exposed. Then he spoke in an uncharacteristic and kindly tone. "You recall everything perfectly, don't you Jones?"

"Of course, sir. It's only natural to remember things you've written."

"And all of us here in this court will always remember your rendering of your verses. We will savour your artistry and never doubt your sincerity. But unfortunately artistry and sincerity do not justify what you wrote. When you wrote those poems you obviously intended that others should see them, and read them, and be guided by them, didn't you? Your objective was to persuade others to share your views and mutiny, wasn't it?"

"No, sir. I never showed them to anyone. I wrote them for myself."

"Indeed! Then how do *you* account for the fact that these verses also appear on one of the sheets of the propaganda you pinned to your company notice board, the sheets under the banner of the *Non-Conscription Fellowship?* How did they get hold of them if you didn't show them to anyone? How do *you* account for that?"

"I don't understand ..."

"Well I understand. You have been actively trying to persuade others to mutiny, haven't you? You must have been."

Major Jordan exploited Jones's confusion and soon had him on a roll. The Fusilier was back to his normal self and Jordan knew he had a witness on his hands that he could get to say or agree to anything he liked. Being unable to answer the simplest of questions, Jones shrank in the witness box, more than ever a garden gnome. Tears of frustration welled in his eyes and his body began to shake, first his shoulders and then his entire torso.

Throughout the court embarrassment and sympathy towards Jones was so acute that Colonel Burrows intervened. "Major, I don't think there is any point in prolonging this cross-examination any longer. Unless you have new ground to cover, perhaps you should leave it at that?"

"Just as you wish, sir … No more questions."

"Captain Simpson, do you wish to further your examination?"

"No, sir."

"Are you sure?"

"Quite sure, sir. And in the circumstances I will not be calling my other witness, Major Hunt. With your permission, that closes the case for the defence."

All that remained was for the two counsels to summarise their respective cases.

Major Jordan spoke first. He was ebullient, knowing that victory was his. He felt he had every right to exploit the situation. He made it sound as though the exposure of a traitor was all down to his brilliance as a cross-examiner. His confidence was so great that he even brought up the matter of 618's intelligence, anxious to forestall anything Captain Simpson might say on that subject, seeking mitigation. He pointed out that medically 618 was classified as A1 when he joined up and nothing had happened since to cast doubts on that.

Jordan concluded by saying: "The prosecution has proved that this is a clear case of a man intent on causing a mutiny. A man who tried to persuade others to stop fighting and this is something for which he must bear full responsibility. While his early record is not questioned, one can only lament his subsequent behaviour. His lack of moral fibre in collaborating with the trouble-maker Sassoon, the *Non-Conscription Fellowship,* and the pacifist Bertrand Russell, is deplorable and must be made an example of. In the circumstances the prosecution demands that a verdict of guilty be returned."

In contrast, Captain Simpson's summary was a brief and sad affair. He referred to the duplicity of the accused in changing his story without prior warning, and how, in the circumstances, there was nothing further to be said in his defence. He didn't say anything in mitigation and at one stage he rambled on so inconsequently that no one understood what he was driving at. At another point his voice became so subdued that no one could hear him and Colonel Burrows wasn't inclined to tell him to speak up, knowing that he would soon dry up anyhow.

When the board members retired to consider their verdict, Captain Simpson found himself with 618 in an upstairs classroom. They stood on opposite sides of the room, staring down on to the playground that surrounded the building. Simpson waited for an explanation. When he didn't get one, his anger exploded. "What the bloody hell have you been playing at?"

618 didn't even look round.

"You could at least have told me you were going to do that. And what's the point?"

Simpson stared across the room at 618's hunched figure, trying to fathom out what had motivated him. He knew he admired Sassoon on account of his bravery and poetry; but it was beyond his comprehension that a man would perjure himself so outrageously and risk jail for someone as misguided as Sassoon. He wondered if 618 had done it in order to avoid death on the battlefield: a way of working his ticket. That seemed more likely. Yet to Simpson even that didn't ring true.

Then a horrific thought struck Simpson: homosexuality!

If there was one thing that could explain 618's bizarre behaviour it was a perverted homosexual relationship between the two men.

Sassoon's sexual tastes were well known in the War Office legal department because of the way his homosexual friends had saved him from a court-martial. Simpson was so familiar with the situation that he turned on 618 and demanded: "For how long have you been Sassoon's faggot?"

618 turned, flabbergasted.

"And I suppose that accounts for those foul limericks, all aimed against women. And it's why your brother hates Sassoon so much. Because he knows what's been going on between you?"

618 stammered a denial but it meant nothing. Simpson wasn't even listening. His mind had clammed up. With homosexuality bursting into the case, he didn't care what happened. He considered himself exonerated from any further responsibilities. As far as he was concerned Jones could rot in jail.

21

The Final Hours

Colonel Burrows and members of the court had no trouble arriving at a unanimous verdict. They returned within twenty minutes. Burrows read from a prepared statement. He addressed 618 directly as he stood to attention at the side of the defence table.

"Fusilier Davey Jones, 1st Battalion of The Royal Welch Fusiliers, you have been tried by a duly constituted and authorised Field General Court-Martial. The verdict of the said court-martial is that you are guilty of trying to incite a mutiny. The court therefore sentences you to death by firing squad."

The guilty verdict came as no surprise, but the death sentence astounded everyone.

Growls of outrage and dissent rose from the Fusilier officers. 618 collapsed onto a nearby chair and appeared about to faint and Simpson was likewise so shocked that he just stood stock still in amazement.

The first Jones 617 heard of the sentence was when a regimental policeman unlocked the door of the headmaster's old study and called out: "All over. He's guilty ... Death by firing squad ..."

"Firing squad?" shrieked 617.

"That's right, boyo. He had it coming to him."

Jones 617 dashed down the passageway to the school assembly hall. Orderlies were already clearing away the court furniture. None of the participants were any longer there. Only a few Fusilier officers were standing around, holding their own inquest. 617 made for the barn where he knew they would be keeping his brother.

At first the regimental policemen refused to let him in but then, as they saw how agitated he was, they relented. "His defending officer is with him," one of them told him. Then, with snide humour, he added, "But I don't think they're on speaking terms."

617 found them staring at each other across the table, both still dumbfounded by the sentence. Simpson was now full of remorse. However much 618 had lied, and no matter what he had done with Sassoon in private, a death sentence was the last thing he had expected. To him, it was completely inhuman. He wouldn't have wished that on anyone, not even a murderer. With hindsight he loathed himself for having been so ineffectual; for not even pleading for clemency or diminished responsibility.

As soon as he saw 617 enter the barn he jumped up, strode across to him, grabbed his arm, and guided him to a far corner of the barn as though it was suddenly vital that 618 should not overhear them. In a whisper he told 617 what had happened.

"And what the hell did you do about it?" demanded 617.

"Do? What could I do?"

"Something ... Anything ... I spent half an hour telling him what he had to say. I convinced him. You must have said something to make him change his mind."

"I never said a damn thing ... He just didn't do as you told him."

"You should never have agreed to them shutting me up in that room."

"I couldn't stop that ... You were out of control ..."

"Rubbish!"

"Anyhow, I did my best. I put your brother forward as a truthful and reliable witness. So the court had no alternative but to accept his evidence."

Simpson went on making excuses, all of which lacked conviction. With every second that passed, and with 617 regarding him with unconcealed hatred, Simpson reverted to a final excuse.

"Don't worry. Things are not definite. There's still hope. The verdict will stand, but not necessarily the sentence. They'll never confirm a death sentence. It has to go through various levels ... Division, Corps, and eventually to the commander-in-chief. And Haig is well-known for his compassion. Nine-tenths of all death sentences are pardoned ... Only the most blatant offenders are ever executed."

617 had had enough of Simpson's bullshit. He lunged forward and grabbed the lapels of the counsel's tunic, his eyes bulging as his temper flared out of control. Despite his lack of inches, and knowing that striking

an officer was a court-martial offence, he shook Simpson like a terrier finishing off a rat.

The sound of their scuffle alerted the military policemen at the rear of the barn and they rushed forward to part the two men. At that moment Sergeant Morgan entered. When he saw what was happening he took control. "Jones!" he yelled in his best parade-ground manner. "Stand fast!"

The discipline of the parade ground clicked in. 617 drew back and stood to attention. Morgan told him to re-join his brother at the table. Then Morgan went over to Simpson. "I'm sorry about that, sir. Fusilier Jones is overwrought. It's best if you just forget it."

"I understand," replied Simpson. "We're all in enough trouble as it is."

"It'll be best to leave them on their own now, sir."

The twins faced each other across the table.

"Oh, Davey, Davey! What have you done now, then boyo?"

Davey started to cry in the silent, pathetic way he always had done when lost and isolated as a toddler, unable to relate to anybody or anything. 617 stretched out an arm and grasped his brother's hand, their fingers interlocking.

"Oh Davey, Davey!"

The process of ratifying the sentence went through a lieutenant-colonel, a brigadier-general, a major-general, a lieutenant-general, and finally Field-Marshal Sir Douglas Haig. It took a few days for the sentence to be confirmed at all levels. There were no recommendations for mercy. The execution of Fusilier D. Jones (618) was set for dawn on the morning of August 25th 1917.

The final night was the worst time.

Captain Simpson was so shattered by the savagery of military discipline and so ashamed of his failure as a defence counsel, that he couldn't face any more. He left for London as quickly as possible. He didn't even investigate the possibility of a little known and rarely used appeal procedure whereby a direct plea for mercy to King George was allowed.

Dozens of men in the Fusiliers sought permission to visit 618 in order to commiserate with him, but the colonel only allowed access to 617, Sergeant

Morgan, and the Padre. The last tried to comfort 618 with a short sermon about accepting the Almighty's will. Then he read psalms and recited numerous prayers. Eventually, 617 tapped him on the shoulder and said: "That's enough, Padre."

"I'll come back later."

"Please don't, Padre. It won't do any good."

The battalion cookhouse put on a special last meal for 618, but he merely shuffled the food around his plate, ate a little of it, and then vomited, leaving one of the regimental policemen to clear up the mess.

Sergeant Morgan sat with him for a time. He knew better than to say anything. After a time he patted 618 affectionately on the shoulder and left.

As Seven Platoon sergeant, Morgan had been ordered to organise the firing squad. He had pleaded to be excused the duty but it did him no good. The only consolation was that he was able to detail a dozen men from other companies, none of whom knew 618. They protested as well, but Morgan took no notice. Someone had to do it and he knew there would never be any volunteers.

The hours crept by. Occasionally one of the regimental policemen peered inside the barn to check that everything was in order. There were no more visitors; no reminiscing or philosophising or flashes of wisdom to bring any relief. Words were pointless. Discussing death had no purpose or solace. Occasionally 617 got up and paced about, only to return to his previous position.

Only twice did 618 speak. "617 …"

"Yes, Davey?"

"I still haven't been able to find a word to rhyme with orange."

"That's because there isn't one."

"There's a pity then, isn't it."

Shortly before dawn, when 618 knew they would soon fetch him, he broke his silence once more. He smiled and said:

> *"There was a young man from the Rhondda,*
> *Of whom his brother couldn't have been fonder.*
> *When his time was nigh,*
> *And he was ready to die*
> *His brother's love gave him plenty to ponder."*

They leaned across the table and embraced.

They were still locked in that embrace, crying on to each other's shoulders, when they came for him.

Sergeant Morgan entered quietly, almost sheepishly. He beckoned 617 to one side. "Everything all right?"

"All right, Sarge? You must be bloody joking ..."

"Steady, boyo," said Morgan. "Don't make things worse than they already are. I know how you feel, but keep your anger for those who deserve it."

"That's one thing for sure, look you! I'll get that bastard Sassoon if it's the last thing I do."

"That's enough! Just keep things dignified for Davey's sake."

617 turned away, fighting to control his anguish. Several seconds passed before he recovered sufficiently to say anything else. "There's one thing Davey has asked for, Sarge. It'll sound daft to you, like. But he wants to keep in contact with me to the very last moment."

Morgan looked puzzled. "That's impossible."

"No, Sarge. All he wants is for us to be in contact. He wants to hold on to a length of string with me holding the other end, keeping it taut so that he knows I'm still there, with him. Just as I've always been. Does that sound daft, Sarge?"

"Not at all. I'll get it organised."

"I won't be able to watch, so I'll be round the back, in the court yard."

"Right ..."

"It'll have to be a long length of string. It'll be like a life-line ... It'll help him to get through it."

"I understand."

As dawn broke everything was organised. The stake at which 618 was due to stand was at the back of the school playground, set against a thick brick wall, lined by sandbags. Morgan ruled that there should be no restraining straps. He wasn't going to bind him up like a criminal. Twelve reliable men were lined up as the firing squad. Their rifles were fresh out of the armoury, eleven loaded with blank cartridges and one with a bullet. None of them knew who had the rifle with the bullet, although the unfortunate man was bound to realise because of the rifle's recoil. Morgan ordered that once the shooting was over it was never to be mentioned again.

Also in attendance was Second-Lieutenant Meredith of the South Wales Borderers. He was in command of the proceedings, responsible for a successful execution. It was his task to finalise matters if the condemned man was not killed outright. Standing beside him was an army doctor whose job it was to certify that the prisoner was dead.

618 was marched out of the barn and into the school yard by a corporal, flanked by escorts. There was the usual shouting and stamping of feet. Sergeant Morgan blind-folded 618 and stood him against the stake. He then placed the end of a length of string in his hand. He closed 618's hand over it and squeezed his fist affectionately. He gave the other end of the string to the corporal who marched round to the back of the yard and handed it to 617.

Morgan waited until the string jerked and became taut. Then he took his place at one end of the firing squad. He stood to attention. He waited for a second to make sure everything was settled. Then he shouted the final orders.

"Firing squad! Firing squad, ready!" He paused momentarily. "Firing squad, take aim!"

Twelve rifles were raised and held steady.

"FIRE!"

Twelve shots rang out.

Jones 618 dropped to the ground, shot in the stomach. The string connecting him to his brother remained taut.

The doctor hurried forward. "He's still alive." He turned to the subaltern in the South Wales Borderers. "Mr Meredith, do your duty."

"Me?"

"Yes ... You!"

Meredith remained stock still. He showed no signs of removing his revolver from its holster. He was shaking. "I can't shoot him. I just can't. You shoot him."

"I'm a doctor. I don't take lives. Do your duty, sir."

They started to argue even while 618 lay on the ground in front of them in a foetal position, his blood seeping over the yard. He was pulling on the string with all the strength he had left. He was trying to crawl along its length calling out: "Rhys! Rhys!"

The firing squad looked on in horror as the two officers continued to argue. When the doctor remonstrated: "I must be able to certify that he's dead," one man found their callousness so nauseating that he rushed forward, yanked the revolver out of Meredith's holster, and sprinted back to where 618 was sprawled on the ground. Then, at point-blank range, he fired a bullet into the back of 618's head.

The string went slack as it slipped from 618's grasp.

Part Five

Revenge

22

A Spur to Ambition

Siegfried Sassoon took some time to grow accustomed to life at *'Dottyville'*. It was a strange, divided establishment. Many men were in a pitiful condition, stuck in a twilight world of horrors, but for those less afflicted and on the mend it was more tolerable. For Sassoon, who was perfectly fit, it was more like an hotel than a hospital. He was waited on hand and foot by nurses and the oak-panelled walls and opulent soft furnishing gave it an air of refinement. Nor did he have any worries. He heard of no repercussions with regard to his protest, and the letters he received from Ottoline avoided the subject altogether, being too preoccupied with love.

It seemed to Sassoon that his protest had been futile. It might just as well never have happened.

Within a few days Sassoon was given a private room on account of his room-mate - one of the more afflicted inmates - suffering from chronic nightmares in which he not only cried out orders and warnings but would occasionally jump out of bed, scream, "Charge, fellows!" and collide with the nearest piece of furniture. That would wake him up and he would turn to Sassoon and say: "Sorry about that, old boy ..."

Sassoon's new room was snug and comfortable and he was able to spend hours in privacy, writing poetry at an antique bureau. Later, in bed, he read either a Thomas Hardy novel or Masefield poems by the light of an expensive bedside lamp.

The grounds of Craiglockhart were expansive with terraced patios and plenty of rolling lawns melding into woodlands. It even had a flat, closely-mown lawn which Sassoon found ideal for practicing golf shots. To start with, things were made all the better when a subaltern in the Argyle and Sutherland Highlanders volunteered to be his caddy and retrieved the balls for him; an ideal arrangement until the Scotsman presented Sassoon with an invoice for five guineas at the end of the month, a sure sign that despite its qualities Craiglockhart justified Sassoon's sobriquet of *'Dottyville'*.

Captain Rivers, Sassoon's psychiatrist, treated him as a visitor rather than a patient. He knew there was nothing wrong with him, that he had been foisted upon him as a patient as a matter of convenience, so he allowed him to come and go as he pleased, whether it was to play golf on one of the many local courses, or to go into Edinburgh to wander around the town without any restrictions, other than to return by 'lights-out'. His treatment-sessions with Captain Rivers took place every other day, but these were never more than conversations between two men who were on a par intellectually. Their views on the war were diametrically opposed but instead of accepting their differences and leaving it at that, they argued politely, with Sassoon refusing to retract his protest, despite being urged to do so.

Dr Rivers took his meals with the inmates and he usually sat opposite Sassoon so that they could carry on with their argument. Other patients listened keenly but never offered opinions, although one or two laughed occasionally if either Rivers or Sassoon scored a good point. One of them liked nothing better than to cry out: "Touché!" but it was impossible to tell which side of the argument he favoured.

Sassoon, having previously suffered hallucinations, had great sympathy for his fellow inmates. He understood the ordeals they had endured and the need for a hospital like Craiglockhart never escaped him. As he watched the worst cases wandering around in confusion, or saw men behaving in a bizarre manner, or causing disturbances in the middle of the night, he was proud that he had tried to bring it all to an end with his protest.

Some of the inmates were beyond help, destined to spend the rest of their lives incarcerated in a Home, but others responded to treatment and were well on the way to recovery, destined to be sent back to the front. These men played chess and draughts and other board games, and had art and handicraft lessons, and contributed to the Craiglockhart Monthly Magazine.

Robert Graves visited Sassoon on several occasions and they wined and dined at the Caledonian Hotel on Princes Street, opposite Edinburgh Castle. The Grill Room was always crowded with staff officers. Like Sassoon's poetic characters (*scarlet majors fierce and bold and out of breath)* they had very healthy appetites. So did Graves and Sassoon and of all the places where they wined and dined during their service the Caledonian was the best.

Every morning Sassoon received a letter from Lady Ottoline. Her output was prolific and she displayed great skill by reiterating how much she loved him without ever repeating herself word for word. She specialised in ringing the changes with flowery phrases and purple patches, so much so that although they often verged on the ridiculous, he found them quaint and amusing, a type of superior fan mail. In particular he loved the way she kept asking for more of his illustrations and he took to heart her insistence that whilst at Craiglockhart he should devote himself entirely to his writing.

He often re-read her letters and then recalled the long conversations they enjoyed as they'd wandered the lawns of Garsington, especially her plans to create an arts commune. Indeed, the more he looked back on his visits to Garsington the more he came to value her many kindnesses, ranging from introductions to cultured men and women to the personal care she lavished upon him during his convalescence. Now, he felt ashamed of the cruel way Graves and he had teased her when they were in barracks at Litherland. Her generosity had deserved a lot better.

He often thought of inviting her to visit him at Craiglockhart but he kept putting it off, knowing that if he did she was bound to regard it as an invitation to become lovers, and despite all she had done for him he still wasn't sure that he was ready for that. Not that his reservations were as entrenched as they had been. He was wavering, greatly influenced by Robert Graves's disclosure after a good dinner at the Caledonian that he was considering marrying a young girl called Nancy Nicholson.

At first Sassoon was appalled. He saw it as a betrayal. Then it set him thinking about his own situation. Graves's argument in favour of a heterosexual relationship was convincing. There had to be more to life than flirting with every good-looking young bloke he encountered. Such affairs were inevitably transitional, whereas marriage had a firmer purpose in life with the prospect of an offspring.

This fundamental dilemma worried Sassoon. He felt he had reached the stage in life where he needed to make a decision one way or the other. It even began to affect his writing and he was forced to admit that if he came down in favour of being conventional, then Lady Ottoline would be an ideal early partner; someone with whom he could feel his way forward, a sort of transitory stop-gap while he learnt the ropes and decided once and for all what his true role was in life. After all, her feelings towards him were indisputable and there would be no complications, no rampaging husband or jealous lovers. He could treat it as a carefree adventure, just as she was always urging him. It would simply be a matter of inviting her to Edinburgh, booking in at the Caledonian, investing in a few stiff whiskies, and then getting on with it, trusting that natural instincts would guide him. If it didn't fulfil his expectations, nothing would be lost.

A main feature of Sassoon's sojourn at Craiglockhart was his meeting with Wilfred Owen. He kept Ottoline fully informed about their encounter and told her that Owen was a meek little subaltern in the Manchester Regiment who was overawed by meeting a real, published poet. He had no way of knowing, of course, that Owen was destined to become Britain's most renowned war poet, and that their meeting would have even greater significance than his encounter with Robert Graves over two years before.

Owen was already a patient at Craiglockhart when Sassoon arrived. He was suffering from shell-shock, but within his regiment he was considered lucky not to have been charged with cowardice. Only his rank had saved him. As part of his treatment at Craiglockhart he was editor of the hospital's monthly magazine and, as such, he was always on the lookout for suitable people to contribute to it. When he heard that Sassoon had been admitted he was delighted, having watched his progress as a poet with great interest and admiration.

It was sometime before Owen plucked up enough courage to introduce himself. A mystique surrounded Sassoon, an aura of distinction. His tall, athletic figure attracted attention and being fit and mentally unscathed, and eager to argue with Rivers rather than be lectured by him, put him in a class of his own, a man who had had the guts to defy the army and the government with a protest many considered to be fully justified. Then, of course, there was his poetry. None of them, apart from Owen, had ever read any of his poems, but a published poet was automatically a man of substance. As for his kit, that was already legendary. He arrived at

Craiglockhart with so many trunks and kit bags that he seemed all set to embark on a continental grand tour. His golf clubs were the finest any of them had ever seen.

Within hours of arriving he was practising shots and in the weeks to come his devotion to the game gave the inmates who exercised in the grounds something novel to watch. He was keenest on chip shots with a niblick but every now and then, when enough patients had gathered to watch, he would peer into his golf bag, rummage around as though making a major decision, and eventually pull out a driver. He would tee-up, address the ball in a protracted rigmarole, and then smite the ball into the distant trees, a ball lost for ever, but of no account to Sassoon, having achieved his objective of impressing his fellow patients.

Against all this, Owen felt very inferior and it was sometime before he plucked up enough courage to show Sassoon some of his work. Sassoon condescendingly admitted that it showed promise and he agreed to read more. When he read Owens's first draft of *Anthem for Doomed Youth* he accepted, if only to himself at first, that here was a talent of national importance, someone who could rival him in the future.

To suddenly unearth such talent drove Sassoon to greater efforts with his own poetry. He was determined that no one should outshine him. He was convinced that he had been ordained for poetic leadership and he resolved that while he was at Craiglockhart he would compile a major work entitled *Counter-Attack* which Heinemann would make into a best-seller. Now that he was able to shut himself away in his bedroom in perfect peace and quiet he was convinced that he was about to write what would become the bench-mark for all future war poets.

He disciplined himself and established a daily routine: he rose at 0800 hours, read his correspondence over breakfast, and then got straight down to two hours of writing. At 1100 hours he took a trip down to the main lounge for coffee and a general discussion with Owen; and then he finished the morning off with a session of golf practice, during which Owen followed at his heels like a faithful spaniel, chirruping away about poetry as Sassoon chipped and putted. Only once did Sassoon break his concentration and speak. Whilst he glanced backwards and forwards, judging the power needed for sinking a putt, he asked Owen: "Do you ever write limericks?"

"No, never."

"Could you?"

"I suppose so, if I tried."

"If I suddenly called out the name of a town, could you write a limerick about it straight off, without hesitation?"

"Good gracious no! I spend ages over everything. I never get sudden inspirations. I spend weeks fiddling about with words."

"Same here. Graves as well."

"I expect we're all the same. Why do you ask?"

"I just wondered."

After lunch, Sassoon had another session of writing until afternoon tea on one of the terraces. Suitably refreshed, he devoted himself to his correspondence, keeping in touch with Ross and others, exchanging what he liked to call 'rhyming letters' with Graves, and every now and then dropping Ottoline a reply, very often enclosing one of his latest poems, suitably illustrated, knowing how much she appreciated his artwork.

Most of all he enjoyed having visitors from the outside world: Ross appeared regularly and very often added distinction to his visits by bringing along famous authors, such as Bennett and Wells and Squire. They would dine at the Caledonian and the staff gave them VIP treatment. It was all very congenial. Sassoon often thought it was too good to be true, and that proved to be the case.

23

Lady Ottoline Confesses

Sassoon's first set back came when Wilfred Owen was passed fit for further duty. It meant he would have another spell in France. Sassoon organised a farewell party for him at the Scottish Conservative Club in Edinburgh and in the course of a riotous evening they became hopelessly drunk and infuriated other members by reciting large chunks of what they imagined to be their latest masterpieces. Owen crossed the Channel the next day and was eventually killed a week before the armistice was signed as he led his men across a canal.

The second thing to happen was that Lady Ottoline stopped writing her daily letters. Sassoon couldn't imagine what had gone wrong. Her letters had become a regular part of his life. Each day he scoured the post but still nothing arrived. At first he thought little of it but then he began to worry. His ego missed its daily massage and before long he became very concerned, even alarmed. He wondered if she was ill, or had suffered an accident. He imagined all kinds of things. It occurred to him that he might have said something to wound her in one of his replies. He racked his mind for anything indiscreet he might have written, but concluded that he was innocent, that his replies had been increasingly friendly, with even a few playful and cheeky phrases slipped in to please her with vague hints that he was ready to succumb to her advances.

He wrote to her several times, asking what was amiss, and what had happened to her lovely letters that he enjoyed so much. He got no answers and he imagined his letters piling up on her desk, unanswered. When another letter from her did eventually arrive it was short, sharp and very uncharacteristic, even though she still couldn't resist dousing the envelope in perfume.

It read:

> *"My darling Siggy,*
> *It is imperative that I meet you. Something utterly dreadful has*
> *happened. I am too devastated to write to you about it. I know you say*

*I am not allowed to visit Craiglockhart, but I must see you! So we will
have to meet in Edinburgh. What's happened is something I can only tell
you about face-to-face. Please book me in at an hotel as soon as
possible and advise.
Love, as ever,
Ottoline.*

He booked adjoining rooms on the 1st floor of the Caledonian Hotel. He
wrote to let her know he was expecting her and he made a point of
mentioning the adjoining rooms, leaving her to draw her own conclusion.

Then, for two days, he waited for another letter, but nothing came,
adding to the mystery. All he could imagine was that Phillip had at last
been certified insane, or that Bertrand Russell had gone too far at one of his
lectures and been arrested for subversive activities. Whatever it was, he
reasoned that if he was able to lavish sympathy on her it would make the
consummation of their relationship all the smoother.

When he eventually met her at the Waverley Railway Station he hardly
recognised her. She looked dreadful, at least five years older and dressed
more outrageously than ever, her most audacious touch being a sombrero-
style hat. Their greeting was cordial but no more. He had never known her
so restrained. She was determined their eyes should not meet and as they
left the station she avoided taking his hand. They walked to the Caledonian
as though they were strangers. They booked in and were taken up to their
adjoining rooms. No sooner had the porter settled her luggage, accepted
his tip, and closed the door, than Ottoline began to talk. She didn't even
bother to remove her sombrero. She sat on the edge of the double bed while
he pulled up one of the easy-chairs to be close to her. He grew more
nervous about what might have happened.

"This protest of yours, Siggy ..."

"Our protest," he reminded her playfully. "Others were involved as well
as me."

"Very well then, our protest. I'm afraid it's had the most disastrous
consequences. What's happened is truly awful ..."

"What, for heaven's sake?"

"Do you remember that you once told me all about the men in your
platoon?"

"Of course."

"There were twins. You told me that one of them was an autistic savant who could remember thousands of rhyming words?"

"That's right … Jones 618. What about him?"

"He's been shot."

"Oh no! Poor old 618 …"

She said nothing else, just watched grief register on his face.

"Poor old 618," he said again. "That's really awful."

He thought about the hours they'd spent together in their dugout, hours he would never forget; hours in which their awful surroundings were forgotten amid 618's stories of the Rhondda and his limericks in response to Sassoon calling out the names of Welsh towns. He was about to explain all this to Ottoline, but he could see she was in no mood for his reminiscing. He looked at her enquiringly, wondering what had made her come all the way up from Garsington. Not just to tell him about 618's death, surely? She had never even met him.

"He wasn't just shot, Siggy. He was shot by his own men."

"An accident?"

"No, no! He was executed. Shot by a firing squad."

"Good God! Whatever for?"

"For supporting your protest."

"My protest? Our protest."

"All right. Our protest." Ottoline stretched forward and grasped his hands, seeking comfort. "Siggy, we are supposed to be pacifists. We're against the taking of life. Life is sacred, every single one. That's the whole point of pacifism. Don't kill! But because of your protest they ended up shooting this poor, wretched young man. It makes a mockery of all we've been trying to achieve. You can't oppose all killing by getting someone executed. Pacifists aren't entitled to sacrifice people for their cause."

Sassoon was slow to respond, genuinely puzzled. He was so taken-aback that the whole thing seemed totally surreal, utterly bizarre. In his mind's eye he saw 618 on his stool. He heard him rattling off more limericks. He visualised it all so vividly that he was left nonplussed. He just sat there in bewilderment as Ottoline rambled on about pacifism, sobbing in her distress. Eventually, he stopped her, desperate for a proper explanation.

"Ottoline, for God's sake! Try to control yourself. Never mind about pacifism. Just tell me what happened. And for heaven's sake take your hat and coat off and settle down. I'll call room service for some drinks."

He managed to calm her and a waiter soon arrived with large brandies. She grabbed one and gulped it down, making her body shudder. He put an arm about her shoulders and held her tight until certain she was in a fit state to explain things properly.

She started by telling him that in the House of Commons her husband Phillip was very active in demanding details from the War Office about the number and nature of General Field Courts-Martial on the western front. He and his colleagues were worried by rumours of executions. After great pressure from all sides of the House, the Secretary of State for War made a statement. The figures he gave the House were horrendous. Over two hundred men had already been executed. Among the information made available to MPs was the case of Fusilier Jones. It caught the attention of Phillip Morrell because of his regiment, the Royal Welch Fusiliers, the same as Sassoon's.

"Up to now all executions have been hushed-up," said Ottoline. "With executed men they even send telegrams to the next of kin telling them that the man had 'died in the course of doing his duty'."

"But how did 618 get into trouble in the first place?" demanded Sassoon.

"How? You should know ..."

"Me? Why me?"

"Because he was one of those on your list to be sent *Fellowship* pamphlets. You should never have involved him. Then none of this would have happened. Don't you remember putting him on your list?"

"Yes, you're right. I remember."

'Ebbw Vale' flashed into Sassoon's mind, his challenge to 618. He'd never given it another thought, but when he racked his memory he realised that it had been among the large bunch of letters he'd sent unsealed to Russell, ready for him to insert his pamphlets as they became available, and then post them off direct.

He dreaded what he would hear next.

Ottoline went on to explain how 618 had been so excited at receiving a letter from him that he had pinned the *Fellowship* flyer on the company notice board and how this led to his court-martial. She told how 618 had been cleared of displaying seditious material since he was merely obeying an order."

"So why all the fuss if he was cleared?"

"Because they searched all his kit and found a whole lot of limericks and poems ... And these were a very different story. Some of the poems were highly seditious and were exactly the same as the poems quoted on the pamphlets which he'd pinned on the notice board. And since all the poems they'd found in his kit were in his handwriting they assumed Jones to be the author. Was 618 in the habit of making copies of your poems?"

"Yes, he did it all the time. He hoarded them."

"That's what the defence counsel claimed. He even tried to call you as a witness. He wanted to prove beyond doubt that you wrote the poems, not Jones. But he was told that because you are in a mental hospital your evidence would not be admissible. You would have been classified as an 'idiot' witness."

"What a bloody cheek! Anyhow, what's that got to do with it? There's nothing wrong with my poems. Some may have been critical, even downright disrespectful, as rude as hell about staff officers, but I've never published anything in the least seditious. Nothing that could remotely justified a death sentence."

Ottoline paused, gathering her thoughts. She had no clear idea of how to explain what had happened without putting herself in a terrible light, making her responsible for everything. She edged around the truth.

"Unfortunately, Siggy, when the defence counsel put Jones in the witness box, he asked Jones to make it clear that he hadn't written the poems. But instead, Jones astounded everyone by claiming sole authorship of all the poems found in his kit. And however hard the counsel tried to make him tell the truth, he stuck to his claim that he was the original author. And being under oath he had to be believed."

"Why on earth would Jones claim that?"

"Phillip has been in touch with the defence counsel and it seems there were two reasons. First and foremost to exonerate you from any blame, and secondly because Jones thought he would merely get a jail sentence which would get him out of any more service in the trenches."

"And for that they shot him!"

"Yes."

"They shot him instead of me?"

"Yes ..."

"Ottoline, this is sheer nonsense! Why should anyone give a damn who wrote the poems? There has never been anything wrong with my poems, for God's sake! None of them has ever had anything to do with my protest. None of them have been in the least mutinous."

Ottoline stood up and went over to the fireplace. She stared down into the empty grate. She had to confess to him, but she couldn't do it while facing him. "Siggy, do you remember writing to me once with what you called your avant garde poems with your lovely illustrations? One of them was called *The Victim*, about a sniper? And two others, *The Warning* and *Wake up to Reality?*"

"Yes, of course I do."

"Well, you obviously weren't to know, but those were the poems Russell used on the pamphlets. And the defence counsel said it was '*The Victim*' that condemned 618 out of hand."

"But none of those poems have ever been published ..."

"I know."

"They were never even meant for publication."

"I know."

"I wrote them just for you - I told you that."

"I know."

"No one in their right mind would ever have published them."

"I know."

"Then how come they were quoted on the pamphlets?"

Ottoline couldn't reply, even though the truth was obvious.

"Answer me, woman!"

Her voice was muffled, hardly audible. "I gave them to Bertie ..."

"Why?"

"For the cause."

"Well you had no bloody right to."

"I know I didn't."

"Then why the hell did you?"

"Because they were so brilliant. And as soon as Bertie saw them he said they were just what we needed. That their impact would be enormous."

"Impact! Who the hell cares about impact? When we met to discuss my protest we spent hours making it reasonable and ambiguous. Not to overstep the mark. Christ, *The Victim,* calls for outright surrender ..."

"I know ..."

"And you gave *it* to Russell to use?"

"Yes, but I had no idea they would ever end up at your regiment. I had no idea that you'd put Jones on your list. And when I gave the poems to Bertie I insisted that your name should not be put to them. No one would ever have known who wrote them if this man Jones hadn't made copies of them. How was I to know he made copies of everything you wrote?"

"Balls! The authorship would have been bound to come out. Sooner or later you or Russell would have let it slip, or someone would recognise my style. Things like that always get out."

For a few moments he stared at her, full of hate. Then he spoke quietly but venomously: "My God, I do believe you did this out of spite. Pure, malicious spite! 'Hell hath no fury like a woman scorned'."

"Siggy, how can you say that?"

"Because it's true and you know it."

"It's not. I swear it's not. I had no way of knowing what had gone on between you and this man Jones."

The intensity of her tears increased. They tumbled down her cheeks. Then she fell on her knees and beseeched him for forgiveness, but her grovelling simply sickened him.

"You stupid bloody bitch!"

"Siggy!"

"How else do you expect me to react? Those poems would be enough to get anyone shot. A lunatic would never have published *The Victim!* No wonder they shot him. Do you understand what you have done, woman?"

"Siggy, I'm sorry ..."

"Sorry! Good God, you as good as pulled the trigger on him. And you call yourself a pacifist ... How could you ever have been so fucking stupid?"

"Siggy, I'm sorry ... I'm so desperately sorry."

Sassoon stormed out of the room, slamming the door behind him. He sprinted along the corridor, down the stairs two at a time, and out on to Princes Street. He walked its length twice and then hailed a taxi and returned to Craiglockhart. He spent the rest of the night lying on his bed fully dressed, thinking about what had happened. He kept jerking up into a sitting position and crying out, "Oh, God!"

He had reoccurring visions of 618 standing at the stake and it made his mind spin in turmoil. Nothing any longer made sense. 618's death left him totally stunned, floundering out of his depth. It destroyed his judgement and he cursed himself for ever protesting. It had been catastrophic, a pathetic cock-up which had achieved nothing. Everyone had told him it would be a disaster. Yet he, a mere second-lieutenant, a lowly platoon commander, a wart, the lowest form of life in the poor bloody infantry, thought he knew better. Just who the hell did he think he was?

Later, he calmed down a little, but even so he couldn't credit how naïve he had been to allow himself to be manipulated by the pacifists, the likes of Murry, Russell and the Morrells. All of them were head-in-the-clouds liberals, free-thinkers who chased impossible ideals. They didn't have the faintest idea of what real life was like; hypocrites who called themselves humanists but who were prepared to sacrifice men to promote their cause. Sassoon suddenly realised how they must have rejoiced when they saw him coming: such a gullible young idiot, so greedy for fame, so ripe for exploitation.

As for Lady Ottoline Morrell, the conniving bitch! Her feelings towards him had obviously had precious little to do with love. Now, he saw her outrageous flirting as a façade, inspired by her loyalty to her lover Russell and their pacifist cause; a so-called Lady who was willing to prostitute herself for the her cause. He wondered how he had ever thought of laying a finger on her.

Yet however much he blamed others, he was well aware of the truth. His protest was the root cause of everything. Without it, none of it would have happened. Worst of all, he now realised that he had made his protest out of vanity, the desire to stir things up, the longing to be noticed and admired, to cause a sensation. He had ignored the advice of his friends and comrades. He hadn't even bothered to evaluate the possibility of the wholesale chaos and carnage that would inevitably have followed if there had been mutinies in the army.

He recalled how he had responded to Strachey's taunts by boasting of his willingness to lay down his life for others; yet never in a millions years would he have been prepared to sacrifice anyone else's life, least of all an innocent and unique youngster like 618. Now, he would never be able to forgive himself for having brought about the death of someone of whom he was so fond and held in such high esteem.

His mind rambled on, a wild kaleidoscope of jumbled thoughts, and he felt as though he was going mad. He knew that for as long as he lived he would be obsessed by guilt and self-hate. Only death would ever bring an end to his torment.

If he'd had his revolver handy he would have put an end to it all there and then. It would have been easy, quick and so thoroughly deserved.

He slept for a few hours and at dawn he woke to a stark choice between suicide and paying due penance by going back to France. He decided on the latter. Suicide would be cowardly, a capitulation, whereas going back to the front and embarking on every mad-cap scheme that cropped up would be positive and might even do some good. In the trenches he would have a chance to expiate his guilt. He needed to suffer with all the others; to go back and re-establish agape love with his men; to serve them and lead them and be ready for his final comeuppance; to embrace death with them like the true soldier he had once been.

24
Another Medical Board

Sassoon needed fresh air and vigorous exercise. He had an urge to stride about open spaces. Even though he had made his decision to return to France, he needed solitude to cogitate over the matter. After breakfast he ordered a taxi and went to his favourite golf course a few miles to the north of Edinburgh. He played eighteen holes and as he progressed around the course his mind was probing the precise involvement of Lady Ottoline. She was obviously at the heart of things, but he was beginning to wonder whether her actions had been as deliberate and malicious as he had first thought. She was certainly justified in saying that he should never have involved Jones 618, and no doubt she had been manipulated by Bertram Russell. His evil influence was stamped over everything

He dreaded that during his row with Ottoline his judgement had become warped and he had been unfair on her. It had certainly been an extraordinary and dramatic meeting. One moment he was steeling himself to sleep with her and the next he was cursing her viciously, then storming out and leaving her to pay the hotel bill.

There were also other things that puzzled him. He couldn't understand why 618 was so confident that he would only be jailed and not get a death sentence, and why hadn't the defence counsel made greater efforts to nail down the real authorship of the poems? It must surely have been possible? And where was 617's evidence on all this?

Sassoon longed to know the exact details of what had happened.

Once back in the clubhouse he perched on a bar stool and sank two quick whiskies. Then he phoned for a taxi to take him back to Craiglockhart. It was only when the taxi driver tried to be funny and said: "Going there to get yourself sorted out, sir?" that it dawned on Sassoon that that was precisely what he needed to do. He needed to see Rivers: he was just the man to help him.

As soon as he reached Craiglockhart he barged into the doctor's outer office and confronted the elderly nurse who guarded Rivers from intruders and time-wasters. He demanded to see Rivers right away but she said it was out of the question. He was already seeing another patient. Angry words followed and eventually Rivers burst into the room to find out what was happening. He told Sassoon in no uncertain terms to calm down and to behave himself, and to come back the following morning when his next session was due.

Rivers was so well-mannered that when Sassoon entered his office the following morning he rose enthusiastically from his chair to greet him. He shook his hand and invited him to take a seat. "Good golf yesterday morning?"

"Excellent ... One of my better days. My handicap will have to be changed if I'm not careful."

"The rate you're going you'll end war as a scratch golfer. Which reminds me. The gardeners have asked if you would be kind enough to replace the divots you keep taking out of their lawn."

"Certainly. But that won't be a problem for much longer, Doc. I've decided it's time for me to leave *Dottyville* and go back to France."

"Really? *You've* decided ..."

"Yes. I'd like you to arrange a medical board for me."

Rivers was infuriated by Sassoon's conceit, his assumption that he could do as he liked, just breeze in and expect everyone to kowtow to him. "So you're ready to retract your protest, are you? What made you change your mind?"

"I haven't changed my mind ..."

"Well you can't leave Craiglockhart until you do. Mr Sassoon, you seem to think you can do as you like. You treat this hospital as a sort of rest camp. I do my best to minimise army discipline but I am not prepared to just let you charge in here and demand to see me. Then tell me what you intend to do. The time has come for you to listen to a few home-truths."

"Home-truths about what?"

"About yourself."

The smile slipped from Sassoon's face. "You know damn all about me."

"I've learned a lot from our discussions. And I have a dossier on you. I know all your movements within your regiment, your leaves, your wounds, your illnesses, and reports from your commanding officers. Are you still an anarchist?"

Sassoon laughed bitterly. "Buffalo Bill!"

"Whatever you call him, he's a very shrewd judge of character. And what he's written gives me a very clear picture."

"Oh, really?"

"Yes, really ... Mad Jack and all that. You've only ever spent a few weeks in the front trenches but to read your poems anyone would think you've spent half your life in them. And your poems are full of snide remarks about the gluttony of staff officers, but you've enjoyed as many gourmet dinners as any of them. You even have a special table held in readiness for you at the Caledonian."

"There's no harm in that."

"I suppose not. But I have never come across a front-line officer who has spent so much time in England, either on leave or convalescing. Nine months suffering from diarrhoea. How you managed that I'll never know. It shows initiative, I suppose, if you're that way inclined. Anyhow, why are you suddenly so keen to go back to France?"

Sassoon glared back at Rivers, amazed that a man he had come to regard as a friend had turned hostile. It made him sullen and despondent. "I have a reason..."

"Really?"

"Yes, really ..."

"Nothing to do with the Fusilier Jones, I take it? The man they executed for trying to cause a mutiny?"

"How do you know about that?"

"The Member of Parliament, Lees-Smith. He's an old friend of mine. He told me what happened. He said there is a theory going around the House that they shot Jones in lieu of you, simply as an example to all other troops. So he advised me to keep you here. To on no account let you go back to France."

"Why not?"

"For your safety, of course."

"They think someone is liable to put a bullet in my back?"

"I hardly think so, but I wouldn't put it past them to give you all the dirty work."

"By which you mean suicidal missions?"

"Something like that."

"Good! That's just what I want. And tell me, is the case of Fusilier Jones common knowledge?"

"Oh no. The government puts an embargo on news of executions. The press aren't allowed to mention them for the sake of the relatives. They don't even know their men have been executed. They're sent telegrams saying that they died doing their duty."

Ottoline's words exactly, thought Sassoon. Then, more to himself than Rivers, he added: "It wasn't my fault ... I had no idea of what was going on."

"Really? I rather thought you'd take that line. You're always the same, Sassoon. You assume you can do anything you like and get away with it. It's time you grew up. Being spoilt rotten since birth is why you were unable to cope with Marlborough and Cambridge. And why you didn't last in the Yeomanry. You suffer from an explosive mixture of immaturity and sexual frustrations."

"Oh good God," laughed Sassoon. "Surely you're not going to drag Freud into this?"

"Why not? Being sexually repressed can lead to all kinds of things. The need for the limelight, having everyone talking about you, rash decisions and acute feelings of disquiet."

Sassoon had no intention of being drawn into a Freudian discussion. "Are you going to arrange a medical board for me or not?"

"Why should I?"

"Because of the torment I'm suffering. I have to go back to France. And the men need officers they trust and love."

"Hardly love, Sassoon. Respect, maybe, but claims of love are a bit exaggerated, surely?"

"I don't mean physical love. I mean agape love - love between men. My men would do anything for me, follow me anywhere ..."

"In the past that may have been true, but certainly not after your protest."

"Nonsense! They still need me. And anyhow, I need them even more. I have to get back there to share their suffering."

Rivers made no immediate reply. He looked hard at Sassoon, his opinion of him shifting. Rivers knew that the hallmark of a good officer was one who was willing to put his men first, to share their dangers and sufferings without any concern for his own comfort or safety.

"Did you know the Fusilier who was executed?" asked Rivers.

"He was my platoon runner. We shared a dugout."

"How long for?"

"Two years or so."

"Was he a pacifist?"

"Good God, no. He was autistic. An autistic savant."

"Then why did he become involved?"

"It's a long story, but he had a unique way with words, memorising rhyming words especially, which meant we became very close. And eventually he took the blame for some outspoken poems I wrote. He made copies of them and then, without me knowing, he claimed them as his at the court-martial in order to shield me. And that led to him being found guilty and then executed."

"And that makes you feel guilty?"

"Of course it bloody does! Christ, fancy you asking me that. It not only makes me feel guilty but as humble as hell as well. Despite all his disadvantages, Jones had the courage to sacrifice himself for someone else. 'Greater love hath no man than to lay down'..."

"St John, chapter ..."

"I know that, Rivers. Don't patronize me."

Sassoon's rebuke brought silence.

"Are you still a pacifist?" asked Rivers at length.

"Of course not. I never have been, as you well know. Pacifists are against killing anyone - or supposed to be. Anyhow, I'm sick to death with arguing the toss the whole time. The time for arguments is over. I simply have to go back to France. Going back into the trenches is my only chance."

"Your only chance of what?"

"Of being able to live with myself."

The two men sat there, motionless, staring at each other.

Eventually Sassoon asked: "Do you have the remotest idea of what I'm saying?"

"I understand perfectly."

"You do?"

"Yes."

"So do I get my medical board or don't I?"

"Yes, you do."

"Despite no retraction?"

"Despite no retraction."

Rivers stood up, indicating that the interview was over. He smiled, a broad, beaming smile which he rarely shared with others. "It will take a week or so to arrange things. But I'll make sure there are no problems. In the meantime, don't forget about replacing those divots."

"Oh yes, the divots! Anyhow, thanks."

"Don't mention it, Mr Sassoon. And rest assured that all of us here at Craighlockhart will be glad to see the back of you."

"Ditto!" said Sassoon.

They laughed, knowing that the bond between them was restored to the extent that they could exchange insults like old-school friends without taking offence. They shook hands and then Rivers watched Sassoon stride out of the room. He listened to him as he apologised once again to the nurse for his bad manners of the previous day. Only Sassoon would have bothered to do it for a second time thought Rivers.

Instead of returning to his desk, Rivers went over to his bay window and stared out across the gardens where men were taking exercise, either wandering around aimlessly, or being pushed about in their wheelchairs. How ironic, he thought. He spent months treating these men, coaxing them back to normality, and then, as soon as he had succeeded, he sent them straight back from whence they'd come to start all over again. Some would be lucky and get a home posting, but most of them would return to France, there to be driven mad again or most likely killed.

Rivers had never known anyone more certain to be killed than Sassoon.

Indeed, Sassoon was the only man Rivers had ever encountered who made it quite clear that he wanted to be killed. He longed for self-sacrifice, to die serving and suffering with his men.

Exactly a week later Sassoon attended his medical board and it went smoothly. He answered questions about his health and assured the board that he no longer had hallucinations and that he slept soundly without nightmares. No one mentioned his protest and he was passed fit for duty.

A sizable crowd of patients and staff saw him off amid much joking about his luggage and how he wouldn't need his golf clubs where he was going. The Craiglockhart charabanc then took him south to his old stomping ground at Litherland to await a posting.

25

Under Threat

The chances of Sassoon and Jones 617 ever meeting again were remote. 617 prayed for the day, but Sassoon never even considered the possibility.

The Royal Welch Fusiliers now had 25 battalions on active service, even though some were so short of men that they were temporarily non-operational and reforming, men being transferred from one battalion to another. Also, the war was forever spreading across the world with battalions of the Fusiliers now serving in places such as Mesopotamia, Egypt, Palestine, Italy and Ireland, as well as the western front.

After his brother's execution, Jones 617 was soon dismissed as Lieutenant Latimer's batman. He failed to carry out even basic duties properly and his general behaviour was so sour and disagreeable that Latimer found it quite impossible to live in the same dugout with him. 617 went back to his previous section. He had no friends there. They had long since been killed or badly wounded; but he didn't much care. Friends, who in the early days had been so important, no longer mattered. Quite a few of the reinforcements weren't even Welsh, just hoi polloi drafted in from the remnants of various English county regiments.

Morgan was still platoon sergeant. In all but name he ran the platoon. Mr Latimer only left his dugout when necessary. Otherwise he spent his time reading and re-reading his wife's letters and eating the Welsh cakes she sent him.

When the battalion went back into reserve, Morgan tried hard to revitalize 617 but he was wasting his time. When he suggested that he should reform the company choir, 617 simply shrugged his shoulders and walked off. All he did was mooch around the company lines, carrying out orders grudgingly, doing just enough to stay out of trouble. He knew all the new-comers in the company despised him. He was, after all, the twin brother of a proven mutineer; a man who had been found guilty of collaborating with civilian pacifists; a man who sought to condemn out of hand all the efforts of those who had already died or been so horribly wounded.

On the rare occasions when Jones 617 tried to justify his brother as a lad who had been misled by others, they turned away, leaving 617 exasperated and isolated, hating all the more those who had been responsible.

Sergeant Morgan used his influence to get him some leave, a whole fortnight back in the Rhondda, but he refused it. How could he go back home without Davey? How could he face them all when he'd failed to fulfil his promise to bring him back safely? How could he walk up Tip View Terrace with all the neighbours pulling back their lace curtains to stare at him as he trudged up the hill, his other half missing? How could he look his Ma and Da in the eye and not tell them that Davey had been shot by a firing squad, having sacrificed himself for the sake of a posturing, upper-crust Englishman.

So instead of going on leave, 617 wrote a long letter to his Ma and Da. Although he suspected that they would ultimately learn the truth, he told them the same lie as the war office had told them in their official telegram: that Davey had died bravely, doing his duty.

When his Da replied it was with sadness and dignity, expressing deep sorrow that their beloved Davey, who had always been such a joy to them, had gone the same way as so many other brave young lads from the Rhondda. Then, with irony 617 could hardly bear, his Da derived comfort by saying that Davey had at least died fighting for a noble cause.

The worst thing for 617 was that he knew in his heart that his Ma and Da would blame him. They would never say so, not even to each other, but they would blame him nevertheless. And they were right to do so. He had failed on all counts. It was madness for them to have enrolled in the army in the first place, and an even greater mistake to allow him to be influenced and misled by Sassoon. He should never have allowed Davey to think that just because he could rhyme words that he had any real understanding of what he was doing. He should have warned him that fraternization between officers and other ranks only ever brought trouble.

Now, Jones 617 was biding his time. He had no idea when or where he would meet Sassoon again, but he was certain that his chance would come.

The moment would arrive when he had Sassoon in his sights, and when that moment came he would not miss. He would murder the bastard without any compunction, inspired and justified by the most basic of all motives: an eye for an eye and a tooth for a tooth; and he would do it in circumstances which made him look blameless. He had no intention of swinging for Sassoon. He would make sure that everyone thought it was an accident, a blue on blue, or friendly fire, just a sad case of a trigger-happy sentry.

The only person who had any idea of what was on his mind was Sergeant Morgan. That didn't matter. He'd known Morgan since childhood. They'd been playmates together and he knew Morgan wouldn't take sides or cause trouble. He would sit on the fence, keep his nose clean, and thereby enhance his chances of promotion.

26

Suicide Wish

Sassoon's desire to get back to France as quickly as possible met with every imaginable frustration. For a month it seemed that the army didn't know what to do with him, or perhaps had forgotten all about him. He sat around at Litherland with no duties, sharing a hut with several junior officers who had recovered from shell-shock, although none of them had been at Craiglockhart. They were a dull, miserable lot who did little but lie on their beds and stare at the ceiling. None of them played golf, which meant that Sassoon spent solitary hours each day hacking his way around the local links.

In the evenings he revised the poems which he intended to be part of his master-piece, *Counter Attack,* due to be published by Heinemann. In the stagnant, odorous surroundings of Litherland he found it difficult to concentrate and he produced very little original work. He had further setbacks when his mentors, who usually praised everything he wrote, implored him to make alterations, even to scrap several poems as unfit for publication. Among his severest critics was the publisher William Heinemann. It was a terrible blow to Sassoon's ego and he couldn't help wondering if it came as a result of his protest, as though they were now on the lookout for work which was too contentious to print. Suddenly, he was suspect, being held at arm's length.

Eventually a rumour circulated around Litherland that they were about to go to France, but when the order came through it was a posting to Ireland. Sassoon was bitterly disappointed and during the few weeks he spent in the Limerick area he did little besides join the local hunts and ride about the countryside, finding consolation by killing foxes. He found the Irish hunting fraternity friendly enough but in barracks and the officers' mess there was a strained atmosphere whenever he appeared. Even the recently commissioned officers adopted a very condescending attitude towards him.

They never spoke to him, except when he addressed them directly, and even then all he got was a curt 'Yes' or 'No'.

It made his life so miserable that when he received a letter from Lady Ottoline he was delighted. He opened it eagerly, never having expected to hear from her again after their awful row at the Caledonian Hotel. The row had certainly left its mark on her as well. Her letter was very different to her previous ones. The crazy syntax, the over-elaborate paragraphs, and the flirtatious innuendoes, were all missing. Now, there was only plain English, remorse and appeals for forgiveness. He was so impressed by her acceptance of full responsibility for using his poems, and how she refrained from blaming Bertrand Russell, that his heart softened. It showed true character; someone of impeccable breeding; and he couldn't help thinking that when he came to know all the facts he would see her role in a different light. More than ever, he was convinced that Russell was the true villain.

Twice, Sassoon started to write replies, but on both occasions he faltered and changed his mind. He decided to leave it for a while; to let things simmer. If he eventually got to France and was killed, as he was sure he would be, writing to Ottoline would be pointless. His death would only add to her misery; and if by a miracle he survived, there would be time enough to forget old differences and rekindle her friendship.

Early in February Sassoon received orders that he was to sail from Southampton for Egypt in order to join the 25th Battalion of the Royal Welch Fusiliers serving under General Allenby. On February 8th he reached Alexandria, where he joined the battalion. It was commanded by Lord Kensington, one of the landed gentry who owned enormous stretches of Pembrokeshire. His Lordship and his adjutant, Captain Wintringham Stable, interviewed Sassoon on his arrival in much the same way as Earl March and Captain Blakiston Houston had when he joined the Sussex Yeomanry, and Sassoon knew from their sour expressions that they drew much the same conclusions. The only difference was that Sassoon was now a Captain and a combat veteran with a Military Cross; someone who had to be given a command. He was appointed commander of A Company, but they made it clear that they would keep a close eye on him.

His service in Egypt and Palestine contributed very little to the war effort: sometimes it was nothing but idleness, swimming in the sea or visiting local archaeological treasures like a tourist. At other times he attended a succession of concert parties laid on for the troops, and the nearest he got to combat was long spells of road repairs on the main highway leading to the real war.

Then news came through of a successful German offensive in France. The channel ports and Paris were suddenly at risk and several infantry battalions in the Middle-East, including the 25th Royal Welch Fusiliers, were ordered back to the western front. Sassoon's morale soared. He'd got his way at last and he wrote to Robert Graves that he was going to make the most of the opportunity or die in the attempt. To emphasise his point he made a new will and left Graves a yearly income of £250.0.0.

A few days before the battalion was due to sail from Alexandria, Sassoon had a letter from Dent, asking him to contact the novelist E.M. Forster who was serving in Egypt with the Red Cross. Sassoon was flattered that such an eminent novelist should want to meet him, not realising that it had nothing to do with them being literary figures, but a recommendation from within the inner sanctum of homosexuals. As it happened Lord Kensington made sure that Sassoon was denied the opportunity and his contact with Forster never got beyond an exchange of letters in which Sassoon explained how he loathed his fellow officers. In his final letter to Forster he confided: "The Hun will do for me this time!" Then, after he had posted the letter, he felt he should have explained to Forster that according to their mutual friend, the poet Robert Nichols, there was a plot in the War Office to make sure that once he was in France he'd stay there for good, six foot under.

When the 25th battalion arrived in France they were shunted about for two weeks but they eventually ended up in the Habareq area. Then, in early July, they were ordered to relieve the East Lancashire Regiment in the front line at Saint Floris.

Sassoon was thrilled to be back in the trenches, within hailing distance of the Germans. As a company commander, and one of the few men in the battalion with combat experience, he felt very much in control of things and he had every intention of living up to his old nick-name of Mad Jack. He had only been in their position a few hours when he went over the top in darkness to explore no-man's-land, leaving his platoon commanders and NCOs to settle the men in as best they could.

He arrived back just before dawn with his usual plan of no-man's-land, showing the major shell craters and prominent objects on which they could take their bearings during sorties against the Hun. He was so pleased with the result that he went back to battalion headquarters to give the colonel a report about no-man's-land, the disposition of the German trenches, and the state of their barbed wire.

Lord Kensington refused to see him, so Sassoon left everything with the adjutant, Captain Wintringham Stable. This brought repercussions. Within hours, Sassoon's sketch got back as far as the brigadier and he went berserk at the thought of a company commander venturing into no-man's-land. Later in the day a runner arrived at Sassoon's dugout with a written order, stating that on no account were company commanders to go out into no-man's-land without permission. Sassoon read it and was just about to crumple it up and throw it away when the runner interceded in alarm. "Excuse me, sir. You mustn't do that. Captain Stable said it was to be signed as seen and understood. And that I was to return it to him."

Sassoon shrugged his shoulders. "Just as you like."

He signed the message pad even though he had no intention of taking any notice of it. He was going to command his company his way, not be told what to do by someone sitting in the safety of battalion headquarters.

That same afternoon there was an unexpected development. The runner reappeared and told Sassoon that 60 survivors from the 1st battalion were due to arrive as reinforcements and that ten had been posted to A Company, which would put them back to full strength. Better still, one of them was an officer, Captain Vivian de Sola Pinto, who was to be Sassoon's second-in-command. Another bonus, which pleased Sassoon even more, was that there was a warrant officer among them, none other than Company Sergeant-Major Morgan, recently promoted from sergeant after having been awarded his second DCM for rallying the remnants of the 1st battalion after they'd been reduced to two wounded officers.

Captain Pinto was a bespectacled intellectual who had read English Lit. at Oxford University. He was delighted to serve under Sassoon, being yet another poet. They hit it off right from the start even though Sassoon was unimpressed by Pinto's verses.

Pinto knew of Sassoon's reputation as Mad Jack so he wasn't surprised by his aggressive attitude towards the Hun. He also admired the way Sassoon had already made his company the finest in the battalion. He found Sassoon's methods highly unorthodox, especially his contempt for his superiors and the Nelsonian way he ignored their orders when it suited him.

As Pinto liked to tell people in later years, Sassoon took the company by the scruff of the neck and moulded them into a fine fighting unit, inspiring them by personal example. He did everything expected of him and then a lot more besides. Every night he took out a platoon commander and several of his men on patrols. His mere presence inspired them with keenness and confidence. He demonstrated the importance of patience and the need to stick to basic field craft. He also taught them to use Mills bombs in preference to rifles since bullets went straight over the German trenches, whereas Mills bombs dropped among them and caused havoc. Grenades also made a lot more noise, and noise - Sassoon told them - was a major cause of fear and panic, especially when coming from different directions.

What impressed them most about Sassoon was that when they returned from their patrols he loved to grab something to eat and drink and then go out again, this time with his protégé Corporal Rowlands. Once out there on their own, they treated it as the serious business of the night, locating and then destroying German machine guns.

As a consequence, Sassoon's company became an efficient fighting unit. His men loved him for it, but he got precious little support from his senior officers. At battalion and brigade headquarters they remained highly suspicious of him, knowing perfectly well that he was defying the Brigadier's orders and going into no-man's-land every night. It was left to Captain Pinto to cover up for him, making ingenious excuses for his absences, but he fooled no one. They all knew what Mad Jack was up to.

When CSM Morgan joined at the 25th Battalion in command of the reinforcements he was able to choose which company he served in and he had no hesitation in opting for A Company. Sassoon was the man to serve under, despite his protest and the subsequent court-martial of Jones 618. Having seen every move along the way, Morgan put no direct blame on Sassoon for 618's execution.

He arrived at A Company in darkness and he had some difficulty groping his way down into Sassoon's dugout. The candle-light was poor, and Sassoon's pipe was issuing out so much smoke that for a moment they stared at each other in doubt. Then they greeted each other with cries of joy, delighted to be reunited. Captain Pinto trailed into the dugout a few yards behind Morgan. He watched their reunion with envy and then sat on one of the bunks and listened as they went straight into a stream of reminiscences, laughing at things which weren't funny and pulling each other's legs as though they were schoolboys. Eventually their conversation settled on the court-martial of Jones 618.

"I knew nothing about it until it was all over, when I was in Craiglockhart," said Sassoon. "Even then, I only heard about it second hand, through a friend with contacts in the House of Commons. And when I heard of the poems Jones claimed he had written I was absolutely appalled. Those poems were never meant to see the light of day ... And they wouldn't have if it hadn't been for that bastard Russell."

"What a balls-up, sir," sighed Morgan. "And the defence counsel didn't exactly help things."

"Were you there all the time, Morgan?"

"Yes, sir. I saw and heard it all."

"And what about his brother, Jones 617?" asked Sassoon.

"He's still going strong, sir. He was devastated by the whole thing, especially since he was never allowed to give evidence on 618's behalf."

"Is he still with the 1st Battalion?"

"No, sir."

"What's he up to, then?"

"He's here. One of the reinforcements."

Sassoon couldn't hide his concern. It was something he had never anticipated.

"Don't worry, sir," smiled Morgan. "I made sure he went to another company. He's with B Company so I don't suppose you'll ever run into him."

"But B Company is right alongside us. Should I have a word with him?"

"Lord no, sir. Definitely not! He's like a wounded tiger, best avoided. He sees you as the villain of the piece."

"Me? That's hardly fair. What about Bertrand Russell?"

"It doesn't make any difference now, sir. But don't get involved with 617. The whole thing has made him unstable. He took it very badly."

Later that night, well after midnight, with thick clouds sculling across the moon to a background of insect noises and scurrying rats, Sassoon went on his routine inspection of the company. He did this every night before going out into no-man's-land with Corporal Rowlands. He chatted to them all and reminded them that he and Rowlands would be arriving back from their usual patrol shortly before dawn.

His inspections ended on the right flank of the company where they linked up with B Company. On his third night he was just about to retrace his steps when he saw something very odd. Ahead of him was a short stretch of trench and then the usual sharp bend, or dog's leg, to minimise shell blast; and right smack in the middle of the bend a man was sitting on the firing parapet, his head and shoulders protruding above the trench wall. He was silhouetted against the sky and the flashes of distant shells. It was a crazy position for a man to adopt, just inviting to be hit by a stray bullet or shrapnel. For a moment Sassoon even wondered if the man was part of a German raiding party which had sneaked through their barbed wire. Then he realised it couldn't be. The sharp outline of a British steel helmet was quite clear. Whoever it was, his rifle was raised, aimed straight at him. He even heard the distinctive, metallic clonk of the Lee Enfield bolt action, a bullet being rammed into the chamber.

"Who's that?" demanded Sassoon.

"Who do you think, you bastard?"

"Lower your rifle, 617."

"By all means." He lowered his rifle from his shoulder, but kept it trained on Sassoon at waist level.

"What are you doing? Why aren't you in your company lines?"

"I was waiting for you. I was told you'd be around. They say you're as regular as clockwork. There's something I want to tell you ..."

"What?"

"I'm going to shoot you."

"Really? Now why would you want to do that?"

"You know bloody well why."

"Go on then. Do it. What are you waiting for?"

"I'll do it in my own good time. I'm not going to swing for you, Sassoon. You did for Davey, but you're not bloody well going to do for me as well."

"Nobody is around. There are no witnesses."

"Good old Mad Jack! The fearless warrior. I'll do it, rest assured, but when I'm good and ready. You just sweat on it, you bastard."

"You don't intimidate me, Jones."

"Really! Well you just remember this. Every time you go out on patrol, and especially when you come back in, I'll be watching you ... Just biding my time ..."

617 didn't wait for Sassoon to reply. He jumped down from the firing parapet and made off down the trench to B Company lines. "Watch your step, Sassoon!" he called out as he disappeared.

Sassoon didn't know what to make of the encounter. Did 617 really mean it? Did he have the guts to shoot a man in cold blood? Sassoon didn't doubt that he had it within him to kill Germans in the heat of battle, in a 'them or us' situation, but shooting a fellow Fusilier in cold blood was murder, not an act of war. There was a difference, a very big difference.

The more Sassoon thought about the incident the more convinced he became that 617's threat was real: that he meant exactly what he said and was merely waiting for the right moment. After all, his motivation was obvious enough, maybe even justified.

Sassoon had no intention of taking the matter to a higher authority. Schoolboy ethics had taught him that 'sneaking' was the last thing to do. One sorted out one's own problems. And what did it matter anyhow? Since he didn't give a damn if he died, why should he worry? What did it matter if the satisfaction of killing him went to 617 rather than a German sniper, or machine-gunner, or a distant artillery crew?

As Sassoon reflected on this, the irony of being shot by his own side amused him. It would enhance his reputation and lead him to be mourned and eulogized as a legendary figure. In Sassoon's contorted mind it had a Byronic twist of noble sacrifice.

On July 11th a warning order came through from brigade headquarters for the 25th to prepare for a move into reserve. Usually, units changed over during hours of darkness, but on this occasion it was to be carried out in daylight, making the night of July 12th/13th their last in the position. Lord Kensington called a general meeting of all officers rather than a conventional orders group. He was determined that his orders should not become garbled and misunderstood, and the one order he stressed and repeated ad nauseam, was that on their final night in the line no one - but no one - was to venture into no-man's-land.

"There are very sound reasons for this," he declared. "We must not get involved in fire-fights and suffer more casualties. We want a peaceful night so that in the morning we can slip off in good order. Is that clear to everyone?"

There was a general murmur of assent.

"And is it perfectly clear to you, Captain Sassoon?" asked the colonel sarcastically, knowing it would bring an easy laugh.

"Perfectly, sir," replied Sassoon.

"It means that anyone seen in no-man's-land during the night of the 13th will be regarded as German and be dealt with accordingly. As for the actual change-over, an advance party from the East Surrey Regiment will be with us overnight. Then, at 10:00 hours on the 13th, A Company of the Surreys will take over from our A Company. Then, on the hour, every hour, other companies will change-over in alphabetical order until the change-over is completed. Are there any questions?"

There were none.

The following morning - the 12th - Sassoon experienced the most unnerving moment of his military career. The Germans unleashed a vicious artillery concentration on the two forward companies of the battalion. Sassoon's company was hit the hardest. Everyone took evasive action as shells cascaded down for over an hour. Men squatted in their dugouts and hoped for the best. Sassoon's dugout took three direct hits in quick succession. The first two shells exploded on impact and tore great holes in the roof. Timbers and supporting sandbags imploded and sealed off the entrance. The third shell burst through the remains of the roof. It landed in the middle of the dugout but didn't explode. It demolished the table and chairs and narrowly missed the bunks on which Sassoon and Captain Pinto were lying. The two officers were so stunned by the blast of the earlier explosions, and so affected by the dust and debris that billowed around them, that they didn't realise what had happened. When the atmosphere cleared they saw a large shell protruding from the floor of the dugout like a giant turd. They stared in amazement, convinced that it would explode at any moment; that it would blow them to kingdom-come and reduce them to a few scattered body parts, ready to be shovelled into empty sandbags in the usual way.

Yet the shell still didn't explode. It was a genuine dud, not a delayed-fuse shell, and once the shelling stopped a squad of men led by Morgan worked feverishly at digging out the two officers. They emerged dishevelled and badly shaken.

Sassoon saw their escape as an omen. A man could have only so much luck, and he'd had more than his fair share. The next time he'd be a goner, but what did it matter? He had paid his penance and justified his return to France. Lord Kensington and Stable might not think much of him, but he had created a fine company. He knew it, and his men knew it, and they would forever revere him because of it. That made death acceptable, even a relief, and with his masterpiece *Counter Attack* completed and published it would be a good time to go, just so long as it was a painless death: a single bullet, quick and clean such as Jones 617 seemed to have in mind. He wondered why he didn't get on with it. Why didn't he stop procrastinating and take his revenge and then go back to the Rhondda with pride, knowing that he had meted out due justice?

Sassoon decided to make it easy for him.

An hour or two later, having settled into a fresh dugout, he wrote another of his rhyming letters to Robert Graves. He had shared so many things with Robert that he felt obliged to share his death with him as well. His rhyming letter was plain and simple. It read:

> *"Dear Roberto,*
>> *Today came a visitor from hell,*
>> *No less than a dud Kraut shell.*
>> *Through our roof it tore,*
>> *Serving notice, double sure,*
>> *That death will soon me embrace.*
>> *So I've chosen my time, chosen my place,*
>> *The day's told off --- the 13th in the month of July.*
>> *There steady I'll stand; undaunted, ready to die."*

He called for his runner, sealed the envelope, and told him to deliver it to the post-corporal at battalion headquarters: a sealed envelope, a sealed fate.

27

Mad Jack's Final Patrol

It was a hot, sweaty night. Swarms of mosquitoes buzzed about, biting and sucking. Men slapped them flat in anger, but always too late.

There was a dense mantle of stars above a full moon. Visibility was excellent, so clear that men were able to use their periscopes to keep an eye on no-man's-land rather than stick their head above the parapets or peer through their loop holes. Nothing stirred ahead of them. Intermittent shelling and small arms fire was confined to their distant flanks. Once stand-to ended, men busied themselves with packing-up their kit and making final preparations for the change-over. The advance party from the East Surrey Regiment arrived and were shown around the trenches. Platoon commanders and NCOs never stopped touring around, checking and re-checking that everything was in order. There was an air of anxiety. A change-over was a tricky time. The Hun had an uncanny knack of knowing what was going on.

Sassoon was on his best behaviour. He stayed in his dugout with Captain Pinto. They discussed poetry, which was all Pinto ever wanted to do. Sassoon was still in shock, unable to control trembling hands. It never occurred to anyone that in his present state he intended yet again to disobey orders and go on the prowl in no-man's-land. They thought his bravado had at last been drawn.

Sassoon's batman made endless cups of tea. CSM Morgan called in regularly to keep Sassoon informed of developments, but he never reported any problems. Everything was going smoothly.

Sassoon waited until 0400 hours. Morgan was in the dugout taking the mickey out of the East Surrey advance party. Sassoon was so amused that he waited for Morgan to finish his stories before stirring from his bunk. He said he was going for a pee and that he wouldn't be long. He'd drunk so much tea that it seemed perfectly genuine. He paused in the doorway and laughed. "I'd better take my steel helmet with me. It's no good lecturing the men on obeying new orders and then not wearing one myself."

Morgan handed him his helmet, noting that he was unarmed apart from his usual revolver.

Sassoon was an inordinately long time having a pee. Morgan looked at his watch as though having a pee should have a time limit.

"Do you think he's all right?" asked Pinto.

"I don't know, sir."

They waited anxiously and when Sassoon still didn't reappeared Morgan said: "You don't think he's gone over the top again, do you? My God, I'll bet he has. There will be hell to pay ..."

Morgan and Pinto hurried out into the trench. Morgan headed to their right flank and Pinto to their left. "Try to find Corporal Rowlands as well," Morgan shouted as they parted. "If he has gone out, he will have taken Rowlands with him."

Rowlands was also missing. The man he shared a dugout with said: "He nipped out a couple of minutes ago with Captain Sassoon."

Two other men had seen them climb out of the trench and disappear through the barbed wire gap. One of them was the sentry on duty in the forward sap on the right flank, alongside Baker Company. He told Morgan: "Captain Sassoon went out about ten minutes ago. He said he'd be back just before dawn."

No-man's-land had several favourable features for the Fusiliers. Halfway across the divide there was an old farm track which they knew as the sunken road, and from there to the British lines the ground dipped abruptly, giving some forty yards of dead ground in which they were out of the sight of the Germans. It meant, theoretically, that returning patrols were home and dry as soon as they reached the sunken road.

Morgan didn't intend to take any chances. He linked up with Captain Pinto and they went round the company warning every man that Sassoon and Rowlands had gone over the top and would be returning before dawn. They ordered men to apply their safety-catches and that as soon as they saw or heard any movement to their front they should report it to an NCO. No one was to open fire without a direct order from Captain Pinto.

Morgan was equally concerned by the reception Sassoon and Rowlands would get from the Germans. They'd harassed them so often during the past week that they were bound to get a very hostile reception once they started bombing. Compared to that danger, returning to their own lines would be straight-forward, despite the order that anyone in no-man's-land was to be regarded as German and shot.

Once everyone in the company had been warned, they could only wait. Several times Morgan went down to the saps on their company front, spending time with those manning them. They were all good, steady lads and Morgan was confident he could rely on them. Then for an hour Morgan prowled the forward trench. Visibility remained excellent so he ordered all the periscopes to be manned, knowing that the lenses attracted all available light. It never occurred to either Morgan or Pinto to warn the companies on their flanks. They assumed Sassoon and Rowlands would return through their normal re-entry point which was in the centre of the A Company position.

Jones 617 had been biding his time for several days: in army lingo, lying doggo. After his confrontation with Sassoon on his first night on the position, 617 had deliberately left it at that. He had been tempted to go into A Company every night to seek out Sassoon and appear suddenly out of the darkness, his rifle levelled at him, keeping the bastard's nerves on edge; but he had decided against it. Sassoon had no nerves and any further threats would only increase the risk of others rumbling what he was up to. Likewise, when 617 was with men of his platoon he never said a word against Sassoon; never even mentioned his name.

Things changed radically in 617's favour when orders were issued for the Fusiliers to be relieved by the East Surrey Regiment. When the order filtered down the ranks that anyone seen in no man's land was to be regarded as German, it played right into his hands. It was a licence to murder. One thing was certain: Sassoon was bound to go out to harass the Hun with Corporal Rowlands, just as they always did. Neither of them would ever forgo a final chance of glory.

617 was on stag duty in the sap on the extreme left flank of B Company, next to A Company. There was nothing unusual in that. He had volunteered for it every night with the express purpose of studying the patrolling habits of Sassoon and Rowlands.

617 watched them as they went out. Later, when the first glimmer of daylight spread over the horizon, there was the familiar sound of exploding Mills bombs, followed by small arms fire: Sassoon and Rowlands were up to their usual tricks. It was a short, sharp engagement, followed by an eerie silence. As always, men knew they would have to wait to find out what had happened, whether they were on their way back or if they'd met their end at the hands of the Germans.

Whatever had happened, 617 remained ready for them. He had adopted a firing position in his sap, his rifle loaded and at the ready, safety catch off, butt pressed against his shoulder. The minutes ticked by and as daylight increased so 617 feared that his chance to shoot Sassoon would never come. The shouting which had come from the German trenches suggested that they might already have done his job for him. Bitter disappointment overcame him. He didn't just want Sassoon dead. He wanted to kill him. He was desperate to kill him.

Then 617 saw movement. Someone was coming up from the sunken road, near the bottom of the slope. He was obscured by bushes but it was a lone, tall figure. He was moving in the same manner as Sassoon, upright and with jerky steps. Gradually, 617 became aware that his hopes were being realised. It *was* Sassoon! And he was walking slowly and steadily straight towards him.

He wasn't making for A Company at all. He was heading directly towards 617's sap, looking around as though to verify his position. When he was some thirty yards away he stopped and stood perfectly still. Then he removed his steel helmet. He still didn't move, just stood there - waiting.

617 had him in his sights, lined up to perfection - the tip of his foresight trained straight between Sassoon's eyes. 617 drew in his breath and then held it. He put the first pressure on his trigger, just a gentle squeeze so that he didn't pull on the trigger with the second pressure.

After the exchange of fire on the German lines had stopped, Captain Pinto stationed himself on one end of the company frontage to await Sassoon's return. He ordered Morgan to take up a similar position on the other flank, adjacent to B Company.

Looking over the trench parapet, Morgan had a clear view down the slope towards the sunken road and the light was sufficient for him to see the saps on the extremes of both companies. He could see the man in B company sap plainly. He had his back to Morgan but even so he recognised something familiar about him. He took out his binoculars and looked more closely. It was Jones 617.

Instantly, Morgan guessed what was going to happen. He knew 617 was bound to see Sassoon coming back in and that under battalion orders he had every right - indeed an obligation - to shoot him. He was fair game, an easy and legitimate target.

"God almighty!" muttered Morgan.

No sooner had Morgan uttered his curse than Sassoon appeared. He was walking up the slope but he wasn't heading for his usual re-entry point. He was making for 617's sap. Morgan watched, mesmerised. He focused on Sassoon through his binoculars. Now, he was standing stock still. Then he removed his steel helmet.

"The bastard's going to shoot him," Morgan said aloud. He knew a shot would ring out at any moment. He turned to the man alongside him who was manning one of their periscopes. "Quick! Give me something to throw," he ordered.

"To throw?"

"Yes, anything ... Quick!"

The man handed Morgan a Mills bomb. Morgan grabbed it and without any hesitation or thought he hurled it at 617. He hadn't pulled the split-pin out to activate it and as he watched it soar through the air he knew there was a good chance that the split-pin would hold fast; but if it didn't, and the split-pin came out on landing, it was bound to kill both 617 and Sassoon.

The Mills bomb landed in the sap, right alongside 617.

Simultaneously with 617 squeezing his trigger his attention was diverted. It was only momentary, but that was enough. As his rifle fired he was actually glancing sideways at the Mills bomb, terrified that it was about to explode. His rifle moved fractionally, blighting his aim.

617 grabbed the bomb and threw it down the slope. When it didn't explode he turned his attention back to Sassoon. To his astonishment he

was still standing there, perfectly upright, apparently unharmed. He was feeling his head and then examining his hand, searching for signs of blood. Suddenly blood appeared in abundance. It gushed from the top of his skull and flowed down the side of his face. Yet he still didn't collapse as any man shot in the head would do normally.

617 operated the bolt of his rifle to get in another shot, but he was already too late. The sound of his shot brought immediate reactions. Corporal Rowlands sprinted up from the sunken road and Morgan and Captain Pinto leapt out of the A Company trench and dashed towards Sassoon as he stood there wiping blood from his eyes. The three men gathered around him and examined his head, giving 617 no chance of another shot.

Rowlands soon located the wound. It was just above Sassoon's right temple. Once the flow of blood was staunched the wound was revealed as superficial. It was no more than a nick or a scratch, but as with all head wounds it was bleeding profusely, giving a false impression of severity.

Morgan called for a stretcher but when it arrived Sassoon refused to lie on it. He kept saying it was all right; that it was nothing, even though he welcomed Rowlands's support as the small party returned to A Company through their usual re-entry point.

As they led Sassoon through the trenches he kept yelling: "It's all right. I'll be back. They'll soon fix this and I'll be back."

When he reached battalion headquarters he insisted on informing the colonel and the adjutant of the same thing: "A few days I'll be back again, just you wait and see."

"No you bloody won't, Sassoon," retorted the colonel. "Get the hell out of here and don't even think about coming back."

In B Company Major Evans was the first to investigate. He soon pinned things down to the sap on their left flank, but by the time he got there Sassoon and the others were already disappearing into the A Company trenches. Major Evans jumped down into the sap. "What happened?"

He got no answer from Jones 617. He was squatting in the sap, his head slumped on his chest and his rifle still propped up in front of him.

"What happened, Jones? Did you think it was a German?"

There was no answer.

"What happened, for God's sake? What were they all doing out there?"

There was still no answer. 617 didn't take any notice of him.

"Jones, why did you fire?"

Again, no answer.

"Jones, I'm ordering you to tell me what happened."

When Major Evans still got no response he looked at Jones more carefully. He was motionless, his head tilted forward, resting on his chest. Major Evans wondered if he too had been wounded. He eased Jones's head up from his chest. There was no blood, no signs of a wound. Yet what confronted Major Evans was a familiar sight. During his time at the front he'd seen it many times: dilated eyes with a wild, haunted look, the whites prominent, suggesting madness; a sagging lower jaw signifying total despair; the look of someone who could no longer cope, a man so traumatised that he was scarred for life; a man who had become a zombie.

Major Evans heaved 617 to his feet and led him away. At company HQ he handed him over to stretcher-bearers and they laid him gently on their stretcher and carried him to the battalion aid post.

Part Five

Khyber Morgan

28

Shadows of War

So that's what happened.

The mysterious events which had so puzzled me during my first meeting with Khyber Morgan in the early 1960s have been explained. They are a mystery no more.

But that was not the end of the story. The shadow of the Great War continued to hang over Britain for many years. Many think it still does. Even with all the old soldiers now dead and gone, the scars remain and refuse to fade.

Sassoon never kept his promise to return and fight again. When he reached the rear echelons he was in such a parlous state that it was obvious that such a thing was impossible. He had no alternative but to return to England. He ended up in the Lancaster Gate Hospital in London. There, for months, he went through troubled times. His moods and general medical condition fluctuated daily, sometimes hourly. His doctors found him impossible to treat. Sometimes he was normal but more often he teetered on the brink of a nervous breakdown, some said madness.

Every day he had a host of visitors. Sometimes he was delighted to receive a select few, but mostly he refused to see anyone and took shelter in solitude.

Lady Ottoline visited the hospital daily but Sassoon ignored her presence, refusing to see her. Those who did spend time with him (among them Khyber Morgan, while on leave) left in dismay, doubtful that he would ever recover. His doctors were adamant that his troubles were purely psychological. It was the shock of his wound that sparked things off, not the wound itself, which caused no problems. The snick made by Jones 617's bullet healed swiftly, as most superficial wounds do. In years to come there wasn't even any evidence of a scar.

Captain Rivers was called in to treat him and gradually, after many sessions, Sassoon emerged from his twilight world and became normal again - at least, as normal as he had ever been. His keen sense of humour was restored; he read copiously; and perhaps most significantly he regained his interest in cricket, always one of his first loves.

Finally, he resumed writing poetry. Rivers maintained that it was the prospect of further literary success that saved him, but most people thought Rivers was being far too modest. Wherever the credit lay, Sassoon's transformation was remarkable, even if slow.

One of the final signs of recovery was that he agreed to see Lady Ottoline again. As one of his doctors left his room, the door remained ajar and through the gap Sassoon caught sight of her sitting on an upright chair in the corridor, her face hidden in the shadow of another outlandish hat. She presented such a poignant and wretched figure that he was overwhelmed by compassion for her. He knew she had been sitting there day after day and he suddenly despised himself for his stubborn callousness in refusing to see her.

Maybe she had made a catastrophic error that led to Jones 618's death, yet hadn't they all made mistakes? The whole war was nothing but a series of ghastly mistakes. God only knew how many mistakes Sassoon had made, so who was he to treat Lady Ottoline as though she was a lone sinner? He thought of all the favours she had done him, especially his convalescence at Garsington Manor, and without further hesitation he waved to her and beckoned her into the room.

Many months later she told her friends that she found him a very changed man. Never again was he the same darling boy she had lusted after; but despite this they eventually patched up their differences and forged a lasting reconciliation. Indeed, when Lady Ottoline found love and satisfaction with her gardener, Lionel Gomme, she and Sassoon were free to become truly platonic friends and in later years they even enjoyed family holidays together.

Sassoon went on to lead a full life. He added to his reputation as a poet and wrote numerous highly acclaimed books, notably *Memoirs of a Fox Hunting Man* which is still in print and widely read. He had numerous lusty homosexual affairs which left him lucky not to have fallen foul of the law. Then, to everyone's surprise, he married and had a son. The marriage did not last but he became a devoted father. In a final volte-face he embraced Roman Catholicism and he eventually died aged eighty, having denounced his protest of 1917 as a mistake. He also denounced pacifism and fully supported the righteousness of the Second World War.

Ironically, he passed away peacefully in bed, just like the generals he reviled in one of his most famous poems.

When Jones 617 was stretchered back to the battalion aid post he still didn't say anything. Nor did he speak at any of the various hospitals he was subsequently sent to. His failure to kill Sassoon had caused such deep-seated psychiatric damage that he was struck dumb. Not a single word passed his lips.

It was a common condition in the Great War, but the vast majority of mutants recovered their voices. Very often it happened when they cried out during nightmares. Others found their voices again after patient work by psychiatrists (Rivers had many successes), and those who still hadn't regained their voices after several months were subjected to electric shocks to the brain, which was little more than a form of torture. (Speak, or you'll get a stronger dose.)

Jones 617 went through this treatment. When he didn't respond he got stronger doses until they very nearly killed him. He still didn't speak and in the end they accepted that he had a mental blockage which they could not erase. It was a case of 'won't speak' rather than 'can't speak'.

He was discharged from hospital and sent to the Veterans Home in Mountain Ash, where in many ways he had a normal life within the limitations of such a place. He read, played the piano, had games of chess, listened to the radio, and went for long walks; but he never spoke. Nor was he ever known to smile or show any signs of animation. He communicated with others through written notes, even though he did this as seldom as possible. Everyone gave up worrying about him and accepted him as he was. He had very occasional visits from relatives and one or two ex-Royal Fusiliers. My wife Megan went to see him perhaps once a year, usually accompanied by Khyber Morgan's wife, Blodwyn.

I only ever paid him one visit.

29
Khyber's Torment

On and off, and between writing several other novels, I spent over ten years researching Sassoon's protest and its consequences. To further my efforts I had many meetings with Khyber Morgan and Blodwyn. Every time my wife and I visited the Rhondda we called in on them and we became great friends.

In many ways the manuscript I eventually completed (in the seventies) was a joint effort. Khyber not only provided the lion's share of the story but both he and Blodwyn were stern but constructive critics. At our meeting to discuss the first completed draft of the story we came across several points I had missed. Among them Blodwyn brought up the manner in which her cousin Davey had been executed.

"What isn't clear," she said, "is exactly how he met his end. Who was it that stepped forward and fired the fatal shot when the officer in charge refused?"

The three of us looked to Khyber, realising that he must have known the man.

"That's not important," he said. "It doesn't matter who it was."

"But it does," protested Blodwyn. "It had me wondering. And as it stands now, it looks as though something is being concealed. And you must know who it was. You were there, watching."

"Not really," said Khyber.

"Oh, come on! You must have seen."

There was a long silence before Khyber got up from his chair and paced about their front parlour. Then he told us.

"I shot him. I finished him off. I had to. No one else was going to. And someone had to do it."

Khyber strode the room twice more. Nothing was said and he kept his eyes diverted.

We were dumbfounded by his sudden disclosure.

Then he turned to us sharply: "Well I couldn't just leave him there, now could I? Not lying in his own blood, pulling on his length of string and trying to struggle toward Rhys, obviously in great pain."

None of us answered.

"In all my service I've killed hundreds of men. But the only one I ever feel guilty about is Davey. All the others were in the normal course of duty. But shooting Davey has haunted me ever since. It always has done. And it always will. The worst thing was that once I'd done it, I bent down and picked up his length of string. I don't know why. I needed to do something so that I didn't have to just stand there and look down at his body with half his head blown away. It was the sort of thing you do when your mind is in turmoil, when you can no longer think clearly. Anyhow, I started to roll the string up and as I did so it suddenly went taut. I looked up and there, standing at the corner of the school building, was Rhys. He was holding the other end. Our eyes met and I can't tell you what a complete and utter bastard I felt. In my left hand was the officer's revolver, still smoking. So Rhys knew exactly what had happened."

Khyber sat down again. His face was blank. He was reliving the whole thing. Then his face crumbled, simply collapsed into a mass of wrinkles. We watched as he broke down.

To see a man of Khyber's calibre weeping like a small boy is something I never want to see again. Blodwyn hurried over to him and wrapped her arms around him, but he was beyond being comforted. He went on crying, his body shuddering, tears gushing down his cheeks. He was making loud snorting noises as he tried to control himself, but years of supressed emotion was something he could no longer hold back.

Eventually, Blodwyn took him upstairs. Megan and I had no idea what to say, so we just sat there, Megan wiping away her tears.

About half an hour later we heard them coming back downstairs. Blodwyn opened the door and beckoned us to join them in the back parlour. Khyber was sitting at the table. He was back under control. He gave us a wan smile and apologised. "Sit down," he said "and I'll tell you the rest. Things I could never mention before."

We did as he said.

"When I started to roll up that string and it went taut, I looked up. Rhys's eyes were full of fury and hate. I knew then that it meant more bloodshed. I knew he would never let things go without getting revenge for Davey's execution. He loved that boy so much, and Rhys had always been a fiery and erratic lad. I expected him to produce his rifle and shoot me, there and then. I felt so awful I wouldn't have minded if he had. But he didn't. Do you know what he did? He just rolled up the ball of string and disappeared back to the school yard again. As he went he shouted out: 'I'll get that bastard! I swear to God that I'll get that bastard'.

"I wasn't surprised that he reacted like that. During the court-martial I often heard him curse and threaten Sassoon. He put all the blame on him."

Khyber took a long drink from the cup of tea Blodwyn had made for him. "And to be honest," he continued, "I knew and understood exactly how he felt, even though I'd always been close to Sassoon. From then on I tried not to think about it, but in my heart I knew something dramatic would happen. That's why, when we were posted to the 25th battalion, I made sure Rhys went to a different company and why I warned Sassoon to be wary of him. I kept telling myself that that would be sufficient."

Khyber paused, mustering his determination to go on. "I closed my mind to the whole thing. I've done some brave things during my service, but on that occasion, when it mattered more than ever, I took the coward's way out. I just hoped for the best. I decided not to get involved."

He took another swig of tea, needing time in which to steady himself. "It was a difficult situation for me. I had such split loyalties. There was no man I respected more as a brave soldier than Sassoon. He was one in a million, but there was no excuse for his protest. If it hadn't been for his damned protest none of it would have happened. So I understood exactly how Rhys felt. And I still do. Especially since Rhys had no idea how closely involved Bertrand Russell and Lady Ottoline were in all this - their treachery in using Sassoon's poems."

Khyber stopped pacing about and faced us. "I was well aware of how the pacifists had used Sassoon, of course. And my biggest mistake was never to explain things to Rhys. It was only on that final night when Sassoon headed straight for Rhys instead of the usual re-entry gap that I realised just how desperate things were. And when I saw Sassoon just standing there, taunting Rhys, I was only conscious of one thought - to stop any more killing. That was why I threw that Mills bomb. I was damned if I was going to let anyone else be killed."

Finally, Khyber looked at each of us in turn. "So there you have it."

None of us replied.

"You'd better work it into your manuscript," Khyber said to me. "It has to be the whole truth or none of it will be worth a scrap."

Blodwyn looked at Khyber pleadingly. "Why didn't you tell me all this long ago?"

"How could I? Davey was your cousin and I know how much you'd always loved him. There are so many things in war that are beyond an individual's control. And when things like that hit you, all you can do is try to forget them. Some men can and some men can't. There's no explaining it. I've always had to cope with the memory of shooting Davey. It's easy to forgive others but not to forgive yourself. Even when everyone in the valleys knew Davey had been executed and had sacrificed himself for Sassoon, I could never admit that I fired the final bullet. Yet I've always known that it would come out eventually. And now it has. So let that be the last word."

The End

Hayling Island 1974.

Epilogue

But it was far from being the last word. That lay elsewhere.

Later that evening I took Khyber's advice and added his revelations to my draft manuscript, being as discreet as possible. It came as a relief when I wrote 'The End' and add the dateline 'Hayling Island, 1974' at the bottom of the page. However, I was being premature. I had no idea that there was another major surprise in store.

When Megan and I got back to Hayling Island we didn't mention the matter again for over a week. It was as though we were trying to digest it all and make sense of it. When we did discuss it we saw things very differently. We even argued about it. I blamed Rhys for everything, seeing his hatred of Sassoon as vicious and revengeful, but Megan maintained that the issue was far more complicated than that. She claimed that the pacifists, Lady Ottoline and Bertrand Russell, were the real villains.

When I made a vague suggestion that it might be just as well to forget the whole thing and leave the book unpublished, Megan wasn't at all pleased. She reminded me of all the years I'd spent on it, often at the expense of family life, and she was adamant that the whole point of the book was to clarify exactly what had happened for the sake of future generations in the Rhondda. They had a right to know the truth, which made it vital to honour my agreement with Khyber and publish when all those involved were dead.

Then she astounded me by adding: "Except for Rhys, of course. We must show him your draft manuscript, and the sooner the better."

"Show it to Rhys!" I exclaimed. "He's the last person to show it to."

"Nonsense! Rhys still has no idea that Sassoon was betrayed by Ottoline and Russell. Nor does he realise that Sassoon would never have allowed Davey to take responsibility for the poems if he'd known what was happening."

We considered this for a few moments before she summed up the despair she felt. "It's always the same ... The rich and famous get away with everything. There's Lady Ottoline, left completely in the clear. She even got herself a young lover, her gardener. She was so besotted that Lawrence used her as his model for *Lady Chatterley's Lover*. As for Russell, although they jailed him for time, he soon changed his mind about pacifism in order to regain his fellowship at Cambridge University. He even went on to win a Nobel Prize. And Sassoon, he got away with God knows how many homosexual affairs, then got married and had a son. Finally, he converted to Catholicism, no doubt to confess his sins and be forgiven everything. But as for poor old Rhys ... He ends up like his Uncle Desmond ... Years of misery, mouldering away like a dumb cluck among shell-shocked survivors from the trenches."

I sympathised, but I remained adamant that no one should get a preview of the manuscript. We had to accept that Rhys's silence was just one of the cruel vagaries of fate. I knew how sensitive Megan was on the issue so I tried to conclude matters with a generalisation.

"The trouble with life is that there's no fairness in it."

Megan didn't reply, so I assumed we had agreed to differ.

I thought no more about it until maybe six months later when I returned from a skiing holiday with our sons. In my absence another of my novels had come back in the post from a publisher.

I had a self-imposed rule of 'ten rejections and scrap', so I stowed it away in my cupboard reserved for work in progress and failures. It was then that I saw that *The Man Who Shot Siegfried Sassoon* was missing. I guessed what had happened and I was horrified.

When I tackled Megan about it, she admitted it.

"Whilst you and the boys were whizzing down the ski slopes, I went back to the Rhondda for a few days. And I went to see Rhys. No one has been anywhere near him for over a year."

"And you took my draft manuscript with you?"

"Yes."

"And left it with him?"

"Yes."

"Thanks very much."

"Does it matter?"

"Of course it matters. Apart from everything else, it's my only copy."

"Sorry! But that's no big deal. You can always go and get it back."

That was true, so I decided to do just that.

I was so nervous of meeting Rhys again that I kept putting it off, but eventually, when I found myself in Bristol on business, I summoned up sufficient courage to drive on to Mountain Ash, having telephoned the matron in advance.

I had never been to the Veterans' Home and didn't know what to expect. I was pleasantly surprised. It had been reduced to a small establishment due to so many deaths but that didn't stop it from being well-appointed and immaculately clean. On top of that, I got a very friendly reception from the matron.

"Another visitor for Rhys," she laughed. "How lovely! Things really are looking up."

"I won't keep him long. I've just come to collect the draft manuscript I mentioned over the telephone. Has he read it, do you know?"

"Read it! My goodness me, he never stops reading it."

A young nurse ushered me into the Home's sun lounge. It was empty except for Rhys, sitting at the far end. He was in an easy chair with an occasional table beside him. He'd gone very grey since I'd last seen him but there was no mistaking him. Before the nurse left me, she said: "If he wants to say anything, he'll write it on his pad. But don't expect much. And don't rush him. He can't stand being rushed."

To my surprise the manuscript was on the occasional table.

"I've come to collect my book," I said.

I reached across for it but I'd hardly moved before he grabbed it and gathered it into his lap, as though reluctant to part with it. I expected him to pull out his pad and scribble out complaints about how harsh and unfair I had been towards him, and what a bastard Sassoon had been; but all he did was flip through the pages to make sure he hadn't left any notes tucked in amongst them.

When satisfied that he'd left nothing behind, he handed the manuscript to me. It was in a very tatty state. Lots of the pages were dog-eared and scuffed and instead of everything being held together by a treasury tag and a couple of rubber bands, the pages were loose and all over the place, some even upside down with various passages underlined.

It showed every sign of having been studied line by line, time and time again. Over the past months he must have examined every aspect and nuance of events, from the treachery of Ottoline Morrell and Bertrand Russell to his own wild rants against Sassoon which led to Davey's bizarre court evidence.

I dreaded to think of what he had made of it all. I watched him closely but he gave nothing away. He stared at me in a very odd and penetrating manner, a glare which was both unfathomable and disturbing.

I tried to come up with an appropriate comment, or a question that might ease matters. When I failed, I decided on a hasty exit. After all, I wasn't a relative or a friend or even an ex-Fusilier, and I realised that if I got involved in any form of discussion I would have to contend with Jones's fiery temperament and be prepared for a long delay whilst he wrote everything down on his pad.

So I turned to leave. I didn't even have the manners to ask him how he was or if he needed anything.

As I reached the door I heard an odd noise.

I turned to see who or what it was, but there was no one else around. I decided it must be one of his fellow veterans in the garden, approaching the open French windows.

I waited for a moment to see if anyone appeared, but no one did. Then the noise came again: a voice, a croaky and hesitant voice.

"On your way out, boyo, would you tell Nurse Davies I'd like a cup of tea."

Other books by John Hollands

The Dead, the Dying and the Damned

"A brilliantly angry first novel. The character studies are masterly ... Unless some genius like Hollands writes a book in which people behave like real human beings ... Some people will demand its suppression. But I would say this: it is only when people as courageous as Hollands dare to write the truth about war that the miracle will come when it will be no more."

Nancy Spain, Daily Express

"Stands with *All Quiet on the Western Front* as the best-ever war novel."

Paul Wigby, Associated Press

"Admirably done! Sincere, conscientious and factual."

Scott-Thomas, Daily Telegraph

"A brilliant piece of writing"

Evening News

"The battle scenes are magnificent and the whole book is a tremendous achievement for a young man still in his early twenties."

James Cameron, News Chronicle

"A remarkable first novel. Bound to become a best-seller."

Yorkshire Evening Post

"A genuinely moving book. There is no mistaking the strength of emotion, pity, indignation and resentment that has driven him to seek an outlet in words."

Peter Quinnell, Daily Mail

"As fiction it is grippingly impressive. As a document it is frightening."

Birmingham Gazette

"It should be read by all politicians."

South Wales Echo

"The best novel of the Korean War"

New York Times

"The battle scenes are perfect."

The New Yorker

"The novel ranks with Remarque's *All Quiet on the Western Front* and Gibbs's *And Now It Can Be Told*.

Robert Barr, Boston Globe

"I have read *The Dead, the Dying and the Damned* many times. The many well-drawn characters, the humorous descriptions of army life, and the masterly battle scenes make it one of the best war novels ever written. It is, without doubt, the definitive novel of the Korean War and, as such, should be readily available to all."

Cyril Coombes

Heroes of the Hook

"John Hollands is a brilliant writer. His book, *The Dead, the Dying and the Damned*, was a runaway best seller, but *Heroes of the Hook* is much better. The first half of the book is hilariously funny, the second half devastatingly sad. His characters are so real they jump off the page at you. The story is so vivid that it made me cry, first with laughter and then sadness. I will read it again when I have recovered."

J.M.B. Clarke, Australia

"Dear Mr Hollands,

... We had a week-end visitor, so on Friday evening I suggested he might like to have a look at *The Heroes of the Hook*. It was a big mistake. We hardly got a word out of him all week-end. He just sat there, his nose buried in the book, laughing a lot and eventually bursting into uncontrollable tears. To cap it all, when he left on Monday morning he took the book with him, explaining: 'I must read it again when I get home. I'll send it back anon'. We are still waiting for anon."

Extract from a letter to the author

"No bull! Of all the war memoirs I have read (and I've read most of them), *Heroes of the Hook* beats them all hands down."

Reg Askey, Korean Veteran (The Tigers)

"I recommend this book to everyone, male or female, with or without any interest in war books."

Hilary Bates

"An excellent read ... It would pay people to read this book to know what went on in the terrible Korean War.

Robert Wall-Pring

The Exposed

"I found *The Exposed* moving and extremely convincing. George was a wonderful character, brilliantly real and fresh, and the Japanese heroine (Katsumi) tremendously likable and convincing. The evocation of the era and the eye for details of that time were most impressive."

Maeve Haran, *Having It All*

"A wonderful story, superbly told."

Guy Bellamy, *The Secret Lemonade Drinker*

"A work of genius. The most moving, wonderful, happy-and-sad book I have ever read."

Trevor Hunt, *Ibiza Shorts*

"Marvellous characters. It's a superb piece of work."

John Pawsey, Lit. Agent

"Quite brilliant! Plot, setting, characterization, all superb and most perceptive of human nature."

Peter Brooke-Smith, Oxon

"A fascinating read. The love story is touchingly told: very funny and ultimately very moving. At times it takes one to the depths of despair but in the end its profoundly inspiring message is dramatically and effectively revealed. A very fine piece of work."

John Hogston, Author

"John Hollands has written the most superb novel. His easy style and well-drawn characters make it a sure-fire winner. The wit and charm of the novel, together with the special treatment of the story, make you want to read it in one sitting. I managed in two."

Ken Fisher, The English Library

"There are three things I found really impressive about *The Exposed*. First of all the character of Katsumi, which was utterly enchanting; and because she was so convincing the final part of the book introduces a spiritual dimension equally as convincing; and thirdly, the story never lost touch with the ordinary world it was set in. The novel is down-to-earth in its presentation - an honest, square-on view with no spin. It is a real achievement. The whole book makes the last paragraph more than just a pious hope."

Jeremy Firth, English Lit. Oundle

"*The Exposed* is best book I've read in a very long time. I have no doubts that the books of John Hollands will be read over and over again."

Brian Walden, Cornish Libraries

"*The Exposed* is a beautiful novel crying out to be made into a film. Finely drawn characters you really get to know and care about. I wish his publisher would reprint his earlier novels. There are few better writers."

Rosemary Cliff

Memory and Imagination Series
Gran and Mr Muckey

"Amusing, enthralling, poignant. I just loved it. I am about to start the second volume ... Can't wait ..."

Amazon critic

"I enjoyed *Gran and Mr Muckey* immensely. The characters are hugely entertaining and the scene where Sajit is in the headmaster's study is masterly."

Robin Lloyd-Jones, Lord of the Dance

"Gran and Mr Muckey kept me roaring with laughter and had me quoting pieces to all and sundry."

Rev. David Quine, St Kilda Revisited

"Quite apart from being very funny, *Gran and Mr Muckey* is a fascinating chronicle of our times, reflecting attitudes which have long since changed. The constructive approach of the Hill Head Prep School towards the Common Entrance Exam is absolutely priceless."

Cyril Coombes

The Man Who Shot Siegfried Sassoon

The Man Who Shot Siegfried Sassoon